"A man's

Frederick Douglas

The Iscariot *Fields*

Michael J. Vines

The Iscariot Fields

Copyright © Michael J. Vines

MJVinesAuthor@gmail.com.

Cover by: VCM Media Group
Judy Vines

Dedicated to Judy, my wife, best friend and eternal companion.
Without her nothing makes sense, especially a rough draft manuscript!
Simply put, she outranks me. I love you wife!

Also, to my Warriors:
Sgt. Major Clifford DuFrain Sr always my hero for your lifetime of service.
Air Force Staff Sgt. Dennis Serbu (LEO Lt.), a brother and noble spirit.
Brother and Editor Clinton Giese - Gunner's mate third class (Vietnam) who
encouraged and inspired me to pick up the pen all those years ago.
Infantry Sgt. Christopher Schenk who motivated me to complete this work,
was my consultant and co-conspirator.
And . . .
To all men and women who would arrest the "beginnings".

To my sister Michele Vines Manning for her good spirit, keen mind and love
of humanity. And for her encouragement and insights.

Finally, to Mr. Robert LaRoque my teacher and friend who took a very young
boy by the scruff of his neck and gifted him the world of literature. My love of
reading, history and writing I owe all to him. It is an honor for me to count
him my friend.

Chapter I

In those beginnings of times was Cain. And every generation thereafter has struggled to wash away his legacy, the bloody, crushed skull of his brother. We've all thought that we were going to be the ones to do it. In our youth we surely knew our generation would possess enough kindness and reason to accomplish it. We would be the Saviors of this insane globe. But in our maturity, we've also come to know the same sour defeat of our ancestors. There's really no hope for success is there? Victory is, as has oft been said, as small as hope in a dead man's eye. In this particular case Carl Walker's dead eyes.

The morning winds blowing across the prairies toward the small farming community of Odell, Illinois carry secrets she won't hear until it's too late to make any difference. A few of America's favorite sons are poised nearby to deliver their contribution to the insanity. And when they arrive all of Odell will be sound asleep except Carl Walker. Carl will be awake, draining the very last drop out of his very last bottle of Jack Daniels.

The Friday morning sky over Odell is a cloudless, endless blue. Newly plowed fields travel in uninterrupted grooves out from the town in every direction towards the horizon. As far as the eye can see long straight rows of pregnant soil wet with morning dew carry the musty fragrance of mother earth. Townspeople begin to stir before sunrise, but long after that Carl remains in a drunken stupor-induced sleep. He's red-eyed, flushed-cheeked, purple nosed and pale livered. Prissy, his grey cat moves lazily from her resting place on his chest where she's been curiously sniffing his whiskey-laced breath to the arm of the couch near his feet. She sits there staring at him with her deep yellow eyes that long ago inspired him to rescue her from the shelter in Kankakee. Staring at him like he's a sad curiosity . . . staring as if she knows something

1

Carl doesn't. She does, earlier this morning he gulped away the last sunrise of his life.

Meanwhile, refilled coffee pots greet regulars streaming into The Dinner Bell, a small diner at the north end of the old town square. It's full of farmers sporting brown, sun-leathered faces. John Deer hats pushed back on wrinkled foreheads, calloused hands pass cigarettes and sugar up and down the worn, faded green laminate counter. The crackle of bacon cooking on the grille, spoons tinkling against the side of thick white and mostly stained porcelain coffee mugs provides background music to the noisy din of conversation. All of these folks know each other, they grew up here, so did their moms and dads and theirs. Eggs and hot cakes, even the omelets take a second seat to the best sausage gravy and buttermilk biscuits north of the Mason Dixon line. It's a scene right out of fifties television as traffic and towns folks steadily fill the town square. There are only thirty-one hundred people in Odell and between Thursday night and Saturday morning most all of them at one time or another seem to make their way to the square. No one would be surprised to see Andy, Opie or Aunt Bee saunter into the Dinner Bell.

At 7:30 every morning Billy "Pudge" Miller opens the doors to his small, wooden-floored grocery and hardware store on the west side of the town square. The service is personal, the lighting dim, the counters low and the variety limited, but the Millers make you feel welcome. It's hi Anne, or John or Bill when you walk into their store. They know you, your parents, who you're married to or dating, why you got divorced, what church you go to or, heaven forbid, don't go to! Yes, everyone living in Odell is a relative or, so it seems and that's how you feel when you walk into Millers, like family. It's the only grocery store in town, if you don't count Casey's Gas Station on Route 17

2

heading east out of town, which, of course, Pudge didn't. After all, he was a butcher "trained up" by his father and no decent man could call his place a grocery store if it didn't sport a proper butcher-manned, meat counter.

Pudge took care of his place without much help, except for his wife, Shelly. She easily did as much work as he, but he'd never admit it. He didn't really need to. Everyone in a small town knows everyone else's business and everyone in Odell knew Shelly Miller pulled more than her share of the load at the IGA. Still, some things were sacred to Pudge. "Never own more store than a good wife is willing to run and take no credit for," he often quipped at the monthly, all night, guys only, poker game. Hosted at the Hamilton Street VFW on the last Friday of the month, the game concerned itself less with the game of poker than it did with a bar full of booze, good food and good ole boy company. Unfortunately, at this Friday night's game none of the good old boys would be smiling and Pudge Miller would regret his oft repeated remark even though it was uttered in jest.

Across town on Frahers Street, not far from Memorial Baseball Park, Jimmy (Gus) Morgan was getting ready for school. He grew up playing ball on that field, as did most of the children in Odell. He's a good kid who quarterbacks the football team up the road at Dwight Central High and is also the captain of the baseball team. A decent student, his college future is all but guaranteed. Big Ten scouts from two sports were keeping tabs on him. Yet for all his athletic prowess he had an endearing personality that invited people to be close with him. His strikingly good-looking face was framed by black curly hair and a perfectly placed dark mole on his right jaw just below the corner of his thin lips. Dark eyes set deep into chiseled high cheek bones gave him a Mediterranean look.

3

His dad, Doc Morgan, the town pharmacist, bragged about him incessantly; to the point of embarrassment for Gus. But he loved his dad and tolerated his bragging on him with a usual "aw shucks" smile.

"Yeah, Gus hadn't even reached my belt when he was helping his mama on shopping days over at Millers. He'd go up and down the aisles with her picking up things that had fallen on the floor or that other folks dropped. Even used to help Pudge stock cans up on the shelves while his momma went about her business." But little Gus didn't get too many years to help Mama with her grocery shopping before heart disease concluded its destruction of her. She was just twenty-nine years old when it took her. Gus was ten. She collapsed and died on the sidewalk in front of Ella Murray's house on the way to a little league game with him. His buddies blamed the whole unfortunate tragedy on Murray who they all believed to be a witch. A truly unpleasant person, she henceforth was eyed suspiciously by them, especially on Halloween night where none but the bravest dared to venture up the steps of her large wrap around porch. And even then, they who made the trip never ever dared consume the offering. Everyone, at least from the ranks of the children knew 'the witch' poisoned it.

Friday morning Gus was off to school, baseball practice and then an evening in Dwight with Adriane Dolan, his girl. Doc lent him the family's pick up, so they could get a bite to eat and catch a movie after practice. There would, of course, be time for some innocent necking on the way home. The flat farmland seems to make the moon bigger and brighter on the plains of central Illinois, especially when you're seventeen and admiring it with your favorite girl. Gus knew and was looking forward to the fact that he could sleep in Saturday until Doc needed a hand at the store. Dad cut him slack these mornings even

4

though it was the busiest day in the pharmacy.

"The boy works hard at school. His mom always whispers to me that he needs some rest."

At 9:15 the county squad car motors east on Scott Street between the Dinner Bell and Millers. A six-foot seven inches, two hundred and sixty-pound police officer sits behind the wheel, his mere presence assures everyone in town that all is well. Sheriff Larry Odell's stock is blue blood with lineage traced all the way back to William Odell who first stopped his covered wagons there in 1852.

The open plains could be a cruel and lonely place in those old days, but Odell knew that the trails west from Chicago and parts east ran right through this land. He could grow produce and would be able to move it to the centers of population easily one day. In the meantime, he'd sell goods to wagon trains, pioneers, scouts, the army, fortune seekers still passing through on their way west; the railroad couldn't be far behind. A general store was a good idea. It was for a while at least, until his wife, Margaret, took off with one of the near do well trail masters headed back east. The plains, her husband nor her children could replace her love of city life, the bustle of New York City. So, one quiet, full moon night she up and left them. The price of the ticket home was bearable compared to the hardships of frontier life. The children were small, too small to really miss her she reckoned.

They were also too small to help with the store and Odell couldn't manage the land and it. The burden eventually became too much for him; he sold the store and kept his land. Passing through several hands, some successful, some not, the old store finally burned to the foundation at the turn of the century. Now, Pudge Miller's IGA stood on the very lot where the original Odell

General Store stood one hundred and sixty-seven years earlier.

The fourth great-grandson of the town's founder was the most respected man in town. Sheriff Odell's eyes were cold, steel blue and could look a wrong doer into a speedy mind set of repentance with "that stare." When he entered a room his presence was palpable, yet, his voice was surprisingly soft for a person of his size. A former defensive lineman for the University of Illinois, he wasn't shy about personal contact if a situation called for it, but he preferred reason. In Odell situations rarely arose that required force and when it did it likely involved someone passing through on the nearby interstate. According to Sheriff Odell, there were only two kinds of people that lived in 'his town', those who respected him and those who fear him. And when it came to performance of his duties, he didn't much care which group a person belonged to.

What Larry pretended not to know was that he was well loved by almost all the townspeople who had witnessed his countless acts of kindness over the years. As big a bear as he was, it wasn't unusual to catch him on the monkey bars at the elementary school just as sixty-eight deliriously happy children were being sprung for recess. The mere sight of the massive man walking the playground was enough to bring them screaming to him. There are no drugs or gang problems in Odell, Illinois.

A year earlier when he locked up Carl Walker the day before Thanksgiving for causing a scrap over at Blintz's Tap, he felt so bad for the family that he drove all the way to Kempton and bought one hundred dollars of groceries for them. No need to let the town's folk see that soft spot. Late Thanksgiving eve, he left the boxes of food on the Walker's front porch and drove off into the night. He didn't notice Carl's teary-eyed wife sitting in the upstairs window,

6

watching his taillights disappear into the cold November night. Larry Odell is not just a man's man, he's everyone's man.

No, nothing much exciting ever happened in Odell, according to the life-long residents of the small farming community, unless you count the fact that one of its now favorite sons, Lorenzo Brigham Odell, is the new President of the United States.

Chapter II

Odell, Illinois, is America. It's not small-town America. It is, at its very core, America. Its 3,100 souls live only 72 miles from the great metropolitan crossroads of the nation, Chicago. It's a decidedly unlikely place for the destiny that awaits her.

She's a farming community sitting all by herself in the middle of the flattest land anywhere on the planet, or so it seems to her young people. "There's nothing to do," they say; "no place to go." It's just flat-out boring no-place Odell. But like all young people who migrate away from their home towns to the great cities of the land or to other places of mystery in the world, they will miss her. They will remember, like those that left before them, the summer days by the Vermilion River or the twenty-five-cent bus rides down Route 66 to Pontiac for a Sunday afternoon movie. They'll sit by fireplaces in faraway, pseudo-sophisticated lairs sipping glasses of fashionable wine and reflect fondly, longingly on the picnic grove off the little country road that runs north past the west side Catholic cemetery. They run away only to return during the loneliness of midnight hours, running back to her warmth, her security and her memories. Odell is sacred land to be sure, an ancient land that supported humankind for thousands of years before the first settlers ever dreamed of unloading their covered wagons there.

# # # # #

In the spring of 1832, Kiwigapawa watched his daughter play on the banks of the Mazon River. It's little more than a large creek, even during the high-water season, but it carries enough fish to nourish his Kickapoo Tribe and the wildlife of the plains.

Kennekuk played in the stream which had yet to warm in the spring sunshine.

Her long, black hair draped around a pretty, round face with big, almond eyes. Her bare feet splashed water as she chased small fish moving lazily with the current toward spawning areas. Most braves wanted a boy child as their first born. So, had Kiwigapawa until the instant he saw little Kennekuk.

Occasionally, she glanced up from her play in the shallows and flashed a heart-melting smile at her father, the chief.

"Father come play with me. Come see the fishes," she called gleefully. "They are moving so slow I can almost pick them up. Why are they moving like that? Is it because the water is still cold?"

"Yes." He began. "When the water is cold, the fishes move slowly. When you are cold from the winter snows, you do not run about very much unless you must; do you? It is not until the sun begins to warm the land and your pretty little face that you begin to run about and make it difficult for your old father to catch you; yes?"

The little girl giggled at the thought of being the object of her father's chase.

"Before the water warms in springtime, the fishes move about slowly and then we can use our arrows, spears or hooks to catch them." He smiled. "But when summer approaches and they become more active it is harder . . . much like it is harder to catch my Kennekuk. You see?"

"Yes father," she replied admiring his wisdom.

"Come here and sit on your father's legs," the chief said as he moved to the top of the bank and sat near his daughter. Casting his eyes about, the chief took in the vast, flat grasslands of his home. Red-winged black birds circled tall, green grass searching for grasshoppers and crickets. A chicken hawk scrolled through bright blue, cloudless skies and the smell of campfires drifted down through the small grove of trees that stood behind him. It was a perfect place, this hunting ground.

"This is your land Kennekuk," he said as he turned to her. "It will always be so, but it has not always been our land. This land has been bought with the blood of your ancestors," he said as he looked out across the horizon. "Never forget, never forget them and their blood."

"Some of the old nations accept the white ways, but not the Kickapoo. Not our nation. This land they will want to take from us someday, but we will not leave it. We'll not leave this ground where our blood is mixed with the soil forever. Never Kennekuk. Never." The young chief took his daughter's face in his massive hands and drew it near to his.

"Remember these things, daughter," he said as his expression changed, and he looked tenderly into her eyes. "You may have its berries and herbs and fishes and wildlife for as long as you like. When you marry your husband will build your wickiup here and the fire inside will keep you warm against the winter snows. One day you will give this land to your little ones and they to theirs. Some day when I go to join the Great Spirit you will feel my spirit near you. I will watch you care for this land like our ancestors did. And I will love you forever and ever."

"Yes, father. I will take care of it, I swear," she said simply as she smiled at him and laid her head upon his chest.

Forty miles to the east near the Kankakee River, Captain Paul Smythe saddled his horse and shouted his men into formation. He would lead the company of horse soldiers and one agent from the Bureau of Indian Affairs to Odell. It was time for the Kickapoo to leave for the barren reservation land one hundred and eighty-seven miles away, far beyond St. Louis, Missouri. When all was said and done history would show that neither Kennekuk, her family nor her

10

descendants would ever see the plains of the sacred hunting grounds again . . . until that is, a little more than one hundred and sixty-seven years later, when Monica Palmer drove down interstate Highway 55 to interview Mary Duke Odell.

That interview began just as a caravan of forty military vehicles neared Atlanta, Illinois where it would stop for the remainder of the day.

# # # # #

It was only noon on Friday, but two of the town elders had already staked their claims on two of the round-red plastic-covered bar stools in Blintz's; they were getting ready for their weekly war of words.

"The Indians ain't got no more claim on this land than my great-grandfather did, stupid!" Jimmy Spencer snarled at his lifelong friend. "Just because they were here first don't mean that they can hold onto it forever. If that was the case, then we all oughta get up and move our boney white carcasses off the entire North American Continent!"

Jimmy took a long draw on his ice-cold glass of beer as he watched the bartender move from person to person taking orders, exchanging hellos and cleaning up spills. Her sweatshirt said it all, "I support the three basic food groups - bottle, can and keg." She was Odell born and bred; had a cute tush on her as well! She was another reason Jimmy loved Friday afternoons in town, Blintz's Tap & Dining in particular.

He smiled as he contemplated the furor his remarks would cause among the liberals surrounding him. Hell, he didn't believe a lick of it. He only said it to liven up the joint. It was Friday, after all, and not much exciting ever happened in Odell. You must make your own fun here and that's just what he was doing. He considered it his job.

11

"James, you are so full of crap, Miller could sell parts of you for fertilizer," Isaac Odell sneered as the small group of lunch patrons smiled knowing the battle had begun. Many came to Blintz's every Friday just to hear the feud between the two area blue bloods. Few knew how close the two men really were or how tightly intertwined their lives had been.

Jimmy Spencer's great-grandfather was half of a two-man partnership that bought the first land from the federal government upon which the town of Odell now sits. It was a little more than one hundred and forty-six years ago. Henry Gardner and James Spencer plotted the land in thirty-one-acre parcels and sold them for nearly thirty dollars apiece. When William Odell purchased 2,100 acres of land, they surprised him by giving the town his name. Now two of their progeny was the Friday afternoon special at Blintz's Tap and Dining.

# # # # #

Just north of tiny Atlanta, Illinois those forty military vehicles pulled onto farm property surrounded, enclosed, even hidden by a large pine forest. The massive estate looked much like a European castle complete with towers. Buried deep behind a ring of tall pine trees it was hid so well most of the people in the surrounding area hardly knew it existed. No one had ever been invited there and no one knew or ever saw the owners. Large iron gates presented a formidable obstacle to the casual visitor, but no casual visitors ever came calling on this farmhouse.

Men parked vehicles in near silence and checked equipment. The crackling of radios could be heard occasionally, but none of the transmissions could be monitored by anyone outside the elite group of eight hundred and sixty-four men in army fatigues. Evil intentions hung in the air and in fifteen hours they were going to release their iteration of insanity on the citizens of Odell and the

12

United States of America. You could smell anger in their camp; see it in the eyes of those boys.

Chapter III

There's a telephone tower on Prairie Street just outside the town limits. It's the tallest structure of any kind for miles. Atop that tower, a body can see nearly every square inch of the newly plowed fields surrounding Odell and on a clear night, the city lights of Joliet, fifty-seven miles away. The shining sun warmed her steel structure as a lineman's truck pulled onto its concrete pad. After a single figure exited, it pulled away driving east to Odell.

Dick Ralph sauntered into Blintz's with Ruth, his wife of 49 years, for Friday lunch. It wasn't often they had a Friday together like this anymore. Though long past retirement age, Dick was still employed full time at Rube's Auto Dealership in Dwight. There was a time when Dick would yank out a transmission as casually as he would open a beer. The pains of arthritis and diminishing strength encouraged him to find lighter duties. These past nine years he just sold cars and decided it was surely one of his better decisions. People loved buying a car from someone who was known in all the area to be honest and a master mechanic. They knew he would see to it that they'd be taken care of if anything were to go wrong. Dick Ralph took care of the customer before and after a sale. He treated those who decided not to buy as if they were one of his best return customers. That's just the kind of guy he was.

Four days a week Ralph made the short trip to Dwight to sell his cars. His schedule was as regular as his strong, healthy heart. "Hell, you couldn't keep him from a day's work if he had the plague," Ruth could be heard to complain good humoredly. At six-foot-three, brown eyes, brown hair, with dark-rimmed glasses, Dick was an imposing figure. Though nearly a decade away from daily work with tools, his hands were still those of a man who had worked hard to earn what small luxuries he and Ruth enjoyed. They lived in a modest,

14

attractive white house on the far east end of Vermillion Street where he was born almost seventy years ago. It was there Ruth and Dick had spent their entire married life raising their two children.

He was and still is the local basketball hero, the sole-surviving member of the 1965 sweet sixteen high school team. This little bit Catholic high school from no place Odell, was playing in the state championship tournament in the days before school teams were separated by school size.

The scrappy little bits played their way through the ranks of schools from Chicago, its wealthy suburbs and other big cities that sported huge athletic talent pools and budgets. There were only sixteen teams left and the boys from Odell stood as tall as any of them. Seasons must come to an end they say and when the boys from Odell walked onto the basketball court at ten a.m. that forever Friday morning to face the enemy from Peoria-Woodruff, it did . . . sort of. But in a real sense it never ended. That season will live on forever for the boys who played and the people of Odell who witnessed it. They lost the game, but these young men were heroes to the residents of Odell and to the entire county.

Four years later, when Odell celebrated the town's centennial, the team was invited to ride in an honest-to-God convertible. . . like real heroes. But Dick Ralph and several of his teammates were halfway across the world in places called Khe Sanh, Saigon and NaTrang being different kinds of heroes. His high school yearbook picture and those of his fellow soldiers rode in the convertible instead. Yes indeed, Odell is as American as America gets.

The roar of the crowd never fades in a real athlete's ear. Sometimes when Dick drives around his beloved town he calls to mind the glory of those days. He can still smell the smells of the locker room, which any athlete will tell you

15

are not all bad - the resin powder, the tape placed on ankles and wrists, sweaty uniforms soaked with victory or defeat - smells that conjure up a smile. Earlier in the day, as Dick drove past the empty lot where the high school used to stand, he longed for her old brick-red walls more than ever. He slowed the car to a halt pausing as if he wanted to be there when she arose, resurrected out of new green grass. Ruth noticed his nostalgic mood but said nothing. Dick moved past the unusual feelings of melancholy and pulled his car into the diner's parking lot.

Blintz's on the southwest side of the town square occupies most of a large white building. The tap room inside is long and dark with video games and poker machines, a pool table at the far end. The walls are covered with posters from the Chicago Bears, White Sox & Cubs. A Black Hawks team portrait with three Stanley Cups hangs in between scenes from the Motor Speedway, the Chicago home of NASCAR racing and a pinup of Marilyn Monroe. The most dominant artifact is the front quarter panel off a 1955 Chevy Bel Air 150! Everything hung was vintage; the most striking aside from the quarter panel a yellow-brown, faded collage of President Kennedy newspaper clippings. Center stage in the collage are the newspaper headlines of his assassination and the subsequent murder of Lee Harvey Oswald. Kennedy was a hero to many in town.

It's no surprise that most of the town held equal pride in the grandson of Mary Duke Odell, Lorenzo. A framed pictorial of equal size detailing the rise of its favorite son from Mayor to State Congressman, U.S. Senator to the highest office in the land hung in a place of honor above the Kennedy collage. Unlike his cousin, Larry, President Odell was a slight man with dark hair and darker eyes. His warm, inviting smile could also be deceptive. He was known

16

on occasion to have a horrid temper and wasn't shy about using it to intimidate his foes. Whether he couldn't control it or didn't want to its a mystery. But this trait hidden by an outward charm and backed by a substantial political power base made President Odell seem, to some, a very dangerous man. He wasn't well liked by everyone in Odell. There were those who'd grown up with him who had seen flashes of a mean streak, but still he was one of them and even his worst detractors would battle furiously for his honor with an outsider.

Saying hello to nearly everyone in the place, eyes quickly adjusting to the dimly lit room, Dick and Ruth made their way to a large, circular table between the bar and the formal dining area. You don't live in a town this size your entire life and not know every soul around.

Dick smiled as he allowed a few sentences from the warring elders to drift his way. He loved those old dogs. A glance out the front window of the dining room caught Carl Walker moving aimlessly up the east side of the town square. No matter how circuitous the route, Dick knew Carl was headed for his favorite stool at the end of the bar. For years the locals chided Danny Blintz until he sent the stool over to Walt Young's custom furniture and had the back of the stool engraved with Carl's name.

Ruth Ralph wasn't from Odell in the blue-blood sense, but she might as well have been. It was her adopted home, and no one had better challenge her on that issue. She was born in a moderate-sized town, fifteen miles up route forty-seven. She was a startlingly attractive mature woman. Clean elegant lines with high cheekbones and piercing blue eyes made it clear that she was, in her younger years, a beautiful woman. Dick and Ruth who had just celebrated their forty-ninth wedding anniversary still held hands wherever they

17

went. He opened the car door for her, she walked on the inside of the sidewalk, he beside her on the outside. That's the way his mother taught him a gentleman treated a lady. That's the way he treated her no matter where they went.

Dressed impeccably, in a white blouse and navy-blue skirt she seemed to glide from one table to another, not a hair out of place. Ruth soon engaged Agnes Mount in conversation about "Odell Days" set for the first week in August. The ladies were conspiring. There was a new radio personality in Chicago with, so it oddly seemed, the last name of Odell. He was no relation that he nor anyone else knew of, but he had become a regular afternoon listen for many of the townspeople. They intended to invite him to visit this year and to ride as grand Marshal in the parade.

"Well Agnes, I understand the young man is a small-town boy himself. He comes from out there in the quad cities and worked in a factory of some sort before he landed his first part time local radio job. Now he's hit the big time in Chicago, and it seems to me just providential that Julie got to speak to him on the show last week. His last name being Odell fits just perfect into an invitation. Besides what wonderful publicity for our little town! I´m just sure he'll come."

"I know Ruth, it's just . . . well it's just, I wonder if we won't regret getting more publicity than we want. You know it's bad enough to have the national press barging in and out of our lives every time Lorenzo Brigham decides to bless us with his presence."

"Now Agnes, after all he is the President of the United States. And while you may have been his fifth-grade teacher, you should be more respectful," Ruth chided her friend with a sly grin.

18

"Hmmpf! He's probably the same little snot he was when he used to hide hard boiled eggs in my filing cabinets. Not that I would ever share that with the news media, but I have to be honest with you, every time I see him, whether it's here in town, on television or in the papers, I just want to scream at him. He was such a little terror!"

"Well yes, I know he was a precocious little thang darlin, but that was a long time ago and I am sure he has changed quite a bit since his egg hiding days. But look here, you have detracted me from the topic at hand. I am going to go ahead and contact that Mr. Odell radio personality up in Chicago and see if indeed he won't come to Odell Days. I spoke with Susan Havlik just yesterday and she thought it was a splendid idea. She told me she would include him on the VIP list as soon as I received confirmation from him that he would join us."

Each year during Odell Days, the town square filled with people from all over the county. Booths and carnival rides helped celebrate the anniversary of the town's formal beginning. Talent shows, tractor pulls, and livestock competitions were as much a part of the fun as the parade that kicked off the week-long festival. Annually, the town tried to get someone special to visit as a way of promoting pride. Most years they weren't very successful in securing their celebrity of choice, but that wouldn't dissuade the pioneer stock these ladies represented.

Ruth's gaze moved about the room smiling each time her eyes met a friend here and another there. Dick was spinning his magic with the men around him as her eyes settled on a stranger, a telephone lineman sitting at the farthest end of the bar feasting on Blintz's famous fried-chicken lunch. Strangers were welcome in Odell, but they never went unnoticed. Everyone in the place knew

19

an outsider was there, but there was no way he'd have known that he was accounted for.

Larry Hurley Odell sat at the table behind Dick and Ruth. He didn't usually take this much time for lunch, but a call from the secret service alerted Mayor Glen Pickett that Monica Palmer had been approved to interview the Presidents' grandmother and a phone call from Mayor landed him the assignment to meet her for lunch. Why he always got stuck with this sort of hand-holding duty was a puzzle to him, but the mayor knew what he was doing. The sheriff was an imposing figure and any potential troublemakers would get the message early that this wasn't the place to look for trouble.

On the other hand, Larry was as charming a fellow as the town had produced. It was always fresh in the mayor's mind that Larry could have gone to any of the bigger cities or towns for a position on the police force that would afford him more professional promise. He thought dealing out some of the sweeter assignments to him was a reward. But Larry didn't see them as perks, they were irritants!

Odell sipped his cup of coffee and half listened to the chatter of the people around him. One eye was on the door waiting for Palmer and the other cast an occasional glance at the lineman. As far as he knew the guns were not standard issue for telephone repair men. A bulge in his jeans above his left ankle could be seen as he propped his foot on the rung of the bar stool. His jeans outlined the rest of the holster. But then again, Odell thought, "he must have to work in some pretty 'dicey" spots up Chicago way."

# # # # #

Carl Walker strained to fight the tightness in his chest and the tremors in

20

his hands as he walked west on Vermillion Street. The sun was already high and the bright reflection off the stark white walls of The Odell Grain and Coal Company caused him to squint as he rounded the corner onto Front Street. At one time he'd been the promised son of Odell. A star high school athlete who had lettered in four sports, he was a shoo-in for one of the big ten schools. But the scouts failed to show up after a junior year knee injury and his family hadn't the funds to send him to school. If only he'd had the good sense to become a farmer or even to claim to be one, he could have avoided the draft that sent him to Vietnam. But Carl Walker considered himself a patriot, an honest man and no damned draft dodger. It was July of 1967 when he stepped off the Northwest Orient troop transport at Ton Son Nhut Air Base just outside Saigon. As he strolled up Front Street toward an imaginary destination, he remembered the look of the airline stewardess who bade him goodbye as he departed the plane. It had haunted him all these years. Barely visible tears formed in her eyes as she shook his hand and said, "Good luck, soldier." It was almost like a benediction as she repeated it with every G.I. that passed by her. A last kiss on the cheek for boys who may very well be marching off into the dark hours of death.

He knew what she was really thinking; she was wondering if she was shaking hands with a dead boy. He wondered how many guys she said that to were dead. He exited the plane and stared out over a city cloaked in a fog or steam, he wasn't sure which. The stench was beyond description, the temperature an unimaginable one hundred and fifteen degrees and it was only seven o'clock in the morning! He knew this was going to be a very bad year, a very, very bad year.

Three hundred and sixty-one days, two purple hearts and a silver cross later he was back on another Northwest Orient flight leaving for home, but he'd left something in those jungles.

Carl continued down Front Street stopping to say hello to people who drifted out of the Community Center and Town Hall in search of lunch. Carl was headed for breakfast and if he didn't get there soon, he thought to himself he was "going to shake to death."

His eyes darted across the square to his real destination. He pretended every day to have just come in from some mysterious place of employment. People knew Carl was unemployed, his wife, Bonnie knew he was unemployed. In fact, everyone in town knew Carl was unemployed, except Carl. Bonnie worked as a secretary at the Women's Correctional Facility in Dwight and was the glue that held the family together. She was small in stature, frail looking, but once she'd been a real beauty and had the attention of all the "right" boys at school. She wanted to be Mrs. Carl Walker as much as Carl wanted her to be, but now she was resigned to a life a prom queen never expects.

Carl made this trip pretending, perhaps dreaming of things that might have been; the same route in his mind and on the streets of Odell nearly every day. Occasionally, he would wander off at night from one of the two bars in town and not get home until lunch time the next day or worse. No one got excited if Carl didn't show up at home for a night or two; he often disappeared, though where to, was a mystery. Sometimes, when Carl was especially drunk and especially paranoid, he would wander off to scale the ladder on the town's water tower. There he would stand, watch the rest of the night with whatever libation he chose as his guard mate. And he would pace around and around and around the water tower until he was certain his beloved Odell was safe, or he just got too damn tired waiting for the enemy to show up. Then he would lay down on the north side of the tower, always the north side, because that's where the city lights from Dwight could be seen and he would sleep there 'til the morning sun would wake him. The problem Carl's guard duty caused for the village of Odell was a sober Carl Walker that was terrified of heights! When the siren atop the firehouse screamed on a Saturday morning, most folks rolled over and smiled. Village kids would scream with delight as they ran up the streets circling the town square. Kenny Eisington would climb the ladder blindfold in hand, swearing under his breath. Once atop the tower, he would talk Carl down from his sheer panic and eventually when he had blindfolded him he would lead him down the ladder to the ground. A grateful Walker would hug his rescuers, proclaim their bravery to the young people standing around and then, without additional ceremony, wander off to his house as if he had just been out for a morning stroll.

After one of those guard duty nights he wouldn't be seen making his daily late morning circuit of the town square. It would be well into the afternoon before he ventured out of his house and when he finally did, he would make a beeline for Blintz's.

Reaching Hamilton Street, Carl crossed the town square and the train tracks that ran just west of it. When he reached Blintz's, he opened the door his eyes struggling to adjust to the dim light within. It didn't matter much that he couldn't see very well, Carl could have negotiated every nook and cranny of that place in pitch blackness. He made his way down the bar acknowledging patrons, saying a special hello to his buddy Sheriff Odell, until he reached the end of the bar.

He wasn't sure what to do; a stranger was sitting on his stool. Looking

23

around the room as if to ask for directions he finally took the stool next to the lineman and awkwardly said a quiet hello. He ordered a draft beer, nervously waiting for what seemed like an eternity before it arrived. He was expert at pretending that it wasn't a necessity, but one could see from the other end of the bar those shaking hands betraying him and knew the lie he was telling himself. That drink was a necessity. And he knew only two things could conquer the shakes - total sobriety or alcohol - and the first was not an option.

He took a long, hard draw on his first beer of the day. It was like a transfusion, he thought. The carbonation scratched his itching throat and the cold liquid screamed peace to something deep inside him over which he no longer had control; some demon who held him captive. All he knew was the more he drank the quieter the demon became until at some point during the day, the demon went to sleep and then he could, too.

Carl leaned over to the lineman, "How ya doing? A great spring day out there isn't it?"

"Yeah, a great one. The kind of day one should be home with his family doing something around the house or packing up the tackle and heading off to the lake." The lineman's voice didn't sound all that friendly Carl thought. The stranger took one long last swig of his beer. "Well, I'm off to keep words flying through wire. You take care, now."

Sheriff Odell also thought it odd that a man climbing telephone poles and towers for a living would have a beer with his lunch. It was just one beer after all, but it was still damn odd.

Carl Walker moved over to 'his stool' and stared for a very long, still moment into the mirror behind the bar. Eventually he whispered to his twin, "you cheated me."

24

Chapter IV

Mary Duke Odell stood at the kitchen sink staring out the window into her manicured backyard. The reporter was in the sitting room, but Mary, in no hurry to answer another round of the same kind of meaningless questions, was staring at the yellow tulips that framed the walkway leading to the back-fence gate. Yet, she couldn't in all honesty deny her pride in Lorenzo and the attention it sometimes brought to her. Who'da thought, a country girl like her, pioneer stock and big city folk knocking at her door all the time? Took an army to convince her grandson that she wouldn't settle for the bevy of secret servicemen who first took up position about her home. Brought more attention than if they weren't there. They were there more often than Mary thought, but not nearly as much as the President would have preferred.

The reporter, a young woman from the Chicago Tribune, shared that her great-great-great-grandmother was a Native American whose tribe once lived somewhere in the area. She'd been terribly excited to land this as her first major assignment, an interview with the President's grandmother and a visit to ancestral lands all in one swoop! And then there was the local sheriff, Larry Odell, another descendant of the original founders of Odell. She just knew this was going to be the best weekend assignment of her young career.

Mary always tried to make time for the local press. It was the national boys and girls that made her feel ill at ease; the CNNs and networks, the News.coms and the such. She was the grand dame of Livingston County. An elegant country lady that loved pretending that she was just a simple country girl, she longed to be outside tending to her flower garden in the morning sunshine. Planted up against the garage the sun's warmth radiated off the west wall of the red brick structure nourishing the best tulips in all of Livingston

County.

"I'll be right with you dear, just want to get this coffee brewing before we begin," Mary called out to the young woman waiting in her living room.

Monica Palmer was an attractive, talented young woman fresh out of Roosevelt University's Journalism program. Her first year at the Tribune had garnered her, the usual gofer assignments but she loved the opportunity and was a diligent employee. Her boss liked her spunk. When the Sunday edition needed some fill, Ron Bradley decided it would be interesting to see how youth would relate to and memorialize a meeting with that "crusty old broad from Odell." When she was called into his office, Monica could hardly believe her ears. Her five-foot, two-inch frame seemed to swell to more than six feet. She called her family that evening to tell them of her good fortune and to remind them to be on the watch for the article in the Sunday edition.

Straight long brown hair and a heart-shaped face with full lips made her look younger than her twenty-four years. She often thought to look young was a pain in the rear for someone in her occupation.

"I have a hard time getting into a stinking night club how the hell am I going to crack doors I need to crack to make a go of this?"

On Friday morning she dressed smartly, business like, in a black skirt and jacket. Her white blouse was complimented with a scarlet red scarf and modest gold necklace. Driving down the interstate her heart rate soared the closer she got to Odell. Her vehicle came to a halt outside the huge red brick home of Mary Duke Odell. The house dated back a hundred and ten years. Surrounded by a short white picket fence the front yard was full of flowers blossoming. It smelled like a flower shop. Yellow jackets were flitting from bush to bush. An old fashion pair of street lanterns sat on each side of the walkway leading up

26

to the front steps that ended at a wrap-around porch. Monica imagined all the folks who must have sat in the pale blue wicker chairs adorning it. Two large ceiling fans recently added allowed Mary to relax in the summer evenings and survey the Odell kingdom and the neighbors she loved as they passed by.

She acknowledged a case of the jitters as she approached her first big assignment. It took a few minutes to gain her composure, to slow her heart rate. And then she was out the door and up the steps to the beginning of the most exciting, dangerous chapter of her life though she didn't know it.

Mary filled the coffee pot with cold clear water and placed it on the stove. Calling Monica into the kitchen Mary said, "I'm not averse to modern conveniences, but no one can convince me that coffee was made to be brewed anywhere except in the coffee pot my mother gave me on my wedding day. Whoever heard of making a good cup of coffee in thirty seconds? My Lord! And everyone who has ever been to my house for coffee swears, by all that is holy, that I am the best coffee brewer they ever met. It's not me honey. It's this good ole stained pot. You know don't you that no matter how many times you use a Brillo pad on this thing that you still can't make it shine? And that's the way it's s'posed to be.

"See that cardinal out by the garage? She came back again a few days ago. She comes back to that same old oak tree every spring; has now for at least seven years. People ask how I know it's the same bird . . . well, not people, just my neighbor Verna Pickett. She's such a pain in the rear sometimes. 'It's the same bird Verna . . . because it is! That's all there is to it.'" Mary mocked.

"Each year Verna asks that same question and each year I answer her with the same answer. Seemingly each time to her satisfaction, but the next year she asks me straight away again. I think the woman's going a bit south if you know what I mean."

Mary decided to steal another quick peek at Mother Cardinal. She loved her subdued red coloring, quieter hues than the weathered red brick of the garage walls. She wasn't as bright as her many mates, but in her quieter colors and confidence she outranked them. She watched her build her nest new every year twig by twig. She'd sit on the back porch watching her arrange small pieces of this and that for her soon-to-arrive fledglings. Then one day as sure as sunrise Mary would take her coffee to the porch surprised to find beautiful eggs present in the nest. It always surprised her no matter how much she prepared herself. Eventually the eggs would hatch, and she would supervise, in her mind, the care of the chicks. There were usually three or four babies to start. Of course, there was no guarantee that they would all make it, in fact, it was most unusual that all would survive the nest. Though Mother seemed to bring the same food every day and the chicks all were fed, some thrived and some did not. Mary wasn't sure if the ones who did not make it were too weak to fight for their fair share of food or if they simply lacked the character to survive. Did Mother know which ones had a chance and which didn't? Did she spend her time, devote her energy and feeding to only those in the nest she instinctively knew had the best chance of perpetuating the specie? Or was she just a mother, saddened by the loss of a little one?

Sometimes it was no fault of anyone that the full brood didn't make it. Like two years ago, when Simon, her cantankerous, rogue of a cat decided to go to Sabbath morning buffet which happened to end squarely in the middle of the cardinal's nest. Mary was furious with him. Simon was the victim of a full week of Mary's wrath, initiated by a slipper that bounced more than three feet off his head. It was the only time one of Mary's friends had ever seen her angry with an animal. When she simmered down, she realized Simon was just being a cat, but it did not make the hurt any less painful.

Drifting back from the window, Mary returned to the young reporter.

"Let's go into the sitting room sweetie, we'll be more comfortable there."

She knew this young lady was going to be different than other reporters who came to see her. In those brief moments looking out the kitchen window she stole glimpses of her. She could see it in her eyes.

As they walked on creaking wooden floors towards the front room Monica asked, "Mrs. Odell, I read that your ancestors were honest-to-goodness, covered-wagon pioneers. Do you know much about them?"

Monica was eyeing a circular table full of very old brown faded photographs.

"Yes . . . after a fashion, I suppose. You see, great-great-grandfather and grandmother left for the far west in covered wagons in the 1840's from Nauvoo, Illinois. It was a long arduous trek of nearly four months. I have their diaries you know. Well I have copies of them. Mr. Odell donated the originals to the museum in Salt Lake City. They were kind enough to duplicate and bind them for us. If you'd like, I'll show them to you later; perhaps someday we can read from them together. They make wonderful reading. Grandmother wrote most religiously every day, so they are rather complete. They drove their teams and covered wagons across the frozen Mississippi in February of eighteen hundred and forty-five and staged in Iowa before the long trek west in early spring. On the open trail at night they had the most wonderful campfires; the camp would come together to dance, sing and share food with one another. And then of course there's accounts of tragedy; Indian raids, children

29

lost to sickness and accident and death out alone on the prairies far from any-one or anything. Our family lost two little ones on the trail. They are buried somewhere on the plains west of Keokuck. I think of their little spirits some days when cool westerly breezes blow across our fields here. I wonder about them, what they were like. Did they laugh a lot, were they happy little ones? Yes . . . you come again another time and we'll read through those diaries if you like?"

"Oh, yes, are you serious? I'd love to! You just name the time. But now I am a little confused. If great-great-grandfather and grandmother drove covered wagons west, how did they wind back up here in what is now Odell?"

"The answer is time tested and true. Men, that's the answer honey, men. They always seem to think the grass is greener in the next pasture. Grandfa-ther Odell thought the west was going to be the answer to all his dreams. After ten years in Utah he decided he wanted to move east. I mean east as in back to the Eastern states. They began the return journey in the spring of 1852. When they reached camp just west of here grandmother decided, she had traveled far enough for one lifetime. I don't know why the historians of Odell haven't cleaned that story up more than a little; for the most part historians are men you know. No matter what they say, grandpa great Bill Odell bought that first 2100 acres because his wife told him to hold still or go on east without her. So, I guess you could say we owe the fact that this little town is what it is to-day because Grandmother Odell decided to put down stakes not grandfather.

"You're kidding! What a great little story!"

"Well, I thought you would appreciate a little bit of a scoop today." Mary smiled at the reporter and then her face became quite sober. "She left you know?"

"She left? Left what, Odell?"

"Yes, but that's another story. Depending on who tells it, you know. Would you like some cookies with your coffee?"

"Yes Ma'am."

Mary arose heading back toward the kitchen with the young reporter in tow. Opening cupboards, sliding in and out of her pantry, she moved about her kitchen as she had done for the past 63 years.

The reporter watched Mary as she made conversation. "She's special; a fascinating woman," she thought as she, for the first time took real physical stock of her. She was a tall woman, nearly six feet tall, with wonderfully bright white hair. Her skin was of medium complexion, covered with freckles; freckles not age spots. Monica looked about the house on their way to the kitchen trying to glimpse a picture of Mary as a young woman. She found none. Mary had slender strong arms and hands. Her fingers were especially long the reporter thought, wishing she had such hands. "No glasses," she noticed, in spite of her age, and a wonderfully perfect smile. The smile was what it was about Mary that made her Odell's treasure and was making her America's. Her eyes were not only a deep ocean blue, as blue as any the reporter had ever seen, but they looked like something right out of a Foster Grant ad staring at you off the page so intensely that you can't help but wonder if anyone could ever really have eyes that blue. Mary Duke Odell did, and they had the ability to pierce a person's soul when she stared at them. The reporter couldn't help but think for some inexplicable reason that they weren't Mary's eyes; it was like a young person was hiding away inside there somewhere. Those young eyes looking out at her from across the kitchen seemed to be calling to her, no inviting her. But inviting her to what she just hadn't figured out yet. Monica liked Mary

31

Duke Odell. She liked her very much.

Mary turned around from the counter with a small flowered plate full of cookies. She said as she handed her a cup, "Come let's sit down in here where we can see the flowers in the back yard, or would you prefer the back porch?"

"The porch, I think. We can see more of the yard from there and it is such a lovely morning isn't it?"

"Yes, it's one of the better ones we have had this spring I think." Sitting down on a long swing seat and patting the spot next to her Mary continued, "Honey, why don't you just put down that pencil and pad. We'll just girl talk. By the time you leave here you'll have more than enough to write about; more than I care to think about!" Mary laughed.

"Ok, you have a deal." The young reporter giggled. "But, please . . . let me turn on my recorder, I have a lousy memory for details, and I don't want to miss or forget anything." Mary nodded her consent. "Mrs. Odell?"

"It's Mary, remember we're just a couple of good ole girls having coffee together and chatting." She liked the young girl. She couldn't be more than twenty-two or three and a good story for her editor would do wonders for her career. She reminded Mary of herself a little bit when she had just graduated from college and was full of the world.

"Was there ever a time when you wanted to leave Odell? Maybe head off to the city, Chicago . . . New York . . . Los Angeles, anyplace?"

"Yes, dear there was a time. I darn near made it, too." She smiled, "I was a young woman. I just got my degree from the University of Illinois. I thought about staying in Odell and teaching at St. Paul's, but I felt a real draw toward a bigger place. You know someplace where I could be anonymous, where you could spit into the wind and nobody gave a hoot if you did. Thought I might go up to Chicago, lose myself in the masses and make my fortune. Oh, I knew I would eventually come back to Odell, but I wanted to give it a shot." She anticipated the next question. "You want to know why I didn't." Mary got up off the swing and moved to the screened wall of the porch. Staring off into the yard, she continued, "I was a young girl, possibly not much older than you are now. And if you don't mind a bit of immodesty, I was not a bad looker." She grinned.

One Tuesday morning April of 1936 I awoke after the silliest dream. There was this big red brick house in it and a white picket fence. It was beautiful and there were three children playing in the front yard. I was walking past the house and as I got even with the front porch the children stopped playing and stared at me. They were beautiful kids really. I was drawn to them and slowed my pace. As I moved past them, they called out to me, giggling, I can still hear their laughter. I turned to them, they beckoned for me to join them, eyes all sparkling, but I didn't accept their invitation. When I had finally passed them a good ways their calls seemed more urgent, so I turned to them . . .poof, they were gone. I looked for them everywhere but could not find them. I woke up upset. Did you ever have a dream like that? So real that when you woke up you were emotional from it? Well, I was, and I felt so silly being affected by a dream that way. I didn't tell anyone about it for a long, long time.

Well later that day Mr. Odell asked me to next Sunday services with him. We went for a picnic lunch afterwards. I don't suppose it's very fashionable thing to do these days, ask a body to church with you, but it was very important in my day. Mr. Odell and I attended St. Paul's occasionally together in those early days and Mr. Odell well . . . he just had to sit right down in the front row. It wasn't that he wanted to be seen by anyone or anything like that,

33

but the truth be known he was a little hard of hearing even as a young man. So, when we attended together, we would march to the very front row. That Sunday, Father Maxwell was giving one of the best homilies. I was enjoying it so much when, suddenly, he stopped right in his tracks and looked down at me from the pulpit. I was so nervous, wondering if I had done something to distract him. He called me out by name and then as clear as a bell declared in front of the whole congregation, "Mary Duke! Don't you dare go running off to some big city. The Lord would just as well be pleased if you rooted down here in Odell as did your ancestors." That being said, he went about his sermon and never paid me no mind until we were leaving the parish. Mr. Odell was wondering what that was all about, and I told him I was sure I hadn't the faintest idea. But when I reached the vestibule father was waiting for me. We said nothing to each other; he just had this twinkle in his eyes. When I got down to the bottom of the steps, I could feel that Mr. Odell was not right behind me. He was standing on the top step engaged in conversation with Father Maxwell. When Mr. Odell first turned towards me and our eyes met, he had that "forever look in his eyes." Do you know what I mean, honey?"

"No Ma'am" the reporter whispered almost reverently.

"Well, no matter, you're probably too young to have seen a "forever look." Mary smiled at her. "Anyway darling, to make a very long story short, I stayed in Odell. I took a teaching position at St. Paul's High School, never looked back . . . never regretted my decision for a moment."

"What a nice story."

"Oh, that's not the end of it honey. A year later Mr. Odell, he was such a handsome man; you would have been just ga ga over him, asked me to marry him and of course the rest is history, except you should know about this house.

This house with the white picket fence is where we raised our three beautiful children, those children from the dream. This is our "forever look" home."

"Omigod!" The reporter whispered in awe.

"I never told Mr. Odell about that dream until after President Odell's mother was born. Until today it has been our secret . . . mine and his. Now you have a scoop for sure, don't you?"

"Oh, yes. Yes, I do, but are you sure you want it told? It's so lovely . . . so personal."

"It's kind of a gift to you honey. You write it up. You treat it with dignity. I know you will."

"Oh yes Ma'am, of course I will. You can bet on it."

"I'm sure. And now it's time to spice up this coffee a bit. What do you say?"

Monica nodded and after a few sips of the *refreshed coffee* said. "Mary, you're right . . . this is the best damn coffee I ever had." Mary smiled at the comment.

The two women sat in silence for a long time, sipping coffee, watching mother cardinal warming her eggs. The reporter reflected on the extraordinary spirit sitting next to her. She learned over an hour and half ago, that Mary subscribed to three major newspapers, The Chicago Tribune, The New York Times and The Washington Post, which she read daily. She did so to keep an eye on her grandson. Impressive for a woman who claimed, tongue in cheek, that the universe ended at the borders of Odell. She read at least one book a month, preferring historical novels or biographies. She was a big fan of historian H. W. Brands.

The western half of the sun porch was dedicated to oil painting. Though not a great artist, she was accomplished enough to sell several paintings at the "Odell Days" celebration every year, donating the proceeds to the library at the women's prison in Dwight. She spent a few hours every other week or so at both elementary schools doing volunteer work. She was an active member of the Odell Library Board and met every second Thursday of the month with the historical society. In secret she called it the hysterical society since the girls who belonged were some of her best friends and laughter dominated the meetings. And finally, once a month Mary Duke Odell, contrary to Secret Service advice, traveled the near seven miles north to the Dwight Women's Correctional Facility where she volunteered as a guidance counselor. The toughest women in the state were sent to Dwight. They adored her.

A day ago, after the initial excitement of getting the assignment to interview Mrs. Odell, Monica became concerned about the content of the interview. Mary Duke had been media'd to death. She was twenty-four and Mary was in her eighties. What could she possibly ask that had not already been asked in dozens of interviews? What would, or could she and Mrs. Odell possibly have in common? What could she uncover or share with readers that would be new and interesting?

In a little less than two hours Mary had answered these questions. She taught her about the sisterhood women have with each other if they will only take the time to discover it. Now as she sat on the quiet back porch, she found it difficult to take her eyes off this grand lady. She didn't want to leave and couldn't wait to come back, but she had to meet Sheriff Odell for lunch. After all she was a professional and she had a deadline to meet. She needed to get to it. She was anxious to get to it.

"Mary, it's getting late, but before I go, may I ask you just one more question. I wrote it down last night. It was the only question I could really think of that I hadn't seen someone else ask you. So, I wrote it down, so I wouldn't forget to ask you."

"Of course, you may." Those blue eyes sparkled at her.

"Ok . . . here it is. After all these years, after all your experiences tell me . . . tell me what the greatest day of your life was." Monica checked the recorder and sat back. She thought to herself, "would it be her marriage, the birth of her children, attending the inauguration of her daughter's son? This ought to be good. It had to be" . . . it was going to be.

"Are you sure the world is ready for this, honey?" Mary smiled at the young woman.

The reporter laughed out loud. "No, I'm not sure they are but what the hell!"

Mary returned to her spot on the swing seat beside the reporter, reached over and held the young woman's hand for a moment. "Ok, one last story from this crazy old lady before I meet the girls for lunch.

When I was a very young girl, things were different than they are for young women today." Looking at the reporter's business dress suit Mary continued, "but I'm sure you realize that. In any event I went to a one-room schoolhouse until St. Paul's Elementary School was built. At the time I was twelve years old. The little school was all the town could afford so all grades, first through twelfth met in that one room. Miss Isabella Murray was our teacher, a matronly ole thang if you know what I mean. She was portly, immaculately dressed and even way out here on the plains she secured the best make up and used it daily. I remember her very stern face, which never smiled, was framed with shockingly white hair. She wasn't that old a woman, but to tell you the

truth, I don't know how old she really was. She was a firm believer and practi-
tioner of the 'spare the rod spoil the child' philosophy. We were all terrified of
her.

And then there was this boy, a ninth grader, his name was Charlie Watson.
Some of his buddies called him Chuckie, but I didn't because I didn't much
care for him. He was a red-haired boy. What you call a 'ginger' nowadays
yes?"

"Yes."

"Well he was a tall lanky young man with bright blue eyes and always
seemed to have the devil about him. He and his lot were always in some sort
of mischief or another. Couldn't trust him as far as you could throw a tractor.
He wore the same shirt to school at least four days a week as I remember and
never went to heavy on the soap and water in between days.

Charlie was a marble shooter, the best marble shooter in the region. He
won a tournament up in Dwight once and even beat the menfolk down at the
county fair in Pontiac. No question, Charlie was a good marble shooter. I
don't know of anyone who ever beat him," Mary smiled.

"The schoolhouse stood on the western side of Odell. There wasn't no
grass anywhere near it. Just one big dusty patch of ground. Had a few big trees
on it though. One just a few yards from the front door. In the spring time it
could get nasty hot out there in that school yard and when it did most of the
young women wouldn't even go outside when recess came for fear of dirtying
up their dresses. Of course, as I've mentioned to you that was certainly no
concern for Charlie and his gang. So, unless it was raining and the whole area
turned into a mud hole, every recess found Charlie and his gang shooting marbles down in the dirt. I think at one-time Charlie Watson owned every damn

marble in a fifty-mile radius of Odell." She grinned.

"Are you with me, Monica?" she smiled at the young girl's look of puzzle-ment.

"Oh, yes. Please continue." The reporter had no idea where this was going, but she was loving it.

"Well, one day in early June," Mary thought for a moment, "June 6, 1924 to be exact. The recess bell rang; the weather was perfect, so boys and girls all piled out to the playground. The boys and Charlie Watson went to one side to shoot marbles and the girls and smaller kids to the other side for a game of kick ball. The boys soon got busy huddling around Charlie as he made short order of Freddie Hewett's paltry lot of marbles. Just as Charlie closed his cloth marble sack and drew the string tight, a voice rang out from across the yard."

"Charlie Watson, you wanna shoot some marbles with me?" The school yard fell silent. Silent as I or anyone else had ever heard it. I know you are wondering what the big deal is honey. The big deal is this. Girls did not shoot marbles when I was a girl." Mary looked into the reporter's eyes. She could tell she wasn't getting it. "Honey . . . girls were not *permitted*. It wasn't that we weren't capable or that we did not want to; we were not allowed to. It was unthinkable!" Monica stared back at her in disbelief.

"You see Miss Murray had explained to us, on many an occasion that there were certain things that were appropriate for a young lady to participate in and others that were not. And getting down in the dirt to shoot marbles with one of those rascal boys was not one of them! We never broke one of Miss Murray's rules. Disobedience was a never a concept to be entertained."

Mary continued "The silence that followed the challenge gave way to a few giggles from the boys nearest to Charlie.

39

I could stand it no longer Miss Palmer. I raised a small cloth marble purse I had been hiding for months in my desk. I swung it back and forth a few times like a pendulum, knowing Charlie Watson couldn't resist 'unowned' marbles. My challenge inspired roars of laughter from the boy side of the playground. Howls bounced off the schoolhouse walls while some of the boys lay on the ground writhing in pretend pain from the very thought of such ridiculousness. All of them, delirious with laughter. In response to the reaction from the boy's side of the school yard, that same voice issued the challenge again with the same result. After this scene repeated itself once again, I had all I could take. I yelled from across the school 'Chicken!' The boys fell into fits of laughter at the thought that such an insult could be hurled at one as important as Charlie Watson, marble Champion of Pontiac County!

"Yes, all of them howled . . . all except Charlie Watson who rose to his feet, face beet red glowering at me as if I had called his mother the foulest name known to us. Then as suddenly as the uproar started it stopped and silence fell over the playground. It was so quiet that I could hear the leaves rustling in the wind on the old oak tree close to the schoolhouse stairs. My own heartbeat sounded loud to me. My mouth was dry, it was hard for me to catch my breath, but I clutched that small purse holding my precious ten marbles and stared Charlie Watson right back in the eye. I put my hands on my hips and then held out the bag.

"Mary Duke! You ain't got the sense yer own parents growed ya up with. Girls don't shoot marbles, don't even know how to. 'Cides, yer wearin a skirt. You, a stupid sixth grader wants to shoot me a round? Are you sick or something?" His face reddened a deep new shade at the very idea of having to address me.

I called to him again, 'Chicken! again raising the purse, taunting him.

"What! What did you call me? I can't believe this kid. Now I know she must be crazy. Somebody call Dr. Gray to come fetch her over to the nut-house."

"You are a *coward* Charlie Watson. A coward and a . . . Chicken!!!"

That was all it took. Charlie could stand no more. "Git over here stupid. I'll show you who's chicken."

I walked slowly across the dusty playground, my heart beating a million times a second. I'd swear everyone in the world could hear that thumping. I was determined though. I was not afraid of Charlie Watson nor any other boy on that playground. I was only afraid of being afraid. The girls, my girls, did not fall in behind me as I expected they would. They were mortified and sort of scooted around me, so they could blend into the crowd, behind the boys. I was hurt by their failure to support me at first. I felt betrayed and then my hurt turned to anger. And this is one woman you don't want to get riled. didn't give a damn. I was gonna shoot marbles with Charlie Watson and I was gonna whup him."

Mary leaned back on the swing and took a long sip of her coffee. The anxious reporter had to prompt her out of what appeared to be a much-revisited reverie.

"And? And what happened? Did you shoot with him? Did you beat him?"

"Honey, I shot with him. I got down on my knees in the dusty dirt of the playground, harlot that I was. I lifted my skirt, so my knees were showing, so my dress wouldn't get dirty and I shot him all right Monica; I shot the heck out of him. When the dust cleared, I owned every marble Charlie Watson brought to school that day."

41

"Omigodddd!" Monica squealed as she stared, her eyes transfixed on Mary.

"It doesn't end there honey. There was no applause when it was over. I dusted my hands and knees off, brushed the dust from my skirt and wiped the sweat from my upper lip. The girls, my girlfriends didn't wait on me. They followed the boys back into the school room. Charlie Watson led them, his face still a crimson red, his nostrils flared, spitting revenge this and cheating that. He was a very angry boy. Of course, the whole class was talking about it when the teacher returned to the room. I beat him alright, but that's not what made it the greatest day of my life."

"Miss Murray was furious and despite repeated efforts to gain control of a class that was out of control, she'd finally had enough. She demanded to know what the bustle was all about. Snooty Cynthia Cook spilled the beans on me. She always was a teacher's snitch."

"When Murray heard the details her nostrils flared, one strand hair came unglued from her perfect hairdo and fell forward over her forehead. She flung it back into place and called me to the front of the class. There she derided me for embarrassing her and the rest of the respectable young women in attendance." "What on earth was I thinking of and hadn't my parents brought me up properly and what was the superintendent going to think when he heard of it? It was a well-established fact that girls who insisted on participating in boys' games grew up to make nothing of themselves. And aside from that, they were generally regarded as trash by most decent folks. Concluding, she demanded that I produce the now bulging, the grey purse and return every marble in it to its rightful owner, Charlie Watson. Charlie, desperately trying to regain his dignity, and his marbles, was more than willing to accept them, the low down no account."

"Oh no! Did you have to give them back to that little weasel?"

"I took one look at Miss Murray and one at Charlie Watson." Mary's eyes, sparkling, smiling blue eyes landed on the reporter. "Then I turned around and faced the room full of students who were at this point quite speechless. And I said to those attending that auspicious occasion, "I will never give Charlie Watson back a single marble he ain't won from me, down in the dirt, square 'n fair. Not now, not ever. Not even if hell freezes over like my daddy says." And with that I ran out of the room and scaled up the swing tree on the far side of the school yard. Mrs. Murray rushed out on my tail and angrily tried, for the better part of a half an hour, to get me down out of that tree. Which of course I refused to do. I cared little for her threats and less for her attempts to sweet talk me. I wouldn't budge an inch and knew she'd never dare come up after me. It would have been unladylike. But she did send one of Charlie Watson's minions scooting off in the direction of my home."

"Soon, from my vantage point in the tree, I could see in the distance the small speck of my father making his way across the fields toward the school. My heart beat so hard again I thought it was going to bust right out of my chest. When he finally got close enough that I could see him clearly, he looked toward the tree with me in it. And that's when I could see a big grin on his face! In that instant I loved him more than life itself Monica! I crawled down out of that tree and ran to his outstretched arms. My daddy kissed me on both cheeks, placed me on his shoulders and carried me off home. He only asked me one question all that way home. "Did ya beat him fair 'n square?" I nodded yes, and he laughed pretty much all the way there.

Mary leaned very close to the reporter's ear. "And that honey, was the greatest day of my entire life. It's remains to this day the greatest thing that

43

ever has happened to me!"

Those beautiful blue eyes seemed to illuminate the entre room, Monica thought, as she stared at the elderly woman.

# # # # #

It's 11:30 Friday night in Atlanta, Illinois and communications and electronics specialist Lt. Robert Lee Cox from Winchester, Tennessee has just completed his final equipment check. It's an interesting array of the most advanced gear he's seen assembled into one place in a very long time. "Thank God for "friends in high places." When a little fear started to rise in his throat he thought, "it's ok, a little fear is healthy. You ain't got no fear, you ain't got no brains." One more cup of coffee and he's ready to go.

Madison T. Vincent, Colonel U.S. Army ret. sat behind a large oak desk staring out of the second-floor arched double windows, amazed that his life had brought him to this moment. A small-town boy from upstate New York, he'd made his way with high honors through West Point, survived the filthy heat of two mid-eastern conflicts, rounded out his twenty-five-year career and had nothing but an easy life to look forward to with the love of his life.

Many thought he loved combat but those who really knew him knew that while he'd been a ferocious warrior and commander quite the opposite was true. He always thought his primary role was a part of a larger plan to dissuade an enemy of the United States from acting foolishly. In the theater of war, he was a hard commander, fair and cared for his men more than anything. He had not sacrificed lives unnecessarily, but he would sacrifice them for the success of a mission; that's what war and leadership are all about the. . .willingness to sacrifice. And as he sat staring at vehicles moving up and down Interstate 55 in the distance, sacrifice was on his mind. The sacrifice that he and his men were about to make once more for their country. "Hopefully, you get the enemy to sacrifice more of their men than you have to of yours," he once told an old non-combatant friend.

Colonel Vincent has an aversion to profanity. He wasn't a prude, but he had high standards and the word went out among candidates for the elite battalion he now commanded that your language had better be held in check, especially when around the "old man".

"A man who has no command over his mouth most likely has no command over his body and thus represents the potential weak link in the chain. Gentlemen, there will be no weak links in any chain I'm responsible for." In the heat of combat though, he sometimes turned a deaf ear.

It is time to address the command group and then the men. This is the season of war that he loves most; the anticipation of confrontation, tree lines darker than the sky at dusk . . . holding what, who . . . glory, resolve, victory, heroism, death, even the non-option defeat? He resented those in the broadcast booths on Saturday and Sunday afternoons who compared the big football games to a war . . . or going to war. They had no similarities. Those players, those announcers and most of their audience would never, . . . never come close to knowing what going to war was like. That knowledge was reserved for his men and men and women like them.

Now is the time when he felt closest to his men . . . just before they were about to spit into brother death's face. "Get the boys ready to go, lay it all on the line, dry mouths, and then when you can hear your own heartbeat in your ears, it's time to go. Time to flip the switches of these good soldiers to 'On.'"

"Sergeant Major?" His voice booms out of the office door. "Light 'em up. Officers and Non-Coms in my office in ten minutes."

45

"Yes, Sir," Sergeant Major Tom Manning responded even as he was moving toward the outer door. "Sergeant Stevens, round 'em up, the old man wants 'em front and center in ten."

In seven minutes, the officers stood in Colonel Vincent's outer office. Alpha Company Commander, Captain Larry Schnecksnider, a Cajun from the bayous of Louisiana, tall with sandy blond hair and blue eyes. He joined Vincent in Iraq and was as good an infantry commander as existed. Captain Mario Petracha, Charlie Company Commander, was a big man. His size was intimidating, and had he not busted his knees playing football at the University of Syracuse, he would most likely have been in some network's commentator's booth instead of traipsing around the world cleaning one mess after another. His dark, curly black hair accents a tanned face where a prominent neanderthal brow adds to an already intimidating persona. His eyes, small for a man his size, are quite capable of boring through a person, especially one who's not completed an assigned task or hadn't completed it up to expected standards. His boys sometimes refer to him as "Stallone", Italian for Stallion. . . but not to his face. Of course, he knows about the nickname and secretly likes it, but he'd never acknowledged that.

Bravo Company Commander, Captain Marcus William Stewart hails Los Angeles, a tough street kid/gang member. When he was given the choice of five years in one of California's finest rehabilitation clinics or two years in the service of his country, he thought the Army would look nicer on his resume than reform school. Shortly after arriving at Fort Dix, New Jersey for basic training he caught the drill cadre's eyes as a young man with leadership potential. Advanced infantry training and another eye caught; he was recommended for the army's Officers Training School. When he graduated first in his class, the Old Man snatched him up as a young second Lt. and hauled his butt off to the mid-east with him twice. There he proved himself with three purple hearts and a distinguished service cross. If not for a wise judge and the Old Man, he'd have been found dead on the streets of Los Angeles a long time ago.

Captain Allen Bell, G-2 Intelligence officer, was a short portly man with a receding hairline and the most unlikely looking of all the infantry officers present. Hailing from central Missouri, he fancied himself a good ole boy whose passion was hunting and fishing. Though he'd earned a master's degree in American Literature, he felt most at home shooting the breeze with the good ole salt of the earth people that were his neighbors. He was the "intellectual" of the group though Petracha often referred to him as having been educated beyond his intelligence. But Allen was one of those rare birds who decided to do what he loved most rather than what parents, friends, professors and eventually an ex-wife had encouraged. He had been around the horn with the Old Man and was delighted when he got the call from him over years ago.

Captain Paul Hauser was the "baby" of the team. A former Navy SEAL, he left the military over a dispute involving a superior officer's wife. It had been an ill-advised mistake and the NAVY was hesitant to suggest retirement to such a superior officer. They invest a lot of money into making a man a SEAL and even more in him as he progresses up the chain of command. But you just don't get caught planking some admiral's young, trophy wife at a base Christmas party and expect your career to blossom. It was the morality clause (the brig) or dishonorable discharge. Hauser decided on the latter and bounced around the personal bodyguard/private investigations business for a few years. He liked neither, but the money was good. For a man with Hauser's special talents, however, most of what he did was nothing more than babysitting "the

47

swells." He'd rubbed elbows with enough Hollywood types to know that too many of them were weak, vain people with too much money and time on their hands and he was glad to be back in the saddle. When Sergeant Major Manning recommended him for the mission, Colonel Vincent never hesitated to extend the most important position of the mission to him. He looked like the original G.I. Joe toy. Tall, with a flat top crew cut and an iron set to his jaw, he never went anyplace without a cigar stuck between his teeth. In Desert Storm he had one shot out of his mouth. He became an instant legend, storming up and down streets firing into any window that looked like it might harbor the son of a **** who destroyed his last good cigar.

Vincent's executive officer was the quiet man of the bunch. All business, logistics and planning he was "The Man" when it came to find out who had what, where so and so was supposed to be and how an objective was to be taken. A master at being able to change game plans on the run, Captain John Coffin would have made a wonderful NFL coach. When he and Vincent put their minds to a task, it was a sure bet it was going to be successfully accomplished. Coffin had a sense of what it was going to take logistically to pull off just about any mission. He relied on Vincent to tell him if and when to make the required moves. They were a devastating team that had met shortly after Vincent was assigned to head up the Special Forces training facility at Ft. Bragg.

Coffin looked like a businessman, with his black rimmed glasses and a pocket full of pens at his constant ready. Cell phones and hand-held electronics to a man like Coffin, were manna from heaven. He'd never been married and never gave it much thought. Married life he reasoned had no place in an Army life. An occasional trip to the "bar of the month" with the guys and a brief rendezvous with a local gal was as about as close to a relationship as he'd ever had with a woman. He was close to his parents who lived in the small town of Sanford, Florida. Dad was a retired baker and mom kept busy keeping track of John's two sisters, one brother and countless grandchildren. Nope, mom n dad didn't need old John to perpetuate the clan; the others had taken that burden off his shoulders, thank God.

Vincent appeared in the doorway with a small pointer in his hand. "Come in, gentlemen, it's time to get this show on the road." The small band of officers followed Vincent into, what was now the war staging room. On a large table Vincent had laid out a map of the target area. "As our training has demonstrated it's going to be fairly easy isolating the target." Pointing to the map, "the perimeter will be laid out here, a two-mile radius of the target, but once we get in there, I do not want to see a living soul of any kind approach within five miles of that circumference perimeter, understand? Tell the troops if it moves shoot it. And shoot to kill it. We are not interested in taking any prisoners. That also means there will be no egress from the inside of the perimeter as well. The same shoot rules apply. Is that understood?" Vincent looked around the room. The question was rhetorical. In preparation for the mission they'd been over the plan a thousand times on paper and in the field. Every man in the room and every troop staged outside knew all the details and the rules of engagement. Each had committed to the mission and whatever it took, for some it might require their lives. They knew that as well.

"Interstate 55 will be cut off three miles below Route 17 on the north. Route 23 on the west, 47 on the east and Rowe Road on the south. Captain Schnecksnider, you have responsibility along with Captain Petracha to make sure that the perimeter is established, fortified and impenetrable immediately upon troop arrival. Robert, I want you to drop what you must drop and get back to your monitoring station. I want you contacting everyone that needs to hear from you. No exceptions; you pick something up on that equipment, I want it warned once and dead if it fails to respond.

"Captain Bell. Your advance man is already in position and in contact?"

"Yes Sir, he's on the tower as we speak."

"Good. You and Captain Lee make sure the communication disruption effort dovetails into his drop effort. Nothing coming in and nothing going out unless it's to our people from our people. Understand?"

"Yes, Sir."

"Captain Stewart, you got the job of babysitter. Inside the perimeter you boys take care of rounding up the goods. You and your boys ready to handle that?"

"Ready as we will ever be Sir."

"Good. Now listen; we follow the plan to the tee. No casualties other than what are called for to preserve the integrity of the mission. Do you understand? I don't want to hear any of this "collateral damage" noise. If someone is dropped it is because they've been so designated or there was a threat to the mission. Remember, these are American citizens. We're all on board then?" There was no need to answer the commander.

"However, that being said, I want no one to doubt our abilities. I will not stand for any civilian heroes. I hope that is equally clear to you men. Now I want you boys to look over these maps and make sure one more time that every detail is accounted for. No mistakes, nothing missing, no questions once we hit the road. When you are through, meet me in the staging building with your men in one hour." With his final instructions in place Vincent headed for

50

the doorway; he needed to find some place quiet to pray.

When he reached the door, he turned once again to the group. "Captain Hauser?"

"Sir?"

"You keep my nephew close to you. He doesn't get out of your sight or protection for one minute. You hear me, son?"

"Sir, yes Sir," Hauser snapped back. Vincent looked over the group of warrior leaders. "Sixty-three point seven miles to freedom men. Sixty-three point seven."

# # # # #

At twenty-three hundred hours, eight hundred and sixty-four men stood in formation in the massive outbuilding located just to the northwest of the main building at Agincourt Farms. The floor was packed dirt, the ceiling massively high. The men wondered what on earth it was used for; certainly, no farm needed such a structure. At the far end of the building a makeshift stage had been constructed. It was empty until Colonel Madison Trace Vincent entered the room from a side door and Sergeant Major Tom Manning screamed "Tennnnnnn Hut!" The men snapped to attention. The Colonel walked stiffly up the stairs and to center stage. Placing his hands on his hips, he did not put the men to parade rest. His eyes surveyed the three companies before him as he walked back and forth to each side of the stage. His eyes seemed to pierce the soul of every soldier in the room. They'd trained under him now for over a year. He was *The Man*, their man. They trusted in him completely and were not only ready to die for him, had sworn an individual oath to do so if necessary.

Vincent came to a halt center stage and stood silently looking over them for a full minute before he started. "Gentlemen, we are about to embark upon a mission for which we will forever have the gratitude of our blessed country. On my way over here a while ago, I overheard a soldier ask one of his fellows if he thought we had enough men to carry out the mission. I wish to address that question for you tonight before we leave this encampment.

"We have enough to succeed, enough to die and enough to fail. If we are slated to die, let it be God's will and if we are destined to succeed let it also be, for the fewer the men the greater the share of honor no matter what the outcome. I for one wish for not one more soul than we have assembled in this room. Not one. I have no need for those who are not here."

"While I don't covet the temporal things of this world, fancy cars, big homes, designer clothes, I do covet honor. I would beg you to forgive me that sin. The glory and honor that will be yours, ours will be coveted by those who wish they'd been with us this night, but chose to stay home in their beds and do nothing to defend their own freedoms."

"Years from now when your bravery is spoken of in history books, talked about on television shows, debated in the halls of government across the world, your names will ring as loud and true as any that walked upon the battlefields at Saratoga, Ticonderoga, Gettysburg, or Antietam. It will not matter to them that you outlived this mission, or if need be. that you bless this good soil with your blood and make the sacrifice God requires of men who fight for liberty. On the anniversary of this day your names will be held high, by your neighbors, family, friends and countrymen. Some will step forward and claim to have stood here among you, but their claims will ring hollow. Your wounds . . . your scars will evidence your honor and you, only you will be able to stand tall and say, 'these wounds I received for my country on that great and glorious day when liberty would have been stolen from us lest I and my confederates stood true to defend it against those dastardly devils who would retch it from us, from our families and our country.'"

"Old men forget. Old soldiers do not. You good men will not forget this day; you will teach your children of it. Time will not be the assassin of our deeds; we will not let it. I know you are ready to march with me into the book of honor and I am proud to be your commander. Now and forever we will be linked one to the other. Each of you, look to your left and to your right. No one else deserves to partake of that portion of the honor that awaits you other than the ones standing here beside you."

"Almost six hundred years ago, an English King stood at the head of his troops on the battlefields of France. They were greatly outnumbered, sick with dysentery, lacking food and facing a massive French Army which stood between them and the port they needed to reach to escape to England. He addressed them with these words:"

> *'We few, we happy few, we band of brothers*
> *For he today that sheds his blood with me shall*
> *Fe my brother; be he ne'er so vile, this day shall gentle*
> *His condition; And gentlemen n England now-a-bed*
> *Shall think themselves accurs'd they were not here,*
> *And hold their man hoods cheap whiles any speaks*
> *That fought with us upon St. Crispian's day.'*

"Victory came that day to the English Forces, peace was restored to the shores of England for many years. And this evening we speak of them, here in this small place so far removed from them by time and distance. Think of them; for you are brothers with them. Tonight, will be the beginning step that will always link you to them. You will share that same kind of immortality."

"We are on the road to honor," Vincent's voice reached a furious pitch of excitement. "I tell you now men . . . it is sixty-three-point seven miles," pointing to the interstate just a few miles east of them, "up that road."

Vincent turned to Manning. "Sergeant Major . . . saddle up . . . move 'em out!"

Then the venue was quiet. Dead quiet with eight hundred and sixty-four determined men staring at the empty stage. Even the officers held still for a few seconds.

Chapter V

Every small town has a town drunk; Carl Walker was Odell's. And every small town, it seems, has a town bully; so, did Odell and he just swaggered into Blintz's Tap & Dining for lunch. Moving past several people he went to high school with, Glen Garnet never cast a glance at any of them. He focused only on the direction of the bar. One had to wonder if he was born angry. His folks were farmers and he ran the farm now that his father was too feeble. His mother was a quiet woman who by all accounts had her fair share of education before she met Glen's father. It surprised some of the locals when they married because there was that disparity between them. The secret embryonic reason though began in the loft of a barn on a quiet, nothing to do, fall Friday evening. Perhaps young Glen, at some point, found out that his parents married to add legitimacy to his name. Not a popular position to be in, in a small town. Aside from this poorly kept secret, people in town didn't know much about the Garnets, except that they paid their grocery bills regularly, attended St. Paul's on Christmas and Easter like all good Catholics and minded their own business.

Glen, a tall and lanky fellow didn't possess the physical characteristics that would inspire anyone to size him up as a fighter, but everyone who knew him knew this was no boy to fool with. He'd a very few friends in high school and his closest friend, Gary Donnell, died of cancer just a few years after he graduated from high school. When that happened, and it happened very quickly, Glen seemed to isolate himself even further from those outside his very small circle of friends. He never quite made it to his senior year in high school being absent more than present during his junior year. He considered it a major victory when he reached his sixteenth birthday and convinced his father, over his mother's strong objections, to allow him to leave school. "What tha heck ya need all that history and stuff for anyway?" He pled his case at the supper table one early fall harvest morning. He knew the farm was getting too be too much for the old man. "I don't need to know who the emperor of Japan is to go out and pull that corn in Dad! I need to be here where you and I can make a go of this harvest, of this farm. Times ain't easy. All that school's gonna get us is the loss of this farm. And I say I have enough education right now to help you run this place and to keep it going."

There was the very real probability of losing the farm his great grandfather had started that settled the issue for Glen's father. He'd hardly looked up from his plate partly, so he could avoid his wife's pleading eyes.

"I reckon he's old enough to make up his own mind about his life, Momma. He makes sense. I am not as young as I used to be, and it would be good to be able to count on the boy being here full time to work with me. He ain't never plans to leave tha farm no way, do ya Boy?"

"No Sir, not now . . . not ever, not for no one."

So, years earlier the deal was sealed over the old wooden dining room table, sealed with the clink of two Budweiser bottles held high above the red and white checked plastic tablecloth. Glen's mother said little, smiled weakly, but did not join the toast.

The next morning well before sunrise Glen, much to his father's surprise, was dressed and ready for school. "A gotta go up and fill out my resignation papers today daddy. Everyone that's gonna be leaving has to have a meetin with Mr. Kletzial, the principal." It was mid-morning though before Glen pulled into Dwight Central High's parking lot. While tractors are not a rare sight in this part of the country, and even occasionally in the school parking

56

lot whenever a hay ride party is scheduled, students on mid-morning gym clas-
ses couldn't help but pause as they watched the tractor and wagon inch slowly
along between aisles of staff and student cars.

Ralph Kletzial was not a nice man. He was not liked by the students, his
administrative staff or his cadre of teachers at Dwight Central. He was a tall
man of imposing character, almost bald with a monk's ring of white hair
wrapped above the ears. Thick black framed glasses added to his aloof, offi-
cious appearance. He dressed as if he were the floor manager of Brioni, instead of the principal of a rural high school. He looked as though he'd just
walked out of an Italian casino instead of his two-story bungalow on Rice
Street. The ladies of the jury swore he wore light make up. Pleasant to look at,
his thin lips seemed to never part to a smile . . . except for the bi-annual visit
of school board members as they made their way down his surgical suite clean
hallways. Kletzial did not make life easy or fun for his students or teachers although in high school one's life should be easy . . . and fun! When he parked
his car every morning in the reserved parking space and walked up the main
entrance to the school, students joked that he even starched his shorts.

On Fridays, Kletzial brought to school his prize possession. No, it was not
his wife. Fridays, football game nights, Kletzial drove his candy apple red
1965 Mustang convertible. He'd spent countless hours in its restoration and a
tidy sum of money to craftsmen who completed those tasks for which he had
no personal talent. This year he'd had a new upholstery project completed. It
was gorgeous. Friday, the day of Glen's "resignation" from high school the
weathermen had guaranteed the best Indian summer day of the year. The Mustang's snow-white top was tucked neatly away.

Best everyone could remember it was around 11:45 a.m. and Kletzial was in a meeting with Dwight's football coach Dean Slayman advising him that if next year's team didn't make the class 4A playoffs he'd fire him. "Mr. Kletzial, please come to the front office immediately, your ten thirty appointment with Mr. Ire is here." This was a code Kletzial had established for emergencies. He ended his chewing on coach Slayman and hurried to the front office.

By the time Kletzial reached his personal assistant, Glen had pulled the wagon dead even with "the mustang" convertible and had nearly filled the entire front cavity of the car with farm fresh, his farm fresh, manure. He was shoveling furiously. Somebody noticed before Kletzial's secretary did and students left the athletic field, poured out of classrooms and formed a semi- circle of curiosity and disbelief a safe distance from the scene of the sacrilege. If Kletzial had a bad heart, it surely would have killed him that day. At first, he could not believe what his brain was communicating to him as he caught a glance of the activity out of the corner of his eye, one hand on the office door. Screaming obscenities, never heard in the dear old hallways of Dwight Central, he ran pulling his suit coat off as he exited the entranceway . . . Slayman wasn't far behind him thank goodness.

"Mr. Garnet! I am going to whup the living heck out of you . . . you SOB!" The principal's eyes were bulging, his face, temples and neck were a crimson red, one could have taken his pulse just looking at the carotid arteries in his neck which were about to explode. As he approached the car ready to haul Garnet off the wagon and give him a good thrashing, he was hit square in the face with a huge shovel of manure. It stunned him, and he fell back a few steps, manure slid down his face, his impeccably starched white shirt, french-cuffed sleeves and suit pants. Only coach Slayman grabbing Kletzial prevented the fight of the century from happening right then and there.

Garnet stood a top of a still formidable pile of manure in the back of the wagon grinning widely and wildly at his tormentor of the last three years. A tormentor who was now being restrained by two teachers and the coach. "I just want you to know, you can't expel me. I quit!" With that pronouncement Garnet reached into his flannel shirt pocket and produced a pack of Kool cigarettes. Lighting one up he said, "I know it's not even lunch time, but I've worked up one heck of a thirst here." With that he produced a can of beer from the side of the wagon and sat down flat in the middle of the pile of manure. Taking long exaggerated swigs on the can at the end of which he punctuated the act with a loud and long . . . ahhhhhhhhhhhh, Kletzial became even more enraged, his face turning a deeper shade of furious red after each long swig and the long drawn out exclamation of satisfaction.

Garnet waited for the distant sirens to arrive. If he'd done anything in all his years at Dwight Central to endear him to his schoolmates, this was it. Kletzial was never the same.

Glen liked to brag that he had never been whupped. Often making reference to that day he filled Kletzial's mustang with cow manure, he bragged he would have whupped that old man had not Slayman and the others held him back. It was not totally true that Garnet had never been "whupped" and the person who had given it to him sat at a table near the door of Blintz's sipping a cup of coffee waiting for his interview with Monica Palmer. It'd been a long time ago and it was far outside the village limits. Odell took off his badge and laid it on the seat of the squad car daring Garnet to pick it up if he could. No one ever heard the details or the cause of the confrontation, but Garnet never laid hands on the badge or the Sheriff. Absent from the local bars for a few

59

weeks an IGA clerk over in Cabrey saw him sporting one heck of a shiner.

When Garnet moved onto the stool and muttered "the usual" to the bartender, he looked around the room for the first time. The only two people he nodded a hello to, was Sheriff Odell and the blonde waitress, Patty Higgins. He hardly even looked up when Monica Palmer walked in the door. Larry Odell sure did.

# # # # #

At the V intersection of West Street and Wolf Road just south of town, John Dewey was just about to begin his Friday Night Lights broadcast. "It's WPLN 560 a.m. on your dial, 'the Plains Speaking' radio station featuring plain talk for just plain people. Up next folks, after a short commercial break and a couple Little Big Town tunes, we'll be chatting up Saturday afternoon baseball. We're gonna take a good look at the Kankakee/Dwight and the Danvers/Watseka match up. Both those games should be real barn burners if ya'll forgive the expression." As soon as Dewy hit the commercial button, the door to the small white building blast open courtesy of two military types sporting automatic weapons. The noise scared the heck out of him but within a few seconds he caught hold of himself thinking he'd been caught up in a drug bust gone wrong or something. These SWAT guys would recognize this soon enough and this would all be cleared up. He thought that until one of them swiftly smashed a rifle butt on the side of his face.

During the short time he was unconscious the second "SWAT guy" taped a sign to the outside of the door "Interview in process - Do not disturb." When Dewy came to, one of the men was at the control board and the other was standing at the door emptying an equipment bag. Little Big Town was still singing so he'd not been out long. His head felt like an elephant was sitting on

60

it. His hands were zip tied behind him and his right foot was zipped to a leg of his chair.

"Sorry about that," one of the two men barked at him. "You need to do what we tell you and you won't get hurt any further. This is about as bad as it's going to get for you. But make no mistake about it Sir, if we have the slightest trouble with you we'll put bullets in you and in your family. Them first so you'll see we aren't fooling around. So, it's not going to be worth trying to be a hero, trust me."

Dewy's mind raced to his wife and son wondering if they were safe. The taller of the two men sitting at the microphone read his mind. "Yeah, the wife 'n kid, they're okay as long as you do what you're told. Understand?"

"Yes Sir, I just don't . . ."

Preempted, "you don't need to know what's going on right now. There'll be a time for that we promise. But for now, just do as we tell you and all will be okay. Your family's wellbeing depends entirely upon you. And just so you know we're not kidding . . ." the soldier shoved a picture in front of him. It was Dewy, his wife and son at the previous week's ball game. "Now Sir, there's gonna be no more talking. Just get your normal programming out and pretend we're not here. And . . . no funny stuff. If there is we'll know, we reckon we've been fans of yours for an over a year now."

# # # # #

"Won't you please sit down, Ms. Palmer?" Larry Odell stood to shake her hand. He towered over her. She did not hide her surprise at his size. "Mayor Pickett asked me to drive you around Odell, give you the five-dollar tour. I expect lunch here is about the best place to get the flavor of our little town.

Usually by Friday afternoon this time, anyone who's anyone is here having lunch or is on their way." Handing a paper, one-sheet menu stained with a few weeks of good cooking he continued. "I might recommend the chicken, best in the state in our opinion. Of course, there are a lot of people up there in Chicago that might not put too much stock in our simple country folk opinions."

"Awwwwww cut the crap, Sheriff. You simple country folk spawned the current President of the United States of America." She grinned. "I bet I can trust your judgement when it comes to chicken." He liked her directness. "Now tell me, is there anyone in this town nearly as wonderful as your grandmother? I just spent a few hours with her and I so totally enjoyed her." She never looked at the menu. "And . . . I'm starved. I'd love that broiled chicken dinner."

Larry motioned to the waitress who moseyed over with a pencil stuck in her hair and a hand on a hip swagger. "Hey ya Sheriff, what's it gonna be today?" She hardly glanced at the stranger sitting with him.

"Well we will both have the chicken dinner, Pat. What would you like to drink Ms. Palmer?"

"A diet Coke will do just fine Sheriff Odell." Her tone was mock business. The waitress glanced down at her for the first time.

"Oh, honey . . . I am so sorry. I didn't even notice you sitting there. How rude of me," she cast a witchy glance at the sheriff.

"Oh, that's okay . . . Pat, I didn't notice you either," Monica slung back at her. "Make that two diet Cokes with the dinner, Patricia." Odell offered quickly.

"You got it." And a swirl of pale pink waitress uniform disappeared from the table.

"Sheriff, do you think Miss Pat will spit on my chicken dinner?"

"Not a chance, not here in Odell," he replied smiling.

"Oh, I'll bet she does. I'll eat it anyway. Now tell me more about your Grandmother. I want to hear about her from you."

"I thought I was supposed to show you around Odell and tell you what you wanted to know about the town?"

"Why, Sheriff . . . Mary Duke Odell is Odell. I imagine she embodies all that is good about it, is responsible for much of what goes on in it and is rarely out foxed by any of you good ole boys that run it."

"Yes, probably so," he laughed out loud, "probably so. Grandmother seemed mostly to raise me. Mom and Dad both worked up in Dwight at the school as early as I can remember. Mom taught seventh grade and dad worked in the maintenance department. Took a lot of hours to pay for our little home, save money for me to go to college. I love my parents. They are my heroes. I have no others except Grandmother. I'm not sure I'm articulate enough to tell you how I feel about her. I remember the little things more than anything. School lunch bags stuffed with homemade cupcakes, a couple of Tootsie Rolls, a note that said she loved me. Little things make life what it is you know, Ms. Palmer?"

"Please, may we settle on first names?" Monica offered. It was an old but fairly transparent trick journalist used to make an interviewee feel as though there was a personal trust relationship in the making and that they could do no harm "sharing" with a friend.

"You bet, yes Ma'am." But he didn't mean it. He didn't mind familiarity, but he didn't like it with strangers, no matter how good looking they were.

"Mary invited me to attend the pancake breakfast with her tomorrow

63

morning at St. Paul's you know. I wasn't planning on staying over, so I'll drive up to Dwight I suppose and pick up some essentials after we take our little tour."

"I'll introduce you to Dick and Ruth Ralph before we leave. Ruth can give you some ideas on what stores to hit in Dwight."

"Great idea. I don't need much really, a change of clothes and some lady thangs you know?" She did her best to slur the end of the sentence, so she sounded 'country'.

"Well Ruth will be your best bet here in town." By the way . . . in case you haven't noticed, there are no hotels in town. Have you a place to stay?"

"Well, yes . . . I do. Mayor Pickett invited me to stay with him and his family this morning. I turned it down, but I may have to phone and retract my earlier rejection. You know this is my first big assignment. I mean really big assignment. I was told that Mrs. Odell doesn't cotton much to the press, so I was very nervous about coming down here."

Sheriff Odell knew this was her first really big assignment. No one comes to town to visit the grandmother of the President of the United States without being vetted like they've never been before and while that's a federal responsibility in some arenas, no one comes into Larry Odell's town without him knowing all about them.

"Everyone's been really great here. Friendly . . . well," she grinned, "everyone except your girlfriend over there." Casting a glance in the waitress's direction, he acknowledged the jab and glanced toward the kitchen doors. The double doors to the kitchen kicked open and Pat made her way to their table carrying a large round serving tray. She slid Odell's plates carefully before him offering an easy view down a generously filled blouse that had more

64

buttons unbuttoned than was necessary. Monica's plates received less gentle placement. A straw was dropped casually on the table next to a fresh drink. Another swirl of pink and white and Pat returned to her station at the end of the bar and lit up a cigarette. Before Larry could pick up his fork and dig into lunch, Monica reached across the table and picked up his plate. She exchanged it with hers. Licking some mashed potatoes off her index finger, she placed her plate down in front of him.

"I know things like that don't happen in Odell, but this is just a little thang I learned from those nasty restaurants up in the big bad ole city," she smiled. Watching the exchange of plates, a sly smile crossed the lips of the waitress.

Glen Garnet sat at the bar working on his fourth bottle of beer. He was drinking himself into a bad mood. It was Friday after all and much like Carl Walker . . . he wasn't happy with the guy in the mirror.

# # # # #

The sun slid close to the western horizon and low light swept over Odell. It was good after a long winter to feel the sun's rays on ones face this late in the day. The stores that surrounded the town square were busy with shoppers. For most of the residents Thursday or Friday was payday and that meant a night walking the square, doing some shopping, driving up to Dwight or down to Pontiac. Gus Morgan and Adriane Dolan decided the drive to Pontiac was a good idea and left as soon as baseball practice was over. Dinner at Panno's, one of the area's authentic Italian eateries, a movie in Pontiac were on the agenda. It would only take them an hour down Interstate 55.

Dick and Ruth Ralph spent time on the square in the evening then headed for home. Dick had to be at the dealership in the morning and Ruth was headed up to Chicago with her sisters. Carl Walker made his way to nearby

65

Cabrey and had his feet cemented to the floor of a local watering hole and was busy shooting pool. It is just another quiet, springtime, Friday night descending on the small town of Odell.

Pudge Miller was busy at work in the store. Friday nights and Saturday mornings Pudge and Shelly Miller earned their weekly salaries. The rest of the week the store was open as pure and simple convenience to their customers. And to keep them from those damn gas station wanna be. And most of the people who lived about the area could just as easily drop into a number of them to pick up essentials. Pudge insisted on remaining open 'til eight o'clock every night except Sundays. On Sunday's they were only open 'til noon.

As the last customer hit the door Pudge asked Whitey Gibbons, a local teen, to sweep the wooden floors. Pudge began tearing down the slicing machine and cleaning up the butcher's department. Shelly was in charge of the money, the accounting and ordering. Closing at eight o'clock on Fridays allowed plenty of time for cleaning and getting ready for the Saturday morning crowds. And this Friday night was Poker night. Pudge had to get on over to the VFW for the card game with the boys. "Shelly, I'll be done here in just a bit. I'm gonna head over to the game. Do you want me to pick something up for you from Blintz's or the Dinner Bell before I head out?"

"No, you go ahead. I'm just gonna do some housekeeping stuff around here then head on home. I'm pretty beat. Now don't you be too late tonight. You know it's an early rise tomorrow and I don't want to hear your guff all day long 'bout how tired you are," she grinned.

"Baby, you know I never complain after being up all night drunk as an ox with the boys," Pudge yelled from the back of the store. "Whitey . . . you gonna be here in the morning bright and early, right son?"

"Yes Sir, Mr. Miller, seven sharp. Mom has a list of groceries posted on the fridge door and if I don't bring it home tomorrow when I get off, my name will be mud. Is there anything else you want me to do before I leave? I've swept the floors and I mopped the snack area floor."

"Nope nothing else, just be sure when you come in tomorrow morning to wipe off the produce with a moist towel when you stack it, okay? We should have you out of here by no later than two or three. Thanks for coming in this evening . . . me n Mrs. appreciate your help."

The young boy with shockingly fair blonde hair liked working at the store. It put cash in his pocket and the Millers were like a second set of parents. Most of the time it wasn't like working at all. He occasionally felt guilty taking the paycheck. The Millers would send home pastry, bread and other groceries with him rather than throw them out when they had to be pulled from the shelves. He had come to love them though he had only worked part time since the previous fall when his father had badly injured his leg in a farming accident.

Miller stepped out of the store into the warm, fresh smelling, night air and walked the three blocks south to the VFW on Hamilton Street. Inside, already at a large, green felt gaming table sat five men. 'Big Ron' Lapinski, Jerry 'Grandad' Pracz, 'Little Ron' Rodriguez, Jimmy Brieden and 'Uncle Joe' Patrick. Big Ron, the local insurance agent, was a tall man with a fast receding hairline. He had small eyes and a prominent long slender nose. He sported a permanent grin wrapped around an ever-present unlit cigar, he thought it made him look important. He was the drinker among a room full of champion-caliber drinkers. Ron's personal motto, he often bragged to strangers, hung in a place of honor on the wall behind the bar at Blintz's. "It don't mean crap whether the glass is half full or half empty. . . long as it's beer in it." His easy-going personality and smile belied a quick minded man who could sell ice in a snowstorm. And at some time in the wee morning hours of every card game, when plenty of libation had been consumed, Ron would grumble between teeth clenching his unlit cigar, "well heck . . . I didn't know deuces were wild!" Always muttered just as a pot was being scooped up, the provocation was made just to invoke the inevitable utterly drunken bedlam that would rage around the table. Having thus inspired the ensuing the verbal melee he'd sit back, chew on the big cigar and gleefully take in the chaos. Often, he'd have a side bet with another member of the group wagering how long it would take to put the matter to rest. This craziness occurred at almost every card game; had for years.

Jerry Pracz, owner of the town's only hardware store, was an immigrant. The short, stocky, rugged man with wavy black hair and sparkling dark eyes, was the elder statesman of the group. In his mid-eighties, no one knew his exact age, he looked like he wasn't a day older than fifty. It wasn't hard to imagine Jerry when he was a young man, strong as a bull working on his father's small farm just outside of Warsaw. He'd immigrated to the United States via England with a storied past full of war medals and heroism that generated quiet, yet considerable respect from his fellow Odell citizens. He spent time in a Russian concentration camp as a young boy with his parents and siblings. When Germany declared war on Russia the camp doors were opened and the thousands of Polish prisoners, of which he was one, were told to go home, all the way home from Siberia, which they did . . . on foot. When Jerry reached home however, he kept walking. Walking all the way until he caught a ship and found himself fighting the Germans along with the British army in the

North African Theater. The young farm boy performed so admirably he was sent back to England, transferred to the Royal Air Force, became a bombardier, and spent the remainder of the war flying missions over Germany. Jerry met his wife in London at the end of the war. After a brief courtship they married and moved to Chicago. Eventually buying land that reminded him of his farm outside of Warsaw, the Praczs moved a few miles south of Odell. His strong polish accent intact, a suave, European demeanor, at least in the eyes of the locals, Odell fast adopted him as their master of ceremonies for all events. He is considered the Patriarch of Odell notwithstanding his home of origin. And he was and forever the affectionate object of Big Ron's good-natured mischief.

Jimmy Brieden, a safety officer, for I. G. Battery Corp, worked forty-five miles east of Odell in Kankakee. A short, squat, bowling ball of a man with a loud voice, beady dark eyes and a neatly trimmed brown beard, Brieden, much to the chagrin of his acquaintances, always had the answer. If Jerry bought a twenty-seven-inch television, Jimmy bought a bigger one. If Joe's lawn looked good one springtime, Jimmy's was greener the next. He was an irritant to everyone in the room, but they'd known him since kindergarten and tolerated his idiosyncrasies. In spite of them, he was a good-hearted soul, so the poker club put up with him. Notoriously loud, even in the largest of crowds, his voice could be heard above all. Jim had a well-established reputation for being late for everything and leaving early before cleaning up and especially if there was a check to be picked up. Unfortunately, this Friday night Jimmy Brieden was on time and had no choice but to stay late.

Ron Rodriguez, A.K.A. Little Ron or 'The Trick', another obvious foreigner, attended the University of Illinois with Big Ron and made the long trip down to Odell from the trendy north side of Chicago for the monthly poker games.

The manager of a Michigan Avenue Men's Clothier, no one at the table looked more out of place than did the young Hispanic, impeccably dressed and bejeweled. 'The Trick' was a genuinely likeable guy, a lady's man right off the cover of GQ. In his mid-thirties he still mostly lived in a small but neat home on the south side of Chicago, but he kept a fashionable apartment in the yuppie neighborhoods just north of downtown Chicago. He preferred the company of his mom whom he adored. She like many single mothers held multiple full-time jobs to put him through college. He wasn't about to leave her alone in the sunset of her years. So, Ron rarely stayed in his uptown apartment unless a particularly wonderful party or nightclub successfully assaulted his sobriety and he was unable or unwilling to make the long trek back to the south side.

Sitting closest to the bar on the far side of the table was "Uncle Joe". Joe Martin, a computer programmer geek, who worked for Sweetheart Cup. A local boy, with roots going back far enough that he was considered one of the real blue bloods of the area. His ancestors settled west of town and raised cattle which were sold to wagon trains heading west in the mid 1880's. Joe was another dreaded cigar smoker in spite of the fact that he had suffered one heart attack at the ripe old age of thirty-five. Medium in build and height with sandy dishwater blonde hair and a walrus mustache, he was the best poker player in the group.

Uncle Joe's claim to fame was making it to the state tennis championships in his junior year in high school. Unfortunately, he drew Norman Proller in the semi-finals. Proller was a Jewish boy from Chicago whom Joe had never beat.

70

Seems like Proller had his number, talking to him during matches, asking the time, commenting on the weather. Drove Joe nuts. Proller never wore tennis attire. Joe swore it was illegal and meant to distract opponents, but there was nothing in the rules against black pants, a white dress shirt and tie and black PF Flyers. Joe knew "the kid did it to piss him off," but could do nothing about it. Proller was a very good tennis player though and Joe knew as did Norman that with or without the mind games Joe was no match for him.

One-year Joe made it all the way to the semi-finals, and he had his measure of glory for a small-town boy from a small-town high school. And then Norman Proller whipped him two straight sets, 6-0. It was the last time they met. Proller moved with his family back to Washington D.C. when his father took a position with the F.B. I. Before he left though, he sent a note to Uncle Joe. All it said was, "never give up, never give up, never, never, . . . give up." Winston Churchill. Uncle Joe still had the note.

# # # # #

Nine thirty p.m. Mary Duke Odell climbed into the four-poster bed and began reading Hamlet for the zillionth time. She loved Shakespeare, Hamlet in particular. She hadn't much time to read tonight because she had to be up early for the pancake breakfast. Each night before reading she knelt at the side of the bed to talk to God and Mr. Odell, not necessarily in that order. The big old house seemed empty these days, but memories of raising her children made her smile. How she missed Mr. Odell, she thought as her eyes raced across Shakespeare's familiar phrases, perfectly placed, combined words. How on earth anyone could write like that? It was beyond her. From her bedroom window she could see the full moon now high in the eastern sky. After an hour of reading she lay the book on her nightstand and turned out the light

71

next to her bed. There never were any alarms in the old house, never needed to be and Mary was dead set against those darn Secret Service folks being so close. Let them follow her daughter around in New York or wherever she was rambling around she smiled to herself, but no need to have them here under foot in no place Odell. Fact was, closest they got to her was a small home down the street and a buzzer should she need them for any reason. She never had.

Long about midnight Carl Walker started back to Odell. "Maybe I should stop in Blintz's and see what's going on before I head to the house," he thought to himself as he headed west down the country road. "Gotta drive straight so Larry Odell don't see me." The thought of the local hoosegow was enough to keep the steering wheel straight and the gas pedal lightly touched. "Million stars out there tonight, like the night of the game." Glancing off to his left he noticed the tree line at the far end of Bullard's farm. He remembered how in the old days, the Nam days, a tree line at night like that would get his blood boiling, his heart to racing. He remembered cotton mouth so bad that no matter how many times he swallowed he could not moisten his lips with his tongue. Death was waiting in the tree lines and walking toward them through an open field was a horrifying experience no matter how heavily armed you were. Knowing there were people in there ready to kill made one's skin feel like it was on fire. "Seems to me," he thought, "I still get that rush looking at the tree lines. Stupid isn't it. Way out here in Odell and I still get the rush looking at the midnight tree lines. Like there was anyone waiting in there for me." Walker was back in Odell by midnight. Rather than drive through the center of town and risk being spotted by Sheriff Odell, he turned his lights out and pulled his car into his driveway. Well, he nearly made it; the car was half in the drive and half across the sidewalk. He closed the door quietly, just enough to make the dome light go out. Leaning on his walking stick, he headed for Blintz's.

Monica Palmer's eventful day ended after the riding tour of the town with Larry Odell, a quick trip up the interstate to Dwight and an even quicker shopping spree. The evening meal with the Picketts reinforced the good feelings she'd felt for the country folk she found herself with. At ten o'clock she headed for the empty bedroom once occupied by the daughter now taking freshmen finals at the University of Illinois. By midnight Monica had been asleep for two hours. Her last conscious thought of the day centered on the interview with Mary Duke Odell. It had been one of the most interesting days of her life. The setting moon would bring a day to replace it.

Chapter VI

No one in the sleepy town of Atlanta, Illinois noticed the convoy pull out onto South Street and head for the interstate. Between the navy training center in north suburban Chicago and the Rock Island Arsenal on the Mississippi, convoys weren't an unusual sight as they traveled up and down Interstate 55. Most convoys traveled at this time of night to avoid the hair pulling traffic jams associated with the Chicago metropolitan area. Gus Morgan and his date paid no more than a passing glance as they overtook Vincent and his men on the way back from Pontiac. "Sometimes boys, the best way to hide from the bogey man is to put on a bright yellow shirt and jump up and down right in front of him," Vincent exclaimed at a planning session eighteen months earlier.

Separating into smaller units, the convoy began drifting off the interstate one unit at a time, peeling away into small towns, back roads, all heading north toward Odell. Some vehicles left the highway where there were no exits pushing on down embankment and driving off into the darkness. Just west of Cayuga, Illinois, Livingston County Sheriff Freddie Reyelts sat bored in his squad car on famous old Route 66. This part of the once popularly traveled highway hardly ever saw a car at this time of the morning. It was a good place to take a coffee break without incessant headlights smacking him in the face. "Kath, this is Fred. I'm gonna take fifteen or so, get some of this coffee out of my thermos and take a few aspirins. Got a blinding headache. Will catch ya in a few. Give a holler if you need me."

Seventeen minutes later a small military unit passed him. It wasn't so much that the lead vehicle started to head off into a plowed field that got Fred to thinking. Sometimes farmers in these parts would allow the National Guard to bivouac in a pasture, tree line or field somewhere. But Reyelts noticed something no one on the interstate had noticed. The license plate on the last vehicle was not a government issued plate. "Damn odd," he thought to himself. "That army truck wasn't tagged with government plates." "Kath, gotta go check out some army boys, looks like they may have strayed from where they're supposed to be. I've got a three-quarter ton truck and one duce and a half. Looks like they're all carrying troops and they're gonna be madder'n heck if they wake up lost."

Reyelts, turned on his MARS lights and drove up within three car lengths of the last vehicle in line. He could not hear the crack of a microphone. "Sarge, looks like that peace officer decided to have a look at us. What do you want me to do about it? He's closing fast, and the lights are on."

"Quiet him. Keep the com down from here on out." The trucks bounced over small ruts of the plowed field as Sheriff Reyelts followed off road in his squad car and closed the distance between him and the rear vehicle. He thought he could see movement behind the heavy canvas flap that covered the back entrance to the duce and a half. He never heard the quiet "pop" of the M16. And then he was dead.

The dispatcher checking with Reyelts began to worry that his radio was malfunctioning. "Fred, are you there? Give me a holler, what've you got going out there. Is everything ok? Fred, if I don't get an answer from you immediately, I'm callin' back up." The radio was silent. The dispatcher sent out a call for another squad car to check on Reyelts.

Radio communications were kept to a bare minimum as had been planned, but Vincent's voice soon cracked the silence. "Alpha Company, Commander, report."

"Alpha's five miles from target and in process of establishing a southern and western perimeter. I've had law enforcement officer disruption, he's been terminated. Will shut down the main artery at the "Go" command Sir."

"Bravo Company, what's going on?"

75

"Bravo passing target on way to northern perimeter, no interruptions. We will be ready in fifteen minutes Sir."

"Charlie, speak to me."

"Charlie is in position, Sir, and ready to go. We've gotta contact the lineman. We can go on the air whenever you're ready. That's all secure."

"Ok. Everyone listen up. Com shut down on my mark. By the clock from now on until command is a Go. On my mark now at exactly 0230, mark and out."

Troops from all three companies began disembarking into fields and around highways leading into and out of Odell at two-thirty a.m. Saturday morning. In less than thirty minutes a cadre of paramilitary troops had established a perimeter around the town. Very sophisticated surveillance equipment that could detect any movement, heat signatures or sound coming from outside the perimeter was deployed. The lineman cut off all telephonic communications to the small town at the Go command. Lt. Cox initiated the jamming equipment that would take care of all wireless service. The lineman was now perched high atop the telephone tower west of Odell and had a visual of north and southbound traffic on Interstate 55 for over ten miles in each direction. Traffic was light; he was about to make it a lot lighter.

No one could see the men in full combat gear setting up their positions, laying down incendiary devices and filling sandbags full of the rich central plains soil. Heavy automatic weapons were placed close to the town on main traffic arteries. Charges were placed a few miles out on each of the highways leading into town. On the go command gaping craters would preclude all normal ingress and egress to and from Odell, Illinois, home of the President of the United States of America.

Twenty minutes later the lead vehicle of the convoy exited the interstate and turned east onto Prairie Street. Vincent whispered into his radio, "For tis'

Tommy this and Tommy that and chuck him out the brute, but tis the savior of his country when the guns begin to shoot." The lineman hearing the Go command pressed the red button on the small black box at his feet causing monstrous explosions two miles north and two miles south of the Odell exit of I55. The five civilian cars in the area, blinded by the blasts and stunned by the shock wave, brought their cars to screeching halts. Troops emerged from the pitch-black night and captured the shocked occupants of two vehicles trapped inside the cut off line. They were made to walk out of the cut off zone, confused but obedient.

Hearing the detonations, Alpha, Bravo and Charlie companies responded with similar charges that destroyed the four other roads leading into and out of Odell. Trees were toppled to discourage any attempts to go around the craters created by the blasts. Several of the town's residents were awakened by the noise from the multiple blasts. Larry Odell hadn't heard them though. He'd just finished a double shift and had fallen asleep down in his family room listening to a late starting Cubs-Dodgers game. This night of all nights he decided to listen to the game through earphones. He wasn't on call. No, he never heard the commotion that had others up briefly for an exploratory walk through their homes and staring out windows. Most chalked the noise up to thunder, their dreams or perhaps a military jet from Scott Air Force Base in Belleville. In any event, no one called anyone and each in his or her own time strolled back to the peaceful security of their respective beds.

Vincent's voice cracked over the battalion's radio. It was 0252 hours, two minutes after confirmation that the highways had been taken out. "Lt. Cox shut down the town of Odell. When that task has been completed, let me know."

"Sir, yes Sir," he responded.

Twenty-five minutes later all electricity was shut off in the small town;

phone lines were rendered inoperable. Cox reported back to his commander, "Sir, all land-based and cell phones are inoperable, and electricity is off. We have one Ham radio operator on the north side of town; we'll be rendering that inoperable momentarily. Our communications network is online Sir. All check points and time coordinates have been executed and report back in the affirmative. We are communications go, Sir.

"Also, be advised, Sir, that we are monitoring state police communications and District Six out of Pontiac has just scrambled six squads. They are headed north on the interstate."

"Have we any movement yet out of Districts Twenty-one or Eight?"

"No, Sir, but it sure as heck won't be too long before we do."

"Alpha Company, this is Colonel Vincent. Are you ready for that northbound traffic?"

"Captain Schnecksnider here Sir. That's an affirmative. We are dug into positions, Sir."

"Captain, you have permission to defend your position. From now on it's gonna be your call till daylight. That's why we pay you the big money son. Shoot small."

"Yes Sir. We'll give it our best."

"Bravo, as soon as we respond to northbound incoming, we can expect company from Eight and Twenty-one and reinforcements from District Six. You be on your toes and take care of anything coming in from the north."

"We're sitting in the duck blind, Sir," Captain Stewart barked back into the radio. "Anyone shows up in our sector they're neutralized."

"Captain Cox, as soon as we eliminate the initial thrusts from those three districts, you hook me up with Sixth District commanding officer. You got that?"

"You bet, Colonel."

"I want just enough time to read our opening statement. Then I want all of us on a communications black out for twenty minutes. We have one hundred percent communications isolation and security Captain Cox?"

"No Sir, that's a negative. I told you we would have 97 percent communications integrity for about forty-eight hours. After that I have no idea how long it will take the big boys to figure out what I am up to here." Vincent smiled to himself. Cox was a good man, never forgot a detail or what he alleged the detail was.

"Good enough, Captain. Keep an ear close to the ground. All companies heads up now. The proverbial crap is about to hit the fan. Today we may be the brutes, but tomorrow lads . . . tomorrow we will be the saviors of our country."

A squad car driven by Sergeant Matt Grey, headed north on the interstate in response to the explosions and the silence from Sheriff Reyelts' squad car. Five more followed closely behind him. It was eerily still as he rolled up on the squad car containing Reyelts' body. Shouting "officer down" into his microphone, brought two squad cars off the interstate to his position. The remaining three raced up the highway toward a growing number of backed up taillights. Whatever had happened up ahead was causing even the light weekend, early morning traffic started to back up.

By the time they approached the area of the blast, traffic was at a standstill, cars sat in line for a quarter of a mile. One squad car took up position at the end of the line to control northbound traffic and to assist in the event people needed to be moved out of harm's way. Two squads drove slowly up the emergency lane as drivers and passengers from stopped cars waved them on. It wasn't long before they reached the end of the road . . . literally. There was a crater forty-feet wide, five feet deep stretching across both the north and southbound lanes of the highway. One vehicle, a semi-tractor trailer lay in the bottom of the pit. The driver was thrown from the cab. His body lay in a position that told the officers that he had no chance of being alive. Someone in the crowd of passengers now standing next to the officer asked about wreckage of an airplane. "We're not sure what the heck caused this Ma'am, but you all gotta move back now," responded Officer Bill Easley. He called to the second officer, Corporal Danny Sullivan, "Sully, we gotta move these people back and call for some help. I'm not sure who's got this above Odell in the south bound lanes, but we need someone over there now. Get on the radio and see if there are any aircraft missing, get us some help pronto. We've got a casualty down in this crater, I'm sure he's not alive. I'm going down and have a look."

Easley climbed into the pit to check the injured driver and to investigate the possibility of a passenger. The driver was broken in two and there was no passenger as far as he could tell. Radio contact made by Sullivan with District Six dispatch advised unknown cause behind significant explosions. They were going to need fire and rescue ASAP.

Sniper Jerry Stevens watched the police officers at the crater site through the scope on his .50 caliber long-range sniper rifle. With an accurate range in excess of one mile, the high-powered weapon had a clean range of nearly five. The cross hairs lay squarely on the rear section of Sully's squad car. Steven's had practiced this kind of shot a million times in his mind . . . waiting for his heartbeat to slow he inhaled softly. Eyes focused he begins his count; it's a timing thing. He will squeeze the trigger, squeezing steadily at that very moment in between beats of his heart, his breath held. Beat one . . . beat two . . . beat three . . . squeeze and whoosh! The round traveling faster than the speed of sound slams into the squad car exploding the gas tank before any officer can even hear the report of his weapon. The second round slammed into Easley's squad car engine bringing him scurrying up out of the crater. As soon as

80

he reached the rim, he hit the ground near his front bumper. Stevens spotted him and eased off another round. It struck the officer squarely exploding his chest despite the bullet proof vest. Stevens turned his scope in the direction of the line of cars backed up behind the two burning squad cars. People were running in every direction. He was looking for the remaining squad car. He placed the cross hairs on the third officer as he screamed at civilians to move back down the expressway away from the fire. He could not get a clean shot and lowered his weapon.

Hearing the explosions followed by what they identified as small arm fire on Interstate 55, Sergeant Grey and two fellow officers at the Reyelts murder scene jumped into their squad's cars and headed to the entrance of the interstate. There was no helping Reyelts. The crime scene investigation would have to wait. As they entered the highway and traveled less than a mile they could see headlights heading in their direction in the northbound lanes. Their radios began to scream with traffic now. District Six had been contacted by the third squad car at the edge of the craters. Officers down, major explosions at the scene and taking fire! The transmissions were chaotic. The squads heading north into the oncoming traffic were frantically trying to communicate with their fellow officer at the crater scene. There was no response.

As soon as the southbound traffic reached the three squad cars racing north a motorist slammed on his brakes and jumped from the car waving his arms frantically. "I'm a Gulf War veteran and those squads up there were shot out. I expect a high-powered weapon, .50 caliber at least. There's nothing left of them nor the officers in them. You better not head up that way because you're way outgunned. Whatever's being fired and whomever is firing it, has written cop names written all over the rounds."

"The shooter could have had any number of us milling around, but he zeroed in on the squads and those officers. They never had a chance!" Grey exited his squad and directed the remaining traffic past him and down off the northbound on ramp. He decided discretion was indeed the better part of valor and heeded the advice of the civilian.

District Six was pure pandemonium. They had three officers down, explosions going off all over the district and no idea what was behind it. Support calls were made to District Eight, in Metamora, Illinois. It would take squads from that area nearly fifteen minutes to reach District Six's territory. Calls for assistance also went out to District Twenty-one. They were sending cars and as many of them as they could, but their headquarters was twenty minutes away. It was going to be awhile before they could be effective support.

Thirty minutes later as squad cars from Illinois State Police Districts Eight and Twenty-one approached within three miles of the craters on the highway they were fired upon. Weapon flashes were not seen, no reports from any weapons were heard, but rounds were screaming overhead. Officers abandoned their cars on high ground and jumped into ditches alongside the highway.

At five minutes after four o'clock in the morning, Alpha Company began entry into the town of Odell from the south. Colonel Madison T. Vincent riding in an open jeep cradled a walkie-talkie in one hand and a cigar in the other. "Robert, get me the commander of District Six. It's about time that Nazi had a lesson about the Constitution of the United States of America."

# # # # #

District Six Commander Mike O 'Brien was born on the south side of Chicago. He was an Irishman with wavy reddish blonde hair, blue eyes and fair complexion. He was six feet seven inches tall. He worked out regularly and ran two miles every morning before sunup. He hated wearing a bulletproof vest, because they never seemed to fit his muscular chest no matter what size he ordered or tried on. He'd considered a custom-made vest and would order it as soon as he could get around to it. At least that's what he kept telling his wife and the district safety officer who was constantly ragging him about it.

He'd finally managed a weekend off Friday and was looking forward to sleeping in with his wife. Then the call came that Reyelts' body had been discovered. He arrived at headquarters twenty minutes later. The radios hadn't stopped crackling since. He was just about to head out in a car himself when the dispatch officer entered his office with a *'you better hear this'* look on his face. "Sir, line eight is for you."

O'Brien hit the button on the speaker phone on his desk.

"Commander O'Brien?"

"Yes, this is Commander O'Brien. How can I help you?"

"As I told your dispatch officer, I am only going to be on the line with you for a few moments. I am a man of few words. I know you want to see the violence that has occurred so far this morning come to an end, as do I." O'Brien took note of the "so far" phrase. "So, please afford me a few minutes of your time so that we might accomplish that end together."

"You have my attention. Proceed."

"My name is Colonel Madison T. Vincent, retired U. S. Army. Active Commander of the First Battalion of the American Revolutionary Militia. Before you doubt me, Sir, I assure you we are in your state in force and plan to stay for as long as we please. I urge you take my advice and have your men withdraw to a radius of no closer than five miles from Odell. We have the entire town surrounded and occupied. As I speak, we are assembling the town's people and will have by our last estimate 3,100 prisoners, including the grandmother and cousin of the President of the United States. That number, Sir, is just a bit larger than the number of American lives lost in the attack on the Twin Towers. Not counting of course, the one thousand, one hundred and forty medically related deaths most of which our government has decided to ignore.

"As you are no doubt aware by this point in time, we mean business. We will not hesitate to execute any or all the hostages if we are not taken seriously. I am going to read two documents to you. Hopefully you are familiar with one of them since you were an active proponent of its creation and participant in its implementation. The other, I doubt seriously you nor anyone in your department has ever read. May I proceed?"

O'Brien's heart raced as he fought to remain calm. He would gather as much information from this nut case as he could, before attempting to ask any questions. "Yes, you have my attention Colonel Vincent."

"Good. Here are the first portions of the two documents I would like to share with you. *We the people of the United States, in order to form a more perfect union, establish justice, insure domestic tranquility, **provide for the common defense**, promote the general welfare, and **secure the blessings of liberty to ourselves and our posterity**, do ordain and establish this Constitution for the United States of America.*" You with me so far Commander?"

"Yes, Colonel Vincent. I am with you and I can assure you that I am no stranger to the preamble to the Constitution of the United States."

"Well, that will be a point of debate for years to come, Sir. In the meantime, allow me the next few short moments to continue."

"Please do Colonel."

"The next are just small sentences to the eye Commander but are a mountain for liberty to the free men and women of this country. We will not let it be plowed asunder, by the likes of you or "the Gods of the East."

"Congress shall make no law . . . abridging the freedom of speech, or of the press; or the right of the people peaceably to assemble, **and to petition the government for a redress of grievances.** Additionally, . . . *A well-regulated* *militia, **being necessary to the security of a free state, the right to keep and bear arms, shall not be infringed.***"

"I appreciate the first and second amendments to the Constitution as well Colonel Vincent, but I don't get the importance of the history lesson while several of my men lay dead or wounded, shot down by your cowardly ambush!" O'Brien's temper was famous around the district and as much as he tried to control it, he hadn't. It was a mistake.

Vincent responded in a slow quiet voice. "It's in your best interest, the best interest of your men and the good citizens of Odell for reason to prevail Commander. Shouting will accomplish nothing I assure you. Enough blood has been shed. Shall I continue, or shall we let more blood just to get your attention?"

"Proceed." O'Brien said in a purposefully lowered tone, desperately fighting to lower his blood pressure as well.

"I'm going to read to you a very small portion of Federal Statute 44USC38 - **"44USC 38- FIREARMS - ILLEGAL POSSESSION- CONTRABAND**. "It is hereby illegal for any private citizen, as defined by this statute, to own, possess, sell trade, purchase, possess or otherwise transfer in any manner any firearm except as defined below:

> "Firearm shall include, but not be limited to
> any pistol, revolver, rifle, automatic weapon,
> semi-automatic weapon or any other weapon
> that operates by use of a projectile shot from
> or otherwise launched from the weapon by
> way of an explosive charge from the weapon.
> Nothing in this article however shall prohibit
> any private citizen from obtaining a license

85

for the purpose of securing and registering any weapon designed specifically for the purpose of recreational hunting from Federally designated license hunting disbursement establishments. Such hunting firearms shall be limited to no more than sixteen gauge shot guns for the purposes of hunting small game and fowl. For the purposes of hunting larger game such firearms shall be limited to .270 caliber weapons. A private citizen for the purposes of this Statute does not include those individuals authorized, under separate sections of this code, to carry firearms for the protection of the citizenry as described in those sections.

(Ammunition restrictions are addressed in subsequent sub paragraphs of the act.)

"You are familiar with this new law are you not, Commander? They're calling it the Scottstown/Brady Bill and indeed were you not one of many law enforcement officers called upon to testify at the ratification hearings?"

"Of course, I'm familiar with it and yes I did so testify. Don't tell me this is all about that public safety bill Colonel Vincent!" The phone went dead.

Chapter VII

It's Saturday morning closing time when Carl Walker left Blintz's Tap & Dining's and headed north on Wolf Street. "Gotta git home, gotta git home. The old lady's gonna have a cow. God, I'm so tired. Seems like every night home gets farther and farther away. Should be there soon, should be there soon." Carl continued to head west in the wrong direction until even he couldn't mistake the lights of the interstate. "Damn! How the heck did I get way over here? Who's messing with me? They know I gotta get home or there will be heck to pay." His mistake realized, Carl made a one-hundred-and-eighty-degree course correction and staggered eastward toward his home. But he decided he was just too drunk to make it to the other side of town. Best place Carl could find to settle in for the evening was, you guessed it, the water tower. Sliding his walking stick into his belt, he began a climb that he would never have undertaken sober. One hundred and eighty feet later he sat down on the walkway surrounding the base of the massive tank and leaned back to admire the clear spring nighttime sky. It was a remarkable feat really when one considered his state of inebriation. On previous occasions when the fire department was called upon to extricate him from his perch there was always a sense of amazement, awe really, that he had been able to make the ascent to begin with. Pulling the walking stick from its makeshift scabbard and laying it at his side he quickly drifted off to sleep.

Odell could rest peaceably now, her faithful sentry standing watch over her.

The poker game over at the VFW was, not surprisingly, in full swing at two thirty a.m. and plenty of booze had been consumed by the men sitting around the table. The game itself had degenerated to the game of *Indian*. Six and a half hours of hard drinking had dulled wits and good taste. Actually, they could not use the drinking as an excuse, to engage in such a sophomoric game, because at some time during every poker evening one could count on some member or another calling the game of *Indian*.

Pudge drunkenly slurs, "Boys . . . it is my observation, based upon a reasonable degree of gender specific experience and certainty, that boys simply have more fun than girls! Think about it. Everything, well most everything that's fun is . . . well is Man's fun. Can't think of anything that isn't." Pudge looks over the table at Big Ron, who has taken the cigar out of his mouth and has poised a beer mug in front of his mouth as if he was debating comment over drink. The former won.

"Pudge, you knucklehead, I do believe you're right. Football, baseball, well, all sports were invented by men. And back in the day. . . for men. Now I'm not taking nothing away from the womenfolk, but I think yer right. Movies was invented by men ya know. Fact is so was television. Now where the hell would we be in a few weeks when the Cubs start playing and there's no T.V.? And what else? Hell, there's gotta be lots of other things."

"Fishin." Pipes up Brieden. Uncle Joe would go nuts if he couldn't get that boat on the Illinois and go fishin. Men invented fishin, I'm positive of it."

The Trick glances in Brieden's direction, cigar posed, grin fixed on the route of two perfect smoke rings drifting in Pudge's direction. "When?"

"When . . . When what?" Big Ron asks.

"When did man invent fishing you morons?" Trick asked. It was silent for a few moments as the men looked around the table for someone, anyone to say something intelligent.

"1775" Brieden said as he looked around the table for support. The place erupted. The game forgotten, the men all threw their cards at Brieden. Funny thing was they weren't sure if he was kidding or not. As a rule, and with him furiously drunk, one could hardly tell. The Trick took a long slug on his bourbon and water, leaned back in his chair and closed his eyes.

"Brieden," the word was drawn out long and slow. "That, you idiot, was the year of the Declaration of Independence!" Trick declared. "Well least I think it was, but I know for damn sure people were fishing before 1775!"

"Well yes of course they were, but I was talking about recreational fishing and I think, well I'm pretty sure some guy named Rappala from Sweden was the guy that started it all. Before that most all fishing was for survival or commercial like. You know?"

Joe Martin's forehead hit the table. His body convulsed with laughter. "God, I hope no one ever bugs this place. If anyone ever discovered the level of pure ignorance to which conversation stoops here, none of us would have a job."

"Well, he could be right," Big Ron grinned.

Jerry Pracz remained silent. He had the ace of spades stuck with sweat to his forehead. It was the winning card for that game of Indian. He knew it because he could see the card in Trick's glasses. He was feeling pretty good about himself and could give a white rats butt about fishing and who invented it or whether men or women had more fun. He'd won the pot and he was gonna get it.

This was the scene when the first explosion on the interstate jolted the room and the men.

"What the good hell was that?" Pudge spoke first.

"Dunno," slurred Uncle Joe. "Maybe an accident on the interstate. Would have to be a hellava accident tho. Maybe a tanker. We'll know shortly if the fire engines start up. Take a look out the window Jimmy; see if you can see anything out there."

Just as Brieden was saying okay another blast sounded shaking painted frames on the wall. Alarmed, the men jumped and went to the window on the west side of the room. They could see flames lighting up the sky. "Air Force is at it again," Big Ron muttered as he headed back to a fresh beer and the half-eaten chicken leg lying on his plate. The rest of the men stayed at the window. It was way too early in the year for a grain silo to have blown. No reason to dismiss Big Ron's explanation. Besides, nothing of any significance ever happened in Odell. No need for alarm.

Half an hour later Shelly Miller awoke to sounds in her back yard. She lay in the bed for a moment before moving to the window to look out on her backyard and freshly planted garden. It was a clear night and the moon shone brightly above the little home she'd shared with Pudge for nearly ten years. Slowly, she pulled back the curtain. To her absolute horror she saw two figures standing in the yard and it was clear that they were holding rifles. She was terrified. Moving across the room to the bedside table she picked up her cell phone. There was no dial tone. Her pulse racing, she ran to the closet where Pudge kept his shotgun and quickly pulled it out. She knew better than to put any lights on, so she struggled in the dark trying to locate the box of ammunition kept on the shelf at the top of the closet. Finally loading the shotgun, she crept downstairs praying it was her imagination and that Pudge would soon walk through the door. He wouldn't. At that very moment Pudge had troubles of his own.

Shelly walked around the downstairs in a low profile, her heart beating so hard she was certain it could be heard by the two figures in her yard. She watched them as they moved up the sides of her house; one on the west side one on the east. She could see them crouching as they moved. This was no mistake. This was no dream or her imagination. She was terrified, but she was also determined . . . she was going to defend her home, their home. Soon one of the figures was on the front porch. She could see him through the large frosted oval glass inset in the front door. He was approaching the door! Shelly raised the shotgun shoulder level and took aim. As soon as his hand reached for the door, she squeezed off a round. The impact blew him right off the porch and onto the sidewalk leading up to the steps. The report of the shotgun was so loud in the entrance way of the home it deafened her. She never knew if the shot hit its mark and eliminated the man on the porch. His partner however, reacted the way any soldier was trained to react. He stepped from the left side of the door jam and opened fire into the house. A short blast from the M-16 lit up the entrance way and Shelly Miller. It splattered her all over her grandmother's coat rack. The noise was loud, but brief. The soldier could neither hear nor detect any other movement inside the house. He waited to see if lights came on in either of the houses next door to the Miller's. Remarkably, there were none and no signs of movement at that moment. A dog barking in the distance was all the soldier could hear.

"Col Vincent, this is Captain Stewart. We have coordinated and are sweeping the town now. We'll have the citizens assembled at the square by 0530 hours. We've taken one casualty and inflicted one. Men will be moving on targeted homes in exactly five minutes . . . Mark 0430 out.

"Captain Stewart, that's an affirmative. As soon as you have the command center secured, advise."

91

# # # # #

When the electricity went out on the poker game in the VFW, the men did what any drunken group of poker players would do they lit up candles and continued playing. "As long as the beer stays cold, I see no reason to interrupt a perfectly decent poker game," Jerry Pracz said. "Besides, I'm up 'bout twenty-five dollars," he grinned. Shortly after Pracz's comment the men could see flashlights moving up the staircase to the second floor where they were. Thinking it was the caretaker, Steve Parillo, Uncle Joe called out, "hey Steve, pay the freaking electric bill will ya? Hell, Pudge's wife would have a heart attack if his fat butt walked in the door before breakfast time." The men laughed. The last time Pudge went home early, he'd gotten ill at the game, lost his keys and had to shake the door to get Shelly to let him in. When he rattled the doorknob at two a.m., Shelly called Larry Odell to come take care of a prowler.

Much to the surprise of the card players, Steve Parillo didn't show up in the doorway. Two-armed infantry men did. One of the soldiers spoke to the group. "Gentlemen, sorry to interrupt your card game, but for your safety we need you to leave the building and move to the town square.

"What the hell for soldier?" Big Ron asked.

"Well we don't know exactly what's up. Sir, all we know is that we need to clear this building and several others in town. The mayor and our commander are on their way there now."

"Well, young pup, you can kiss my ass because I ain't going nowhere 'cept right here where the beer is cold, and the food is hot."

The soldiers lowered their weapons from parade rest position and aimed them directly at the men seated around the table. "Gentlemen, we are not

92

fooling around here. Do yourselves a big favor, step away from the table." The men were so surprised that they didn't obey at first. Big Ron stuck a cigar in his mouth leaned his chair back on two legs and said "Like I says . . . kiss my big ass General. Just who the hell do you think you are, boy. This is America. You want us to do something for Uncle Sam, you better say please, and you better have a good reason why we should be doing what you ask. "What the hell is this all about? 'Til we know, we ain't doing nothing. We ain't going no-where."

The soldier moved toward him until he had closed the distance to a rifle's length. With one swift swooping motion the soldier slammed the butt of the weapon hard into Big Ron's face. Teeth flew, and the clear snap of a jawbone could be heard by the rest of the now shocked and terrified group of men. Big Ron fell out of the chair like a sack of potatoes. The soldier turned his attention to the others around the table. His partner raised his weapon to a shooting position, pointing the muzzle at that group. "*Please*, put your hands in the air gentlemen," the first soldier said. Big Ron lay on the floor unconscious as the rest of the men stood and placing their hands above their heads. "Now, gentlemen, we're going to frisk you for weapons and then escort you down the stairs and out of this building. As soon as we get you outside, move up the street to the square. When your friend there wakes up, we'll see that he gets the medical attention he needs. Now move out."

Shadowy figures and the dark of night did not compute for a fog brained Carl Walker. He woke with the first explosion, but soon fell back into a drunken sleep. It wasn't odd that the subsequent explosions didn't wake him, but the small arms fire had. Most military will tell you that you have to learn to sleep through the sound of artillery, well at least through the sound of your

93

own, but small arms fire sounds exactly the same no matter where it's coming from and you never sleep through that. He finally awoke on the water tower at the north end of the town square and grabbed his walking stick. He couldn't figure out if he was dreaming or if there really were soldiers in full battle gear and weapons running around below him. He did the only thing a stewed brain would allow him to do under the circumstances. He screamed at them. "Halt! Who goes there?" Expecting a password . . . "I'll open up," he threatened to one of the soldiers on the ground, the warning looked to be accompanied by a real threat. At least the walking stick Walker cradled across his chest at port arms looked that way to him. He raised his weapon, aimed and squeezed a few rounds off. They caught Carl right in the mid-section. Belly wounds are the worst and this one was horrid. Carl fell back against the side of the water tower and then keeled forward in a kneeling position. As he fell off the ledge toward the ground his foot caught on one of the grates and hung him upside down. Hanging there caused the bleeding to be more profuse than could be imagined. It would make for a horrible picture for the people in the square as the sun rose hitting the first thing it always hit in Odell, the water tower. Carl Walker, hometown boy, husband, football hero, war hero bled to death in less than five minutes. "Shall I go up and get him down, Sarge?" the soldier whispered to his squad leader.

"No, leave him there. We have too much to do and besides he'll remind our fellow citizens how serious we are."

Glen Garnet had fallen asleep in the arms of the Pat Higgins, the blonde waitress from Blintz's just before the first blast that tore up the interstate. They'd both had too much to drink and way too much of each other to hear any of the subsequent blasts or the small arms fire that had occurred earlier. At four-thirty in the morning however, they woke to banging on the front door. Glen rolled over as if to ignore the noise. Pat reached for the lamp on her end table, but when she turned the knob no light came on. Grabbing Glen's denim shirt, she put it on and ran to the front door. When she pulled it open, she was surprised to see the soldier that stood there. "Ma'am, we have an emergency and need you to get your family together and move on over to the town square as soon as possible. How many of you are there?"

"Well, what kind of emergency? Just me and my boyfriend. What's going on?"

"We don't have time to explain to you Ma'am, but we need you to move fast. Are there any weapons in your home? Any explosives or anything like that?"

"Well, no, but what the hell does that matter? We ain't under arrest or nothing like that are we?" Looking past the man on the porch Pat could see others . . . shadowy townspeople moving along the street. She could make no one out, but as her eyes adjusted, she could see other soldiers moving about as well. Not waiting for the soldier's answer her eyes returned to him. "Well ok, but it will just take us a minute. She moved to shut the door, but the soldier had moved in behind her and had placed his foot in the way of her closing it. "Do you mind?" she asked somewhat annoyed.

"Yes Ma'am, as a matter of fact we do. Now, please, just get your boyfriend and get on over to the square so everyone is safe okay?"

"Deep down inside Pat knew something was wrong, but she had a queer feeling not to question too much, nor to resist. She didn't like this guy's tone. He was young, sometimes young soldiers with weapons in their hands can be full of bravado. Pat moved into the bedroom and shook Glen awake. He was not happy about it but picking up on her sense of urgency he knew something was up. And if it was that serious it might mean a fight and Glen, drunk or sober, was always ready for a good fight. He quickly put on his jeans, boots and T-shirt. Pat was dressed before him and sat on the bed waiting. As soon as he was dressed, they moved down the hall toward the front door. "What the hell is going on?" Glen asked of the soldier standing in the doorway.

"Really can't say for sure right now, sir, except we have been ordered to clear all the residents out of the homes and move them to the town square for their own safety. Looks to me like this is no drill either 'cause we have been brought in from a long way off."

"Oh Really, a long way off from . . . like where?"

"Can't tell you from where, but we ain't from no place around here. Now, please move on over there to the square. I'm pretty sure our commanding officer and your mayor are on the way and will be speaking with the town shortly."

"Well okay, but I don't like it. C'mon, Pat." Garnet took the startled waitress's hand and started down off the porch. Pat had the second shock of the early morning. Garnet had never held her hand in front of anyone before. Now they were walking up the street to the square like they were an old married couple. Sure, it was early and the sun not up yet, but he's sober, least she thinks so. And he's still tugging her along. She smiled.

# # # # #

The sun rising on the water tower slowly revealed the blood-soaked body of Carl Walker to the three thousand plus townspeople gathered in the town square. His blood had dripped down onto the Odell Coal Company sign. Mothers shielded their children's eyes from the sight the best they could.

96

Carl's wife knelt in the dirt on the south end of the square not able to look up at her husband's body. He may have turned to alcohol, but God you should have seen him when he was a young man. He was . . . the love of her life. She forgave his shortcomings, his demons and yes, even his neglect. She still loved him and her heart broke as she looked loathsomely about her at the soldiers encircling the square.

A hundred men stood silent with weapons at port arms, held at an angle across their chests, but they looked like they meant business. News spread quickly. Shelly Miller was dead. Carl Walker hung from the water tower and Ron Lapinsky, lay on the entranceway to the VFW with his face bashed in while two military men with red crosses on their sleeves attended to him. Pudge Miller received a pistol whipping when he tried get past the guards to his wife. People were milling about in small circles mumbling, dumbfounded. Had someone invaded the United States? Who were these men who looked to be every bit American, but whose actions were every bit un-American? Jeeps with machine guns sat at each corner of the square and while the guns themselves were pointed skyward, there was little doubt that they would be used on those gathered if the orders came.

At five a.m., Larry Hurley Odell awoke to a loud banging on his front door. Rolling his massive body off the couch, he struggled upstairs wishing for just one Saturday morning when he could sleep in. The electricity's off and all he can think of is coffee. That's what he needed a nice big cup of coffee Mary Duke Odell style. He loved his with lots of cream and two or three spoons of sugar. And a cinnamon roll, yes . . . a cinnamon roll home made from Grandmother's kitchen. The banging continued . . . annoying him he yelled. "Okay, okay . . . I hear ya." "Maybe it's got to do with the black out," he thought.

Odell opened the large Mahogany door. Surprised to see the military men standing there his officer persona kicked in. "Sheriff Odell, what can I do for you?"

"Yes, we know Sheriff, that's why we are here. Mayor . . ." the soldier looked at a piece of paper for effect. ". . . Pickett? Yes, Mayor Pickett asked that we get right over here and pick you up. You're needed at his home ASAP Sir."

"What's it all about? What's going on?"

"Well we're under orders not to discuss, Sheriff. Best let Mayor Pickett explain things to you. All we know is that it is important for you to hustle over there with us right away."

Well, let me swish some mouthwash and put my gun belt on and I will be right with you."

"Sorry, Sir, there is no time for that believe me. It's urgent you come with us right away. We will come back for whatever you need."

The sheriff looked down on the young man and then to his companion. "Men, I don't go anywhere without my weapons. Be with you in a minute." As he turned to head back down the hallway, he felt the muzzle of the M-16 touch the nape of his neck.

"Sir, I am afraid we must insist that you come with us immediately. No need to bring your weapons. We will come for them later."

"Son, you better remove that gun barrel from the back of my neck if you know what's good for you." Odell's face was hot with anger.

"I appreciate your advice, Sheriff, but I want to assure you of one thing. We are under orders to use lethal force if necessary. We have our orders to bring you to the mayor's home as is and if you refuse to come, we are under orders to bring your body. It's your call now, Sir. Now, please do us a favor and back out of the door with your hands behind your back." As Odell did so the other soldier moved past him into the house. He returned soon with handcuffs and placed them on the Sheriff. "Figure this will make all of us a little more at ease. Sorry to have to do this, Sheriff, but you give us no other choice.

"Well, boys I hope for your sakes you got this planned out real well, cause I can think of about a half a dozen charges right now, and that's before I even get into the federal stuff."

"Well Sir, we do have this planned out pretty well we think, and I bet there are more charges connected to this than you ever could dream of. Now, what say we just take a nice early morning stroll over to Mayor Pickett's little place, shall we?"

On the way to the mayor's house he noticed for the first time the absence of electricity throughout the town. The sun was on its way up, it was still dark, but one could still move around well enough without lights. He could see people walking up Richards Street in the direction of Pudge Millers IGA. Odd that they would be heading off in that direction at this time of day.

It only took ten minutes to walk from Odell's place to the home of the mayor. Moving up the stairs of the white, wrap-around porch and through the front door Odell found Mayor Pickett, his wife and children on the couch. Monica Palmer, in pajamas, was sitting on the floor next to them. Odell took note of two armed men standing guard on each side of the small living room. Soon however, a third man appeared from the kitchen. He was wearing a Sergeant major's insignia. The Sergeant pulled a radio from his waist band and spoke into it.

"Colonel, this is Sergeant Major Manning. We have the mayor's residence secured and are ready to transport in ten minutes or your command." The radio crackled back.

"Sergeant Major, we are just entering the command headquarters. We will probably need twenty minutes or so. Please see that the mayor and his family and Sheriff Odell are made comfortable. I understand we have a casualty in the square. I want you to have him brought down ASAP, do you understand Tom, ASAP? Who the hell had the dumb idea to leave him swinging up there so the whole town could get a view of him? I want to know whose bright idea that was, and I want to speak to him as soon as I am off the flatbed. Got me?"

"Yes Sir. I understand, sir. I am aware of the casualty. We've been busy with the house to- house sweep, Sir, but we'll correct that mistake pronto."

"Okay, I'll be back to you in twenty."

Manning turned to Odell. "Sheriff Odell, forgive us for having to bring you here under a pretext. As you overheard, in just a few minutes we will be moving to the town square, where we are hopeful we will be able to make plain to you and to the good people of Odell just why we're here and how much we would like to conclude our business and move on from here as soon as possible."

Addressing the troops that brought Odell to the house he said, "Men, if you have the keys to those cuffs, please take them off Sheriff Odell." Turning his eyes back to Odell he continued, "Sheriff, I'm gonna cut you loose from those damn things, but I expect you'll behave yourself and that we'll have no problems. For your information, we already have much of the population of Odell in the town square and are inviting the rest to join us as I speak. So, as an authority figure here in Odell we need you to cooperate. Any miscue on your part could result unnecessary violence and in death or injury to innocent

100

civilians. There has already been some bloodshed and we wish very much to avoid anymore. And to be perfectly honest with you, we'd prefer not to have to shoot you, but we will.

You're valuable to us, obviously very valuable and it doesn't take a rocket scientist to figure out why. But don't take that fact for granted, it's not a get-out-of-jail-free card. We prefer your cooperation with us, even if it is only very passive."

Odell stared at the tall muscular man measuring his enemy; his voice was calm as he responded to him, almost subdued. "Well Sergeant, looks like you have a slight advantage. I assure you I don't want anyone hurt. So, let's just see where this takes the two of us okay?"

"Yes, that's a very good approach. We knew you were a prudent man and we both seem to have the same goal. The less bloodshed the better."

There was, at five-thirty in the morning, only one resident of Odell who was not standing in the square with the rest of the townspeople . . . Mary Duke Odell. Her home was surrounded by troops. Her secret service detail was disarmed, handcuffed and sitting on the sidewalk at the end of the block. She was advised that a threat to her safety required her to remain inside the home until the Mayor and the commander of the troops could come speak to her. Inside the big red brick house Mary paced back and forth, not so much concerned for herself as she was for the town. She'd heard the explosions and her futile attempts to call her secret service agents began to worry her earlier in the morning. It wasn't until the soldiers knocked on her door and explained that she was in danger and that they were there to protect her that she really began to pace between the small kitchen and living room. Two or three times she had offered her famous coffee to the nice young boys on the front stoop who while

101

polite, declined. She'd have felt much better if they had accepted. Could there be something wrong in Washington? Was her grandson okay? They had assured her he was, but she knew how they hold things back from people until family can be gathered when something goes wrong. She was doing her best not to let her imagination get the best of her, but it was so difficult being all alone as she was.

A knock at the door startled her. She moved to the curtains in the living room and pulled one aside to see another military man standing on her front step with his hat tucked under his left arm. He appeared to be an officer. Moving to the entrance way, she opened the front door.

"Good morning, Mrs. Odell. I am so sorry to interrupt your day. May I please introduce myself to you? My name is Colonel Madison T. Vincent. I'm afraid I am going to be your next-door neighbor for the next several days. May I come in?"

Chapter VIII

At six thirty a.m. Colonel Vincent walked slowly down the front steps of Mary Duke Odell's home with his executive officer Major John Coffin. Vincent was looking somber as Coffin gave him a status report. Three police officers confirmed dead, unfortunately, two members of the town were casualties. One, a local woman, accounted for the sole casualty the battalion suffered. Vincent spoke into a walkie talkie, "Lt. Cox, you check with Captain Bell. I want to make sure when I step to that microphone that Commander O'Brien gets an earful and that goes for anyone else who is listening in. We've got about thirty minutes."

"Yes Sir. Power's on to the flatbed and will be restored to the town as soon as you give the order."

Coffin had been busy since the invasion overseeing the movement of troops through the town, making sure everyone responded to the bull horn's announcements. Poker central was now command headquarters just half a block away from Mary Odell's house.

Company commanders verified the absence of activity from the state police who appeared for the time being at least to respect the five-mile radius demand. It would only be a matter of time now before the National Guard was called out. There was little chance of a full assault. No one in their right mind would give an order that could jeopardize the hostages and the family of the President. But there was also little doubt that once the next contact was made the ante was going up.

"Ok. Let's go. It's time to kick this pig." Knowing his comments would be recorded and almost simultaneously broadcast by the local radio station to the nation and having received full report on the status of the operation, Vincent moved toward his jeep and gave instructions to the driver to take him to the flatbed truck parked at the north end of the town square.

Mayor Glen Pickett, frightened to death, was cooperating just as expected. He sat on a chair on the flatbed, parrying questions from friends and neighbors waiting for Vincent to arrive. His wife and children stood off to the side of the truck with Monica Palmer. They all looked haggard, scared . . . worried. Larry Odell sat, his massive arms crossed, on a chair immediately to the left of the mayor. He looked out over the crowd with his steel blue eyes, making direct contact with no one, except Dick Ralph. His lips pursed tight, his cheeks bright red. He was angry and humiliated that this had happened to him . . . to his people. He remained silent, almost statuesque until he heard the distant noise of a jeep heading towards them. He couldn't wait to get a gander at this guy.

Col Vincent's jeep moved east on Scott Street until it came into the north side of the town square. All eyes were on the American flag bedecked vehicle, necks were stretching to get a look at whomever it was that was running this show. A podium with a microphone stood mid-truck. Vincent exited the jeep, placed leather gloves on his hands, picked up a riding crop given to him by his beloved wife many years ago, and walked up the steps. He moved first to Mayor Pickett who stood and shook his hand. Larry Odell cast the mayor a glance that would have killed the poor man had he seen it. When Vincent turned to approach Odell, the Sheriff looked at him with a look that said, "Don't you dare try that with me." And Vincent was smart enough to know when not to pick a fight. He simply nodded to Odell who looked away and continued his stare out over his people.

Vincent stepped to the microphone. "Good citizens of Odell, my name is

Colonel Madison T. Vincent. Under any other circumstances I would bid you a good morning, but I understand that from some perspectives this is not a good morning here in Odell. I would like to answer all your questions, share more information with you than I am able to. But there have been placed upon me certain limitations that preclude me from doing so at this time. I must be exceedingly careful, prudent as to what I share with you and even how I say what I dare to share. Lives depend upon it, your lives, the lives of my men and the lives of many others who may become engaged in this mission. As you know, lives have already been lost here in Odell. That's as tragic as it is unfortunate. Two of your people gave up their lives this morning, three state police officers and one of my men will not return to his wife or children. Believe me when I tell you that it is the sincere desire of my heart that we not suffer the loss of one more soul. I am committed to preserve life as much as I am to preserve liberty which is the essence of why we are here."

"You stand here before me this morning on the dawn of a day that may ring as important in the history of our country as the very morning that our forefathers declared with defiant voices to tyrants distant, no more! We will have our liberty, or we will have death, but we will have no more tyranny."

"There will come over the course of the next few days, perhaps even weeks defamations, lies and other harsh words about me, my men and those other patriots who sent us here to your town. We expect and accept that and all that will eventually come to us."

"Look around you. You see these good Americans dressed in the combat fatigues of your country. Every one of them, yes each of them has at one time or another served you, our country on the fields of combat. Each one has excelled, many have been wounded and decorated for their acts of bravery, for their sacrifices on those fields. There are no cowards among them. They are all proven men and women of valor. You should know and anyone else who may be listening, should know, that we are willing, perfectly willing to lay down our lives for our cause and country. Hoping we will gain your trust and eventually have your support, I tell you that any man or woman who hasn't a cause so sacred that he will lay his life down for it, has no life worth living nor cause worth believing in. We're ready and willing to fight and to take our enemies with us to dust and grave. This country's future is of greater value than any of our lives and frankly yours as well. I have prayed to God; my men have prayed individually and with me and I know many more will pray to God that not one . . . and I mean this fellow Americans. Not a single one of you or ours are lost."

"Any real soldier will tell you that war is horrible. Battle is the worst nightmare imaginable. Violence, injury and death are not what we want. I want it to be clear to those distant, yet listening to my words this morning, that we do not care what others may say or think or do, as long as we are sure that we are right with ourselves. There are many millions who seek refuge on the popular side of a cause because, and only because, there is safety in numbers. We're not afraid of our small numbers. Had our forefathers stopped to count numbers, we'd all be sipping tyrant tea and bowing to a crown."

"If I were able to carry you off to Washington, D.C. this morning and examine the Congressional directory, you would find page after page of cowardly politicians, misrepresentatives of the people, as I like to call them. Most are liars and crooks, idiot sons and daughters of the elite rich claiming to have *risen-up out of the ranks of the common folks*, those common folks like you and I who really make this nation of ours as great as it is. We haven't enough

106

representation in Washington who have risen-up *through the ranks* of those they purport to represent. Think about it. When is the last time you really had a choice other than what the two major parties shove down your throats every four or six years?"

"In the course of my professional career this is the only office to which I have aspired, to have command over the brave sons and daughters of this country. No higher office has ever been sought, though many have been offered. To be counted among your ranks has, is and always will be the highest rank I have ever needed."

"I know you are cold, tired and frightened. I wish I could say something to allay your fears. I'm truly sorry for your discomfort and the losses suffered on both sides so far. Forgive me for being wordy, I did not intend to make this a long-winded political diatribe. Soon you will be able to return to the comfort of your homes. The power will be restored but of necessity outside communications will remain restricted.

Let me get more directly to our reason for being here."

Sheriff Odell perked up leaning a bit forward in his chair and for the first time since Vincent had begun to speak, shot him a quick glance.

"I wish all of you could look past me, past the Odell Coal Company building. Look off northward past the newly plowed fields that lay just outside your beautiful little town. Look to a distant place called Stern Park Gardens? Have any of you ever heard of that little town?" The people stirred, some even craning a neck as if they really could see the place Vincent was alluding to. Many looked at each other and shook heads in the negative. Some didn't move an inch and stood arms folded, eyes narrowed, staring at the curious figure on the flatbed truck. Dick and Ruth Ralph were among those. Dick thought

107

Vincent looked much like the figure in the opening scene of the movie 'Patton.'"

"No, you can't see it, but it's there. If you were able to leave here today and drive only seventy miles to the north, you would run into it, though it no longer bears that name. You've much in common with it. And it has much in common with another small town like Odell that I want to tell you about this morning. It is a place far from here; four thousand five hundred and forty-three miles. A small town, ten miles west of the City of Prague, Czech- Republic. The town is called Lidice."

"In June of 1942 the village stood on the land it occupied for more than six hundred years. It was a mining village a mile off the main highway with some lovely old inns, a black smith or two, a cobbler, a wheelwright and a tailor. It had a few small shops and a market for vegetables, meat and other goods."

"Above the ninety roofs of the town rose the spires of St. Margaret Church, built in 1736. I've seen it while in that country. Last evening as I was contemplating what I would say to you here this morning, I looked out to the southwest side of your town and saw the spires of St. Paul's Church. It reminded me of St. Margaret's and the small town I visited a few years ago. The vision of St. Paul's spires brings home to me the parallels that exist between Odell, Stern Park Gardens and tiny Lidice.

"That little town in Czechoslovakia was remote, peaceful, almost like a village in a fairy tale. But it was not the pretend village of a fairy tale, it was a very real place that tasted freedom a long time ago and upon whose streets a future President of the United States of America walked as a young man. They even named a street after him. They learned of freedom from him, dreamed of it and saw the visions he painted of it for them."

108

"But the Nazis came to Lidice in those days and with them brought the misery and horror and hardship that their evil thrived upon. One of the first things the Nazi's did was to disarm the villagers. Then they took away their books and told them when to get up in the morning and when to go to bed at night. They barred public gathering and destroyed the little newspaper that used to come to them from Prague every Saturday morning. Oh, they didn't do this all at once mind you. It was just a little bit at a time. Then one day they closed the church. The altar of St. Margaret's would never be used for worship again. Sacramental wine and bread would never be placed upon that sacred table. Two hundred years of worship in her warm embrace came to an end. Men and women were no longer free to speak their minds, to worship their God the way their ancestors had; they could no longer be free. In their hearts, however, the hearts of the tailor, the farmer, the blacksmith, the schoolteacher and even the small young children beat the stubborn independence of those ancestors. And the people of the town of Lidice were not about to give that up to anyone . . . ever. No matter what the price."

"In May of 1942 one of Hitler's most feared, ruthless, arrogant henchmen, the appointed Governor of Czechoslovakia, known as *The Hangman* to the people of Czechoslovakia and as *The Blonde Beast* by his colleagues in the SS, SD Commander Rheinhold Heydrich went for a ride between his country home near Lidice and his headquarters in Prague. He did this in his open top, dark green Mercedes touring car without an armed escort as a show of confidence in his intimidation of the resistance and the successful pacification of the population. It was the 27th of May as his car slowed to round a sharp turn in the roadway that it came under attack from free Czech agents who had been trained in England and dropped into the area for the sole purpose of assassinating him. They were successful, and he died in agony several weeks later. He was 'one of the best Nazis ever', according to Hitler who was infuriated by his death."

"It took the Nazis but a few short days to apprehend the members of the assassination team and to execute them. But Hitler was not satisfied. Heydrich was number two in command of the SS, second only to the hated Heinrich Himmler. He was the senior officer in charge of the 'final solution' the extermination of the Jews of Europe. Hitler was not going to let the death of one of his prized Generals go unpunished, so he gave the orders for retribution. Though the villagers had no part in the attack, the Nazis extracted a ton of flesh in exchange for his death. On June the tenth an official German statement was read to the world. I want to read it to you this morning:

'It is officially announced that in the course of the search for the murderers of General Heydrich, it has been ascertained that the population of the village of Lidice supported and assisted the murderers of General Heydrich . . . Because the inhabitants, by their support of the perpetrators, have flagrantly violated the law, all the men of the village have been shot. The women have been deported to a concentration camp, and the children sent to appropriate centers for re-education. All buildings of the village were leveled to the ground, and by order of the Supreme Commander the name of the village is immediately abolished and will be removed from every map in existence in the Third Reich."

"The people of and indeed the town of Lidice has been wiped not only from the maps of The Third Reich, but indeed from history itself. It is as if they never existed."

"They came in the night, those men in high black boots. They took the tailor, the butcher, the blacksmith. They took every boy over the age of sixteen

110

and they shot them dead in the town square in front of mothers, wives and sisters. A square, my friends, just a bit smaller than the one we are gathered in here this morning. They piled their bodies high in the street . . . all two hundred of them. And let them lay there to rot as they leveled that sweet village to dust. They hauled the women away to days of brutality, rape, torture and death. And they stole the children away from all that was safe, sacred and serene to them. Almost all of them were never to be heard from again. They bragged that they erased the soul of that village. The ninety homes were burned to their foundations. St. Margaret's Cathedral was ground to dust. They literally plowed the ground level removing all trees and shrubs and evidence of any kind that a building ever stood on that soil. They eventually planted grass, so it would appear as though the town never existed . . . and then the last great insult. The name of the little town of Lidice, through which ran, Wilson Street, named after a President of the United States, they rubbed out of existence. At least they thought they'd erased it from the countryside, from their maps and indeed from history itself."

"Why am I sharing this with you and what does it have to do with Odell . . . and our presence in your hometown this spring morning? It has everything to do with it. Why? Vincent's voice was loud echoing off the building surrounding the town square. The town's people were silent and still. "Why I have often wondered in the past, did those men-beasts do that to those poor people . . .why? I'll tell you why they did it. They did it because they were afraid. They were afraid of the freedom that rested in the breast of every man, woman and child that lived in Lidice. They did it because the system they represented was one of hatred, fear, force, terror and control. And Lidice, her people and people everywhere like them, who treasure freedom, were a threat to them."

111

"I gaze over the square this morning, Odell's town square and look into your questioning faces. I can see the fields you have plowed, all around me the small neat homes you've built with the fruits of your honest labors. I look into the faces of your children. Children like those from across America. They are no different. And my friends I look into the eyes of the women of this village called Odell and wonder. What your women would say to me . . . to us, if ever we were to allow that which happened in Lidice to happen here, to their men, to their children, to their homes, to their town."

"The people of Stern Gardens Park, Illinois thought about that same thing when they heard of the plight of Lidice from Wendell Willkie when he spoke there just after the United States entered World War II. It so affected them they vowed the Nazis would not erase the name of the village of Lidice from off the face of the earth. Hitler would not be successful in his brag that they had been erased from history. And so, the people of Sterns Garden Park changed the name of their town . . . to Lidice. They swore to always remember and to never allow such an atrocity to ever occur again. That little town kept that name until it learned a few years after the war that a very few of the survivors of the concentration camps migrated back to their original village and began rebuilding Lidice. Then Sterns Garden Park gave the name up because it was decided that the world deserved only one Lidice. The little American sister village is now called Crest Hill. You can almost see it from here.

"I have spoken to you longer than I had anticipated, and I promise that I will speak to you no longer than five more minutes. But the horrors of Lidice beg a question that surrounds all the horror of World War II. How could we, how could the world stand by and let what happened in Lidice happen? Surely something could have been done in the beginnings . . . *In the beginnings, when the smallest of liberties began to be trampled upon under the guise of what was best for the people.* I need not remind you that *nothing was done*, not for the people of Lidice nor a thousand others like her until it was too late and millions, literally millions of men and women had been exterminated. And I remind you in the words of another, 'it only takes good men to do nothing for evil to succeed.' And it succeeded because no one lifted a finger to stop the evil in the beginnings of the hell it brought to our world."

"Before you judge me, my men and our cause, I want you to remember those people of Lidice. I'll bet you not one of them ever expected the first day they took the books away that it was just the first step in their extermination. So, nobody did anything in the beginnings.

"A few months ago, factions disloyal to the great majority of the people of the United States of America took those 'beginnings steps.' Yes, the beginning is couched in fine statutory language, cloaked with tender feelings of protection and window dressed in the silks of treason just as it was for the people of Poland, the people of France, the people of Czechoslovakia and the people of Lidice. Patriots, such as the men you see standing around this square this morning are poised across this country to rise-up and to take back the liberty that has been stolen from us, guaranteed us by the blood of our forefathers and by the second amendment to the Constitution of the United States of America. *We will not lay down our arms, we will not give up this town until the usurpation of those liberties is restored.* We will fight the *beginnings*, no matter how subtle, no matter how veiled, no matter how placed before the public. And I shout to you . . . beg of you to add your voices to ours . . . our defiant voices as we scream from the plains of this great country loud enough to be heard at the tops of the Rocky Mountains . . . No more! We will have our liberty, we will

113

have our liberties, or we will have death, but we will have no more of your tyranny."

"Our demands will be made known to the President and Congress of the United States within the next twenty-four hours."

"Thank you, citizens of Odell. Forgive my long windedness. You may return to your homes now, but I should note only a few small things for you. Some of you in defiance of the federal government's attempt to disarm the citizens of the United States, may have retained rightfully owned weapons. If you have, for your safety and ours, we ask you to temporarily relinquish them to us. We've accessed the State of Illinois firearms owner's database, so we are aware of every individual in Odell who owns a registered firearm, but we want to collect those that have not been turned in. Our men will return to your homes with you and begin the collection. Now, we don't intend to replace one tyrant with another. Your arms will be returned to you as soon as it is safe for all the parties involved."

"Absolutely the worst thing that can be done is to brandish any firearm for whatever reason. Already this morning a stalwart of Odell mistakenly fired upon two of our men, killing one of them. As a tragic result of that mistake she became an unfortunate casualty herself. Likewise, a resident pointing a walking stick at our men in the dark early morning hours threatened others of our command. He is also a very unfortunate casualty."

"If there are any medical emergencies, our men will be of assistance to you and a physician is located at our command headquarters in the VFW. Removal to local hospitals will be considered on a case by case basis and will be approved by our physician. We have been able to enlist the cooperation of your local radio station, so please keep tuned in so that you can receive further instructions and information. We think this will be the best way to keep you fully informed. It is my sincere hope that we'll have a positive response from Washington and that we'll be leaving Odell within the next few days."

"All we ask for now is calm and cooperation. We want no more harm to come to any member of this community nor to any of our troops. Conduct yourselves like good patriots and show our men the same respect and courtesy you would like shown you and yours. Thank you for your time and patience this morning. God bless you and God Bless the United States of America."

Glen Garnet stood with his arm draped over the shoulders of Pat Higgins. During the long address delivered by Colonel Vincent, Garnet never took his eyes off Larry Hurley Odell. The sheriff was one peed off young man. And when he finally glanced back at Garnet their eyes locked. Glen thought, "somebody's looking for another fight!"

Chapter IX

Mary Duke Odell sat in her favorite rocking chair close to the open window at the front of her house listening to the curious man's voice over the loudspeaker. He was an enigma and while he pled his position expertly and with passion, he was wrong, and she had let him know so. This spring morning at this point in time was a far cry from her day when people loved and respected each other. Then was a time when you could disagree with someone without disliking them. It was a time when Mr. Odell walked the streets of his hometown as if he were a hero. Respect, that's the basic ingredient missing from today's society . . . respect. "I remember when a person's word was as good as scripture," she thought to herself. "When a police officer said something to you, it was met with a yes Sir. Oh yes, there were the rare moments when authority was questioned like the marble contest incident, but that was the exception to the rule and Mrs. Murray had been so obviously wrong. "Yes," Mary thought, "we just don't respect, love one another enough these days."

Earlier she'd watched the two Secret Service men being led to the VFW in handcuffs. It wasn't as though they were being treated roughly, but they looked sad, tired and surprised. She sensed their embarrassment that they had failed to protect her. They didn't lift their eyes until she called out to one of them by name. The agent responded with a weak smile. The other man never took his eyes off the sidewalk. There was a large laceration on the swollen left side of his face. His shirt was drenched in blood. Clearly each was ashamed that they'd been surprised by the men who captured them. It was over before they knew what was going on. Complacency had bested them in a small town where nothing ever happened.

And then there was poor Shelly Miller. Vincent had told her of the two casualties. "Poor Shelly! She was a lovely lady, always so kind to everyone, but especially thoughtful when it came to the young girls of the town and the

116

senior ladies. How am I ever going to go to that store again and maintain my composure? I just know Pudge must be dying a thousand deaths."

Mary's eyes drifted toward St. Paul's and while she listened, she wondered if they would let her go to church like she did every Saturday night. She was a traditionalist; loved Mass on Sunday mornings, but since Mr. Odell passed, she couldn't avoid the beautiful red brick chapel on Saturday evenings. "Know I'm dang well double the Catholic anyone here in town is," she'd joke.

She heard Vincent say something about a St. Margaret's Church, but could not remember any in the area. Was it a new parish over in Limestone or maybe that was the church he went to? It would be to the benefit of the people if Vincent were a Catholic. He'd certainly understand and respect the importance of getting to Mass.

After a few more minutes at the partially opened window, Mary headed back to her kitchen for another cup of coffee. "What of Lorenzo?" She wondered. "Will he do something rash because Larry and I are caught up in the midst of this? No of course not. He's the President of the United States for goodness sakes. He would be cognizant of others here in Odell, friends and parents of friends he grew up with. Now is the time for calm. He will do just the right thing, but I wish I could speak with him for just a few minutes." Mary took her cup of coffee to the front porch and watched as townspeople walked past her on the way back to their homes. No one looked up at her as they passed. No one waived, smiled and said hello to her like they always did. She felt as if they were blaming her.

# # # # #

The crackle of a radio snapped Captain Coffin from his duties at the VFW. "Captain Coffin, this is Colonel Vincent, we're done here. Please get Captain Bell over to your location as soon as possible. I'm going to tour the perimeter and will be there in about twenty minutes. If the men haven't had a chance to

117

chow down, make sure the mess unit get some out to them ok?"

"Yes Sir, Colonel. We've already fed the men and have changed watch. Far as I know all's quiet on the western front."

"Roger that, Captain. Will touch base with you on my way in." As soon as Vincent signed off Coffin's radio went off again.

"Captain Coffin, this is Captain Petracha. We've got movement on the eastern perimeter. Looks like a swat team moving down a drainage ditch. They're still a way off and may just be a probe. It doesn't appear to be a full squad, but I don't like what I see."

"If they've violated the restricted zone, you have authorization to engage as soon as they are in range. Do you hear me? They are not to be inside the perimeter. I don't give a damn what they're up to."

"Affirmative Sir. If they close range, we will eliminate the threat."

"Keep me posted. I'll be back to you in a few minutes." Coffin rang Vincent on his radio and received instructions.

"Get on the horn to O'Brien. Tell him he is about to lose five men. He'd better move them back. Tell him this is the first and last warning he or his men will be the beneficiary of. I want to talk to him and the Chicago field office agent in charge. We'll call at 0830 hours. But you make it clear, John. He moves those men back right now or we'll take em out."

"Yes, Sir. I'll make contact immediately."

Mike O'Brien was in the district's command center with three FBI agents when Coffin's call came through. They'd not been able to tap the internal communication network of the group holding Odell but listening in to Vincent's address to the townspeople was easy. When the phone rang in the large command center, all eyes flashed to it. O'Brien moved quickly to the speaker button. "Commander O'Brien speaking."

118

"Commander, this is Captain John Coffin speaking. I'm calling on behalf of Colonel Vincent with whom you spoke earlier this morning."

"Yes, Coffin, go ahead."

"Commander, perhaps you didn't hear me correctly the first time. This is *Captain* John Coffin. Please address me as such."

O'Brien paused for just a moment, biting his lip, "yes of, course Captain. No disrespect intended. As you can imagine, we're all a little frayed around here. We've a lot of people's lives in jeopardy and certainly don't want words to set off any incident."

"Well, you don't have to worry about that, Sir. We're professionals on this end of the line. We expect to be treated as such and will return the courtesy. But now let's move on to the purpose of my contact. First, you have a small squad of men in a drainage ditch just off Prairie Road about five miles east of town. They appear to be a paramilitary unit or SWAT team of some sort. If they have not reversed course within two minutes, our men, who are locked on them, are going to take every last one of them out. Believe me . . . we have the fire power to accomplish that. And this is the last time . . . and we mean the absolute last time that you will receive a warning before we commence fire. Colonel Vincent also wants me to remind you that we have hostages. and lots of them. The next time we detect movement in our direction of any nature, you will find yourselves responsible for one of them being placed in a body bag. Are we on the same page, Commander?"

"Yes, we are Captain. Is there anything else"?

"We also want you to know that we will not accept any flyovers, an invasion of our air space of any kind. Any aircraft violating a ten-mile radius of Odell will result in civilian casualties. You have satellite technology that will give you as close a gander as you want; we don't care about that. But I assure you, if we can see it and it's inside the ten-mile radius, we will attempt to

119

shoot it down. That failing, we'll execute hostages. Are we clear on that issue also Sir?"

O'Brien looked at the FBI agent in charge who nodded in the affirmative to him. "Roger that Captain Coffin. I don't know who ordered that SWAT team to move into the radius," O'Brien lied. "But I will get them out of there ASAP." Choosing his words carefully, "there have been and will be no flyovers I promise you that."

"Very good Sir. I will tell my men they have a two-minute no-fire restriction. But if the unit moves closer or fails to withdraw immediately, I'll give 'em a green light.

"Commander, Colonel Vincent would like to speak to you and the FBI agent with you at 0830 hours. Is that acceptable?" Surprised that Vincent knew the FBI was already in place, O'Brien agreed.

"Yes, Sir Captain, that would-be Agent Daniel Barrett. I will see that Agent Barrett is available for the 0830 call. Is there anything that we should talk about at this time? Are the townspeople safe?"

"Nothing at this time Commander. As you have undoubtedly heard, Odell has unfortunately sustained two casualties. We will be releasing the identities of those individuals and the circumstances surrounding their demise later today."

"Oh, and Commander, O'Brien, I am not for one moment under the impression that you don't know who ordered that squad to move up and probe our perimeter. There are only two possibilities; you did, or your men are out of control. Either case is unacceptable to us. Just so the record's perfected Sir. Now, I have other duties which require my attention. Good morning." The conversation ended.

O'Brien turned to Agent Barrett, "will somebody tell me *who in Sam Hell* these SOB's are?"

Dan Barrett had an hour and forty-five minutes before speaking with the crackpot in charge of this mess and he had to learn as much about him and his cause as soon as possible. Satellite images that would be available in a few minutes would give him a better picture of the situation on the ground. With them he could better advise Washington and the governor whether to call out the National Guard or whether the situation could be controlled and dismantled with a lesser force. All intelligence so far, which was yet very limited, suggested a sizeable, well entrenched band of thugs. How sophisticated they were he was not sure, but he had suspicions that they're a few guys who knew how to handle some very sophisticated weapons and communications systems. Barrett was concerned. . . real concerned.

If his hunch was right the United States hadn't dealt with a hostage crisis of this magnitude since the 1979 embassy crisis in Iran. The number of possible hostages being held in Odell could be more than fifteen times the embassy employee numbers. And the elephant in the command room was the fact that this time members of the sitting President's family were locked up solid in the mess.

Barrett moved to another room to examine the satellite images arriving over computer screens. "What's it look like Mike?" Barrett asked as he filled the doorway to the command center.

"Well none of us have as much training as we really need with this. We'll have your link with Washington in just a few minutes. We'll have a better handle on what we're up against shortly. Meanwhile, come have a look for yourself."

"Not sure I am going to know what it's showing either, but we also have a guy in a chopper on the way down from Chicago who can interpret anything

121

on the screen. Plus, he can call in for shot adjustments that'll allow us to see the label on a shirt collar. Something tells me we are going to need 'em to do just that."

Barrett moved to printed images already covering the large conference table. He moved slowly about the table looking intently at each image. Occasionally, he picked one up and examined it closer. He exhaled a few times with a low whistle. After fifteen minutes of circling around and around the table, he stopped at the far end of the room and leaned back against the wall. He took a toothpick from his shirt pocket and placed it between his teeth. He looked at O'Brien who was still trying to make sense of the images.

"Mike. I've got some bad news." O'Brien looked up from the images on the table.

"What is it?"

"Looks to me like they got a small battalion up there. Dug in real good too. I don't need any expert to tell me that much. They've got the town surrounded and there could be a couple hundred of them or more. I know I'm not *the man* when it comes to imaging, but I've seen enough satellite pictures to tell you based upon the number of vehicles they have and the number of positions they look to be covering that it's a damn good-sized bunch. A small battle group at the very least, maybe battalion sized. How they got in there with no one noticing is beyond me. We got one situation here my friend. One hell of a situation."

"After this Vincent guy's call, we'll have a little more to go on then you can get to the governor and I'll get through to Washington so that the President can be briefed. And I need some time to think . . . about forty days and forty nights worth. You know, looking at this on the surface as it stands right now, this may take more than a national guard unit to resolve."

"Let's see what they're looking for, what their demands are, and we'll know better what it's gonna take to defuse this. If we could just get a quiet up-close look at these guys . . ."

# # # # #

Dick and Ruth Ralph sat in the living room staring out at what was otherwise a beautiful April Saturday morning. They sat in silence for the longest time, numb from what they had seen, still having a hard time believing what was happening. It was like something out of a B-grade movie, one you would tolerate during the early morning hours between infomercials for thigh shapers and kitchen knives. Both watched jeeps circling the block every fifteen minutes or so. When Vincent drove by in his open jeep, Dick stood and walked to the window for a closer look. "Nazi Bastards themselves," he muttered. Ruth heard him and saw the blood rise in his cheeks.

Shelly Miller was one of Ruth's best friends. The very thought that they'd no longer be able to stroll the square on hot late summer evenings talking about grandchildren and exotic places they'd still love to visit, was nearly more than she could bear. Poor Pudge, whatever would he do without her? The guys from the poker game had to carry him to his house just a few blocks down from Ruth's. She wanted desperately to go down to comfort him and to see what she could do, but Dick insisted they stay at home for a while. Dick Ralph stared out the window at young men who moved about with weapons and grim faces. Their presence caused his thoughts to drift to the M1 rifle he'd stashed in the rafters above the one car garage in the backyard. It was the kind of weapon he carried throughout Korea. He never ever intended to use it again, but the image of Vincent standing at the podium looking all of Mussolini made him wonder if it could still fire and fire accurately.

# # # # #

Dan Barrett watched the phone with one eye and the photos spread out on the table with the other. "Mike, come in here will you? Take a look at this."

123

He called out to O'Brien. O'Brien dropped the phone and entered the command room. "Look here," he said pointing to a recently downloaded satellite photo. "This is a gap in their perimeter. This is the, the southwest side of town. There's a small local radio station in this building right here and nothing else in the way of fortifications for maybe eight hundred yards to the north and west. It's a big gap. I bet we could get a team in there for a closer peak at what is going on. What do you think?"

"No. We can't send anybody in there, Dan. They'd get chewed up. We don't know what they might have laid out there. What if there are mines, trip wires planted in that gap? Not to mention what they might do to the hostages if our guys are spotted. I'm not for it at this stage. I think it's just too damn risky."

"I'm betting they haven't had time to lay mines. They've only been there since late last night, early this morning. They've been busy putting up that perimeter, rounding up the townsfolk and such. My guess is that the gap is there because they don't have enough men to fill it. Every defense has its Achilles heel. And by God . . . Michael, I think we're looking at one. If we can get men into that gap for a short distance without them noticing, it may be the key to getting in there under cover of darkness with a bigger contingent. And then you and I will have something positive to report when we speak to the powers that be."

"And look this doesn't have to be a super intel gathering effort. All we really want to know is if we can get a force of some kind in there under the cover of darkness. First sign of any trouble, we'll yank em out."

"It's too early. Let's wait until nightfall. And what if they do discover the probe and execute one of the hostages?"

"Nightfall isn't going to give us that much more cover. In fact, we'll light up like flares with any infrared technology which they must have. Besides that, if we wait any longer it just gives them that much more time to set up and dig in. Just a quick parry Mike."

"I don't like it Dan. Under cover of darkness might be different, but in broad daylight without knowing what we're up against, I'm against it, makes me nervous. I can't send a SWAT unit in there against those guys. We don't know what their weaponry strength is, and our last little incursion was discovered in short order."

Thirty minutes later just as Col Vincent was waiting for the connection with Commander O'Brien, Coffin flew into the room with his hand gesturing a throat cutting movement. Vincent quickly ended the call. "What's up, John?"

"Can you believe it? Those crazy S.O.B.'s are probing the southwest perimeter! They're crawling men right up the tunnel!"

"Cajun on the line?"

"Yes, Sir."

"Let me talk to him." Vincent picked up the hand mic and spoke into it calmly. "Captain I hear you got movement on the perimeter?"

"Yes, Sir, five men moving down the tunnel, Sir."

"Push the button Captain."

Weapons Specialist Alphonse Bertillion lay on the roof of the old Route 66 gas station just south of town with his spotter. They were the perfectly camouflaged guardians of the tunnel. If you want to know the sophistication level of the enemy leave what looks like a weak spot in your defenses and see if he attempts to exploit it. When Vincent told Captain Schnecksnider to push the button, Bertillion heard nothing more than a click in his earpiece. His arms cradled an M40A3 sniper rifle married to a Unertl 10x tactical scope. One thousand yards away, Sergeant Don Bean of the Illinois State Police motioned his men still. When he raised his binoculars to scout further into the perimeter surrounding Odell, Bertillion squeezed off the first of five rounds. The round smashed through Bean's binoculars taking his head off. His second in command, Pete Boldock, began moving to his side to see if he could assist when the second round struck him in the neck killing him instantly. Neither Bean nor Boldock heard the shots that took their lives. Each of the three other men were struck down as they attempted retreat. In a matter of a few short minutes five bodies lay in the fields west of Odell. All of them except Bean had at least raised their weapons in self-defense, but none got a shot off. No one ever saw the sniper that killed them. It happened so fast there wasn't even time to radio for support. All five members of the SWAT team sent into a "tunnel" were dead.

A few moments after the last shot Bertillion called in the kills to Schnecksnider. Vincent was back on the air.

"Colonel Vincent, Captain Schnecksnider here. We have no movement. We're checking southwestern perimeter and tunnel for additional movement or survivors." After a few moments the radio crackled again. "Sir, no survivors."

Vincent's jaw set hard; his cheeks turned bright red as he turned to Coffin. "Get those morons on the phone."

# # # # #

O'Brien burst into the command center screaming, "I told you it was a stupid idea! We've got five good men dead, blown to hell out there. And what the hell do we have to show for it? Nothing is what we have and who's going to tell the families of these guys that they just walked into a slaughter because we couldn't be patient and do our homework first. Not to mention that we've placed nearly three thousand hostages in peril. Listen, Barrett, I've made an executive decision, and this is going to be the way it is until I get orders to the contrary. Keep your federal ass out of this mess until you're invited back into it. Observe, advise. That's it. The governors on his way and he's madder than hell." With that O'Brien stormed back to his office and a phone ringing off the hook.

Barrett sat silently staring at the command room monitors. He screwed up for sure, but he was just trying to get a handle on these crazies' level of sophistication. He had a taste of it now.

Underestimating the enemy and for going forward before he had all the tactical information necessary were stupid mistakes. The results of the misguided excursion was deflating, but . . . but at least now he knew for a surety and all doubt had been erased. They weren't up against a bunch of amateurs. The cost of that information was enough to make him sick to his stomach though.

Ten minutes after the short firefight, if it could even be called that, the phone rang. "Barrett here." The answer was short, terse.

"Get O'Brien in there with you. I'll wait."

After a few moments, O'Brien entered the command center. "Colonel Vincent, this is Commander O'Brien."

"What were you morons thinking? You just murdered five of your own men! The next time you pull a lame stunt like that, I hope to God you have the guts to lead the charge yourselves." Vincent was furious. He was above all things a soldier, an officer who loved his and respected soldiers, even enemy combatants.

"That was a mistake that should not have happened Colonel. I accept full responsibility for that move. I've personally gave orders that nobody is to move into the five-mile radius as long as the townspeople remain uninjured. However, if we hear of casualties in Odell, I'll have to defer to my superiors. I know you understand."

"Horse feathers, you baboons! That was worse than a mistake, it was

127

murder and if you try a stupid move like that again, you'll not only lose the men involved you have my personal word, you'll lose one resident of Odell to match each man you send. Do you understand me?"

"Yes, Colonel. We understand."

"Good. It's good to know that we have the rules of engagement on the record. Now get someone here from Washington who knows what the hell they're doing. This situation is obviously way over your heads." With that the phone went dead as fast as it came alive.

# # # # #

An hour later the phone rang in Commander O'Brien's office. It was Colonel Vincent. "Hopefully we can speak without the Fed for a few minutes."

"Yes Colonel. Go ahead."

"We haven't been formally introduced, though I'd expect you've read my military personnel jacket by now. I am in command of a very elite group of men. Probing our perimeter is futile and as you've seen, dangerous. I'm sure you have satellite images that have given you some idea of our positions and strength, tactically most of what you need to know."

"Our demands are fairly uncomplicated, and we intend to outline them tomorrow at 1200 hours. We're inviting a major news feed to cover that disclosure. We'll advise you of the conditions that apply to their presence in Odell. If either the state or local governments attempt to gag this effort, we will simply accomplish it through internet broadcast. We have a reporter from the Chicago Tribune among the citizens of Odell. She'll do just fine as our media host; in fact she's volunteered. We'll proceed at exactly 1200 hours unless you have some compelling reason for us not to."

"I'm sure you understand, Colonel." O'Brien replied, "that we'll have to have some time to discuss it here. I suppose my first question to you is are you prepared to send some hostages out with the news crew when it leaves? Perhaps some of the women and children?"

"There's nothing as yet to inspire us to consider any negotiations." O'Brien took mental note of the "as yet" portion of Vincent's response. That meant that at some point in time negotiations for the hostages was possible.

"We'll not be releasing them for anything other than medical emergencies. As we've shared with the citizenry and as you know, we do have a physician in our ranks as well as several properly trained medics. The townspeople will have access to them as they need. If we cannot attend to the medical needs of a resident here in Odell we'll either allow supplies in or, upon approval of the medical officer, we'll send the resident out. Other than that Commander, we'll not be bartering with the town's people."

"Now, I know you have a report to make to the governor. The Fed has to be in communication with his director in Washington. Just two last things and you may share these with him. Trust me when I tell you the President has more at risk here than a few relatives. It's very important that he specifically hears what we have to say and responds positively to it. As for now, you may tell the Fed he may legitimately communicate to Washington grandmother is well and unharmed as is his cousin the sheriff, who shall we say, is somewhat subdued."

"And . . . I want, you to know and my record will reflect that I want nothing more than to avoid any more violence. Though a military man, I am, for the most part a peaceable man. I detest violence of all kinds and wish to see no more of it. In fact, it is the last thing I want. But I'm also an American and a soldier who has served his country for many years. Now I'm a soldier for a cause. One that I deeply believe in. I'm a patriot as are my men. And though you might not believe any of what I've told you, believe this; we are not afraid to die for that cause and country. The men with me are just a small contingent of tens of thousands of others, watching, waiting . . . poised to strike in a similar fashion across the length and breadth of this country. Let's strive to avoid further bloodshed if possible."

"Colonel Vincent, you and I may disagree on a good many things, but I assure you that I don't want to see any more bloodshed than has already taken place. The prevention of further losses, on either side, is of paramount importance."

"I appreciate the opportunity to speak with you and thank you for your candidness though I wish I could prevail upon your good sense and patriotism to lay down your arms and to make your case before the lawful venues of this country. Now when emotions are high, and weapons are a great part of the mix, life as precious as it is, is bound to be lost. Surely, Sir, you understand that this isn't the way to effect change in our country?"

"Now is not the time for debate. I suggest it's time to move back to our respective camps."

"But, Sir. . ." O'Brien waited several seconds for a response before he realized the line was dead. He wanted to tell the traitorous, murdering bastard how wrong he was, but his training told him to keep away from confrontation. He had to do the best he could to appease the opponent until he could come up with a plan to neutralize him. The thought made him smile . . . "neutralize" him. This guy has a freaking army occupying a small town in the middle of some of the flattest land in the mid-section of America. A physical approach to the small town without being detected was near impossible. He had to be able to appeal to Vincent, to negotiate, there was no way this could come to an end by force. Any attempt at it would make Waco look like a trip to Disneyland.

Needing fresh air, O'Brien walked out the front door of the state police building, placed his hands on his hips, looked skyward and took a long deep breath. Recalling how he used to smoke back in college, he wanted one now or was it a drink he needed? Couldn't be a drink, it was only 1030 hours! Yep, it was a drink. He wanted a long, tall, cold glass of beer. He never drank during the day, rarely drank at all. Mostly liked to knock a few back on a Saturday afternoon after mowing his big backyard or while sitting in the stands at Wrigley Field watching his beloved Cubs. It was the beginning of baseball season. The Cubs would be playing at two o'clock this afternoon and he had tickets to take his three children and wife to the game. Wide blue skies, not a cloud in em. The breeze would be blowing out at the park. Would be a great day for a ballgame. Yeah, he really, really wanted a drink now.

# # # # #

Ending his call to O'Brien, Vincent called out, "Sergeant Major, have we made contact with Fox News?"

"Sir, yes Sir. We've told them that we have our own media rep. And just want their crew of cameras and tech guys. They're insisting on sending one of their own in but that's just, so they can scream exclusive. I'm pretty sure they'll give in to our request."

"Our reporter's name is Monica Palmer. She's a junior writer for the Trib. She's green, but I figure that'll work to our advantage. The fewer outsiders the better. We'll draft the questions she will ask, and you've got the answers. It's all coming together well and after your interview with her we're confident she'll cooperate. What do you think, are we a go on that?"

"Sounds good. But I want to meet her right now. Have one of the men fetch her so I can have a look."

"And it's been awhile since I heard from Bell. What's he up to? Get him on the air and get a report from him. I wanna see how we're doing? Looks like the com blocking systems are doing the job, doesn't it?"

"And Bergeron picked up the attempt at the tunnel pretty fast. Couldn't have worked out better if we issued an invitation for them to walk up in there. Sooner or later they'll try something and take another shot at the perimeter. Something's gonna happen. So, keep our eyes peeled and make sure the men are kept alert. This is sorta like riding a lit stick of dynamite. We all know its gonna blow . . . no putting it out . . just a matter of time."

"We're ready Colonel."

"I'll get the reporter over here and raise Captain Bell. Is there anything else you need Sir?"

"Yeah, I need to speak to Hauser too. I want to make sure my nephew's ok. Will you get him on the air? In fact, get him online before Bell, will you?"

"You bet, Sir."

Vincent moved about the large first floor reception room of the VFW now converted to the central command center. Men scurrying around the building were still setting up communications equipment, computers, plotting positions and listening for the listeners. It looked chaotic, but there was method to the madness. Vincent watched with a critical eye as the command center took shape. A radioman broke his concentration.

"Sir, I have Captain Hauser on the line.

"Ok. Corporal let me take his call in my office."

"Colonel Vincent, this is Captain Hauser Sir. Anything I can do for you?"

"Captain I just want a report on my nephew. How's he doing?"

"He's doing just fine, Sir. Came in here without a squeak of a problem and is tucked away out of harm's way. Don't you worry, Sir, I'll take care of him like he was my own kid. Nobody's going to get anywhere near him. You can count on it."

"I know I can Captain. I have every confidence in you and your men. And I know you'll tolerate me wearing the hat of a worried uncle. Do you need anything? How are the men doing? They are holding up okay. All in good shape?"

"We're just fine, we don't need anything. We're dug in pretty good. Morale's high . . . almost too high, but I've got a handle on it. They trained well, Sir. We got the best of the best and we're set to go."

"I'm counting on every one of 'em and I'm not worried. They're good boys and will do the job."

"Well, the kid's just fine . . . you're gonna be real proud of him."

"Thanks, Paul. His momma would be real upset with me if I ever let anything happen to him. Keep me posted and check in with Captain Bell, will you?"

"Yes Sir, will do."

"Okay. I'll talk to you later tonight. I want to have senior cadre in for mess and an intel briefing at 1800 hours. Coffin's going to speak to the townspeople on the radio at 1600 hours but should be free by then. That's all for now."

Vincent ended his conversation with Hauser just in time to take report from Bell. The communications system, as far as Bell knew, hadn't been tapped yet. Vincent congratulated him and clicked the handset off.

As solid a soldier as he was, Vincent had his eccentricities and weaknesses. Upon being offered command of the operation he insisted that his favorite leather chair and massive desk be transported to Odell with him. Though an odd and cumbersome request those offering the command position, indulged him. If he was likely to die during a mission it might as well be while sitting behind that desk in that chair. It was a small luxury request. Now he flopped down into the high-back burgundy leather chair with brass tuck buttons running along the seams. He placed his hands over the grooved, mahogany-wooded paws decorating each arm of the chair. His head leaned back against the soft, coolness of the leather and he closed his eyes, rubbing them with thumb and forefinger, before reaching into the right top drawer to pull out a long Cuban cigar. The drawer to the left contained antique tinted photos of his wife, children and grandchildren. He slid each one out and stared at it for a long time before placing it in the same spot it occupied on the desk back home in the Adirondacks. After they were arranged perfectly, he leaned back in the chair and put his feet up on the desk. Two days without sleep was starting to wear on him. He would've fallen asleep but for the lit cigar and the sound of Sergeant Major Tom Manning talking to the female reporter in the hallway. He needed just five more minutes of rest before he tackled her. Just five minutes of sanity amidst the insanity.

Chapter X

Barrett could see the small town of Odell in the distance from his helicopter as he flew toward Chicago. After brief calls to superiors in Washington, D.C., he'd scheduled video linkage for more detailed meetings that evening. A brief press conference was scheduled for three o'clock that afternoon in downtown Chicago at the State of Illinois building. The federal government had jurisdiction with the host of federal laws already broken, the murder of innocent citizens and law enforcement officers, weapons violations, crossing of state lines and a list to long to contemplate, but it was also important to respect the sovereignty of the State.

He knew the media would be swarming all over his first stop, the Federal Building. Unlike some of his colleagues who loved camera time, dealing with the media and standing in front of the lights and cameras was the part of his job he disliked the most. He just didn't like the spotlight, he'd rather be chasing bad guys. He knew he'd have to choose every word with the utmost care. He couldn't afford to make even the smallest mistake. It's not often that the President of the United States is watching your every move.

There hadn't been enough time to develop as much information as he would need, but every instinct told him not to lump Vincent in with just one more bunch of wackos. The initial information he did have indicated this was an extraordinary man. His dossier was impeccable; indeed, his career had been stellar. There wasn't a hint of involvement with any fringe groups. He attended West Point and graduated in a respectable top ten percent of his class. Towards the very end of the war he'd served his first assignment as a young second lieutenant in Vietnam. Once stateside Vincent's orders carried him to several assignments during mid-eastern conflicts where he rose in rank, having earned the respect of his superiors, with his no-nonsense, way of organizing and utilizing troops.

Colonel Vincent led ground troops into Al Jubayl, Saudia Arabia. As the head of that small liberation force, he was honored by the Royal Family personally. He'd taken the time to learn and speak several arab dialects which endeared him to the allied forces and the locals. Seven years post Desert Storm, Madison T. Vincent retired, more than honorably discharged with three purple hearts and one distinguished service cross. Since retirement he'd traveled the world with his wife Gretchen, his high school sweetheart, and accepted an appointment to the faculty of Schuyler Military Academy in upstate New York.

Nope, this guy was no wacko. In fact, the whole group was a puzzle to Barrett. These S.O.B.s were Americans! How could they draw down on and shoot fellow Americans? What were they thinking? His biggest challenge was to determine the real motivation of these men, the ones who sent them if indeed Vincent was honest about other potential cells and the money boys behind the whole operation. Personally, he didn't believe the force was any larger than those entrenched in Odell. If this had been a larger more organized group, the FBI would have had intelligence that could have been used to prevent the occupation in the first place. Of course, they and others missed the boat with 9-11. The word occupation startled him. Occupation of an American town by Americans was something that hadn't happened since the Civil War! And now he and his men were going to be in charge of rectifying this soon to be historical black spot.

He knew the force was well organized and well equipped. How and where they secured the sophisticated communications systems and weaponry, they had was a real enigma. Securing it, buying it was one thing, taking physical

136

possession of the kind of weapons showing up on the satellite pictures was another thing. Their communications and encryption equipment are high tech and they had to have a pretty bright boy to rig it up. It shouldn't be too difficult to identify who he was. As the chopper moved off towards distant Chicago, Barrett thought to himself, "we got some pretty damn smart boys ourselves and we are gonna whip these jokers. Soon as we crack the communications of that rag tag outfit, we're gonna bleed them out of there."

One of the things that impressed Barrett as he flew back towards the office was that Odell was a perfect target. From his position in the air over Herscher twenty-two miles east of it he could see a hundred miles in every direction. At ground level the approach to Odell would allow an entrenched force to see line of sight fifteen to twenty miles in any direction easy. Barrett knew they'd had spotters positioned with snipers the way they took out officers on the interstate and the SWAT team he'd convinced O'Brien to send in. His eyes were drawn to the highest spot in a fifty-five-mile radius of Odell, the telephone tower on the west side of town. It was contiguous to the interstate, no doubt there's a body lodged in that tower armed with a high-powered sniper rifle. Barrett's guess was he had to be the shooter who got this underway, taking out the officers the night before.

As the chopper peeled away to the northeast, his gaze fixed on Chicago's skyline in the distance. He loved this city. It was, without doubt, one of the most beautiful large cities in the world. Sure, it had its poor neighborhoods, but for the most part, it was clean and exciting. It's best quality, the diversity of its people. The only city in the world that had more Polish citizens than Warsaw or Chicago! The lakefront on the Fourth of July looked like a United Nations office party.

137

# # # # #

Like many of the residents of Odell, "Gus" Morgan and his father sat quietly in their living room talking, wondering what the hell was going on. The young man knew one thing for sure, they needed help. No one in Odell even knew if any was on the way.

"Surely, the authorities are working on it, Gus. The explosions last night, people have lost their lives, all that would instigate a response from the authorities. You just have to be patient son. There's not a dang thing we can do about this. And even if we had our hunting rifles, we would be no match for what I see running up and down these streets. All we can do is wait . . . wait and see."

"But Dad! Didn't you hear what that character said this morning? He said all that had to happen for evil to succeed is for good men to do nothing. And it seems to me that's just what we are doing . . . nothing. We turned in the rifle you and mom bought for me for my tenth birthday! And how does the government know who has guns and who doesn't anyway?"

"Well, son, you got to register a weapon when you buy one. That's the law and somehow, they got access to gun registration records. That's how they knew who had what. Now we're defenseless and it don't matter. No amount of hunting weaponry would have helped us out of this mess. The only thing that would have given us a chance is if we had the same kind of fire power that they do. Perhaps it's good that we don't. Who knows? That being the case, what would you have the good people of Odell do, pick up their broomsticks, pix axe handles, shovels and go off to fight men armed with modern weapons of war? Sometimes good men can do nothing. Do you understand that? There was nothing those villagers of Lidice could do for

138

themselves either. By the time the Nazi murderers came to their town, they were sitting like ducks on a pond. Totally unprepared, totally unaware. And if one tried to take off, he was a goner. No one was able save them. Makes you wonder how their circumstances degenerated to the point where they were defenseless. Perhaps . . . just maybe something that old bastard on the truck bed said today made sense. Maybe. . . just maybe we weren't as vigilant as we should have been "

Gus' dad sounded old to him for the very first time ever.

"I'm gonna go lay down for a bit and take a nap son. Feel like a little rest before I turn the radio on at four to see what those fellas have to say for themselves. You need anything before I hit the sack for a bit?"

"Nope, I'm fine, Dad. You have a good rest. I might go up and open the store for a bit, see if anyone needs anything. Make sure all's okay, if that's alright with you?"

"Yep, that's fine, but you watch yourself now and don't be getting into any trouble. Think you'll still see Adrian this evening?"

"She's s'posed to come over for a while, but I guess it'll depend on how her parents feel about it now. Most folks seem like they wanna stick close to home 'til they figure this out. So, I guess I'm not gonna really count on it. Now you go on up and rest. 'll check out the store and be back at four."

"Okay later son."

Gus had no intention of returning home at four o'clock. After his father went upstairs for a nap, Gus changed into his sweats and cross-country running shoes. He closed the front door quietly and stepped down off the large front porch. While he stood in the front yard limbering up, a jeep carrying two soldiers turned the corner at the north end of the block. As the jeep approached

Gus didn't take his eyes off the men. The jeep rolled to a halt near him. One of the soldiers nodded and motioned him over to the jeep. "You planning on going for a run son?"

"First all Mister, I ain't your son. And second, in case you haven't heard lately, this is a *free country* and that's exactly what I plan on doing."

"Well you see that athletic field across the street. Feel *free* . . . to run around that track until you drop. But don't let me catch you jogging anywhere off this block, you understand? And while you are at it, you might want to lose the smart attitude. We're here to help you, since you're too stupid to help yourselves." The sun's reflection off the window of the jeep blinded Gus. It was impossible to see the face of the soldier speaking to him. He wasn't young though. He could tell by the base in the man's voice.

"Yeah, I'll take a run around the VFW field all right. But don't try to sell me the crap your Colonel was peddling this morning. Seems to me you don't fight Nazis, by becoming them. We don't need your help Mister. so as soon as you drag your ass out of our town or . . . someone drags them out for you, it'll be just fine with me."

Gus moved away from the jeep and ran across the street pass the park's baseball field. The soldiers watched him jog the perimeter of the field for a few minutes before moving on down the road. As soon as they were out of sight, he made his way back across the street. Moving through his backyard into the neighbors behind his house, it seemed that all that stood between him and the small neighboring towns of Cabrey or Herscher were open corn fields. He couldn't have been more wrong.

# # # # #

Fifteen men and women sat around a conference room table on the

37th floor of the Federal Building in downtown Chicago. The room was warmer than usual, the air seemed thick and heavy. Those present were trained for crazy days like this, but that training didn't grant them immunity from the pressure that side kicked with days like this. It did give them the tools to cope. Someone had placed tall pitchers of ice cold water at regular intervals down the middle of the long cherry wood table. Watching condensation form on and run down the sides of the pitchers reminded everyone how warm it was in the room rather than serving to reduce the discomfort and closeness.

Barrett strolled into the room with his administrative assistant, Judy Kaye, in tow. Looking down the table at Bob Swanson and Charlie Lovemoney, his two most dependable agents, he said "Okay Gentlemen, I've got a phone conference with the Assistant Deputy Director, the Director and the Vice President immediately after this conference. They're scheduled for a briefing with the President in two hours. What've we got?"

Swanson, a fifteen-year veteran of the FBI, headed the intel gathering task force. He was a short man with the physical remnants of a NCAA Division I one-hundred sixty pound-wrestling champion. He wasn't much off his competitive weight and according to Lovemoney, his weekly tennis opponent, was still fast as lightening. His hair was cropped close, military style, and he always dressed in a navy-blue suit with pin stripes. The joke around the office was that he slept in one. When it came to his job, Bobby Swanson was all business and an agent that got results. He carried the highest solved crimes and conviction rate in the country three years running. Swanson took a long swallow of ice water from a sweating glass. "Here's what we got, Chief."

"We haven't had much time to work on this. As you know, we've given you as much as we have so far on Vincent. We've got a team taking a closer look at him, his family and close associates as we speak. We have a prelim report from his office at that small military school. Not much so far, but his computer, papers, everything are being examined on site. Phone records, credit cards and banking records are being gathered for examination. As soon as we get a more substantial report back from them, we'll let you know what we have. We're not expecting much of a paper trail though, Chief. Everything we know about him so far indicates he's a pretty smart fellow, but he's not perfect. He's got to have made a slip someplace. With a little more time, we'll plug him. I'll bring you up to speed as soon as we have something solid."

"As for the gang he's got entrenched in Odell, we don't have a damn clue vis a vis what or where or how. We're looking at known associates, people who served with or under Vincent, all the routine avenues, you know. We're combing the woods looking for the sponsors. They must be there lurking in the background somewhere, but we just don't know who's behind this, yet. We have some ideas thanks to the phone calls made to you and O'Brien. First, there's no doubt the actions beginning last night are tied to the Brady law. So, we figure radical militia's gotta be behind it. But who the unit is or if there's, God forbid, several of them, as they claim, we simply haven't nailed that down yet. We're beating the bushes hard; just need a few more hours of communications tap to see what the buzz is out there."

"Bad news is that the force in town is pretty sizeable and pretty well armed. Our satellite images confirm a battalion-sized outfit with very sophisticated weaponry. They've got stingers in there, .50 calibers, M40A3 Sniper rifles, a ton of C4 plastic explosives, and a vehicle convoy large enough to transport approximately eight hundred men. It looks like they're carrying AK47s and M16s, who knows where they got any of it. We know from the size of this group, that this didn't happen overnight. This has required a long planning lead time."

"They're dug in pretty good and have all access to the town blocked. It's cut off pretty good, Sir. As far as we can tell the Presidents' family members are unharmed. Grandmother seems to be one of the only residents not required to leave her home for the round up on the town square. Sheriff Odell was identified in the crowd. He's been placed under guard at the mayor's home along with the Tribune reporter, Palmer. She's just a kid fresh out of college."

"The best angle we have so far is that there must be some connection through the military school. Or at least there must be some connection between it and the money people behind the school. We're pursuing that one real hard. It's almost too obvious though isn't it? We have to make sure we don't have silo vision on this one. Could be that it's a red herring. The only other thing we have to share right now is that we are picking up some gibberish on the taps that may be a good lead. We're not sure if we're hitting encoding and encryption buffers or if the recordings are straight and we just haven't figured it out. Only good phrase we've picked up clearly sounds something like "nephew". One radio transmission between an officer and perhaps Vincent signed off with that call and it was repeated back by the other party to the conversation if it was Vincent. I know that's pretty damn light, but so far it's all we have."

"Yeah you're right . . . that's pretty damn meager with me having to go to the top brass in a few minutes. I don't care how many men we have on this Bobby, double it. I hate to state the obvious, but we need to get more information about these people pronto! Anyone else have anything that might be of use to me when I go to briefing?"

Charlie Lovemoney, a crusty old veteran of twenty-one years, was Barrett's second in command. He was the visual opposite of Bobby Swanson. At six feet nine inches tall and two-hundred- and fifty-pounds Charlie's huge frame could lull an unsuspecting criminal into a false sense of, 'I can out run this fat boy'. Nothing could be less true. Even at his current weight, he played tennis once a week and worked the barbells regularly. It was not unusual to see him standing over a suspect who was laying on the ground gasping for air with a look of incredulity in his eyes. Charlie had run him down. It was an embarrassment so great in some instances the suspect would nearly jump into custody so that spectators couldn't see who caught him."

Lovemoney combed his dark brown hair straight back revealing a perfectly round face. Barrett didn't much care for the beard, but he tolerated some rule bending because Lovemoney was such a good, hard-working investigator. Now he sat next to Swanson staring at a lunchtime stain on his light brown tie. He cussed like a truck driver, especially when anything disrupted his impeccable style of dress like some marinara sauce had just done. When Charlie walked into a room it looked as though he'd just come from a shoot for Gentlemen's Quarterly. But his distinguishing fashion statement was a pair of black plastic framed glasses that dimmed automatically in the sunlight. Problem was they never really returned to clarity when inside a building. Therefore, Charlie seemed to be wearing sunglasses no matter where he was. He didn't seem to mind though and if he did, he never took them back for a different pair or to complain. They were an odd fit for a fellow who spent hours looking right. "It's more important to look like you know what you're doing than to really know what you're doing" was Charlie's mantra. Charlie knew what he was doing.

Flicking the stain on his tie with his right index finger he briefly glanced about the room as all went silent at Barrett's plea for more information. "The wife's the key." All eyes in the room moved towards him. "Yeah, I'm not kidding. They've been together since childhood. I've done a little digging on my own and so far, my info shows a more than average love affair between these two. No matter how sweet this little foray into Odell is, he can't be as hot for it as he is for her. And vice versa if you don't mind me sayin so. She's the key all right. She's gotta know something that'll pop the lid off this case".

"Bobby's right, a mission like this took tons of prep time. My bet is soldier boy didn't wander off too many times for too long without telling her where he was going or where she could reach him in case of an emergency. Possibly he even took her along sometimes, so they could be together in the off-training hours. We'll get more info on her and see what pops."

Swanson grinned as he watched the old veteran spout off without looking up from his tie. The younger agents admired the older man who had seen it all . . . or who nearly had seen it all until this morning at six o'clock when Swanson called to tell him about "civil war lite".

Individual and group discussions surrounding what needed to be done, who needed to do it and what was underway filled the room for another twenty minutes of brainstorming before Barrett addressed the group again. "Okay people. That's about it. Let's not kill any more time talking about what we need to do, let's get to it. I'm heading back to ground zero as soon as the briefing is over and as soon as I can get out of the press conference."

Turning to Judy Kaye he said, "by the way let's get out of there as soon as possible. After the governor reads his statement and answers questions, I'll read a brief statement to the media and take no questions. It's an ongoing

145

investigation, governor's covered as much as can and should be addressed, that sorta thing." "Ya got me Judy? As soon as I'm done, I want you to move up to the microphone and close the day. People let's get moving we aren't gonna get a lot of sleep till this deal is wrapped up."

# # # # #

Barrett stood stiffly with eyes fixed behind the governor looking out over the mass of press personnel. He knew that when it was his turn at the microphone that every word he uttered would be measured and re-measured. Not only would the brass be watching this performance, soon millions of people would be taking stock of him. His statement had to be measured, vague yet enough not to put the wolves in a frenzy. Could the day get any worse?" He didn't know it yet, but the answer to that question was yes. And it would be before the press conference ended.

"Good afternoon. I'm Agent in Charge of Homeland Security. Dan Barrett, Chicago Office of the Federal Bureau of Investigation. Thank you for coming this afternoon. I have a brief statement for you but don't feel that I can add more than the governor has already shared with you."

"At approximately three o'clock this morning central time the downstate community of Odell, Illinois was infiltrated by an unidentified group of armed men. They've taken the entire citizenry of the town hostage and have isolated the area with heavy weaponry. All roadways into and out of town have been blocked. We haven't received any demands from the hostage takers at this time."

"There have been ten casualties that we know of. Last evening three state police officers were gunned down without provocation. This morning about 0930 hours CST, five members of a special response team were also

146

ambushed. There are no survivors of that attack. To the best of our knowledge, two citizens of the town of Odell have been injured or killed. However, we cannot confirm those fatalities or for obvious reasons release their names. When we can of course we will release them pending notice to next of kin".

"We've advised each of your organizations to observe an air and land no-intrusion zone equal to a twenty-mile radius around Odell. We have instructed air traffic controllers at O'Hare, Midway and regional airports to keep traffic out of that area. You television people, especially, who have the eye-in-the-sky coverage, be sure to observe that directive. Talk to your pilots and make sure they are aware of and respect it. If anyone breeches the no-fly zone they are subject to being arrested or worse yet shot down. We want you to know that the hostage takers have the capability of downing your aircraft as well. These people mean business and we can't impress upon you enough the gravity of disobeying the prescribed radius. The weaponry in place in Odell is sophisticated and represents a clear danger to anyone who breaches this limit."

"This is a very dangerous situation for the hostages, and we want no outside events to complicate matters. Any member of the general public that compromises, in any way the discussions currently taking place, will be dealt with severely. We know you'll respect the delicate nature of this situation understanding that the smallest transgression represents serious danger to our officers and the hostages. So, ladies and gentlemen, we are telling you to stay away from the target area. We'll keep you informed as best we can."

"Now, as to the identity of the individuals responsible for the events occurring in Odell. We are pursuing active discussions with the leader of the group. He has been identified as retired Army Colonel Madison T. Vincent of Bemis Heights, New York. More information about Colonel Vincent will be released

147

to you in due time. Several other members of the immediate command group have also been identified and their names will be released to you by our communications officer as soon as the press conference ends. We are early on in this situation, as you can well imagine, so please bear with us. We have an ongoing investigation to conduct during all this."

"The governor has been briefed and is in contact with the attorney general. I've personally just concluded a briefing with the assistant deputy director, the director of the FBI and the Vice President. As a result of that meeting it has been determined that the Homeland Security Director will work in concert with us for the duration of this situation. The Bureau of Alcohol, Tobacco, Firearms and Explosives will be called upon to assist in the investigative efforts. I will remain, at least for the time being, in charge of communication and if necessary, negotiations with the hostage takers. The situation appears to be stable at the moment and our communications with the leaders of this group have given us reason to be optimistic that we can avoid further loss or injury."

Just as Barrett was about to make his exit from the scene and Kaye was about to conclude the press conference, the governor stepped to the microphone and called him back.

"Dan, I know you're pretty wrapped up, but now that the Federal Government has stepped in to assist us in this matter could you see your way clear for just a few moments to answer some of the questions I know our media people have."

Barrett bristled. The governor knew he hated the media spotlight and this was his way of throwing it in Barrett's face after learning that he and the local national guard units wouldn't be 'in charge'. This was, after all, a mid-term election year.

148

"As you wish Governor. I'll field just a very few questions, perhaps five or six. Okay, let's begin."

Barrett did not see a reporter from a local affiliate leave his colleague's side and hastily slide out the door at the rear of the room.

"Agent Barrett, Robert Rickhard from the Trib. What can you tell us about those responsible for this hold up or whatever it is? How many are there and what they expect from all this?"

"We can't tell you much about the group other than to say that they have identified themselves as the American Revolutionary Militia. As I indicated earlier, we're investigating the group, which is one not currently known to the intelligence community. As far as the actual numbers of persons identified with the group in Odell, we are unable to share that with you at this time. What do they expect from all this? Your guess is as good as mine. It's our understanding that a list of demands will be given to us tomorrow. We expect to have them in our hands by noon."

"One follow-up Agent Barrett. Are you telling us you don't know how many of these guys there are or that you won't tell us?"

"Both. We're not sure of the strength of the group and if we were, we wouldn't share that with you. Next question?"

"Jill Westergard, Daily News. You said the ATF is coming in? This is beginning to sound an awful lot like Waco. Can you tell us why they have been called upon?"

Barrett cringed the moment she said the word.

"First of all, Ms. Westergard, that we know of, this has nothing to do with, nor is it anything akin to the challenges faced in Waco. Currently, officers from several state police districts have responded to and are containing the hostage situation. We must relieve those men soon. The policing coverage for their respective districts has not been compromised, but the officers will need to be relieved. And, of course, that must be done without causing unnecessary strain on Police resources. So, after consultation with the governor, the Director of Homeland Security has agreed to send in ATF to assist in the management of the situation. Next question?"

"Follow up, Mr. Barrett?" He didn't like the reporter and her allusion to Waco.

"Let's give someone else a chance, Ms. Westergard."

"Agent Barrett, Mike Sullivan Fox News Chicago Bureau. It sounds like these guys have taken this entire town hostage! Is that the case and if so . . . just how many people do they have? And in follow up to your response, what are you doing to secure the release of the hostages and to verify they are unharmed at this time?"

"Thanks for your question, Mike. The situation, as it stands, has not permitted us to enter the town to determine just how many hostages have been taken. I don't think it would be inaccurate to suggest that a large portion of the town is under the direct control of these armed men. Just how many hostages have been taken is unknown at this time. As soon as we have a solid number, we will share it with you. As far as determining the well-being of the citizens of Odell, I can tell you that we have an understanding with Colonel Vincent that the avoidance of bloodshed is of paramount concern and in the best interest of all parties concerned. They're well aware of our determination not to allow injury to come to any more hostages. We've been told that the two civilian casualties were the result of an unavoidable accident. We're cautiously optimistic that no harm will come to any more of the citizens of Odell. I have time for two more questions."

"Okay. Next and last question?"

"Diane Bruster, ABC News. Agent Barrett, I know this is a delicate issue with you, but could you clarify the role of ATF in this situation. What I'm wondering is if this hasn't any similarity with the Waco situation, won't their presence just exacerbate the situation?"

Barrett knew he'd taken one question too many. "ATF will be supplying manpower and the necessary weaponry to match up against the force in Odell. Waco is a long time ago and a long way away. We have no reason to believe this current matter has anything to do with Waco, so it's a moot issue. This is another time, another day and a different group altogether. We're very comfortable with and appreciate the support and expertise the ATF brings to the mix. Now folks if you'll excuse me, I've got to get back to work. Thank you for coming. We will be holding daily briefings and information officer, Pat Zidlicky, will keep you up to date and answer as many of your questions as possible." As he left the podium, Barrett shot the governor a look that let the man know he'd better not do that again.

"One more question Agent Barrett, Pam Anderson U.S.A. Today"

# # # # #

In Odell, Bravo Company Weapons Specialist Lt. Richard Bruner was on the radio with his company commander Marcus Stewart. "Captain Stewart, I'm telling you they're closing on the fly zone. I make them at twenty-seven miles."

"They come in seven miles more you tell Baker to take 'em down you hear me Lieutenant?"

"Yes Sir, out." Bruner turned to Specialist Fourth Class Larry "The

Reverend" Baker. Specialist Baker, on my order you take your best shot."

Brunner fought the adrenalin rushing through his body. He had been here before, done this a million times in his mind. He waited three minutes and twenty seconds, forty seconds, sixty seconds. They were inside the fly zone by two miles.

"Take 'em down."

Baker steadied his arms and waited for the heartbeat to slow. He leveled the cross hairs on the helicopter headed directly at his position and pulled the trigger on the Stinger surface-to-air anti-aircraft rocket launcher. A loud blast, a recoil followed by a trail of white smoke lit off from his position. The chopper had been warned. The evening news producer, however, decided that just one overhead shot of Odell would make the "film at ten" boys pee their pants with glee. The reporter and cameraman never knew what hit them. The pilot saw it coming, but could do nothing, no maneuver he could attempt would avoid impact. He'd been a combat pilot in Vietnam. He knew what incoming fire looked like. He just couldn't believe his eyes. The last thought that came to his mind wasn't of his wife and children oddly enough. He couldn't believe after the tour of duty in 'Nam and thirty years of civilian flying, that he "was going to be shot down two thousand feet over a friggin cornfield in north central Illinois!"

# # # # #

Gus Morgan stood at the side of his neighbor's house looking out over the newly plowed field to the east. He could see no evidence of troops except the two he'd run into twenty-five minutes earlier. Listening carefully, he heard the jeep round the corner at the far south end of the park. He was timing them, as he had been from his living room window while talking to his father. It took

152

seventeen minutes for them to make the circuit around the blocks they were patrolling. As he listened for the sound of the jeep to fade, he saw the helicopter blow up in the northwest section of sky and decided it was time to make his break for freedom. He lit off running straight down one of the corn rows, head high, arms and legs pumping with the precision and speed of top-notch athlete he was. He could see nothing but daylight ahead of him and if he could make it to the far end of Bullards' field he could seek cover in one of the small creek ditches that ran through the fields surrounding Odell. His nostrils filled with the freshness of the newly turned soil. His young legs pumped, and each step seemed to pull them up and down higher, faster. He didn't know if it was pure adrenalin, the exhilaration of his current daring or fear. He had little time to consider the possibility that he could be caught. The troops would be focused on that downed chopper, they wouldn't pay any attention to him. But what if he was caught? What would they do with him? Screw it. His legs kept pumping. He wasn't going to sit around and do nothing like the old men of the town. He loved his dad, but he was old and couldn't be expected to do anything as daring as this. This was a young man's decision, a young man's job.

When a person is shot from a distance, they rarely hear the report of the weapon firing the round that hits them. It's not like it's portrayed in movies. Often the shock of the impact erases any memory of it and sometimes the weapon's so far away that the projectile finds its mark before the sound waves do.

Second Platoon leader Burton Brigham from Charlie Company spotted Gus Morgan first. Brigham was only a few years older than him, but he'd been in the mid-east twice already. He was no sissy. "Captain Petracha. We got a runner at three o'clock. And he's making pretty good time. We're locked on him.

He looks like a young buck though."

The concern was evident in Brigham's voice. Men who can think in combat are invaluable and Brigham knew that a kill like this could do more harm than good. It pleased Petracha that Brigham made the call before the shot.

"Shoot small take him down." The order came back.

Brigham took the shot that ended Gus Morgan's dream of ever playing professional sports. The M-16 round completely shattered his right knee. The kneecap exploded off the front of his knee as the round entered the back side of his leg. The force of the blow blew his leg right out from under him. To Gus' utter amazement his right leg was just not where it was supposed to be when he went to plant it on the ground. Milliseconds later he heard a 'pop', then the pain shot up the inside of his thigh all the way to his groin. He sprawled out face down in the dirt. He could feel his heart pounding in his ears, his temples throbbed as he struggled to make sense of what had happened to him. He looked down at the hole in his sweat suit and the blood pouring out onto the ground and realized he had been shot. He grabbed his knee let out an agonizing scream.

A few moments later, Charlie Company's medic reached him.

"You'll be okay kid. Now lay still while we get you some help. That was a dumb ass thing to try. You could've gotten killed. Didn't we tell you not to pull any stunts like this? If you weren't as young as you are, you'd be dead."

Brigham put a pressure bandage on what he knew to be a very serious wound. He had to get this kid into town to the medical tent before he bled to death. And he didn't have a lot of time. Another medic and the battalion doctor jumped down out of a Humvee and ran to Gus' side.

"I'll take over Sarge."

"We got a good wound here. Let's stop the flow and get the kid over to the MASH. In a very short period Gus Morgan was moving toward medical treatment and a surefire exit from Odell. It wasn't going to be the kind of heroic exit he'd planned on though. The pain was excruciating. He passed out before he ever made it back to the edge of town.

# # # # #

On his way down the hall one reporter who had made it past the press conference room yelled to Barrett. "What's the current situation in Odell. Does the government have control of the situation?"

"I can assure you that the situation is stable. We have given our word to Colonel Vincent that we will respect the requested radius of the town until we can come to a better understanding of what it is they want and establish some level of trust. Our approach now is to talk, to be patient and to resolve this conflict in a peaceful and sensible manner. Now that's all the time I have to answer questions really." Barrett saw Judy Kaye well in front of him frantically waving him forward. "What the heck could it be, now?"

# # # # #

All hell broke loose in the Morgan house when Doc was told his son had been shot trying to make a break for it through the corn fields. The young corporal who delivered the message caught a right cross square in the jaw. He fell to the side and over the coffee table. He no sooner hit the floor than Doc Morgan was on top of him swinging. Two soldiers moved quickly toward him, but not before he landed several blows to the man's face. A rifle butt to the side of Morgan's jaw knocked him to the floor unconscious. The men dragged the downed corporal to his feet and out to a Humvee waiting at the curb in front of the house. When Doc Morgan was assisted out of the house dazed and

155

handcuffed, neighbors gathered outside of his home.

"You people go back inside your houses right now!" Barked one of the soldiers. "Everything's all right. e're taking Mr. Morgan to the doctor."

"What the hell are you guys doing?" An old man standing near the curb yelled. "You ain't got no right coming in here and beating people up. What do you think this is Nazi Germany?"

The soldier turned around to face the man asking the question. He lowered his weapon and pointed it at his chest. "That my friend is just what we are trying to make sure doesn't happen here. Now you move on into your home on the double. Do you understand me?"

Defiantly, the old man straightened his cardigan sweater, puffed out his chest as if to make it a better target and said, "Go straight to hell young man. I am a veteran of World War II and what you are doing . . . is the same thing the Nazis did. And I am going nowhere until I am damn ready to. Do you understand me?"

The corporal lowered his weapon. He looked at the old man for a while. Respect precluded the soldier from doing anything about the insolence.

"Yes Sir. I understand you and I'm gonna let it pass from one soldier to another. I have business to take care of. We have two men injured here and a third back up in town. Now . . . please go on about your business and don't push me no more."

He didn't want the confrontation he'd started by pushing the old man. It was a mistake he was not going to perpetuate. Jumping up into the Humvee, he screamed at the driver to get them to the MASH tent.

Thirty minutes later as townspeople began tuning into WFRM 565 Doc Morgan sat on a stretcher next to his son's, holding the boy's hand. Gus's

156

knee was bandaged, his pant leg cut away and an intravenous line flowing into the back of his right hand. A doctor approached the two men, a stethoscope hanging around his neck bouncing off his dog tags.

"Well young man, you're very lucky. That was a truly dumb stunt." Looking at Doc Morgan, he continued, "we gotta move him out, Mr. Morgan. His knee needs surgery quick or we'll have some real trouble with that leg later on. We don't want him to lose it now do we. We're getting ready to transport him and Colonel Vincent has given permission for you to accompany your son. Do you need to get anything from your home before we move out? We really need to be moving as quickly as possible."

"No . . . no, I don't need anything from the house. Let's just get my boy to a hospital. He's all I got."

His jaw ached, and it was painful to talk. He was sure it was broken but was more concerned about his Gus' injuries. Luckily it looked very much to him like the doctor was combat experienced. He had Gus stabilized and comfortable . . . the morphine drip was doing the job. But Doc Morgan knew that if that leg didn't get some surgical intervention quickly, he was indeed likely to lose it.

A few moments later a Humvee drove up with a white flag flying above each headlight. Gus and Doc Morgan were moved into the back of the vehicle and it sped off in a northerly direction towards Riverside Medical Center in Kankakee nearly thirty-five miles to the east.

A few of the townspeople moving about the square saw the Humvee with the two white flags on its hood rush up Front Street. Some thought that must be a good sign that whatever was happening was soon going to end. They didn't see or couldn't see the white circle containing the red cross on the top

157

of the vehicle. When the Humvee reached Prairie Street it turned west and headed off toward the interstate. State Police officers perched in the Bell Tower of the County Court Building in Dwight watched the vehicle move up the fields through high powered scopes. This was going to be the first good up-close look at these boys. Was there a possibility that they had recovered bodies . . . or maybe even survivors of the downed helicopter? The officers on the eastern perimeter swore there were no survivors, but you always want to hope . . . even against hope itself, that someone is a miracle survivor of a blast like that.

The Humvee moved steadily across field after field to the outskirts of Dwight. When it came to the junction of Route 66 and Odell Road, it came to a halt. The officers on the northern perimeter near Dwight watched through binoculars as a figure exited the vehicle and walked another fifty yards north of the vehicle carrying a white flag. "Looks like they are surrendering Captain," said one of the officers.

"I wouldn't count on that my friend. But I'm gonna see what they're up to. You keep eyes on that vehicle. Anything looks snaky you light em up? You got my sixes?"

"Yes, Sir. . . You bet."

The senior officer ran down five flights of stairs and out of the County Building onto the street below. He walked swiftly across the paved street to the south and began his trek out into the cornfield. When he'd gone twenty yards, he came to a halt and let the uniformed man move to him. He didn't take his eyes off the vehicle and his weapon hand was on the handle of his service revolver.

The young man dressed in army fatigues came to a halt a few feet from the

158

Police Officer and snapped a quick salute. "Good afternoon, Officer. I am Captain David Drew, medical officer, First Battalion, American Revolutionary Militia. We have two injured in this vehicle, both residents of the town of Odell. One is a gunshot wound to a lower extremity, a very nasty wound. He took an M-16 shot to the back of the knee and there's considerable damage. He needs surgery as soon as possible or I fear he'll lose the leg. The other is his father. He has a broken jaw. We are willing to turn these civilians over to you for transport to Riverside for assistance. Will you take them Sir?"

"Yes, of course. Have your men bring the vehicle up to the pavement so we can affect transfer. Let me get an ambulance over here. They're on standby."

The police officer spoke into his mic, requesting an ambulance for the transfer of the two men. While the Morgan's were being moved into the ambulance, the Policeman turned to the young officer standing near him.

"Captain Drew. You're an educated man. What in God's name are you doing involved in this?"

"I'm just here to deliver two patients, Officer. Let's get this done so I can get back to my unit. If someone in Odell needs attention of any kind, I'm it. The boy will be fine with proper medical attention. We're heading back to town now."

Drew snapped to, saluted the Captain again and moved into his transport. The Humvee backed off into the field. As soon as it was clear of the pavement the Humvee spun about and headed at breakneck speed toward Odell.

"Mike, we just had contact with a medical officer from Odell. They delivered two injured to us and we have them on the way to Kankakee for medical attention. Scary thing is they didn't have one ounce of fear that we would cuff them. They knew the name of the medical facilities we would be taking the

159

injured to and while they were loading them up this green kid has the gall to suggest what orthopedic and vascular surgeons would most likely do the best job of repairing this kid's leg."

Mike O'Brien was still trying to recover from the news that a media helicopter violated airspace and was plucked out of the air by anti-aircraft weaponry . . . most likely a stinger class. "How in hell had they gotten their hands on a Stinger?"

"I'm trying to get through to Barrett. The Governor called and he's screaming that we need to call out the National Guard. He's holding a meeting right now to decide whether to do that or not. Things are getting worse . . . just when we thought they were going to get better. Only thing I know we can't sit still while they continue to inflict casualties in that town. By God I am not going to stand for it." O'Brien's cheeks were crimson.

A few miles up the road in Odell while Major John Coffin was addressing the people of Odell via the radio station, Colonel Vincent sat behind his desk listening to a report from Allen Bell. The unit clerk walked into the office pointing him towards the next room.

"Colonel Vincent. I think you better take this, Sir."

Vincent got up out of his chair and walked into the communications room. A communications specialist was standing there with a funny look on his face and a phone in his hands. He handed it to Vincent.

Chapter XI

In the sunroom of the large colonial home on a high bluff overlooking the Hudson river Gretchen Vincent sat with tear-stained cheeks holding a letter, a cup of tea in one hand and the epistle Vincent left for her a few days earlier in the other. She wept so continually since she discovered it that her eyes ached. They'd been together forever it seemed, in reality since high school. Lovers all through his days at the academy she more than loved him, she adored him and he her. She'd followed him all over the world and when she couldn't be with him it was like part of her had gone missing. Through blurred eyes she read the letter for what seemed like the hundredth time, but it didn't make all that had and was going to happen . . . not happen. She stared at his handwriting.

Darling Gretchen,

I never closed my eyes last night.

I sat in the love seat across the room by the balcony and watched you as you slept. Each breath you took seemed to draw me nearer to you, make me more a part of you than I already am, if that's possible. And sometimes when you exhaled, I imagined parts of you, atoms even, floating across the room toward me. Timing it perfectly I inhaled. I drew you into me and soon I thought I could feel you swimming around, pulsing through my veins. I studied you for the millionth time over the course of our lives together. You looked to me more beautiful than the day I first met you. Do you remember us then on that silly hayride . . . and how you tricked me into going? How stupid young boys are, but how absolutely blessed I was and am to have been the victim of such a wonderfully clever stunt. I still smile when I think of it. . . and your fragrance on that October night.

We have so many wonderful memories together, don't we? Remember the trips we took to that old bed and breakfast on the other side of Greenwich, the one with the stone fences wandering through the fields? What was it called?

'The Owl Barn.' It had that lovely antique book barn with the potbellied stove. There were high back rocking chairs on each side of it and an old coffee pot full of hot cider sitting on top. How many hours did we pass rocking away as we read? It was the first time you wore that white cotton print dress that I love so much. Do you remember it? And remember how we hiked up the mountain and made love by the stream under that ancient oak tree? How the children would howl if they knew, huh? I thought about that trip and all the others sitting here watching you rest in dreamland. I also thought about the midnight hours. The tough times and challenges and throughout all of them how you've taught me to overcome and endure. Simply put, you outrank me.

You've been my deepest part, my other layer, my eternal companion and lover, the completion of me as an entity. You must know that I cannot exist without you. There must be some way, some ordinance to formally connect us throughout the eternities otherwise life must be a joke, a big joke.

Yes, we watched you all night long, me and the enemy full moon. Then when night started to die, and the birds began their songs, I walked around the grounds one last time. It was too soon that the sun rose over the mountains. I so wanted to wake you, to hold you and to kiss you, but I could not bring myself to do it. I simply could not say goodbye to you.

So, remember this. No matter how many sunrises we've shared a million lifetimes could not render enough of them to satisfy my need to share more of them with you. I crave you. There has never been a time since the day we met that my essence hasn't, like a narcotic, demanded you. How often, when I was distant from you . . .off to school, off to war, off to meetings . . . just away, I would close my eyes, look out a window and imagine your breath upon my chest or the flutter of your eyelashes against my cheeks. And while that would temporarily pacify that part of me addicted to you, it was never enough.

Only in your presence am I complete, content, you settle me. We've been

162

so blessed with this pearl of great price, our love.

I walked into your closet about four o'clock and ran my hands over your clothes. I held some of them to my lips, spilled a few tears on and stained others. You will no doubt have to have them to the cleaners before wearing them again <grin>. I played with your perfume and if you think some has gone missing you will have to forgive me. I sprayed some into one of your handkerchiefs and have stolen off with it. Please promise not to prosecute me?

And now Dear Wife, to the matter at hand. One has to ask what would drive a man from the arms of the most cherished thing in his life? What could pull me from the essence of my very being most likely never to enjoy such society ever again in this life? And to beg her to discover, uncover some process, some sealing process wherein we will be linked forever if our lot is to cease that society here and now.

Nothing, nothing less than God and country, both of whom I've complete faith in, call me to just such a terrible sacrifice. It is a conscious sacrifice, laid down gladly to ensure that you, our children, grandchildren and millions like them would not have blessed liberties plucked from them, in the still of the night, were good men to do nothing in the beginnings of tyranny.

It matters not that my life, the lives of many good soldiers and, I fear . . . the lives of some innocents may be lost in our cause. My only pause . . . when I lose mine will be the temporary inability to reach out and hold your hand, to walk with you on the banks of the river, to chase the geese from the fountain to the music of your laughter and all those other enjoyments that make us . . . us.

> *C'est un jardin dans l'esprit d'un homme*
> *Ou croissent les fleurs de ses pensees,*
> *Mais tu n'est pas le violet, ne le rose;*
> *Tu les chauffe tout. Tu es le soleil.*

163

I've written too much, but I didn't know what else to do with myself that would not have awakened you and made this parting ever so much more difficult. I don't want this letter to end, but now, sweetheart, it's time for me to go. To leave you for this season. God grant my only wish that you and I will be reunited someday soon and if not remember this sweetheart, I will be close to you always. When the wind caresses your cheek, think of my spirit needing to be close to you once again. If time wears on and you feel as if you can carry the burden no longer, catch the sun rise over the Mountains, as we have done for all these years together, and know that the warmth that gentiles your lips is nothing more than my soul pressing against yours once again. . . my soul seeking the comforting warmth of your strength.

And lastly, remember that old Negro spiritual we enjoyed so much at Deron's wedding last fall. When it most seems like the legions of hell will prevail against us . . . when there is no escape, when all avenues are closed, and the cause seems destined to be a lost cause . . .

God . . . *will trouble the waters*.

Forever Your love,

Madison

p.s. I just couldn't resist, I kissed you this morning before I left.

Just as Gretchen Vincent finished reading her husbands' letter, two black sedans pulled around the circular drive at the front of the house and came to a halt.

# # # # #

Pudge Miller sat in his favorite easy chair in the living room of his home.

"A few weeks ago, Shelly and I went to a high school concert in New Lenox. Our niece, Sarah sings in the choral group. They had a couple different outfits there ya know? A couple all girl choir groups that sounded just lovely

164

and they had a boys' choir. Now the young men sounded not so good, but they sure gave it the ole college try. The boys' voices are changing, and you could hear them straining. Funny thing is Ron, when they put those kids together, when the ladies were added to their effort, they flat elevated them. And the sound that came out of those kids was pure heaven. Like angels singing it was. I been sitting here thinking, it wasn't till they sang together that the music came to life. . . had the fullness, the harmony."

His eyes fixed on the picture window watching the soldiers drive past back and forth in jeeps. And then as tears welled up. "Shelly was my harmony; she elevated me. I never could make anything work without her."

No one responded.

Blood stained the white staircase, the floor, walls and parts of the ceiling in the foyer. Karen Ells and Mary Conrad scrubbed angrily at the offensive crimson with tears streaming down their cheeks. Their knuckles red, like the rags in the bucket of blood tinted water stung. It seemed like they were trying to wipe away Pudge's pain along with the blood. He was a good husband. He was hard working, a steady provider and honest to the bone. They'd a happy life. Shelly adored him and while he loved to tease about the "state of marriage", he was as delighted about their relationship as she was.

He'd been her beau since his post-grad days. He was a conservative guy who never did anything to cause a stir, except when he sold his home to Jimmy Ellis one mid-July Saturday afternoon. The two men feeling the effect of one too many bottles of beer were extolling the virtues of the each other's home.

"Let's trade."

"What?" Ellis laughed as he tossed his head back and drained the remainder of his beer.

"Hell, I'm not kidding. We've had the same discussion before. We like your corner lot and fence. Shelly likes our vaulted ceilings, skylights and pool. Let's do it. Who says we can't?"

"Well it would be pretty damn strange moving next door wouldn't it? How do we price?"

"Simple, we don't. We trade straight up. You get our house, we get yours. No money need change hands."

The sale made for the dandiest transaction ever in Odell, maybe the state. Two months later the two families moved . . . switched homes. Millers into the Ells homestead, and Ells' into Millers'. They claimed, and the Dwight Herald lent credence to the declaration, that it was the shortest move in the history. Not a dime changed hands and the only attorney involved waived fees. Locals declared it the second miracle of Odell! A large number of townspeople turned out to help with the move and celebrate the odd transaction with a block-wide barbecue. Though the move was short it actually took the families several months to stop pulling into wrong driveways and picking up each other's mail. It was the "hoot" of Odell dinner conversation for months. Such was life in the quiet town of Odell. It was fun living there.

And now, the three of them sat close to one another, Pudge, Karen and Jimmy Ells straining to hear Shelly's voice calling out from the kitchen, her laughter bounding down the hall in response to some wise crack from Pudge. They sat still for a long time staring out the window at soldiers who'd come to destroy their lives and the sanctity of their peaceful existence.

"Those Bastards! Those bastards in the square this morning mouthing liberties this and liberties that. Lidice my ass. Those Nazis are no different than the ones that raped that little town. It's no different. It's just what they did here. They come in here spouting liberators this and defenders of the constitution that. Ask my Shelly how liberated she feels, damn their souls," Pudge muttered.

"Beasts, vulgar Nazi beasts alright Pudge; wrapping their agenda in pretty words but . . . you mark my words, they'll sell that crap to someone. Someone in town will buy it, some of our own I fear." Jimmy Ells responded his voice quivering with grief and anger.

# # # # #

The town of Roxanna sits near the Mississippi river in Southern Illinois. It's hot there by early spring. It can be intolerable during July and August.

Roxanna had one claim to fame. It's not a big deal to anyone of course unless you're from Roxanna. And if you were you knew the name Robert Waldo. In fact, hardly a kid in Roxanna hadn't been over to the Madison County Museum to see Waldos' shoes. No one of real importance could be claimed as a favorite son until Dan Barrett stepped up to the microphone for the governors' press conference at the state building in Chicago. And when he did he would forever replace Mr. Waldo, the world's tallest man, as Roxanna's claim to fame.

Barrett's grandfather, Ronald, also known as 'Runner,' was a moonshiner. He was one of eighteen children; seems there's not a lot to do in Roxanna after the sun goes down but . . .!

Everyone in Madison County knew "Ole Runner" Barrett who even served as mayor for eight years taking his first term of office when he was seventy years old. And now just about everyone in the United States knew his grandson. Earlier in the day he sat in his rocking chair in front of an old black and white television and watched him handle the press. Runner didn't like the media any more than Dan did. They were constantly hounding him about his colorful past. Yeah, he'd made a few mistakes as a young man, but who hadn't? Some said it was because one of his major political opponents found himself at the bottom of a very deep well one fine Sunday morning. The authorities never did figure out how "Bubba" Weider got down there all tied up like he was, but many a suspicious eye cast a glance in Runner's direction.

Dan Barrett wanted nothing to do with Chicago politics, though some of the older Chicago Democrats had tried to tap him into service over his course of tenure with the FBI. Dan always wanted to go into law enforcement. He knew he'd never make the kind of money many of his lesser talented colleagues eventually would, but he didn't grow up with money, so he figured he wouldn't miss it much.

Barrett was angry when the chopper lifted off the Dirksen Federal Building. Up to that point in time he'd been too occupied to feel the anger. The work yet to be done and the parties that had to be brought into the mix hadn't afforded him the opportunity to let emotions surface.

As best as could be counted, three thousand Americans had been taken hostage including the grandmother and first cousin of the President of the United States of America . . . lives, lots of lives were at stake. And the thing that kept eating at Barrett was that Americans were behind it all. Not just the paramilitary group on the ground in Odell, but a significant support had to be in place to sponsor treason of this magnitude. And if indeed their claims that other units were in place and at the ready the support might even be foreign. And that was one hellava scary thought.

International terrorism conjured up images that flooded the airways for years after the World Trade Center. But he'd never considered that such irrational terror could come from within. It was hard to take serious or to even entertain the thought that one or some of our own could initiate such a dangerous exercise. "But, thought Barrett, "every time I think I've seen it all . . . I see it all, all over again!"

The differences, between this assault and that of the World Trade Center attack, was the size of the numbers, the logistics and close to home secrecy. This was no small ragtag outfit. This was obviously a command group with considerable experience, planning and execution. The physical taking over and isolation of the town was accomplished with little effort. It had been well planned and financed. And it took very sophisticated sponsorship to keep an operation of such magnitude quiet. Was there foreign support and or involvement? Intel was working that angle. The very thought of that possibility nauseated him. One of the quadrillion reasons it turned his stomach so was the fact that the boys over at the CIA were sitting on a fence like buzzards watching roadkill waiting for traffic to clear.

He pinched his eyes with thumb and forefingers while he thought to himself "Someone in the intelligence community is going to get a real down-home ass chewing for missing this one. How could they? And most unbelievably the target was right in the Presidents backyard, the Presidents' hometown!

"It was gonna take some doing to clean up this mess once the 'terrorists' were unseated." There, he said it . . . at least to himself. He dared not. He knew better than to use such inflammatory rhetoric in public, but that's how he felt. The months leading up to the crucial vote on Scottstown/Brady were horrid months for the United States. Bad blood seemed to dominate the airways, social media was a battleground spuing venom from both sides of the argument. Violence or threats of violence swept through many states. Fires, vandalism and hot tempers were common. The threats were obviously not taken as seriously as they should have been. No one imagined the pot boiling over to this extent.

Were they rebels, dissidents, terrorist? They'd killed innocent Americans. As far as Barrett was concerned there wasn't a label strong enough but talk of "rebels" isn't something that could be thrown around without dire consequences. He'd have to watch his tongue. Nope, for now terrorists would have to do.

The chopper moved away from the landing pad atop the Dirksen building out over the waters of Lake Michigan, past Miegs Field. Following the coast south two miles the chopper banked right and headed inland. Flying over Soldier Field and lining up almost directly above interstate 55, it began its short flight southwest toward Odell.

Intelligence reports from various agencies began to flow into the District Six command center just south of Odell. Satellite photos confirmed the battalion size of Vincent's group. The communications team was catching words here and there but were far from cracking the sophisticated encryption being used. Bits of information needed were starting to fall into place. The vehicles, fuel, weapons, 'munitions, electronics, communications equipment, food and medicine needed to support a group this large would be enormous. Knowing the size of the group gave the experts some idea of its resupply needs. If the good guys could find out just how much they had of those crucial supplies, they'd be one giant step closer to finding out what these boys were up to. Figure out supply levels you can take a pretty educated stab at how long this group intends to be in place. Once they ran out of rations, they had only what was left in the town. It wasn't like they could call up Pizza Hut and order a few thousand pepperoni only pies. Once those rations drop to critical levels they have to resupply or make a move on their objective.

This was not going to be like any other hostage situation he'd ever dealt with. This time the plan had to be larger more sophisticated. Let them ask for millions of dollars, offer twenty-five thousand. Never say no to the millions, but never say yes either. Don't insult them, but never give them what they really want. Or if they get you in a corner, give it in small increments that make them think you are giving in to them. When you're weak, make them think your strong. When you're strong let them think you're weak and see how they try to take advantage of you. It's okay if they *think* you have promised them the world as long as you don't promise it. And when you do make a promise of any kind or magnitude, be sure you deliver. If you don't deliver get the body bags ready. And finally, in exchange for every ounce you deliver extract a pound of concession. That rule's carved in stone.

As the chopper continued down the southwest corridor, Barrett received word that the governor and President had decided to move troops into the area. More fire power was needed to stand off what intelligence reports confirmed as a significantly armed force that far out gunned the local and state police. In an early plan reversal, it was determined that even the force of ATF agents wasn't going to be enough to contain those dug in in Odell. Companies from the First Army Division, the Big Red One were on standby in Ft. Dix New Jersey. The Screaming Eagles airborne division from Ft. Campbell, Kentucky was also a possibility. Governor Hinshaw suggested the deployment of the National Guard headquartered only one hundred and sixteen miles away in Springfield. That suggestion made the most sense to Barrett as much as he hated to admit that Hinshaw ever said anything worth two cents.

Barrett placed a call to O'Brien from the chopper. "Mike the President has decided to bring in more fire power. I'm sure the Governor's office will be on the horn with you in a few minutes, but I wanted to give you a heads up. No doubt we need it to match whatever the hell these boys have in there. The good news is that your men will be getting some hot food and the rest they need. Have them hang in there for a few more hours. Fortunately, or unfortunately, depending on how you look at it, I've been given command over the Odell matter, at least until or if the President makes the call to utilize federal troops. And then command may convert to pure military. Both you and I know what that'll mean, and I pray to God we never reach that level."

O'Brien sounded relieved. "Well, the boys are sure edgy out there. They are outgunned, and they know it. Right now, if the troops in town decided to do anything there wouldn't be much, we could do about it. Not to mention this is putting one hell of a strain on our coverage of the surrounding counties. Far as I am concerned, the sooner we get boots on the ground the better. Frankly, I don't care who's filling 'em as long as we get some support."

"I've briefly spoken with and gotten some suggestions from General Kubosumi of the Illinois Guard. He wants situational containment. They'll cut roads into town above the checkpoints established by the terrorists and limit all exits from the area all avenues of escape will be closed off. Vincent's got several vehicles in there but not that many can negotiate off road really well. Our troops will be covertly positioned to cut off anyone trying to escape through the fields".

"The NSA has been called in to look for any foreign ties. We gotta get to Vincent, remove the leadership of this group. The rest of his staff, at least those we have identified, while competent, well more than competent, are operations guys not big picture people. They are the executive officers. The key is to cut the dragons' head off and, right now, we're in the process of hammering out the sword. We'll know what he's made of when he hears the whisper of our blade."

"In the meantime, Michael, we have to get him engaged in dialog. Someone said, 'Diplomacy is the art of saying 'nice doggy' until you can find a big rock.' Let's pat him on the head and say nice doggy."

Just as Barrett was concluding his conversation with O'Brien, the Channel 7 news chopper was blown out of the sky. Barrett's pilot banked hard to the left sending papers, personal effects and coffee cups flying around the passenger cabin. The intercom crackled with the pilot's voice, "we got trouble up ahead Agent Barrett."

"What the hell is it?" Barrett barked back, irritated that the sudden maneuver had spilled coffee all over a fresh suit.

"Looks like some jackass violated air space, Sir. They shot it down, a news chopper I think."

172

"Damn, damn, damn! Did I not just tell people to keep the hell away? Have we got to get the bloody air force in here to make sure that no one else flies into that area? That's the kind of crap that's going to get innocent civilians killed!"

Turning to one of the five agents that accompanied him, "get on the horn to the office. I want someone paying a visit to every news organization in reach. Let them S.O.B.s know if one of their staff members . . . just one, moves anywhere near a restricted area again, I'll have the entire frigging bunch of them hauled off to a federal prison. I'm not going to let anyone jeopardize one more life, not our men, not any civilians'. Make sure . . . make damn sure no one else decides to get cute."

Barrett turned to one of his aids and asked, "Do we have her, yet?"

"She's in the car now, Sir. Should be in the Washington office within an hour."

Chapter XII

President Lorenzo G. Odell sat behind his desk in the Oval Office listening to the director of the FBI, the Vice President and General Todd Vanderjack, the head of the Joint Chiefs of Staff. What he didn't need one and a half years away from election was a mess bigger than Scottstown/Brady had already produced. He was a hunter himself, a lover of guns, having grown up on prairie lands that offered plenty of game shooting opportunities. But the proliferation of guns in America had gotten out of hand. Too many people were walking into schools, malls, workplaces and destroying innocent lives. Strong as the National Rifle Association was, a clear mandate had been delivered to the President upon his overwhelming election victory. And he delivered on his campaign promises when he kicked their ass with the passage of the gun regulation bill.

A promise to end the madness polarized the country no doubt, but common sense prevailed, at least it had until now. It was time to disarm America to the extent that such disarmament did not trample upon the right to own "reasonable" firearms. And the Supreme Court Upheld Congress' passage of Scottstown/Brady by reaffirming "reasonable" as defined by the act itself. It was now the law of the land and people had to learn to live with it. He expected anger, some violence, but had not anticipated what was going on in Odell. Who could have?

Years earlier President Odell or "Lorenzo G" as he was known to friends, family and the townspeople of Odell, sat atop the monkey bars on the playground at the elementary school. He'd often go early Saturday mornings when it would be deserted, climb to the top, lay back against the bars, still cold before the sun could warm them, and watch clouds drift across the sky towards the east. On those mornings Lorenzo G dreamed his dreams and planned his getaway from the little town of Odell. He loved home, but something deep down inside of him told him he was meant for another place and that Odell was just a stopover. Even then, he had aspirations that he could only identify at that time as "being special." He lay in early morning sunlight atop the playground world rehearsing speeches, accepting accolades, distributing kindnesses. What he was headed for was unclear, but it was going to be quite a ride he knew that for sure. At the end of his day dreams, either when he ended them himself or when some intruder would startle him back to the beginning of his journey, he'd look around the small square that held the school and the library and a few historic homes and think "I love it here, but it's not where I belong."

Grandma Mary Duke gave him the moniker "Lorenzo G". She only called him that though in moments of pure affection or pure exasperation. He was capable of inspiring both. The inaugural naming arose out of a game of cowboys and Indians. Lorenzo, his cousin sheriff Larry, several other boys and girls had been playing in a grove of trees just south of the VFW baseball field. The play was innocent enough, cowboys easily overpowering Indian maidens confiscating peanut butter and jelly sandwiches, a box of Hostess Twinkies and two cans of Coca Cola. All the kids hurried off towards respective wigwams and ranches when cries of dinner time abruptly brought them back to reality. Lorenzo and Larry were slouched on the couch watching Friday night television when the doorbell rang. Grandma Mary Duke was surprised to find two state police officers standing on her porch.

"Ma'am, we're sorry to interrupt your evening, but we got a problem on our hands here and hope you might be of assistance."

"Why yes, sir, whatever can we do? What's wrong? Is somebody hurt?"

"Well, we sure hope not. But we got a missing child. Cecilia Quihonis is missing. Parents haven't heard from her since school let out. Her mom and dad got home a bit late tonight from Dwight. She was supposed to go to Liz Brown's house, but she never showed up. Now we've been canvassing the

175

area and folks are assembling at the town hall, but just now one of the children said they thought she was off playing with your grandchildren earlier today about 4:30 p. m. Was wondering if we could talk to the boys?"

"Why yes, yes, of course. You come right on in."

Mary led the two officers into the living room where the two boys having overheard the conversation, sat at attention on the couch, eyes wider than silver dollars, perspiration beading up on foreheads and wetting upper lips.

"Boys, you get up off that couch and come over here. These two policemen are looking for Cecilia. When's the last time you saw her?"

Dropped jaws gave them away.

"Oh my God Grandma!" Lorenzo was the first to speak. "She's well. . . she's tied up! We catched her. She was an Indian maid. We captured her and took the Twinkies she had. We tied her up. She was a good capture, you know?"

That was the first time Mary Duke uttered the "Lorenzo G" moniker. "Lorenzo G . . .!"

Seems the boys tied up their quarry and when the dinner bells rang simply forgot the poor girl. When the police officers and parents rushed to the grove, they discovered a dutiful captive squaw patiently waiting in the dark for the boys to return and release her. And that caper was one of just two times Lorenzo G and cousin Larry felt the wrath of Grandpa Odell's belt. Cecilia forgave the boys and was back on the playground the very next day. She became a cowboy; she never played squaw again.

The other time "Lorenzo G" and cousin Larry felt the belt was the cool, misty fall day they decided to warm up their new fortress with a small campfire. A neighbor ratted them out with a call to Grandpa Odell. "Lorenzo G and Larry are building a campfire Brigham."

176

"Well, so what Kaye, boys around here build campfires. It's one of the pleasures of being a boy and growing up in the country. I'm sure they'll be just fine, but thanks for the call."

Mr. Odell was just about to hang up on the neighbor when Kaye Du Frain spat out the next sentence.

"Well, you'll probably change your tone, Brigham Odell when you smell the smoke, cause they're building that campfire right under your front porch!"

Seeking refuge from the September mist and locating the only dry wood they could find, a campfire seemed like a good idea at the time. Both Lorenzo and Larry sat gingerly for the next few days.

# # # # #

It was a well-known by those close to him that President Odell had a fast temper. He'd fought that enemy throughout his life. It had nearly cost him the Presidency during the elections, when a reporter had asked a question about the death of his young wife and what was a shorter mourning period than some considered appropriate. Saturday afternoon's briefing nudged him perilously close to another battle with his old adversary. Most times intellect won over that negative emotion and he knew this had to be one of them.

The events in Odell were just what he didn't need considering the hundreds of global fires that needed attention. Upon hearing the news his first emotion was incredulity, then anger, complete with flushed faced and a few expletives. Those gave way to real concern for the residents of his hometown, people he'd grown up with, knew all his life and then of course his mind raced towards the matriarch of his family and indeed the entire town.

Grandmother had raised Lorenzo G after the untimely death of his father drove his mother to the depths of every bourbon bottle she could get her hands on. . . and worse. She'd not been a particularly strong nor healthy woman to begin with and when Lorenzo II died, she just couldn't cope. She was a small-town girl and he was the only man she ever really loved. Lorenzo G never blamed his mother. He knew she'd not been well most of her life and aside from losing her husband, she never really had the closure everyone talks about because there is no such thing. 'Closure' is just a stupid myth some media hack invented because it has a nice ring to it. Lorenzo's body was never recovered; that didn't help.

While on a fishing expedition with his best friend and family attorney, Lorenzo's father dove into the cool and inviting waters of Lake Michigan. It was a wonderfully warm sunny summer day and the lake was as smooth as a looking glass. The men had consumed a few beers and one dare led to another. They were only a few hundred yards off the Indiana Dunes shoreline when the dare and the refreshing invitation of the crystal-clear water were too much to resist. Father stood on the boat's starboard gunnels, shirt and shoes removed, saluted his shipmates and plunged off into the water. He never resurfaced.

Lake Michigan can be an unforgiving body of water. Everyone knows that it can be as calm and flat as a mirror one minute and pushing ten to twenty-foot waves the next. The fact that the captain of this boat did not know they were in the midst of a well-known undertow field enraged Lorenzo G's mother. Four days of search and rescue frustrated the coast guard and volunteers. Most likely, Lorenzo II dove far enough to be snagged by current that pulled him down and several hundred yards away from the boat. While friends and crew desperately looked over the sides of the craft for any sign of him, he was most likely hundreds of yards away at the bottom of the lake

So, with no body to claim, no cemetery to visit, no grave to fall upon nor to grace with flowers, Lorenzo's mother collapsed mentally and emotionally. Once a withdrawn, quiet woman who for the most part kept to herself outside of church, she started drinking. Her first drink of choice was wine, but she

178

complained it gave her horrid headaches. Bourbon on ice became the numbing agent of preference. Initially, she made efforts to keep the addiction to herself, but as alcohol is wont to do, her intellectual capacity and judgement quickly deteriorated. It wasn't long before she could be seen nearly as often as Carl Walker in Blintz's, a cigarette in one hand and a short, squat glass of tannic-colored liquid sloshing around reflecting cubes of ice in the other. She pretended to be interested in the television no matter what was on it, but her mind was miles away, hating that lake

One day she simply disappeared. Where she went no one ever knew. Oh, there were several theories and speculation from the residents of Odell, but the most popular and probable was that she had become one of the five or six Chicago suicides a year that throw themselves into the icy-cold, winter waters of Lake Michigan. The President was only five years old when she was last seen two days after Christmas.

His mother flashed through his memory banks occasionally, but always in the context of a trip back to Grandmother Odell. She'd been his real mother and now she was in peril. His mind quickened with memories of the big red brick home she and Grandfather Odell had raised him in. The lessons of love tutorials about life and honor, and right and wrong. He couldn't let anything happen to her, he could never forgive himself if he failed her. And now she was in the hands of God knows what. . . who? What must she be thinking? Would she expect him to ride to her rescue? No. She was a strong woman, the grand dame of the county. She would never crumble no matter what these guys pulled.

The President turned to FBI director, Louis Cellini, "well one thing's for damn sure. There's money behind this operation and one big pot of it. So, we need to identify the bankers immediately. Finding the money is imperative. There has to be communications going back and forth between Odell and their co-conspirators and between them and the people or, God forbid, the governments, bankrolling this mess. We must intercept communications between the various camps. It's best to do that rather than interrupt them. Do you agree? Have we done that yet?"

Cellini responded, "Mr. President, this goes to the level of sophistication of this operation. So far, they seem to be operating in a communications vacuum. There's been no outside contact that we know of, or that we've identified. It's been dead silent, at least up to this point. But it's early on. They've only been engaged in Odell less than twenty-four hours. Of course, that doesn't mean they don't have outside command, they have too. We just haven't seen evidence of it. If this drags on, and don't get me wrong Mr. President, we don't plan on this situation lingering for an extended period of time, all I'm saying is as time passes, their need for external Intel and support increases. They will, at some point, have to contact their support group."

"Stay on top of it," turning to the Vice President "and I want that money trail nailed down. It's gotta be there. I don't care what you must do to identify it. I don't want to know about bending rules, side doors, even back doors. Just do your job. These boys are getting paid and I don't mean mercenary "getting paid." They have a bunch of professionals in there and someone has to be paying for lots of groceries."

"In the meantime, what's our current response plan?"

"Protect the hostages and contain the terrorist, if that's what we feel comfortable calling them," said Vice President Ron Daley. "Who knows what the hell their demands are gonna be, but we have received information from the Chicago Field Chief that they want to hold a press conference tomorrow at noon. They've told us that they want Fox News in there with a camera crew, but no reporters. Apparently, a cub reporter from the Tribune was there to do another human-interest piece on your Grandmother and she was caught up in this with the rest of the town."

180

"A press conference? That seems like a pretty dangerous thing to allow. I mean, for God's sake, isn't that giving them carte blanc to send out whatever message they want? And what worries me more; to whomever they want? If they are operating on a communication island right now, won't that just allow them to send info out to whomever? Possibly to other cells positioned across the country. There may be others poised to support them. I want to make sure we aren't the conduit for messages that might trigger a wider action against the government. We don't know what these boys are up to yet and I'm not sure it's a great idea to allow them access to the airwaves."

"We think it best to go along at this point, Mr. President. Though you raise legitimate concerns, in balance the more they expose themselves, the more we'll know about them and what their agenda is. And look at it this way, they can do anything they want already via a web broadcast. The information will make its way to mainstream media anyway. It will just take longer to accomplish that, even if it's only a matter of a few hours. Letting them have the crew can be used as a bargaining chip if we play it correctly and we'll get to the heart of their demands quicker. A good broadcast quality picture may reveal more than meets the eye."

"You can bet this isn't going to be a blind interview either. They'll prep that reporter and she'll only be allowed to ask questions they've given her. By analyzing what they want broadcast, we'll have a better idea how to respond on several fronts".

"And if we use this demand capitulation appropriately, we might optimistically think about squeezing a few hostages out of them in exchange . . . most likely women and children. We're pretty sure they won't let Mrs. Odell go; she's too big a bargaining chip." The President shot the Vice President an angry look.

"Let's not refer to her as that. I know what she is."

"Yes, Sir, I didn't mean any disrespect. Just trying to call it as I see it Sir."

"I know you are; I know you are and I'm being a little too sensitive. I understand what you mean, and my expectations will not be unrealistic should some hostages be released. They won't release her until this is resolved one way or another."

"We think Mr. President, that we can negotiate first an exchange of cameras and crew for hostages. Part two that the feed will be broadcast, but they will be on a several-minute delay basis. No live shots. That way our boys can have a look see at what's on the video and decide whether it can go out. We will check for any back-door code, encryption, anything like that. We've got to have at least twenty-four hours to give any video a real go over, but the actual time required will depend on the length of the message."

"I think Director Cellini and I agree on this Sir. No hostages, no cameras bottom line. What do you think?"

"Agreed, let's go with it. No hostages, no cameras and no live show. Make sure Agent Barrett understands that position. We gotta have live, unharmed bodies or we will shut down every possible means of outside communication with the general public. And I mean it! None. Now one more thing is troubling me. What the hell was the deal with that news helicopter flying into Odell. Didn't you guys shut down the air space?"

Cellini responded, "Yes Sir Mr. President. We gave direct orders to every media outlet in the country that there would be a no-fly zone surrounding the area."

"Then what the hell happened?"

"Far as we can tell, some smart-ass young pup producer with INT News sent them in to get an aerial shot of the area. Guy's name was Braco. Young kid clawing his way up the corporate ladder. The pilot was a Vietnam vet.

182

Chopper also carried a young camera man and a female reporter, mom with two kids and a husband now wondering what the hell happened."

"Just great! See that Braco's in handcuffs before his ten o'clock news airs. Don't care what the charges are, don't care if they stick. Get a hold of justice and have them draw charges up today. I want a clear message sent to the media. No one's to jeopardize another single life in or out of Odell again, especially not so some jackass can impress his network news director. Understand me, Louis?"

"He'll be the lead story on the evening news tonight, Sir. I'll make the call as soon as I leave. In fact, Mr. President, I think this will paint a grim picture for the what . . . occupiers of," Cellini hesitated. "Hell, I don't know what to call these guys in Odell. Terrorist?" He looked back and forth between the President and the Vice President.

The Vice President spoke first, "I don't think that's a good label. Lends too much ability to them. They're militia, renegade militia perhaps, but it's my opinion we stay away from the label terrorist so as not to excite foreign interests who might want to claim alliance."

"I agree with the Vice President. Let's keep this as much a domestic squabble as we can. Renegade militia works for me. They already have a bad image with mainstream America. Let's capitalize with that best we can."

Cellini responded, "I think our move on the news producer may bolster our credibility with the militia leaders in Odell. They'll know we mean business when we agree to one of their demands. The sooner we put the cuffs on the news guy the better."

The President moved from behind his desk. "Well, that's it then. Keep me posted and let's make sure we have no more bloodshed. We've got a lot of innocent lives on the line here. If there's nothing else gentlemen let's get moving."

Cellini was almost out the door when he spun back towards the President. "Oh, one more thing, Sir. We'll have Vincent's wife in our offices in less than an hour."

Chapter XIII

Monica Palmer sat in silence in front of Vincent's desk for what seemed like an eternity. He hadn't even acknowledged her presence when she was ushered into his office and introduced to him. He said nothing for several minutes until he looked up from several photographs spread out before him on the desk. They looked to be aerial views of downtown Chicago, but she couldn't be sure. They could be of another large city. Except for a few quick glances, she defied all her training and kept her eyes focused downward staring at her lap and the wooden slatted floor of the old VFW. She knew this man had killed several law enforcement officers and two civilians were shot, one dead. She was terrified.

"Ms. Palmer." Vincent stood up and reached an outstretched hand towards her as if she'd just entered the room instead of having sat in that chair in silence for a very uncomfortable length of time. Vincent wanted to see how easily she could or could not be led. She was easy. "Hello Sir" she responded softly, meekly shaking his hand.

"Ms. Palmer, I am about to make you one famous young lady. I understand that you've been with the Trib for a very short time. First job, junior reporter actually, right?"

"Yes Sir. This is my first real important assignment."

"Well, after this is all over, you'll be one of the most sought-after reporters in the country, perhaps in the world. You'll have opportunities like you never imagined. I can already see you sitting behind an anchor desk on the evening news! Electronic media Ms. Palmer. That's where the fame and money are. Oh, it's good to make your bones in print; it's an expectation really. Best to have your name associated with the streets and hardcore investigative, down-in-the-gutter dirty news first. And you can only call yourself a reporter if you come up through the print media. All the rest of them long-haired, perfect white smile, dimple-cheeked boys and girls reading teleprompters on the six o'clock news are just scatterbrained robots. Well, most of them. Some of them are closet intellects, but they know the only way they can make their names household familiar is to parrot the gaggle of gangsters who run the networks. I do have disdain for the media, Miss Palmer, so I tend to get carried away, lecture a bit when it comes to them, forgive me."

"Yes, eventually you wanna look into the camera that will bring you into millions of homes every night. But you want to do that as a smart, independent, educated, unbiased woman, not as a talking head parrot. And guess what? We're gonna help you get that done sweetie. We're gonna make you famous!" His voice became friendlier, even excited and he had a killer smile. She oddly found herself a bit taken with him. He had her off guard. Yet something deep inside warned her to be careful. This was no man to trifle with.

"But first things first Miss Palmer. You my young friend, are part of the reason that I and my men are here in Odell. Did you know that?"

He didn't give her the chance to answer, but he noted the surprise on her face. "Do you know why that's true? Because right now you my dear new friend, are part of the problem. Despite that unfortunate fact, I'm now going to give you the opportunity to be part of the solution. Not many people guilty of such treachery and treason are given such a second chance. You know, or at least I hope you know, that neither I nor any of my brave comrades here today expect anything beyond our mission here. Our lives are over as we know it, but yours Miss Palmer, yours despite your criminal associations is just about to begin."

"Why, Sir," she responded feeling a bit indignant at the accusation. "I don't know what the hell you're talking about. Criminal associations? The worst I've ever been guilty of is a few traffic tickets and an underage drinking thing that happened in college and I'm pretty sure none of those events qualify me as a traitor! Frankly, I'm more than insulted that you accuse me of such a thing when you, Sir, you are the ones holding several thousand-people hostages in order to affect your own sick end. I don't know how on earth I could be either of the things you accuse me of. I'm twenty-three years old on my first-ever job out of college. How could I possibly be a part of the problem, whatever the problem is, or the solution whatever that is? Don't get me wrong, if you think I am somehow a part of either, I'm willing to do anything I can do to help avoid any more loss of life or the spilling of blood, I'll do whatever I can to bring that about, but I'm sure as hell not part of your problem." Monica had a little spunk to her. Vincent liked it.

"Excellent! Excellent!" Vincent responded loudly, "because that's just exactly what I wanted to hear from you."

And Vincent wasn't blowing smoke. He wanted to know that this gal had some fire in her belly. If she could be converted to the cause, even just a little bit for a little while she could be useful.

"Yes indeed, that's exactly what I needed to hear from you, assurance that you have the right 'attitude' to help us avoid any more violence. And, yes, you are those things that I accuse you of, but because you are a fledgling traitor, you are salvageable. With time and repentance, perhaps even valuable to your country.

"Do you know who Walter Cronkite is? Of course, you do! What a stupid question of me. Ask a journalism student if she knows who Cronkite is! Your age, youth threw me for a bit. I'm sure if you asked a hundred-young people your age who he was, they wouldn't know him. But you do. So, the question I really meant to ask is do you know why people loved him so much? Why he was not only the most respected journalist of his time but likely of all time? Do you know?"

She didn't hesitate, "His delivery was masterful, he doggedly worked to research those stories he presented, and his voice was like warm honey. He looked into those cameras every night and made people feel like he was talking to each and every one of them individually. I think that's why he was one of the greatest journalists of all times."

"Of course, you're right. But that's gravy, all gravy. One of the blonde Bimbos could fake their way through that. Some do, some do," he said shaking his head. "The reason Miss Palmer, the real nuts-and-bolts reason and don't you ever, ever forget this is this . . . he told people the truth. He didn't tell them his truth. He didn't tell them his political party's truth. He didn't tell them the network executive's nor the owner's truth.He had no agenda other than reporting the honest-to-God truth. So, when he went to Vietnam in February of 1968 to have a look for himself, he knew America had been lied to by the generals, by the President and a host of other politicians. And he came home and told America so. And from that point forward public opinion began to shift and the war started to end. It was that same public opinion that forced Johnson not to seek reelection and Nixon to make a campaign promise to end the war."

"For the most part we've lost individuals like him. And his kind have been replaced with your kind. Your kind is the problem. Your kind bites onto some perceived social problem, decides to advance your position even if it's contrary to the vast majority of public opinion. Then you push your agenda and push it and push it until people are so damned tired of hearing it, they succumb to it. And then you sit back and lick your lips and bask in the glory of the enlightened masses. You are their hero, the champions of your own minds. I sound like I'm lecturing you, don't I? I'm not, I'm educating you, sharing with you some of the facts your pretty girl college overlooked."

"So, let me be more specific about what I mean about you being part of the problem. The passage of the Scottstown/Brady Bill was promoted by, shoved down the throats of Americans across this country, pounded into the psyche of

188

liberal, traitorous senators and congressmen by the President and his minions in the left-wing press. Minions . . . that would be you dear Miss Palmer. You and thousands of scoundrels like you pound the media gavel, night after night after nightly news, day after day after day. Good Morning United States. Pound, pound, pound." Vincent slammed his fist on his desk so loud it brought Sergeant Manning into the office only to be shooed back out. "Until, until finally, the most basic of American freedoms, by an outlaw Congress and the likes of you, have wrenched from us under the guise of public interest; the greater good as President Traitor refers to it, that which is dear and most precious to us."

He was angry but controlled when he walked around from behind the desk and leaned against it right in from of Palmer.

"You, politically correct, big city, cosmopolitan, slickly dressed, smooth talking, viper hissing, Nazi. You and your Follywood porno kings and queens, hypocrite media hypes". Leaning in so close to her face she could see the pores in his skin, "You, little girl, are responsible for Mrs. Millers' brains and blood being splattered all over the staircase in her house. Because if it weren't for you darling, she'd be happily shoveling out portions of hamburger in her store as we speak."

By the time he'd finished with his tirade Palmer was petrified. He had to be mad! Mad as a hatter. "Oh my God, the man in charge of these criminals is a stark raving lunatic!" She thought. Not true, but that's exactly what he wanted her to think. Colonel Vincent straightened up and then straightened up his pressed dress shirt and his tie and returned behind the desk.

"Ms. Palmer" he said in a calm, quiet voice. "Do you know what a gig line is?"

"No Sir," she replied still trying to catch her mental wind. "No, I've never heard the expression. Is it an expression or something else?"

189

"I knew you were a smart gal. Intuitive. It's not an expression." Lifting his tie, he pointed to his dress shirt and its row of buttons down the front.

"A gig line is this line. The shirt buttons line up with the right edge of the belt buckle which lines up with the zipper on the trousers. The knot in the tie I'm wearing must be front and center in my collar and as you can see the tip of the tie must come exactly to the top of that belt buckle. Not one eighth of an inch high or low. And the buckle, it better be so polished that you can shave in it. Well not you personally, but you get the point."

"The gig line is taught to every soldier in the very beginning of military service because it depicts uniformity, the beginning of getting things in order, getting things straight, getting things right, in good working alignment. It's all about getting men and women in good working order. Order is Godlike Ms. Palmer. Where there is no order, there is no God. And right now, your gig line appears to me to be all screwed up and that's one thing about you that scares me a little. In fact, Ms. Palmer your gig line is so far screwed up I'm surprised you can sit upright in that chair. I'm half expecting you to fall out of it and plant your butt on my floor at any minute," he said lighting a cigar and blowing a large puff of smoke at the ceiling.

"Is he completely crazy or what?" she thought.

"Never mind Miss Palmer. Don't you worry your pretty little traitorous head off. I'm gonna straighten it out for ya. I'm gonna fix your gig line good. And if you pay attention and obey orders, you're gonna be so damn grateful . . . and straight. You're gonna be right and in good working order for the rest of your life. And . . . if you don't straighten out, well if you don't, I'm afraid you're gonna be dead." Vincent's eyes narrowed as he looked at the now terrified young woman. "As dead as that poor fellow that was swinging from the water tower this morning. So, if I can't freaking straighten you out young lady, I'll see to it that your tombstone reads 'Her Gig Line Was All Screwed

190

Up.' Got me?"

Palmer was so scared tears welled up in her eyes. Her throat and mouth were so dry she couldn't utter a sound if she tried. Aside from that she didn't know what to say or even if to make a sound if she could. He was mad, he surely was a crazy madman.

Vincent's eyes softened, and a small smile appeared on his face. He looked compassionate even fatherly to her suddenly. "Now don't you worry none too much. We'll fix you. You just go with Sergeant Manning here. He's going to go over a list of questions you're gonna ask me on Fox News tomorrow afternoon. You're not going to be stupid and ask or say anything beyond that list. One more thing, you're gonna look just as pretty as you can. You're going to smile often and talk to me like I was your favorite uncle. And in exchange, we're going to fix that gig line and make you famous all at once. I promise. And I never break my promises. I assure you once the interview is finished, we'll send you home with that Fox News crew, Monica."

He confused her once again using her first name in what she interpreted as almost a fatherly tone!

"I know it's going to be the beginning of a very successful career for you. Be excited and I'll see you again tomorrow afternoon."

When she got up to leave her legs were weak and shaking. She wasn't sure she would make it to the door. Manning was compassionate coming to her aid, taking her by the elbow and escorting her out of the room.

The interview with the Colonel lasted less than fifteen minutes. The Fox News interview with him was scheduled to take place at noon the next day across the street from St. Paul's just as the people of Odell would be leaving 11:00 o'clock mass. They'd look great in the background walking through the town square dressed in their Sunday best.

# # # # #

"Captain Coffin, are we ready for the 1600 hours radio broadcast to the citizenry of Odell?"

"Yes Sir. I have the transcript right here."

"There's a change in plans. I'm going to address the townspeople this afternoon. There's considerably more anxiety than I expected. Naturally the civilian casualties are largely responsible for this level of angst. I'm best to address that. You, however, will be the chief interviewee for Fox News tomorrow. You can articulate our position as well as I can and yer a damn shot more handsome than I am. I don't want the Feds to see much of me for now. I'm going to stay here in the office and watch from this vantage point. I want you to present in full battle gear. Give 'em an eyeful," he grinned.

"Yes, Sir, if that's what you want. Here are the talking points for this afternoons broadcast. Though the station will have free broadcast access, it's not on the air regularly and hardly anyone outside of Odell and the surrounding towns have ever even heard of it. We doubt audience numbers will be up much except for Barrett and company."

"I've got a few hours and need some rest. You can have all the rest you need after dinner tonight. Suggest you turn some logistical responsibilities over to Sergeant Major Manning and start preparing for your television debut!" Vincent smiled at the officer briefly.

# # # # #

"Ladies and Gentlemen of Odell, this is Colonel Vincent speaking and hoping not to cause too much of an interruption to your Saturday evening activities. Unfortunately, we've had to limit some planned events and cancel others. After conferring with Father Moore we've decided to cancel Saturday night mass, hoping to see all of you tomorrow morning bright and early at the 11:00

service. Father Moore has graciously extended an invitation to St. Johns Dutch Reformed Church congregation and those who attend the Odell's First United Baptist Church to meet with his parishioners for a special prayer service for Odell and indeed all the United States. The pastors from each of those churches agree that worship in unity will be best for the citizens of Odell for the time being and encourage their parishioners to attend the united worship service. Hopefully, by next week, your lives and ours will have returned to normal or as close to normal as it's ever going to be again."

Of course, Vincent had never spoken with Father Moore or any of the clergy of Odell. There wasn't time and there was a need to minimize any assembly of the townspeople. To let them think they had their freedom but to keep it under rigid control. It was only temporary anyway.

"There will be a curfew this evening. No one is to be out after sunset unless there is a medical emergency. Pamphlets have been distributed to each home and are available here at the VFW headquarters that provide medical care information, how to notify authorities about any needs, medicines etc. As unfortunate as this curfew is, we are hopeful it will help prevent any more of the type of unfortunate events that occurred earlier today. Sadly, those resulted in the accidental injury to two other of the town's finest citizens including a teenager. We still do not have a medical update on the young man but are working with local authorities to determine his status. As soon as we know more, we will, of course, keep you advised."

"While cell phone coverage has been interrupted temporarily, phone service is available to those with real need to contact relatives outside of Odell. A dedicated phone has been placed here at headquarters. The pamphlet also describes the application process for the use of the phone."

Vincent knew that no one was going to qualify to use that phone or any other until the 'Listeners' made some movement towards the group's

193

demands.

An old mentor had given Vincent some advice a long time ago that he never forgot. Once while composing a scathing report outlining deficiencies in the plans of a group of superiors, the mentor advised cutting the report by seventy-five percent. "The less you write, the less they have to shoot at," he had said.

"Ladies and Gentlemen, fellow citizens, this has been a difficult day for all of us. I can only imagine the gamut of emotions running through your village. I assure you and the young men brought here to protect you share them. It has not only been a difficult day; it's been a long day for all of us. All of you are in need of rest and some time to catch your breath. There may be circumstances wherein you'll need some assistance. If a problem or need of any kind arises reach out to the first soldier you see and seek his assistance. He will direct you to someone who'll take care of whatever you ask. We will be there for you. You have my word. For now, good night and God Bless Odell and God Bless America."

After his radio address, Vincent took a brief jeep tour of the town's perimeter. He wanted a first-hand look at the fortifications even though he trusted his men implicitly to execute the military schematic that had taken years to design. A few words with the men reaffirmed the level of morale and the professionalism he knew would be there. After consultation with the noncom officers, Vincent made his way back to headquarters and a couch temptation that he could no longer resist. He only had an hour before dinner scheduled with his officers. He collapsed into the soft welcoming leather and was fast asleep.It seemed like only passing seconds before Coffin was knocking on his office door to let him know it was time to meet the cadre for dinner.

The second-floor poker venue had been transformed into a dining room. A series of long folding tables covered with plastic tablecloths liberated from the

194

downstairs kitchen held dinner fare, the same that the troops would eat that evening. A mess hall no different from any army field kitchen provided a hot meal of roast beef, mashed potatoes, gravy, white beans, cornbread and peach cobbler. Vincent insisted on hot meals for the men at least twice a day. Breakfast and dinner hours were necessary to maintain mental and physical fitness. If they at some time needed to "tighten" their belts they were prepared to do so. They also had supply lines the Feds wouldn't dare touch if it came to that.

Each of the unit commanders gave quiet status reports. Captain Drew advised that attempts to secure injury updates for Doc and Gus Morgan were unsuccessful. Lt. Cox had even put a request in to O'Brien. Excuses were made in spite of Cox's suggestion that a favorable report back to the citizens of Odell would calm their fears. Vincent acknowledged the effort, but it was apparent it wasn't something he gave a hoot about. As the meal conversation wound down he rose at the end of the long row of seats. "Gentlemen, we've had a successful day. Collateral damage is never desirable, but sometimes unavoidable. I want you to make sure the men know that I do not want, under any circumstances, to sustain one more casualty amongst the ranks. Civilian loss is a price we accepted long ago as an unfortunate probability. Hopefully, we can keep that kind of loss to a minimum, but and this is a big but gentlemen, if in doubt. . . shoot. And if a weapon has to be fired . . . shoot small. Shoot to kill. When you brief your men this evening, make sure that's the message. I know our guys. I know we don't have any hot head triggers out there dying to shoot fellow Americans. I know it will be distasteful, but we've all answered that question in our hearts and during our interviews for the posts we enjoy. No more casualties among the ranks. I simply won't have it. Is that clear men?"

"Sir yes. Sir," filled the air. Vincent left the room with Coffin to go over his national television debut scheduled for noon Sunday outside St. Paul's.

"John, make sure Ron Cox is all over the Fox News thing. You and he should also be in touch with O'Brien and Fox News to address the logistics of

195

how we want to get them in here and out of here. I told the Trib reporter she'd be leaving with them, but that's not going to happen. She'll make a good mouthpiece later on. And one other thing, before the interview, I want her in the Jeep with me when we take the drive through the streets. Make sure the camera crews with us and you tell her she better be smiling like she was the homecoming queen at a Friday night football game. Make it real clear to her, John. After the ride through, we'll head back here to watch your interview. Tell the men I want the town as peaceful as a sleeping baby. I want as near zero visibility as possible. Keep their heads down and out of sight. Remember, 'when you're strong make them think you're weak, when you're weak, don't let them see it.'"

"Let's go over your statement, our demands and Palmer's questions. Then I need to get some shut eye. We all good?"

"Yes Sir, Colonel."

Neither Colonel Vincent's battle plan nor Captain Coffin's wildest imagination could prepare them for Sunday's most poignant sermon.

Chapter XIV

By the time Dan Barrett's helicopter touched down outside of Mike O'Brien's headquarters, O'Brien knew he was no longer in control of the mess taking place in his state. And he was damn grateful. The ironic thought that neither he nor anyone else was in control of anything in Odell except the thugs who were entrenched inside her boundaries, came to mind. O'Brien's conversation with the governor was briefer than he thought it was going to be. Washington and Springfield decided that units of the National Guard were to be poised to surround Odell as soon as the governor gave the order. He would await word from Washington before deploying them and, at least for the time being, Dan Barrett was the word from Washington.

Notwithstanding O'Brien's lame-duck status, Barrett understood the value of keeping the local boy on the team and involved as much as possible. The first thing he did when he entered the building was to ask O'Brien to join him in what was now designated as the 'war room.'

"As long as there's no additional loss of life, Mike, I'd rather not move the guard into position at this point. The insurgents know what our military assets could be if we choose to use them. There's no point of getting into a "my pee pee is bigger than your pee pee" contest with them. There's nothing to be gained at this point except a lot of chest pounding and that's not going to accomplish anything. Agree?"

"I do. As difficult as it is, I think the best course is to let these folks have their little fifteen minutes of fame tomorrow and see what we can learn from that. We may see something that they don't want us to see or hear. We might just learn something that exposes their underbelly."

"That's exactly what I'm thinking now. Until we have more intel on the players any move, we make will be premature. What I can tell you is that they not only have the town in a pretty secure net, according to our eyes in the sky they're hot wiring it with a truck load of explosives. Looks like C4 all over the place. Office says it was done quite nicely. Had to be a pretty covert exercise to not elevate the civilian anxiety level any more than it already is. It had to have been rehearsed repeatedly for them to lay down that kind of quantity in such a short period of time. They must have left a trace somewhere. There simply can't be this many people involved without communication and money trails left somewhere. We'll track them down and flush them out when the time comes, but right now what we need most is time. Time to investigate and time to let them make a mistake."

"What scares me, though is this. What if these clowns have a suicide option on the table? If so we're in real trouble. Think about it, Mike. We'll have more casualties than 9-11 and Oklahoma City combined. It's a pretty darn scary scenario and right now I'm having trouble seeing the end game. I'm praying I'm up to this."

"It's just like any other hostage situation, Dan." O'Brien lied to him. "You keep 'em talking until you can find that opportunity to end the situation. Give them something, but not what they want. Let them think they're making progress as long as they're really not. Buy time. Let the answer come to you as the days develop. Whatever you do, never let them see any weakness. Don't feed the beast."

"Of course, you're right, but right now I can't see extricating these guys by force without huge civilian casualties. If we're too passive we're gonna get creamed, if we're too aggressive, people, lots of people, good people are gonna die. And if that happens it's gonna look like Waco on steroids. Then you and I can both kiss our keisters goodbye. We'll be lucky to find ourselves in front of a senate subcommittee instead of a firing squad. We'll be the lambs invited to the wolf's buffet," Barrett said with an obviously concerned tone.

"Don't think that hasn't crossed my mind. And forgive my mid-western mind. We're not stupid enough to believe that Washington will have our backs if this does go south. We can't trust the Feds one lick."

O'Brien almost added "present company excepted" but both he and Barrett knew that wasn't true, neither Barrett nor the FBI was an exception. Neither had proved worthy of one.

"I understand, believe me."

"Couple more things I want to bring you up to date on. First, thought you should know that the news producer is in federal custody, screaming like a girl when they hauled him out of the newsroom. Couldn't count the number of times he whined freedom of press until someone in the elevator explained to him with a stun gun that sometimes those rights are on hold. He'll be out by the end of the week; it will take that long for the network's lawyers to find him."

"The other thing is that we've picked up Vincent's wife. She's in Washington now and will most likely be flown to Chicago in the morning. After we get what we can out of her, we're going to need to explain to Vincent that two can play this hostage game. Let's see how he likes the other side of the pancake. There's no such thing as fair in war, there's only winning. I will win this war and put Vincent and his gang of thugs where they belong, in a federal prison, for the rest of their lives. Or deep in the ground dead. Either way it's not going to end well for them by God."

"I'm looking forward to interrogating his wife. We're putting a complete dossier together on her and it should be ready for us by the time she arrives. I'll see that you get a copy as soon as it's available. We're gonna hit her first thing in the morning before she has any time for rest. It's going to be a long few days for her as well. And that brings me to the next little deal here."

"Mike, I'm going to have to move the war room downtown. We have more intel access and quicker response to needs than we'll have here. You're welcome to come if you like. I'd frankly like to have you there. I had my people check and they've already been in touch with the governor and State Police Commander, Waldrop. They've approved the TDY assignment if you'll come along. I think your knowledge of the district; the people and your officers could be of invaluable help as we go along. So, what do you say?"

"Is there a pay increase involved somewhere here?" O'Brien grinned.

"No, but the benefits are gonna be something once this is all said and done!" Barrett responded.

He was only half kidding. Once this was over the major players would be some of the most famous and sought-after villains or heroes in the country. Depending on which side of that coin one found oneself, it could be very profitable. It was only a fleeting thought, but it was there nonetheless, and it was honest.

"The prospect of no raise stinks, but the benefits may be intriguing. I'll come along and hope I'm not an unwelcome presence. The last thing I want to be is a token, cooperative headpiece."

"If I didn't think you could be helpful, I wouldn't have extended the invitation."

# # # # #

Vincent had always been an early riser and this Sunday morning was no different. He'd slept well. Though he had much on his mind, he felt at peace. No one likes to see civilian casualties, but they are a fact of war, a fact he'd never get used to, but a fact that would not deter him from his appointed and determined role, nor keep him from a good night's rest.

The sun hadn't begun its rise over the eastern horizon, but he'd finished breakfast and was now about to go for a stroll through the streets of this Odell. When he left the VFW building, he thought he was alone, but Coffin, who knew his commanding officer's early morning habits, assigned two men to follow him at a discreet distance. He inwardly objected the minute he saw them but understood and appreciated the precaution. Pretending not to be aware of their presence he slowly walked up and around several streets in the neat little town. Eventually he found himself wandering in the direction of the interstate on its western boundary.

Springtime in Illinois can be blessed beautiful or just another nasty extension of a long, won't-go-away-no-matter-how-much-you cry-about-it, winter. This Sunday morning was perfect. Inhaling he could smell those wet pregnant rows of dark black soil. It was sweet he thought, refreshing. Not the same but memorable like the scent of a new perfume on a first date. It woke you up. The breeze was cool, but the promise of warm sunlight could be felt in the air. Knowing crops would surely be peeking through that soil in a few weeks, he imagined row upon row of corn as far as the eye could see. And that's one of the reasons he and his men had to be there in Odell, before the crops grew. As he approached within sight of the phone tower, he expected to hear the crack of radios, but he heard none and concern filled him for a second. That second was followed by Jerry Stevens, the sniper stepping from behind the tower and addressing him. "Good morning, Sir. Is there anything I can do for you?"

"Those guys in the jeep let you know I was coming?"

Stevens grinned, "Sir, yes, Sir. I knew you were headed this way I think before you did."

"You're probably right. Anyway, now that I'm here all safe and sound under your watch, I want to have a look." He glanced up at the walkway that encircled the very top of the tower. "I want to have a look for myself just as the sun shows itself."

"That'll be in a few minutes, Sir. So, if you like, I'll lead the way."

"Let's do it."

Soon Vincent was scaling up the ladder behind the "line repairman". When they reached the top, Vincent accepted a cup of coffee from Stevens and sat down on the east side of the tower waiting on the sun. Soon the blacks, greys and purples of morning began to fade surrendering to the colors of springtime. This time of day always reminded him, no matter where he was in the world or back home in New England, his love, Gretchen, and his youth. He let the rising sun bathe his face for a few moments in silence before he rose to his feet and slowly walked counter clockwise around the circumference of the tower. Occasionally ducking his head under a wire here and there he stopped several times to survey the flat farmlands stretching out in every direction. He watched crews of Robins pecking at the earth, fresh from their journeys in the south. Now home grabbing seeds and earthworms to reinvigorate themselves after their long flights. Hawks were absent this early in the morning. They'd wait for the sun to warm the black soil that would warm the air, that would give them lift, that would allow them to glide to and fro across the fields with the least amount of effort. Then they'd locate the prey they needed to feed themselves and their young. The order of nature intrigued Vincent. Its perfect order is what first captured and then held his belief in a higher creative intelligence. How anyone could hold to the "blow-up the universe and-see how it-fell back together" theory, puzzled him. But to each his own. That's what made this country so unique, that we could all hold to whatever we wanted to if our individual perspectives didn't take away the other guy's.

It was going to be a long, eventful day. It was time to get back to the headquarters, get dressed and meet with his officers again. Of the eight hundred and sixty-four troops in Odell very few of them were going to be visible this Sabbath day. He'd ordered the men who would be in town to be in pressed fatigues, weapons clean and to look sharp. Some were going to be spread throughout the population in civilian dress. There was method to that madness as well. Where there was expected to be the largest gathering at St. Paul's for the 11:00 a.m. Mass, there would be extra troops, but not so many as to make it look like an occupying force. Monica Palmer was to be brought to Vincent's jeep right after the service and would accompany him for a ride through the town before the Fox News interview with Coffin.

The jog back to town with the jeep following only took a few minutes. Soon he was in the shower rehearsing in his mind for the millionth time the events about to unfold in Odell.

Colonel Madison Vincent, Captain Larry Schnecksnider, Captain Mario Petracha sat in full dress uniform, each sporting enough real service medals to sink a battleship. They'd reserved the second-row center of St. Paul's Cathedral with the seat right next to them reserved for the town's matriarch, Mary Odell. Sheriff Larry Odell sat next to the mayor and his family in the third row with the entire town council. The rest of the town's three congregations jammed into the remaining pews. Overflow seating had been arranged in the loft where the choir usually sang. Speakers were set up on the steps for those unable to fit inside the building where a large crowd outside sat on lawn chairs and blankets wherever space would accommodate them. Father Moore had been given strict instructions that mass was not to begin until Miss Mary had taken her seat.

At ten minutes after the hour, as regal as any royal, Monica Palmer thought, Mary Duke Odell entered the back of the chapel. Normally not one to seek attention, this morning she was all about attention. In her best Sunday go to meeting dress she walked up the aisle, head high, looking neither to the left nor to the right. She ignored old friends with whom she'd lived and grown up all her life. Her eyes were dead set on the altar and the figure of the Savior hanging on a large wooden cross. When she approached the front of the chapel she genuflected and made the sign of the cross; Vincent and his men arose and stood at attention. She never looked at them. She took a seat in the row in front of all of them. The front row was far from her regular place at the rear of the church. Mary Duke Odell wasn't buying this crap for one second.

203

# # # # #

Colonel Vincent sat motionless through the entire mass. If Mary Duke's slight affected him, no one could tell. Captain Mario Petracha, however, would like to reach across the pew in front of him and drag her by her skinny wrinkled, neck into the place reserved for her between him and Vincent. If she didn't feel his eyes burning a hole into the back of her neck, Petracha thought, it would be the first miracle of St. Paul's that Sunday morning. How dare she be so arrogant when he and his men had laid the remainder of their lives on the line? It wouldn't matter what the outcome was going to be in Odell. Petracha was a wiry old veteran who understood the end game better than any of the young ones. The best-case scenario would be a federal prison, the worst a firing squad or the preferred, death on the field. This adventure might accomplish the statutory goals they desired, but nobody was going to get away with a stunt like this without serious long-term consequences. And this witch, this witch that spawned the dog that occupied the White House, had the gall to turn her back to them? He'd like to put her on the ten o'clock news alright. She wouldn't be doing one of those "aw shucks" country gal interviews if he had his way.

Monica Palmer sat in the back of the chapel in a spot reserved near the end of a pew, so she could be escorted to Vincent's jeep as soon as mass had ended, and salutations could be offered by Father Moore and the town fathers. She wasn't surprised when she saw Mary Duke ignore Vincent and his men, in fact it seemed to fit in perfectly with the character she thought she discovered during her interview with her the day before. Indeed, she quite enjoyed the snub reveling in it so much that she could barely remember anything the priest said during his entire twenty-minute homily. Her strikingly black hair supplied the contrast against a pale-yellow business suit that she felt would make her look her best on camera. As bad as things appeared to be this was no dull-witted young woman. And the more she thought about it through the course of a

204

sleepless night, if Vincent was right and she was going to be famous at the end of all this, no matter what that end was going to be. She damn sure wanted to look the part of a professional newswoman. Like the event or not, this was her big break and she determined to make the most of it.

As the mass neared the end, Monica's eyes shifted from Mary Duke to Vincent and back. She also noticed the two young men in civilian dress sitting across the aisle from her. It was obvious to her from their military style haircuts that they were not locals. The camera crews might not pick up on it, but she had. There were several pairs of them scattered throughout the congregation. None of them paid a lick of attention to what was going on or being said. Their heads were on a swivel the whole time.

When the mass ended, Mary Duke waited for the recession and then stood up. All of Vincent's men followed suit just as they had when she entered the building. All of them except Petracha. He remained seated, red faced and eyes front. That is until Vincent shot him a glance that he immediately responded to. He then rose slowly to his feet, but his eyes never left the altar. As soon as Mary Duke went out the front door Vincent and his men made their way through the large congregation to the back of the chapel. They nodded occasionally and in a friendly manner to many who were standing allowing them to leave first. Vincent noticed that they'd even garnered a few smiles and nodding heads as he proceeded down the aisle. That pleased him. He'd not expected any converts early in the mission and these may not be converts at that moment, but he'd bet a nickel they'd be before the smoke began to clear.

The Vincent entourage walked slowly out the front door, indulged in overly friendly handshakes with Father Moore and the town's other two clergymen. American flags had been posted around the town square and the church the night before. The whole area looked as if it were the morning of the Fourth of July. Vincent turned his head back over his shoulder to affirm the mayor, sheriff, council members and their families were being properly escorted back to

205

their respective homes. When he got to the bottom of the steps, Monica Palmer was waiting for him with a camera crew from Fox News Chicago. Vincent gave her a mock salute and a smile that would melt a brick as he approached her.

"Miss Palmer, I do believe you are the prettiest, smartest and most fashionable reporter I have, in my very long career, ever met! You and I are going for a ride around town. We'll let those cameras follow us in the next jeep. You all wired up?"

"Yes, Sir, I'm wired and ready to go, Colonel Vincent," she smiled. And when she smiled, she smiled broadly, showing perfectly aligned white teeth. It wasn't just an 'I'm going along' smile. Coffin met with her earlier that morning to explain what Colonel Vincent's expectations were relative to her appearance and demeanor. And there wasn't any beating around the bushes in that exchange either.

"You're going to be delightful; you're going to smile and pretend this is the best day of your life. You might want to think this is your first date. That's how happy you want to look. Miss Palmer, if we don't get that out of you, this is going to be your last day here on God's good earth. And if that doesn't put a twist in your panties, we have two cars looking just like the local police sitting in front of your parents' home. One short text message and they'll be in heaven to greet you when you get there. Do we quite understand one another."

A quiet "Yes, Sir," muttered in disbelief, resignation and fear was all she could muster. It was only six o'clock in the morning and already they had her sick with fear. However, was she going to pull this off?

"Good, very good. Now the upside of all this Miss Palmer is that if you do just as we ask you. If your debut is a good one, you'll not only be leaving here with the Fox crew, you're going to be one famous cub reporter with a leg up on every other cub reporter in the whole frigging country! This is your ticket.

This is an opportunity of a lifetime. There are reporters out there who've been at it for thirty, forty, even fifty years who would cut off an arm to be standing in your high heels young lady! Now look at me." She raised her eyes from the floor, dabbed at the beginnings of tears and tried to smile. "We gonna do this? You and me. We gonna put that pretty face of yours all over the world today? We gonna have you on Good Freaking Morning America tomorrow morning? We gonna have you on Sixty Minutes next Sunday night? We are gonna have your mug all over the talk show circuit this week. Are we gonna allow you to tell all those people, all those people who told you, you couldn't make it . . . to go stuff it?" Coffin gave the last question with smile and a reassuring hug. She bought it.

"Sir, yes, Sir." she smiled faintly.

"Ma'am, yes Ma'am. You bet your sweet butt we will. Now go get ready to be famous."

And now, with all their preparation for the press conference, Monica Palmer offered her hand and a huge smile to Colonel Vincent as he assisted her into the back of the command jeep. She sat on his right with a small microphone in her hand. She wasn't to ask him any questions during the ride through town, but if he were to make conversation with her or to point out a landmark here and there, she'd be able to answer, and the friendly chit chat would be carried over an open microphone. It was made to appear almost as if the millions watching over the news network were able to ride along and listen in on a conversation between the two. No one was a monster here. Just a kid reporter really and her fatherly figure military hero out for a Sunday morning drive. Perhaps they'd even stop at Sulli's and get an ice cream cone.

People were making their way home from mass. All three of the town's congregations and some who'd probably not been to a Sunday service in two decades milled around, drank in cool air, satisfied curiosity and started in

207

some cases to debate the sides of the argument. Up Southwest Street in a north easterly direction the jeep moved slowly through the town, almost at a snail's pace. As they passed pedestrians on their way home from church and the Dinner Bell, Colonel Vincent waived to several of them. Some waved back. Some of the little children who'd been given little American Flags as they exited the church, waived them at the soldiers in the army jeep. The jeep took a sharp left turn on Elk and then a right on Old Illinois Highway Rt. 66 heading north towards the main east west street that ran through Odell. Vincent took time to question Palmer about her knowledge of Rt.66 and when she confessed, she had only the slightest idea of its historical significance, he filled her in. A right turn on Prairie would bring them back to the center of town through the north side of the town square passing by the Dinner Bell Restaurant where a boat load of business was being done. Some of the patrons could be seen looking out the window as Vincent's jeep and the news vehicle with cameras pointing passed by. Some stopped on the sidewalk to witness a scene that they'd never expect to see in Odell. Vincent's jeep followed by the media jeep proceeded east on Prairie through the town square. Vincent shared with Palmer some of the more ancient history of the town including the fact that she, according to his sources, had a dog in the fight! Seems she had some Native American blood cruising through her veins and the tribal ancestors she descended from were native to that region of Illinois. Most likely some of her ancient ancestors camped right here on the banks of the river before the first white men ever stepped foot on these fertile plains. She was genuinely surprised to hear about her ancestry and its connection to a land she heretofore knew little about. And she was even more surprised to know that Vincent had taken the time to learn that about her. Maybe he wasn't such a complete jackass after all. It brought a broad "camera moment" smile to her lips and she knew Fox was focused all over the two of them.

The jeep turned right on North Wabash Street wherein lied another surprise, a small monument erected to the memory of those ancestors, the First

208

Nations, who once occupied the land upon which Odell sat. Vincent wanted her to see it and more importantly wanted the cameras to get an up-close shot of her reaction to it. Knowing what they were approaching they zoomed in on her.

Just as they made that turn and just before they reached that small monument, right there in front of Dick and Ruth Ralph's house the first shot rang out. It missed its mark but slammed squarely into the right temple of Monica Palmer blowing her brains all over Colonel Vincent's dress uniform. And Fox news was there with a zoomed in, full color, live-for-your-viewing-pleasure picture as it happened. A second shot immediately followed the first, the shooter never realizing the accuracy or inaccuracy of the first attempt. The second shot caught Vincent in the face.

This was not the Sunday morning drive Colonel Madison T. Vincent had hoped for. But then "the best laid plans of mice and men . . ."

Chapter XV

Gretchen Susan York-Vincent was born in Saratoga Springs, New York. Her moderately wealthy family lived in a town known for its more than wealthy residents and New York City out-of-this-world wealthy, summertime residents. A tall, slender elegant looking girl she made fast friends and found herself whirl winding through her early years of education. Then, the exclusively female, Skidmore College, if you have the sixty-thousand dollars a year to enroll, was Gretchen's school of choice. Dr. York was able to easily send her and her two sisters, Elizabeth and Ann to Skidmore. The sisters went on to successful professional lives in York City and Denver respectively. Gretchen however stuck close to home. There was a good reason for that, and his name was Madison T. Vincent.

It all started across a bonfire. A Friday night high school football pep rally included a bonfire over which an effigy of the opposing school's mascot was ceremoniously hung and burnt to the squeals and delight of all present. It was at the apex of one of those shrills that Gretchen looked across the glow of the bonfire and saw him for the very first time. He was staring at her. Maybe she thought she felt his eyes on her and that's what distracted her from the fun of roasting the opponent's effigy. She stared right back and then when he smiled and turned away and faded into the darkness of the crowd behind the glow of the warm autumn fire she knew just as well as he did that, he had her.

And he knew as well that she had him. It was the beginning of a lifetime romance that never ever seemed to cool beyond those early days. Gretchen had read about, had listened to girlfriends who'd describe that classic "seven-year itch" of relationships, but she never really understood it or had to deal with it. Madison and she never could keep their hands off each other. They were as passionate now as they had been all those years earlier when the bonfire's ashes were still warm. Their lives together were as good as it could be. It was a romance too good to be true, one that could only be found in some cheesy paperback with a picture of a physically perfect couple embracing on the front cover while wind whipped hair, or a fire burned in the background. But it wasn't cheesy, and it wasn't all physical. The bond between them went way beyond that. There had been tough times while he attended West Point and she Skidmore. Distance never helps a relationship. But even so there were never any concerns, nor was there a need to have them, about loyalties. Once when asked by his classmates why he wouldn't dance with a young woman at a Point social function, Vincent snapped that he'd met his future wife and thus it wouldn't be fair to her nor to the lass in question to engage in deception. He never dated another woman from the day of the bonfire to the day of their wedding when that issue was resolved forever. Gretchen, however, dated a few times before she reached the same conclusion. It was pointless.

Soon after her graduation from college she took a teaching post at a local prep school until Vincent waited for his first duty assignment. They were married within the year and then the real whirlwind began. Life was a series of adventures, children, normalcy, empty nesting, more adventures and more adventures. There were lonely times when he was away doing things he never spoke of. Times were frequent when she didn't even know where he was let alone what he was doing. Those were the toughest times and placed the most strain on their relationship. Being alone with the children, having to make decisions that would impact their lives without his input was at times daunting. Vincent knew she was capable and though those times and absences were difficult, the reunions always reignited the fires that burned in each of them for each other. He used to tell her, "I believe in no God that would bring us together, allow us to love each other to the depth that we do, create the families that we have created only to separate us at death. I am no harp wielder. I will not let you go. Ever." When their wedding vows were written, language speaking of the eternal nature of their relationship was incorporated. And they shopped around until they found a clergyman who was good with it.

Gretchen found it so funny that now after all these years, this wife and lover, this mom and mother, this teacher and friend would find herself handcuffed and bound to a chair in the Federal Building in downtown Chicago. She hadn't been told where she was but had overheard conversation where the location had been mentioned. She'd been isolated from all communication since the black unmarked cars pulled up in front of her house the day before. Big men in dark suits barged in screaming search warrant as soon as she cracked the door. Others grabbed her, handcuffed her and put her in the back seat of a car with an ape of a man and another woman. Neither of them spoke to her, answered any questions nor would even acknowledge her presence, except for the initial "sit still and be quiet."

Gretchen wasn't a person that could be pushed around, bullied, but she wasn't an idiot either. She knew something was drastically wrong when she asked to see the warrant and was shoved to a chair and told not to move. She also knew that something terrible was afoot when she was not read her Miranda rights after she was cuffed and tossed into the back seat with the Ape. After what seemed like a very long time, Ape pulled her out of the back seat and forced her to stand. He then placed a blindfold over her eyes, shoved her back into the vehicle and they sped off to who knows where. She guessed that she was taken to a small private airport near Albany most likely. She began

212

counting time and turns. Once they'd reached their destination, she was hustled out of the vehicle, loaded into a small private jet and rushed off. She had no idea of the destination, heck she didn't even know for sure who these guys were. She'd never seen any identification cards, badges flashed, warrants waived past her face if indeed they were legitimate warrants. A little more than half an hour of flight time she found herself on terraform once again, transferred to a larger plane and off to parts unknown. All this time she never was addressed other than in the most curt and succinct way. Sit here, watch your step, stand up, turn around. An hour later by her estimate they landed, she was loaded into another vehicle and transported somewhere where she felt for some reason that she was underground for a short while. Then the elevator ride, the rush down a hallway and now cuffed to this chair. She was at their mercy whoever they were and wherever she was. She estimates she's been in this room for about two hours before she heard a door crack open.

"Take her cuffs off take the blindfold off." The voice was loud and unnerving.

The light in the room was very bright or it may have been that her eyes having been cloaked for so long had difficulty responding to the fluorescence. Her wrists were sore, she ached from sitting in the chair, her throat was so dry she wasn't sure she could make a peep of a sound. She wanted to be angry and indignant, but something told her that was the wrong tact given the treatment thus far, so she held her peace. It was contrary to her nature though.

"Mrs. Vincent, I have had the blindfold removed so you could witness this." With that the big man with loud voice slammed a large, blue three-ringed binder down on the table that separated them. She looked at it and then around the fairly stark room. A microphone rose out of the center of the table,

213

a flat-screen television mounted on the wall at the far end of the room was dark; eight chairs were on each side of the table and one at each end. That was it; at least all she could discern with her impaired vision.

The big man walked to the table and picked up the book. He unfastened the clips that held its content in place and removed pages that were perhaps two inches thick. With that he turned his back to her and violently threw all the pages against the near wall, but not close to a wastepaper basket. The crash and fury of the papers scattering in every direction more than startled her. When he turned around, he had his hands on his hips. He lowered his face so that it was near hers. "Mrs. Vincent," he paused for a what seemed like a very long time as he stared into her eyes. "Mrs. Vincent, that was the rule book. That's what I think of the rules. There go your Miranda rights. There goes your right to make a phone call. Want an attorney present while I question you? Go to hell! You haven't got any rights!" He screamed at her. "You want to know why you haven't any rights Mrs. Vincent? You want to know why?"

She didn't dare answer him at this point. "Yes, you want to know, you're too scared to ask. You want to know alright so I'm gonna tell ya. You haven't got any rights because . . . you . . . aren't . . . even . . . freaking . . . here! Nobody knows where you are. Your kids don't know, Dr. York and momma doesn't know. None of the folks from the church know, your literature club gals don't know, your paddle boarding instructor doesn't know, even your damn postman doesn't know. Your husband doesn't know, but he's going to. He's going to very soon, if he makes it."

The last sentence perked her ears up, her blood pressure jumped, and her heartbeat went nuts. 'What did he say?' she thought.

Dan Barrett was an excellent interrogator and was waiting to count the beats in her carotid artery as soon as he could visualize them. And it didn't take long in her already agitated state to see the steady pump of a good healthy heart. "Oh, I am sorry, how absolutely indelicate of me to have broken the news to you in such a coarse manner. Colonel Vincent was shot in the face by one of the hostages he'd taken. Yes, it happened about four hours ago. Completely blew the brains out of a young innocent, beautiful reporter. Yeah, she just graduated from college a while back. Pretty yellow dress all covered with blood and brain matter. Shouldn't have broken it to you that way. What the heck is wrong with me? Well, I can tell by the look in your eyes and expression on your face that I have zero credibility with you. I don't blame you right now, but before we're done with each other, you will know if you know nothing else, that I'm not going to BS you.

"Here's what I'm going to do. I'm going to have a laptop brought into this conference room. A Fox News video will be keyed up. You watch it. You tell me if that isn't your husband coming out of that church and getting into his jeep with that poor kid. You watch it and tell me if that isn't her brains splattered all over that jeep and his pretty dress pretend army uniform. And then you tell me if that isn't his blood flying out of his mouth and nose when that round catches him square in the face. After you watch that little movie, Mrs. Vincent, you push this little button right here," pointing to a button on the side of the table well within her reach. "And you tell me if you want to know more about your husband's condition, whether he's dead or alive, or if you want to speak to some attorney. I'll be back in a few. They'll bring you some water to drink and a puke bag before you watch that video."

With that Barrett opened then slammed the conference room door. He leaned against the wall outside the conference room and stared down the hallway at Mike O'Brien. He looked at Barrett, gave him a thumbs-up and headed to the coffee room.

Gretchen Vincent sat in the chair staring at the conference room table trembling. She knew this was going to be difficult, but she'd not counted on this.

# # # # #

Any soldier who's ever been in combat will tell you that you don't look for the shooter the first instant you hear the report of a weapon, you duck. And that's just what Vincent's combat instinct told him to do. And he had only a fraction of a second to duck, but it was enough to save his life. The round from Dick Ralph's old M1 smashed into the side of his mouth, took out two top teeth and exited through the other cheek. It knocked him out cold, but he had enough time to feel the pain before he lost consciousness.

Lying on Captain Drew's surgical table Vincent remembered nothing of the bedlam that ensued as soon as his driver and the men standing nearby understood he'd been hit. The young reporter was gone the instant Ralph's misguided bullet smashed into her temple. If she hadn't leaned forward to brush some lint off her new dress the bullet intended for Vincent may have found its mark. Now all her dreams of success and a full life were smashed in an instant. Fame, fame would come, but posthumously.

When Vincent began to regain consciousness in the surgical tent, Captain Drew had finished closing and suturing the gaping hole where two upper molars once resided. The exit wound was nasty, the entry round changed direction when it hit his teeth and luckily for him ripped the corner of his mouth as it exited. Drew had that laceration closed-up and bandaged. An IV filled with antibiotics, a pain killer and a sedative was hung and still running. Vincent felt little pain aside for a throbbing headache. That would change over the matter

216

of a few hours when the pain killers would be lessened. They dull the pain, but they also dull the senses and the colonel didn't have time to be dull witted. His eyes looked like he'd just gone twelve rounds with a heavyweight. As soon as the packing was in place, Drew wrapped gauze around the head of the Colonel so that he looked like something out of a 1950s "Mummy" movie.

"Colonel, you're a very lucky guy. Lost a bunch of blood but you're going to be just fine. You'll feel weak and need to rest for a couple days before you can be up and about. Have a heck of a headache to go with all that I'm afraid. But the good news is a few days of rest and recuperation and you should be good as not quite good as new, but good."

Through a clenched jaw Vincent responded weakly, "The girl?"

"She took a round in the side of the head, Sir. Nothing left to put back together really. She's been bagged and is waiting your orders to send her home."

Through a clenched mouth he said, "See that it's done right away." He couldn't erase the image of her smile.

"You bet, Sir." Just as Drew was responding to Vincent's order Lieutenant Cox slipped into the room.

"I've got to speak to the Colonel."

"He's in no shape for a conversation."

"I know, but he needs to hear this."

"All right but make it short." Cox approached Vincent whose eyes had opened and were searching for him.

"Sorry to share this with you just now Colonel but I knew you'd want to know as soon as possible. They've picked up Mrs. Vincent and have transported her to the Federal Building in downtown Chicago."

Vincent closed his eyes and smiled briefly. "Good," he whispered and then

217

surrendered to the sedative.

# # # # #

In Vincent's headquarters office, John Coffin was issuing orders to Sergeant Major Tom Manning, aid decamp to the Colonel, "Tom, you get that crazy SOB in here as soon as you can. Have Juan Rodriguez take command of Charlie Unit and for God's sake see that the Colonel doesn't hear about this until I give the word."

Colonel Vincent's driver turned around as soon as he heard the report of the M1. Monica Palmers brains were already splattered all over the Colonel. The second shot caught Vincent two seconds later. He turned back around and floored the gas pedal knowing that no matter how serious Vincent's wound was, if he didn't get him to the field surgical tent immediately, he could and would most likely die. Military coverage for this sector of town belonged to Captain Petracha and his men. They weren't far away when the colonel's car rounded the corner. Marksmen were watching civilians drifting home from St. Paul's even though Vincent had ordered the men to step down and make themselves less visible. Petracha had a bad feeling about this motorcade tour of the village from the very beginning and tried to talk Vincent out of it.

"Sounds too dangerous to me, Madison," they'd been long time friends before this mission. "You can't go tooling around this town like yer the mayor! Be easier in hell for some crackpot to take a pop shot at you. Just too careless and unnecessary in my opinion. What's it gonna prove?"

"I understand Mario, but we've got to win over these folks. We're fellow Americans come to liberate them from the inevitable oppression that's taken residence on their doorsteps. We're here to assure their freedom. They'll understand that. These are not violent people, these are good salt of the earth,

218

hardworking, law abiding citizens. We'll be ok. And you'll be in the area. Just keep it toned down a bit. I don't want the news boys giving the feds to close a look at us and I don't want America to look at us like we're an occupying force instead of a liberating one. We've got to convince the public watching the broadcast we're not foreigners come conquering."

"Captain shots coming from that house. Second floor upper right window," a voice called out to Petracha

"Pin em down. Light that damn place up. Get that jeep out of here! Let's go. I need two men. Cover us."

"Keep that SOB's head down. Blow those windows to hell." Automatic orders flew out of the seasoned combat infantry officer.

Dick Ralph had contemplated this response all night long. The last thing he could do was to get in a fire fight with this crew. It'd be suicide. He was no match for what was outside, and he didn't want to put Ruth in harm's way anymore than he was already going to. She fought him tooth and nail about dragging that ole gun out of the attic. It'd been behind boxes in a wooden crate for years.

"Who even knows if it will fire. You're just gonna get us killed. Let the authorities deal with these men."

All sound advice from a good wife. But Dick had a response.

"I understand Ruthie, I understand, but the one thing that murdering Nazi said yesterday while he was up there on the bed of that truck that was right was this. . . nobody did anything in the beginnings. Nobody did a darn thing. He was right. No one did. By God, I'm going to take his advice. I'm not going to stand by and do nothing while these thugs take over our town. Shelly Miller's dead, our best friend! You've known her, we've known her for how

219

many years? Dead gone. Shot fifteen or twenty times. They riddled her body! Doc Morgan and Gus are lying in a hospital over in Kankakee in who knows what kind of condition. And you want me to walk around here like a puppy who just got caught peeing on the living room carpet? By God, no! Emphatically no, never, a thousand times no. I may not survive this thing Ruthie, but I'll be boiling in hell damned if I'm gonna sit on my butt and do nothing. Kill the leaders. It's simple. That's the way it is, the way it's always been.

And I caught Sheriff Odell's eye. He gave me the look. He knows damn well I'm not going to sit on my hands while these thugs take the town hostage. No, he gave me the look alright. He knows I'd never turn all my guns in. When I saw that stare, I knew what I have to do was the right thing to do by God and I'm going to!"

And with that Dick Ralph began cleaning, oiling and loading his Korean War vintage rifle. He was all about removing Vincent from God's good earth and in the morning, that's just what he was going to do.

But the amount of fire power his house received in response to the two shots he did get off tempered Ralph's enthusiasm immediately. Terror for his wife's safety replaced anger and patriotism in quick order. Automatic weapons chewed the upstairs front bedroom to tiny pieces. The devastation was so complete that it looked as though termites the size of dogs had just ended a month-long fast. Ruth was hiding downstairs inside the bathtub in the guest room of the old house. She was safe. Dick moved as quickly as he could downstairs to a pantry just off the kitchen, but when the firing continued, he knew he had to give himself up to ensure Ruth's safety. The rounds were going through walls like paper. She could be hit by any one of them! With that thought he grabbed a white towel in his hand and had determined to surrender as soon as there was a lull in the fire. He didn't have to wait long.

As soon as Petracha felt the cover fire had done its job, he called out to the home's occupants.

"You better throw out your weapons and show yourselves or I'm going to have this house leveled to the ground. I'll wipe it off the map and you with it."

Sensing this was the time Ralph crawled to the couch located beneath what was left of the front window and waived a white towel.

"Don't shoot. My wife is in the guest room in the bathroom. She had nothing to do with this. She knew nothing about it. I'm coming out just please don't hurt my Ruthie. Give me five minutes to check on her and I'll come out."

"You get your ass out here right now. You don't get five minutes for anything. If I don't see you on this porch in twenty seconds, I'm going to turn these guys loose again and you and Ruthie can stroll the heavens together right away. Now get out here."

Ralph called out to his wife, "Ruthie, you okay?" He heard a small frightened voice call out to him. "Oh Dick, whatever on earth have you done? Yes, I'm okay. I'm okay but look what you've done!"

Ralph tied the white towel to a broom stick and stuck it out the front door, which he'd cracked open. Neighbors who'd ducked for cover upon hearing the first shots, began to peek from out behind window curtains now that all was quiet. Some of them across the street and down the block even ventured out onto porches. Reminiscent of Dallas footage when the Kennedy assassination occurred, those who had been on the sidewalks returning from church, could be seen scattered all about on lawns, behind trees and cars and whatever cover they could find when the shooting started.

221

Petracha yelled to Ralph to come out the front door.

"Get out here, this is the last warning I'm giving you. Throw down your weapons and get out here now."

Ralph responded slowly. Discharging that weapon in such a closed space not only distracted him from a more accurate shot, it partially deafened him. He wasn't quite sure what the military guy was yelling but he conjectured that it had to do with surrender and tossing out his weapon, so that's what he did. He tossed the M1 out the partially opened door onto the porch. But he did not follow it as he was ordered to do. His mouth was dry, and his heart was pounding so hard it was double beating. He had trouble catching his breath, so he dropped to the floor and tried his best to calm down. Sweat dripped down his forehead into his burning eyes.

He still didn't know if his shots had hit their mark. His eyes had involuntarily shut because of the loudness of the report of the rifle in such a confined space. It was so thunderous that his hearing immediately dulled, his ears filled with pain. All he really had time to do was to aim again and fire. He didn't know what or who he hit, but he was hoping the good Colonel got his share of lead.

After a few seconds of hearing the screams of Captain Petracha, Ralph walked out his front door, his hands raised fingers locked behind his head. When he stepped onto the front porch he looked to his right and his eyes made contact with his neighbors, Jerome and Pam Swanson. He'd known them for years. They were partially hidden by the neatly trimmed bushes surrounding their porch, but he could still see the shock and terror in their eyes. People were screaming at them to get back into their house, but Dick and Ruth Ralph were among their best friends and they had to see if there was something they

222

could do to help. to find out what the hell was going on.

Their presence distracted Ralph from seeing Petracha as he came around the left side of the porch, his pistol leveled at Ralph's head. Unfortunately, at the exact same time Dick Ralph reached inside his shirt to retrieve one of Ruth's handkerchiefs to wipe the sweat now pouring down his face. Petracha shot him dead on the spot.

The report of Petracha's pistol drew Ruth Ralph through the front door screaming, "No, no, no he was giving up! What are you doing, oh my God?" as she raced to her dead husband's side.

There she lay screaming, rocking back and forth for the longest time, at least it seemed that way. And then in a fit of rage never witnessed by anyone who knew her, she rose to her feet and threw herself at Petracha who was now holding his weapon shoulder high pointed towards the sky. "It was a reflex action," he would later say about the blow he gave to her left temple with the side of his weapon. It laid her out on the porch unconscious. Her hand reached instinctively towards her beloved husband of some forty years.

Petracha turned towards the villagers now looking on with gapped jaws, dropped in shock and horror.

"Do you people think this is a game?" he screamed.

Even his men were surprised at the quickness with which he dispatched the two civilians. They knew no matter what the rationale was going to be, there was going to be hell to pay for the way this was handled.

# # # # #

As Vincent was getting the news that his wife had been kidnapped by the Federal Government, Ruth Ralph lay in a coma, still unconscious on the other side of a bed sheet divider in the same surgical tent. Captain Drew had done all the neurological tests necessary to determine she wasn't coming out of that sleep. Her eyes were fixed and dilated, she had no response to sound or deep pain stimuli, her breathing was shallow and erratic. She was as gone as one can get without having both feet on the train. It really was just a matter of letting her go. Soon her breathing would be more compromised than it already was, her heart would starve from the lack of oxygen and finally the brain would just give up and she would go to the forever sleep.

"Captain Petracha, what in living hell were you thinking? You just murdered a civilian. Maybe two! These are the people we're here trying to liberate, to save, to protect! Good God man, have you taken leave of your senses?" Captain Coffin screamed at him the moment he was shown into Vincent's office where Coffin had taken up temporary residence.

"Captain Coffin, that wasn't no innocent civilian there. He'd just shot and killed that reporter and for all I knew had killed the commander of our forces. Who was to know who else was in that house, what they were armed with and what their intentions were? I was protecting myself, my men and our mission, Sir. And the old woman, came at me. Hell, she coulda had a body bomb on for all I know. It was just reflex to swing at her to keep her off me. If you were there, you'd have done the same thing. What the hell are you grilling me for, you should be interviewing the civilians who saw it and my men. My men will tell you it was self-defense in both instances. There was no choice and if I was faced with the same circumstances again, you'd have the same body count. The Colonel will tell ya when he's able, it was a good shoot. The old woman was unfortunate collateral damage."

"Bull, Captain Petracha. You gunned down a civilian in the posture and process of surrendering. The men say he'd thrown out his weapon and had

224

produced a white flag. An old man reaching for a handkerchief to wipe his brow. Hell, Captain he'd wet himself, he was so scared. And then you beat a seventy-year old, one-hundred-and-ten-pound woman in the head when you could have used any manner of defense moves to neutralize her. Death, that's who's doorstep she is standing on right now. Drew tells me she isn't going to recover, so now we've got to explain two more fatalities to the outside world. Colonel Vincent isn't going to be defending you, because your actions are indefensible. I'm relieving you of the command of you unit, disarming you and confining you to these headquarters until Colonel Vincent is well enough to rescind or perpetuate that order. It's my sincere wish you cooperate with it, and if you don't these young men" nodding to the two heavily armed soldiers who'd fetched him, "will enforce my orders if necessary."

"You know me Captain. I bleed olive drab. I know what it means to follow orders. I'm not here because I'm some egotistical blowhard. You can have my weapon and I'll remain in the building, but you are BS wrong, Sir. I was doing what was necessary to prevent further acts of sabotage and to prevent injury to my troops. You, yourself heard the orders directly from Colonel Vincent. He wanted no more troop casualties. He said he didn't want any civilian casualties, but if that's what it took to protect the men then let it be. No, Sir. You're dead on wrong and when the Colonel is up and running you're going to see who's right and who's wrong here. I'm sorry about the old woman; that was just reflex. But the gunner, I'd blow his ass away in a New York minute if the circumstance presented itself again, Sir. And I'll be waiting for your apology when it's all over. And when you give it, I'd like it in front of my men since you saw fit to cause this injury to me in front of them as well."

"I wouldn't count on it Captain, not as long as I'm in command. Let me

225

have your side arm. Sergeant Major Manning show Captain Petracha to his quarters. Then I want you to send the Fox team in here and I need to speak with someone downtown."

Coffin not only had to deal with the murders of Dick and Ruth Ralph on national television, he had the American audience to attend to, plus the Feds and townspeople. Day two of Odell's liberation wasn't exactly going according to plan. But then good commanders respond positively to that. If everything went according to plan leading troops would be easy Coffin thought. It would be a good forty-eight hours before Vincent was in any shape to make any decisions and some things just couldn't wait.

"Tom, as soon as you have Captain Petracha settled in get back in here. We've got to go ahead with the press conference. I'm also gonna need to talk to Barrett as soon as possible. Ask Lt. Cox to step in here on your way out."

Yes, Sir. He's waiting in the outer office right now. Thought you'd be needing to speak with him."

# # # # #

Winchester is a small mid-state Tennessee town with the traditional town square, not unlike Odell. Except Winchester is a live, vibrant destination of thousands of tourists headed to nearby Tim's Ford Reservoir. The town shuts its doors one day a week to give local merchants a chance to be home with their loved ones because some must cater to those tourists on the Sabbath. Ten minutes out of town in any direction and one finds oneself in country farmlands. Where Robert Lee Cox got his name is no mystery to anyone from that part of the country. His great-grandfather fought at and was killed during the battle of Stones River in Murfreesboro, Tennessee. Cox was proud of that and proud to have the southern heritage that bragged patriotism and spirituality at

226

the same time. Paradoxically, Cox and his people also harbored a healthy distrust of all things Washington D. C. "There never was any good that came out of there, that couldn't come out of home," he often argued.

It surprised many of his friends and family when he decided rather later on in his life to get his degree in communications from Middle Tennessee State University and to run up to Nashville and work for one of the news stations a staggering sixty plus mile from home! He now found himself standing before his new superior officer and commander Captain John Coffin.

"Lt. Cox, due to the unfortunate demise of Ms. Palmer you will now have to be the new field reporter for the Fox News network. You will interview me live in about two hours. I want you to take a detail of men and go find some civilian clothes. You should be in a suit and tie and should introduce yourself with an alias. Make it something common that will sell itself. You drew up the questions Ms. Palmer was to ask and set up most of the arrangements with the Fox crew. I'm going to speak with them in just a few minutes to explain the change in plans. Now go ahead and get some things together and go over those questions. On your way out have one of your guys get me Barrett on the line will ya?

"Sir yes, Sir." Cox's voice was steady but neither his legs nor his stomach was.

"Any questions?"

"No Sir."

"Alright then, let's get to it. Get Barrett and then set up a meeting with the Fox people for a half an hour."

With those instructions, Cox walked out of Captain Coffin's office and onto the highway of newfound fame or infamy whichever side of the coin one

227

was about to view his national television debut.

Chapter XVI

"Agent Barrett, this is Captain Coffin speaking. As you know, Colonel Vincent sustained a gunshot wound at approximately 1220 hours this afternoon. In an attempt to disarm the responsible individuals, the sole gunman and his wife, they became casualties. We have taken appropriate measures to calm the citizenry and to prevent any further attempts of violence. I think, if you were watching the broadcast prior to this unfortunate event, that all was calm and peaceful in Odell. We are going to proceed with the news conference in approximately thirty minutes. We've had complete cooperation with the Fox news people and all seems to be in place in order to proceed. I thought I'd give you the courtesy of a call to see if there are any questions that I might be able to answer before we go on the air."

"Why yes there are a few Captain Coffin. What in Sam Hell is going on in there? I told you we'd not tolerate any more civilian casualties. And I meant what I said. I've got hawks breathing down my neck to go in there and haul you guys out by the scruff of your dead necks. You have to know that!"

"Yes, Sir, we do. And I can assure you we've planned for and are prepared for that eventuality if it comes to that. It seems to me that your job and mine is to do everything we can to make sure that doesn't happen. I'll answer the question that you certainly must know the answer to. A gunman and his wife opened fire on our commander. Return fire killed them both. We want no more civilian casualties any more than you do, but as long as we're here trying to accomplish our goals, we're going to protect the rest of this town, its citizens and our men. You have my word and Colonel Vincent's that we will and are doing all that we can to eliminate injury on either side. Is there anything else?"

"Yes, I need to be assured, have some convincing evidence that the townspeople are okay, and between you and me, that Mrs. Odell is in good health."

229

"You will see for yourself during the broadcast that life is as near to normal here in town as it can be under the circumstances. There's enough food on hand for the civilians for at least a week, maybe more with rationing. Medical aid is being offered and provided, medications are in good supply and except for the unfortunate, yet necessary isolation, all seem to be taking the situation in good stride.

"Now that's about it. I am next in command to Colonel Vincent who is resting comfortably. You may personally inform Mrs. Vincent that he is expected to make a full recovery aside from having a hellava headache, a nice, manly scar on each side of his face and the need for a good dentist when this is all over."

Barrett was surprised to hear that Coffin already knew Mrs. Vincent was in custody. Did they know she was in Chicago? They must. He had the strongest feeling that these guys knew more than he thought they did. No one outside the Bureau and the White House staff knew she'd been picked up. At least that's what he thought until that misinformation was just dispelled.

It was important to Coffin that Barrett's vision be clouded, distracted. Now he not only had to wonder how ARM's tentacles reached into the dark places they shouldn't have access too, he had to focus on correcting that while he dealt with the immediate threat in Odell.

"Okay for now Captain Coffin. We'll be watching the news conference. Make sure there are no more civilian casualties. Don't put me in a position that will force me to act even if I personally don't think it's the thing to do. When will we next hear from you?"

"After our news conference Agent Barrett, that ball will be in your court."

# # # # #

"Good afternoon. This is Edward Morrow reporting for Fox News Chicago, coming straight to you from Odell, Illinois, a small farming community located 67 miles southwest of Chicago. It is perhaps the scene of one of the most remarkable events to have taken place in the history of this country, certainly since the report of cannon on Ft. Sumpter, South Carolina in 1860."

"No doubt you all have been following this developing story for the last forty-eight hours. We are resuming our exclusive coverage of events from inside the town. Coverage that began earlier today before an unfortunate incident involving a mentally ill, elderly resident of the town resulted in the death of one of our own, a beautiful young Chicago Tribune reporter, Monica Palmer. We love and respect this young woman who just a few months ago began what was obvious to everyone, a sparkling career in journalism. Our prayers and sympathies go out to her family, her Trib family and friends and all who knew and loved her. We apologize that our earlier live broadcast so vividly captured the violence resulting from this man's insanity. We've turned all media that captured that event over to the authorities for investigation."

"It was our intention this afternoon to interview Colonel Madison T. Vincent, the commanding officer of the Central Division of The American Revolutionary Militia. Little is known about this patriot organization, but we do know that they have moved in numbers and in force into the town of Odell. For what purpose and to what end we do not know currently. We were hopeful that Colonel Vincent would give us the answers to those questions. Unfortunately, the same individual who assassinated Ms. Palmer also tried to silence Colonel Vincent. He was unsuccessful. However, Colonel Vincent received a serious bullet wound to his face, arm and neck. He is resting comfortably and is expected to make a full recovery after undergoing some surgery."

Cox didn't feel constrained by truth. This was the electronic media. Those exposed to it weren't used to the truth and if a little hyperbole put people in the right frame of mind, then it was for the greater good and the hyperbole was justified. Ask any gaggle of media hypes; they'll tell you that's the *honest truth*!

"Our prayers are, of course, with him, his family members and friends as well. Colonel Vincent's executive officer, Captain John Coffin, has graciously agreed to sit in for Colonel Vincent. He will read a brief statement that will include a list of demands and then time permitting, respond to a few questions. Captain Coffin welcome to Fox News. First before we begin, might we inquire as to the health of Colonel Vincent and the civilians who were responsible for the attack on him and Ms. Palmer."

"Thank you for having me, Mr. Morrow and yes you may inquire. As far as I know, as far as I've been told, while Col Vincent is in some significant degree of discomfort, he is under expert care and everything that can be done with limited medical facilities is being done to manage his pain. He is alert and able to communicate but will need some rest and mending. We expect it will be only a short time before he is up and about his normal duties as our commander. But as you know with all things medical, it's a day to day thing."

"As for the individuals who executed this unprovoked assassination attempt, the murderer of that delightful young lady, Mr. Richard Ralph was shot dead after attempting to fire upon one of our men during the arrest process. While focused on that assault another one of our officers was violently attacked from behind by Mr. Ralph's wife who was wielding a deadly weapon. Our soldier did all that he could to defend himself while executing significant restraint. Unfortunately, she fell during that struggle striking her head on the sidewalk in the front of her home. She is now being observed by medical personnel, receiving treatment in the same field hospital as Colonel Vincent. Indeed they, lay side by side just feet from one another. She is resting comfortably and being attended to with the same professional care as him. We expect her to make a full recovery at which time she will be turned over to local authorities. I hope that answers your questions and thank you for your concern."

"We'd also like to thank the executives at Fox News for inviting us to be on your broadcast after such a traumatic Sunday morning. We appreciate the important platform you are providing ARM and for allowing us to state the reasons for our presence here in Odell and of course our demands for remedy."

"You're welcome, Sir. Now, shall we get to it? You have a statement to share with us after which you agreed to a few questions. Is that correct?"

"Yes, that's correct."

"Go ahead."

With that green light Captain John Coffin turned away from his interviewer and faced the television cameras in front of him.

Townspeople gathered around the center of the town square had a clear view of the north side of the Founders' monument where Captain Coffins stage was set. One camera showed the national viewing audience an image of ordinary people milling around the sidewalk in front of the Dinner Bell. The scene appeared to be pacific. Some residents were craning necks to get a look at the cameramen and the whole television hubbub, others to get a gander at Coffin. As he began to speak all appeared to be very interested in what was being said. A few were seen nodding their heads in agreement with what had been or was being said. Fox cameramen were "encouraged" to show those folks *often*.

There was a significant contingent of young men in civilian dress scattered among the citizenry whom the locals had never seen before. It was obvious that though they might be dressed in civilian clothes they belonged to the ranks of ARM. They all carried small American Flags and waived them vigorously whenever the camera focused on them. Negotiations, or rather explicit instructions assured ARM that Fox cameras would show them often as well.

233

A second camera was placed in the back of a jeep and driven around the small town. This allowed the American public another view of peaceful, cooperative, supportive Odell. It was also calculated to give the Feds a brief look at the entrenchments that would be overlooked by the civilian eye. Vincent wanted to be clear what the consequences would be, civilian and militarily, if any rescue attempt were made.

The third and last camera focused on Captain Coffin as he began his statement. He reiterated nearly word for word the chastisements of Colonel Vincent the day before when he introduced himself to the people of Odell. He embellished upon the circumstances of poor Lidice, explaining the punishments went far beyond Lidice extending to other communities and that thousands had been executed in the final tally. And where once his voice had been friendly, agreeable, even pleading in tone it soon hardened and his eyes steeled.

"Over the last few days and on possibly into the next several weeks you, our fellow Americans, will have heard and will hear many things about the nearly 1,000 souls who have laid their lives on the line for liberty and freedom here in the beautiful farming community of Odell, Illinois. Freedom, freedom from tyranny right here in these precious United States of America. Liberty, liberty to take up arms and defend it. Make no doubt about it. The lives of the young men of ARM are in grave jeopardy. They may end violently here in Odell or they may end slowly, rotting away in some federal prison far from here. Either way, we are perfectly willing to pay that price, to lay them down for your sakes and for the sakes of your posterity."

"We have been accused of treason by the real Traitors in Washington and we may not outlive that slander, but that's not important. What's important is that which Colonel Vincent explained to the people of Odell yesterday and which I have reiterated to you today. Let those traitors know there will be no sitting idly by campfires of apathy while the very vestiges of freedom, your freedom, our freedom are ripped from our bosoms. Even if this is just the beginning of the "Beginnings" we fear, we will not have it. My fellow Americans, this is just the beginning. This is not the end of the thievery we've warned you about, there is more to come. This is just to test the waters to see what they can get away with before someone screams 'enough' at them."

"Last November, those real traitors were wide afoot in our country. Special interest groups, supported by duped media outlets and crooked, devious politicians rammed down the throat of the American public the Scottstown/Brady Act. An act that took a hundred million dollars of marketing, campaigning, backroom deals and under-the-table payments, to garner barely enough votes to become the law of the land."

"When legitimately proposed, supported and democratically installed by the citizens of this United States, we are bound to obey the laws of this great country. Except, and this is a big except my fellow Americans, when votes are bought and paid for by scoundrels with hidden agendas, those very same citizens of this great country have a sacred duty . . . yes, I said sacred duty, to stand up to those responsible and to reverse those votes by any way possible. If that requires blood, our blood, then we say let it flow. No country, no free country, no free peoples ever gained or maintained that freedom without the free flow of blood. And we members of the American Revolutionary Militia offer our wrists for the slitting if that's what it takes."

"In the hearts of the great majority of this country this act is thought to be a wrenching away of a basic constitutional freedom. Certain of our lawmakers ignored that sentiment and voted contrary to the wishes of their constituents and in almost each case reversed previously held, positions. The right to bear arms is as basic as part of our guarantee to freedom as the breath of life is to our lungs."

Make no mistake my friends, as I alluded to earlier, there will be other

235

infringements upon you. Your freedom to express yourselves openly, free speech, even movement about this land without interference is on their agenda. If you think our position radical, craziness, look at those who opposed this act openly. They were branded traitors, killers, racists, dullard backwoods witless people. Every attempt was made by the media, some subtle some not so, to destroy and discredit them. They were laughed at, made the butt of jokes by half-witted, hypocritical, late-night talk show hosts, discriminated against by retail outlets and restaurants. Oh, you're free right now brothers and sisters . . . as long as you agree, are agreeable. But we promise you, your books and Bibles and statues will be next."

"Soon the government will tell you what God you may worship. And if it offends some minority, perhaps the day you worship on or the place you worship in or the very tenants of your religion will become suspect. You may be sitting comfortably in your living rooms right now thinking "impossible, not here in America". Well, we say to you, ask the people of Lidice if they thought, in the beginnings, what happened to them was possible. Ask them if they ever saw it coming. Ask them, ask them."

"Oh, that's right, you can't ask them. You can't because ninety-nine percent of them never survived the beginnings 'end game!' Smashed into oblivion as a people by government brutes too big for them to stand up to. Burned, shot, gassed dead down to nearly the very last of them. Of several thousand less than fifty survived. Friends, fellow countrymen and women, we cannot let these "Beginnings" become the endings of our liberty."

"Those villains in Washington will know for a surety that we are not going away, no matter what the cost, no matter how long it takes. If it takes our blood, our last breath, the loss of our families, our way of life, our work places, our homes, our wives, husbands, brothers, sisters . . . our very all. . . we are not going away. We've made the decision to sacrifice all those things and more if necessary, for the cause of liberty and freedom, our cause, your

236

cause."

"And if our love of country is so strong, so deep that it makes us traitors, then we join heroes with names like Washington, Jefferson, Franklin, Hamilton, Adams and the rest of our patriot ancestors who proudly wore the same title when confronted with tyranny from across the ocean. We will wear that same title proudly as the badge of honor it was and is."

"Not only will we not go away, my dear countrymen and women, neither will thousands of other brothers and sisters currently poised to strike in strategic locations across this great country. We are not alone. We are more than the few the government thinks we are. We invite you to join us. Perhaps not on the fields of blood that may be required of us. But to join us in whatever way possible to repeal this dastardly law, throw the real traitors out and replace them with honorable men and women. We've had enough of the lawyers and politicians."

"It is time to close my remarks. The following list of demands is intended for those traitorous decision makers in Washington. They are non-negotiable. There is no room for discussion, there is no room for reduction, there is no room for removal of any item."

"**First**, we demand the initiation of a popular vote process to repeal the Scottstown/Brady Act. That will require a special national referendum that we demand be monitored by representatives from the international community. Those representatives *must not* emanate from the United Nations and must meet approved criteria set forth by the American Revolutionary Militia."

"**Second**, we demand the immediate resignation of the following government officials. In each case we have incontrovertible evidence of bribery, influence peddling, favoritism and other nefarious activity directly tied to favorable votes that contributed to the very narrow passage of this bill and processes behind it. At the appropriate time, this evidence will be turned over to a special prosecutor which we demand to be named in the near future. We will not turn this evidence over to the Attorney General because of her close personal relationship with the President and our suspicions that she is also culpable or duplicitous in the vote rigging. Please note the following:

> Senator Louise Frang, Illinois,
> Senator Janet Johnson, Massachusetts,
> Senator Jacob Humphries & Congressman - Harold Washington, New Jersey,
> Congresswoman Anna Sanford, Governor Ronald Riccio, California,
> Senator Robert Lewdan, Senator Joseph Marketta, Florida,
> Congressman Umberto Rodriguez, Congresswoman Melissa Frank, Arizona,
> Congresswoman Jennifer Thomas, Senator John Foley, Illinois,
> Congressman Martin Frank, Congresswoman Mary Eig, Maryland
> Governor Daniele Slayton - Michigan."

"Thirdly, at the successful conclusion of our patriotic effort, we demand complete amnesty for all patriots who have participated or will participate in this liberation and restoration process of American liberty, including but not limited to, all support persons, organizations or entities public or private, foreign or domestic."

"Fourth, we anticipate an extended occupation of the town of Odell, Illinois. While we have adequate provisions for our patriot soldiers we anticipate a depletion of food and necessities for the townspeople. We expect re-supply of food, medicine and necessities to be provided by the State of Illinois, who is one of the main supporters of and culprits in, the passage effort of the Scottstown/Brady act. Let them bear some of the expense of the necessity of our effort. In concert with this demand the authorities should know that we will allow only two such re-supply efforts no matter what the duration of the occupation."

"**Fifth,** we demand full financial reparation for the cost of our effort of liberation. The government of the United States of America to bear the restitution of funds, wages, properties, costs and assets sacrificed to the faithful patriots who provided from their own coffers to support this liberation."

"**Sixth,** and lastly. We demand the immediate impeachment or resignation of the President of the United States of America who has violated his sacred oath and duty to uphold the Constitution of The United States of America. He has willingly and willfully violated the Second Amendment to the Constitution."

"The Second Amendment to the Constitution to the United States Constitution protects the right of everyday citizens to keep and bear arms. The right to protect our homes, our families our lands and properties from enemies foreign *and domestic*, private and public and if necessary, to throw off the chains of a tyrannical government, is a sacred right. This amendment was adopted over two-hundred and twenty-five years ago! Think about that, fellow Americans. Our founding fathers, men without special interest, backroom deals, money under the table, hushed up gifts or political donations or support or trips to vacation destinations adopted that amendment on December 15, 1791, to protect you from thugs just like the ones we've listed for resignation. Make no mistake about it, those men, our forefathers are your forefathers, whether you are generations an American or a new citizen of this country. These men are your forefathers, by bloodline or adoption, and they knew the dangers of a government that disarmed those for whom it was created. They understood the fact that some men imbued with power first exercise it with abuse of it."

"The tyrants in Washington have weaseled and fenagled, bought and sold favors and prizes, made promises for future behaviors and support to swing just enough votes to pass this legislation. They have stolen a portion of the Constitution of the United State right out from under you. They robbed it as surely as any thief creeping through the backdoors of your homes at midnight.

At least they've tried to, but the issue is not finished, we promise you that it is not, and we assure them that it is not."

"My brothers and sisters of the United States, the frightening thing about this attempted thievery is that it won't stop here; we promise it won't. Just look at the history books. They reaffirm that this is just the "beginnings" and we don't have to look but a short distance into the past for proof of that."

"We are not immoderate men. We understand the need for some regulation. We understand that the problems in the urban areas of our country, relative to the right to bear arms, are different than those faced in the rural counties of Tennessee, Alaska, or Georgia or Alabama for instance. Inner-city statistics tell us there is need for common sense regulation. The United States of America ranks third in murders by handguns in the entire world. However, if the yearly murders just in Chicago, Detroit, Washington D.C. and New Orleans were to be extracted from those numbers . . . the United States would rank fourth from last in the world. These four cities have among all U.S. cities the tightest gun-control laws and still have the worst murder-by-gun records. What does that tell us? It tells us the problem doesn't lay with gun availability or ownership, it lies with the owners, the wielders, criminals *and those who fail to raise, teach and discipline those committing these murders*. Selling the great lie that passing a law prohibiting the private ownership of guns will solve our murder rate problems is like telling the public passing laws against the consumption of drugs will do away with our ongoing addiction crisis. Lies, lies and more lies."

"Perhaps, I have spoken too long. I am a military man, not an orator. Colonel Vincent would have made our argument more convincingly. Though, I am not naturally a persuader of people, I have spoken my heart and I am convinced my heart reflects those of millions of silent hearts who beat in unison with us, our demand for liberty and our right to defend it will not be stolen. We will not go away, we won't. We will not sit idly by 'in the beginnings."

240

"God bless you all and God bless America."

The cameras panned back in time to show Robert E. Lee Cox, in his civilian dress, lean forward with a clipboard in hand and address Captain Coffin.

"Thank you, Captain Coffin for your impassioned presentation of your position. I'm sure there are many out there who have a million questions and you've agreed to answer a few. We appreciate your taking the time to do so."

"Well, I know, Mr. Morrow, that I said I would make myself available for questions, but I've changed my mind. I think I've said about all there is to be said at this stage of the game. The American people are not stupid. They understand what I've said. The talking heads will talk it to death well into the night anyway. So much so that the people will be as nauseated as I would be if I had to suffer the rehashing and conjecture that will follow."

"Sir, I understand, yes. Well these are extraordinary times Captain and we understand that they're fluid as well. If you feel best to forego the question answer period at this time, perhaps we can do it soon at another time?"

"Absolutely, sure. Perhaps in a few days, a week at the outset Colonel Vincent will be able to sit with you," Coffin lied. The Fox News boys were going to be in a caravan headed out of Odell before he'd even got back to Vincent's office. With that he concluded the interview and caused the camera feeds to end.

Dan Barrett looked at Mike O'Brien, a host of other field agents and television flat screens holding the images of the President, the Vice President, Director Cellini and Illinois Governor Peter Hinshaw. "These guys are frigging nuts!"

Chapter XVII

No commentary accompanied the video Gretchen Vincent just finished watching. All she saw was the shot that blew the left side of Monica Palmer's head off and the force of the blow that jerked her back and to the left. Next, she saw the shot that caught her husband. His face twisted in pain, his hands instinctively rose to protect himself and blood flew in the aerosol spray halo around his head. It reminded her of the Zapruder film. Then as abruptly as the video began, it ended. She felt vomit rise in her throat, but she'd not let it happen, she'd not let them have this moment. She swallowed hard, choking it and holding tears back. Her hands gripped the conference table, while her mind raced past a thousand scenarios all of which seemed improbable.

This whole film could be a fabrication. Digital imaging could make the brain believe you could visit galaxies and civilizations light years away; it could take you to island amusement parks that featured dinosaur rides. It could just as well make your husbands face explodes in front of you. Yet something among all the possibilities and probabilities that raced through her mind told her these sick SOB's weren't trying to maneuver her. Her husband was either gravely wounded or already dead on some cot sixty-seven miles away. It might as well be sixty-seven-million miles. She hung her head taking in long, deep breaths, but hiding them from whomever might be watching, gauging her reaction to the video. Silently, she dealt with the fact that indeed she was likely never to see him again. Her heart sank. The pit of her stomach revolted against her again at the very thought, but she steeled herself for that very real inevitability.

Over the years, they'd discussed death and separation many times; all military couples do. It could happen at any time during the dozens of different deployments Vincent made during his career and it may have this time. As she reached to close the lid of the small laptop computer, a young, mid-twentyish woman walked into the room dressed in a navy-blue business suit. Her jet-black hair pulled back into a tight bun framed an attractive face. In a compassionate tone she said, "I'm sorry Mrs. Vincent about your husband. I need to collect this laptop now. Is there anything I can do for you?"

Gretchen looked at her without response.

"Do you have any questions? Can I get something for you to drink? Maybe refresh that water for you?"

The prisoner stared at her in silence.

"You look awfully tired; probably nothing a cool washcloth and a sink wouldn't help. I'll ask if I can get you down to the lady's room for a few moments if you like."

She wasn't wasting her breath. Barrett, O'Brien and the rest of the audience came to the same conclusion as they observed the one-sided exchange on the closed-circuit screens before them.

"She's tougher than she looks. She's not gonna be easy." Turning to one of the agents in the room Barrett said, "Take her to a room with a bed, get her cleaned up, bring in some food. Let her stew in there. Once she's settled in, nobody goes in, nobody responds to any contact from her. Right now, we've got other issues to attend to."

# # # # #

In summer months Chicago's population, almost three million, swells to four million. Add to that the almost five and a half million who reside in the greater metropolitan area the Feds, have quite a number of people to look after. Odell just added another eight hundred and sixty-four out of towners that

243

Dan Barrett wished had stayed home.

There's a unique room on the thirty-seventh floor of the Federal Building in Chicago. Located only a few blocks east of State Street, the room offers a clear view of Grant Park, Lake Michigan and many of the beautiful lakeside landmarks that make the city one of the top tourist destinations in the world.

The room is used for high-profile interrogations and occasionally negotiations. Chairs on the west side of the conference type table look out over the lake and parks; they are taller than the chairs placed on the east side of the table. There's a reason for that. The smaller chairs were reserved for people being interrogated and their lawyers . . . always. The glass wall behind them gave the occupants of the west side chairs the great view of Chicago's lakefront.

The westerly wall of the room featured hideous wallpaper. Vertical lines filled the wall, floor to ceiling, the entire length of the conference room. During extended questioning, the occupants of the eastern chairs had to stare at that hideous wallpaper sometimes for hours on end. Most victims' interviewees thought their headaches came from the stress associated with being in the room, but a bevy of government employed psychiatrists and ergonomic experts collaborated to design the room. They guaranteed the visual banquet on the western wall would cause, with enough time, both physical and mental discomfort. It worked wonderfully well.

This uncomfortable ambiance was most effective in the pre-noon hours. So, whenever an interrogation was significant enough to warrant use of this special "conference" room, it always started as early in the morning hours as possible. The window blinds opened slightly and lowered create a checkerboard patterned shadow on the already hideous west wall. Stare at that for a few

244

hours and you'd have a headache, too!

The air conditioning control for the room was set to extremes. Female interviewees got cold air blasts; males got heat. The shrinks came up with that ploy as well. Miserable temperatures in the room were blamed on incompetent building engineers who never could seem to get it just right. Juice, coffee, rolls, pastries always brought in for the western chairs. Those across the table were made to ask for them. This room is where Gretchen Vincent would next meet Dan Barrett.

# # # # #

In a conference room on the forty-third floor Dan Barrett, several agents, Louis Cellini, Governor Hinshaw, Commander Waldrop, and a surprise, secret guest, Frank Halderman watched the broadcast from Odell with intense interest. Copies of the broadcast were being analyzed by intel organizations from both state and federal governments. Halderman, the President's chief of staff, also considered by many to be his best friend, let out a low whistle just as the monitors went black and Barrett pronounced insanity on the lunatics holding Odell captive.

"Okay, let's give ourselves a few minutes break then we'll have another look at it. There's a ton of information there and perhaps some disinformation that we'll need to go over."

"We also need to call in some media chips, Agent Barrett. We can't have this craziness go un-responded to for any length of time," Halderman piped up.

"I suppose you're right, Mr. Halderman, and I understand where you're coming from, but that's your bailiwick more than it is in mine. I'm not saying our areas of responsibilities won't blend at some point in time and I really

245

need to be kept in the loop, but my main focus right now is to learn as much as I can from these guys, detect any weakness in their fortifications and exploit it to affect their removal from Odell. Or . . . to get them to surrender. And at this stage of the game, that looks like quite a long shot."

"If you'd like to speak in private with the President to address your need for a response, please use my office to do so. The phone lines are secure. If you need anything else, let me know. After you're through, please feel free to come join our roundtable."

"Thank you, Mr. Barrett, I'll do just that. If you'll now excuse me for the time being, I do need to speak to the President and see what his wishes are."

Halderman left the room in a blaze. Mike O'Brien, though he'd been invited to the party, understood his position well enough to stay sequestered in a corner of the conference room. He was restarting the entire news conference.

When Barrett finally looked his way O'Brien said, "Well let's get it up on the white board. What do we know, what do we suspect, what don't we know?"

With that the men in the room began to scour the video footage. After several hours the white board was full of notations.

Halderman who'd been holed up in Barrett's office for most of the video review time returned to the conference room. "Dan, bring me up to speed. What have we gleaned from the broadcast?"

"Yes, Sir, I, we have some new information, some questions answered and lots of new ones as you can imagine." Having said that, Barrett wheeled the white board around to face Halderman's chair. "First, we know their commander's down. We don't know if he's alive or dead. Coffin could be bluffing, covering up on that issue. My best guess is that Vincent is gone. He took

246

that round right to his face. If not dead, he's no longer our main target, Coffin is."

"Our guys are working on Coffin's bio, relatives, history, known associates, travel history all that. Likely he's not as dynamic as Vincent, but he did a fair job of playing the patriot role. Again, based on the video of the actual shooting, we know Vincent's facial wound is pretty darn serious, so we need to focus right now on the man in charge and that appears to be Coffin."

"If that's the case their mission won't be in much danger, they had to have a contingency plan should leadership be compromised, and it's crippled a bit. I think having Vincent out of the picture, we can be a little tougher with these guys when it comes to negotiations. The backup quarterback is never the guy you want running the offense in the Super Bowl. And that's just what they're faced with now."

"We also picked up the reference to other cells poised across the country. If true, and it's our consensus at this point that's a red herring, we should direct some focus on specific parts of the country. Since they made demands for removal from office of political leaders from six different states, those are the states our intelligence efforts are going to drill down on. We have also increased security for each of their targets."

"This is where we are going to need your cooperation, Mr. Halderman, and that of the office of the President. We don't know whether there's any veracity to the allegations posed by the terrorists, we're just not sure. But a separate investigation into any alleged wrongdoing has to be launched immediately. If we can take a bullet out of their gun, reduce their demands, negotiations become a tad easier. So, we've got to determine if any of these members of congress are culpable of any wrongdoing. And we need to fast track that effort.

247

We won't be able to get much done in time for the government's rebuttal broadcast, but we'll keep you advised of our progress. Hopefully, you'll be able to use the intel we develop to shut these boys up. That is," Barrett looked over his cup of coffee, "if there's no evidence that any of these folks had their hands in any cookie jars."

"We can only hope," Halderman responded with a concerned look on his face.

"They claim to have nearly one thousand troops in Odell. Our estimates place their troop strength at closer to eight-hundred men; mind you that's a significant number of well-armed men inserted among 3,100 unarmed civilians. Their embellishment however lets us know that they are not opposed to hyperbole if it fits their agenda. Thus, we don't know if Vincent is dead or alive. We must take anything they say with a grain of salt until we have one-hundred -percent verification.

"They've made a big deal about the Nazi occupation and obliteration of Lidice, Czechoslovakia when in fact they've almost perfectly mirrored that occupation to the tee. Even down to the arrogance of the commander taking an open-air ride through the area and being shot as a result of it. So, if their plan is not perfect from an ideological perspective, it's most likely to have holes in it from a militaristic one. We now need to find those and exploit them in case we have to go in there."

"One of the things you will have to discuss with the President and his cabinet is, and this is hard to say, but must be said, how many civilian casualties are acceptable should we have to use force? It's a tough question, Mr. Halderman, but if we have no choice but to initiate an action for the liberation of that town, we have to face the fact that a lot of people are going to die, non-combatant people. Perhaps the President's grandmother and cousin."

"The town is fortified to the extent that physical extraction of these guys looks to be a real nightmare without significant civilian casualties. Many of the troop positions inside the perimeter are nestled right up next to residential buildings. Any ordinance lobbed in there will take out innocent people. The only way we look to have resolution at this time is to talk them out. But we've got to boof up our position and someone will have to respond to their demands. We'll have to wait on you before we can do that."

Halderman turned around from the window.

"The President wants to give this a couple of days to percolate before he responds directly to the claims of the terrorists. There will be a brief statement to the nation tonight, but a more specific message will be presented in a day or so when we have more information. Right now, we don't want to say or do anything that may exacerbate the situation and increase the risk of injury to anymore of the townspeople. We're looking at Wednesday night. That should give you people some time to do your thing, perhaps learn a little more about what we're up against and give these nut cases a chance to get reasonable once we do approach them."

"I agree, but remember, we don't want these folks in there for a long time. The longer they're in Odell the worse it is. And it looks to us like they've counted on that scenario; it looks like they're wanting that. They're supplied to the hilt with rations and necessities for their troops. A salt bin out near the interstate, but within their perimeter looks to have been the destination for supply vehicles for the last three months as far as we can make out. So, they've been stock piling supplies in there for a very long time. I don't think they're planning on sharing. We've been told they will let two re-supplies of

249

food, medicine, etcetera to the civilian population and then here's what my second worse fear is, Mr. Halderman."

Halderman sat forward in his chair "What's that?"

"I think they mean for us to starve the population of Odell until it turns real nasty. If we don't cave to demands they'll strangle the town all the while blaming us, the government, for not getting food and supplies to them. The scenes coming out of there will be horrid. If that's their plan, it's masterful. It's just what the Nazis did. Starve the people, turn them into dogs, willing to do anything to feed their dying children, even turn against one another, join the men who finally give them enough sustenance to survive. When they're weak enough, desperate enough, pour any indoctrination down their throats one can think of. Make them hate us, blame us for this whole mess. The longer it goes on the worse the outcome is going to be I assure you."

"Good God! If that's your second worse fear Dan, what the heck's your first?

"They do something to force us to come in with troops. If this goes on long enough, there will be public and political cries for immediate resolution, chest beating, advance for the greater good. And if we must use the guard or even regular army forces it's going to be a royal blood bath. And then, Mr. Halderman, the casualties will make it look like Waco on steroids. Political heads will roll no matter what side of the aisle one sits on. And, Mr. Halderman, notwithstanding the President's personal interest in Odell . . . he himself may hear the whisper of the axe!"

"There is one other danger more dangerous than both those scenarios my friend," Halderman replied.

"Oh, yeah? What's that?"

"That we provide this movement, if indeed it can be called that at this stage. If we provide this movement with martyrs, that my friend may prove more dangerous than either of your worries."

Everybody in the room turned towards Halderman knowing full well the implications of what he proposed. The silence was painful.

Chapter XVIII

Wednesday morning found Mike O'Brien in Dwight, Illinois standing alongside one of his sergeants, peering through binoculars as he spotted the military ambulance driving up Route 47. White flags flying from each side of the vehicle and a red emergency light flashing from the roof of the cab; he thought it was moving at a pretty good clip. All he knew was that a request from the state police district headquarters had arrived downtown for Barrett. O'Brien was specifically requested to receive the ambulance and its occupants who were civilian residents of Odell. The vehicle came to a stop twenty-five yards from the police barricade which had been set up near the town limits. Captain, David Drew exited the passenger side and walked towards O'Brien.

"Captain O'Brien, Sir. We wish to transfer to you two residents of the town of Odell. The first unfortunately, is the body of Mr. Richard Ralph who was killed during an arrest attempt after the assassination of Monica Palmer and the attempted assassination of Colonel Vincent. The second, is the wife of Mr. Ralph, who was seriously injured when she assaulted one of our cadre who was attempting that arrest. I'm afraid her injury is very grave. We've done all we can for her. She's in desperate need of a detailed neurological work up. Will you accept these civilians?"

"Yes, we will, Captain Drew, but in the future, we hope we'll not have to receive any more, not one. Agent Barrett has asked me to remind you that we've already expressed that to you. Let me reiterate. There better not be any more civilian casualties. If that were to happen our limited options become even more limited. We may, you may force us to exercise military options."

"You needn't remind me, Captain O'Brien. And we have no desire to bring additional casualties to you but let us be equally clear with you. If you and the

252

rest of that gang in Washington don't believe we mean business, that we will succumb to force internal or external then you and they are very mistaken. Any decision to move against Odell, we assure you, will result in fields of blood from which none of your men, or the townspeople, will survive. And let me make you a promise, the civilian population of Odell will need more ambulances than you or we can supply. And just in case you boys didn't get the entire message Sunday afternoon, this is just the genesis, just the genesis."

Two men in combat uniform with M16s slung over their shoulders came from the rear of the ambulance carrying a stretcher with the body of Dick Ralph on it. They set it at O'Brien's feet and immediately returned to the rear of the ambulance. This time when they returned, they carried Ruth Ralph looking very pale, connected to IVs, clearly unconscious. Drew's eyes had never left O'Brien's face. When the second stretcher was lowered to the ground, Drew saluted, did an about face and returned to the cab of the ambulance. The engine raced as the vehicle made a quick turnabout and headed back to Odell. Mike O'Brien was stunned to see Captain Mario Petracha handcuffed to Sheriff Larry Odell standing where the rear of the ambulance had been, both men blindfolded! Apparently, Colonel Vincent wasn't a fan of murder no matter what the rationale was. But what were they up to releasing Odell?

# # # # #

Washington D.C. Wednesday night 9:00 O'clock p.m. - The White House.

"My fellow Americans, some have suggested that it would not be wise to address you this evening and that I would be better served if I were to hold off for a few more days. I suppose there are many valid reasons why they would be correct, but this is not about my being better served politically, it's about

253

the best interest of America and liberty. I cannot remain silent any longer. I must address you and to those who are responsible for one of the most heinous acts of treason in our country's recent history may listen in."

"Whenever there's an attack upon the liberty of this great country, no matter how large or small, whether foreign or domestic, whether it targets our largest city or our smallest community, your President will not stand idly by. And if needs be, the most terrible resources of the United States will be brought to bear to eliminate such threats."

"Over the past few days criminals, whom we know to be from various parts of our great land have conspired to drag down into the deepest gutters the very liberty this country was founded upon; liberty they claim to cherish. They do not cherish it. The liberty we know is exercised through a democratic form of government which has become the standard for the entire free world. There is no rationale, no complaint, no alleged misdeed or perceived wrong so great that it cannot be addressed through our democratic processes. These processes have been the appropriate venue for redress from any and all injustices for nearly two hundred and fifty years. The very essence of our Constitution, the fabric from which our democracy has been woven, is to preclude force from rule. Tonight, however is not a forum for debate. Tonight, is a night for a message."

"And this is the message. There can be no cause that excuses the hostage taking or murder of fellow Americans. To justify those dastardly acts under a banner of some alleged defense of those very liberties strangled by the cause itself, begs the lowest form of failed reason. Any demand for the removal of honorable, duly elected government officials emanating from these traitors claiming scurrilous, unsubstantiated allegations of wrongdoing pushes past the boundaries of the absurd. I promise you my fellow Americans that the elected officials you place your trust in, the real patriots you voted for, will not be removed from their offices except by the very same electoral process that put them there to begin with. We will never surrender to the demands of these criminals."

"There is no price for which Liberty, freedom and democracy can be purchased. They are gravely mistaken to think there is. The message I want these men and all those who support them to know is we will not bow to treason nor to those who abuse their fellow Americans, no price can make us do so."

"Naturally our hearts and minds are focused on the good people of Odell, Illinois. I want to assure them and all their friends and families that we will do everything within our power, the power of the federal government, to secure their safety and freedom as soon as possible. There will be every effort made to rescue them from the jaws of this tyranny and to return them to their rightful status as peace loving, law abiding, free citizens of this country. There has been some speculation, concern that I will not exercise "all" options available to me because there are family members close and dear to my heart living in Odell. That is true, there are. But once again I want to assure you that every single soul held captive there is as precious to me as any other. Odell is my hometown. In addition to relatives, I have many lifelong friends there; schoolteachers, coaches, barbers, grocery store operators, all those people who make our lives growing up so special. Precious it is to me."

"But you all must know that just as I am your President, I am its President. Every hometown in these United States is just as precious to me as Odell is. And to be frank with you and with those holding Odell hostage, if the very gates of hell were to be opened upon her or any other of our towns, you will

255

find your President ready with sword in hand if necessary, to do battle."

"As in any grave situation saber rattling never accomplishes much. We will do our best to convince these men to lay down their arms and listen to reason. There is a peaceful avenue to address any perceived grievances and we, being reasonable men, will listen to and speak with reason in an effort to avoid more bloodshed than has already taken place. It is our daily prayer that the end of this matter can be accomplished in a peaceful manner and by this message direct to those in Odell we invite discussion. But at the same time warn that further injury to our citizens is not acceptable nor will it be tolerated. And in the final analysis, if we must go into Odell and take those tyrants out of there, we will."

"Good night my fellow Americans. God Bless Odell and God Bless America."

# # # # #

On the ninth evening of the occupation of Odell using the local radio station One American News was granted exclusive interview rights with Colonel Vincent. "Colonel Vincent, thank you for taking the time to speak with us. We've agreed to a non-video interview because you are still recovering from your wounds. We hope you're doing well and if we might inquire about the status of your health before we ask a few other questions. How are you feeling?"

"Well, right now I look like a raccoon who's just staggered out of a barroom brawl, but I guess you can say I'm doing pretty well all things considered. Thank you for asking."

It hadn't seemed like a week since he'd been shot in the face because he remembered little of it. His face was still swollen, both eyes black and blue and he felt like he'd been kicked in the head by a mule. He told Drew he felt like the entire Russian army had bivouacked in his mouth. Though still eating food processed with a blender he'd decided he needed to stir up the President a little after hearing his Wednesday night slander.

Surprising, even to Vincent, a delegation of the towns' women brought over soup and home-made ice cream. He tasted it with some reluctance, but finally devoured it once he knew it wasn't intended to kill him. He was making daily progress and Coffin had things under control, but he'd spent an hour or two out of bed each of the last two days and could feel his strength beginning to return. If his jaw would just stop aching like the toothache from hell.

"We're glad to hear that, Colonel. Now we'll get right down to business because we know you have limited time with us tonight. First, we want to ask you if you've had any contact from anyone outside of Odell. For instance, and we're not asking you this to cause you any concern, but we've reached out to Mrs. Vincent and frankly we've not been able to make contact with her. Have you had any contact from her or any other family members?"

"Well none of us expect to hear from the outside world for a while at least. We surely don't expect to hear from our families while we're engaged in the business of war. So, the short answer to your question is no, I haven't heard from anyone in my circle of friends or family."

"We don't mean to press the issue, but aren't you concerned that she seems to be missing? At least we haven't been able to contact her?"

"Again, the short answer to that question is no; I am not worried."

"Should we take that to mean she's in hiding or her absence is planned, perhaps expected?"

"You shouldn't take that to mean anything, but to be honest with you, I

257

didn't agree to the interview to spend so much time on my wife's present location. She's not a part of this and we should move on."

"We surely didn't mean to imply that she was duplicitous in your effort Colonel Vincent, perhaps I didn't word my question appropriately and hope you will accept my apologies, if that's the way it came across. I really do feel bad about that."

"You know what? I think you do. I think I'm a pretty good judge of character and while I might thumb my nose at that apology coming from a lot of guys in the media, I think you really are concerned about the way your question was phrased. So, here's what I'm gonna do and then we can move on to the reason I've agreed to this short discussion. Okay. Ya ready?"

"Sir, yes, Sir," the reporter barked with a smile.

"If you want to know the location of my wife, you may want to call Agent Dan Barrett, Agent in Charge of the FBI's Chicago Office. Ask him what room he's got her detained in and if you might have a few minutes to speak with her. Now, good sir, let's move on." The reporter was stunned that Vincent knew where his wife was. He wasn't the only one listening in who was!

"Well, Colonel, I suppose you watched or have had a report on the President's message to the nation Wednesday night. Would you have any response to his remarks?"

"Yes, yes, I do. First, let me say one always tries to avoid personal attacks. Positions may be different and in more civil times one would agree to disagree, but these times are not civil. War never is. So, I will be personal in my retort. The President of the United States, unfortunately for America, is a liar and a coward. Never addressing any issue of contention, he comforted himself with slings and arrows directed at myself and my men. Vicariously, he drew back on thousands of others poised to execute arms in the defense of liberty as well. He has no guts for war. He lacks courage and if he has the sword poised as he claimed, let him swing it. We dare him to. We challenge him. And if he does, he might remember that there are more civilians in the town of Odell than there were casualties in Pearl Harbor, more than were murdered in the twin towers. If he wants to let blood, come to these fields and see how furiously it will flow."

"If he thinks our demands are ludicrous, come dispel them. We will erase him with that mythological sword he so boisterously promised to swing. We will utterly destroy whatever forces he sends and if the entire town of Odell is wiped temporarily from the maps of Illinois and these fields have to run red with blood, then so be it. It can and will be rebuilt and its progeny will curse his name and the name of the family who spawned that traitor."

"However, as I have said, and Captain Coffin has reiterated, we are reasonable men and are willing to talk to traitors if it will right the wrong."

"There are limited supplies of food, medicine and other necessities for the residents of Odell. We have granted Washington permission to resupply these good folks this coming Wednesday. After that onetime supply, they will have nobody but Washington, their favorite son to blame for any un-pleasantries they'll experience. So, if the President wants to rattle sabers let him do it. If he wants to starve these folks so he can uphold the tyranny that brought this upon them and the rest of the nation let the blood, be on his hands."

"We will not leave here without result and . . . this is very important my friend. He cannot remove us no matter what he puffs out his chest about. Let the coward come here and try it."

"Well those are what we call back home . . .'fighting words' Colonel. Do

259

you really intend to challenge the might of the armed forces of the United States?"

"No, we respect our honorable men and women who serve in the armed forces. We think they will not draw arms on fellow Americans. They by their profession know the amount of collateral damage that will result from an all-out military assault. Their commander may not know but they and their officers will. And if it comes right down to following direct orders, we will understand and engage them as the honorable warriors they are. There will be heroes buried on both sides."

"Well we seriously hope for the sakes of all those innocents in Odell, for the sakes of you and your men and all others that it doesn't have to come to that Colonel. I'm hearing in my ear that our very limited time is up and that it's time for you to return to your post. Once again, we wish to thank you for your time, your response to the President's message and the courtesies you've extended to us here at One America News."

"You're welcome and God Bless America."

Dan Barrett shot a glance at Mike O'Brien that said it all. How in the heck did Vincent know they had his wife on the 37th floor of the federal building? Somebody's talking who shouldn't be.

# # # # #

For the next several days communications between the two camps were minimal. One restating demands and asking for progress towards meeting them, the other vowing that investigations were taking place, they took time and needed hostages in exchange for current efforts. As for Odell as the occupation entered its second week its good citizens and the occupiers soon settled into what only could be described as a rhythm of respect and peaceful co-

260

existence. There were patrols and drills alongside children on swing sets, monkey bars and teenagers tossing baseballs. The sun continued to rise and set, rise and set. People ate meals, televisions were back on and most watched the news though there were times for laughter. But no one went to work if they worked outside of Odell. This gave them time for . . . for whatever they wanted; reading, sleeping, thinking, praying, planning. The more the townspeople saw of the soldiers as seemingly young American boys, the calmer they became. But their souls were never really calm, at peace. Deep down inside everyone knew this wasn't going to end well. Everyone.

# # # # #

Aside from regular plates of what tasted like hospital food, escorted trips to the showers and restroom, Gretchen Vincent had, had no human contact for 2 days . . . or was it three, five more? She had no idea. Her watch and phone were confiscated the instant the FBI picked her up. She had no idea if it was day or night. Breakfast, lunch and dinner were mixed up in her mind. Were they doing that on purpose? She could swear she was getting breakfast at night and lunch for breakfast. Were they trying to mix her up, confuse her, put her off guard, dull her? The single answer to all those questions was yes. She was in that dazed, confused state of mind when the door to her sparsely furnished room flew open. It was the female agent from the first day who offered conversation.

"Mrs. Vincent, will you please follow me."

Gretchen rose and followed her out of the small dimly lit room into a series of hallways that eventually led to a main hall with three banks of elevators. She noticed no other bodies walking about as she followed the young woman in the dark blue business suit. Was it the same suit? Funny what things come

261

to your mind when the stress is so intense. She almost wanted to laugh and ask the woman if she'd been home to bathe and change since she last saw her or if she just had a very limited wardrobe. Humor and curiosity left her when she saw the elevator doors open and the woman stepped aside to let her enter first. She wondered if handcuffs were necessary. She wasn't exactly a threat to anyone.

"I'm Agent Susan Randolph. If you need anything in the way of a bathroom break or refreshment, just ask for me."

Gretchen Vincent remained silent; refused to acknowledge her. After all wasn't this the twit who brought that horrid video of Madison being shot?

The ride was a short one down to the 37th floor to "that" conference room. When she first entered, she thought it was almost laughable. Who in hell was the interior decorator? The wallpaper almost distracted her from turning around and looking out on the beautiful lakefront. In the dim almost light of predawn she made out dots of people moving about, seemingly headed off to workplaces. Streetlights were still on in the park below. Buckingham Fountain was still illuminated with multicolored lights. Steps leading to Lake Shore Drive and Grant Park could barely be made out in the shadows.

On the lake, she could see all sorts and sizes of boats bobbing up in down in the Chicago Yacht Club harbor. No one seemed to be stirring there. It was too early and peaceful to be doing anything but sleep, she thought. Only the increasing foot traffic in the streets below told her it was morning and not dusk.

"Please, have a seat right here, Mrs. Vincent" the young woman said holding a chair out for her. She moved to the chair from the window and took a seat. "Mr. Barrett will be here in a few minutes."

An hour later, Dan Barrett and Mike O'Brien walked into the room with steaming cups of coffee and took seats in the chairs on the western side of the conference room. Neither said anything to her when they entered the room, they didn't even acknowledge her presence. She decided to return the favor, staring at the wall behind each of them. After they'd been seated for several minutes, the young woman returned with two sweet rolls and placed one in front of each man. Neat napkins and a canter of coffee also set before the men No one said anything to Mrs. Vincent.

Finally, . . . "Mrs. Vincent, my name is Dan Barrett. I am the Agent In Charge of Homeland Security for the Chicago Federal Bureau of Investigation. My associate here is Captain Michael O'Brien of the Illinois State Police. We are here to speak to you about the unfortunate events taking place in Odell, Illinois, and of course your husband's participation in those events. We want to be up front with you. We are also interested to know if you are a willing participant as well."

"Well, I suppose you do want to talk to me. But what I'm not sure of is why I have been so shabbily treated over these last several days. I don't even know how many days it's been since I was dragged out of my home. Or for that matter Mr. Barrett, why I was dragged without warrants or explanation. I don't even know what day this is!"

Gretchen was livid mad, but she wasn't going to show them any emotion, she was determined not to. "And aside from the miserable violations of my constitutional rights, Mr. Barrett, I have on several occasions advised your miserable underlings that I demanded my right to counsel, all of which have been ignored. And so once again for the last time, I demand my right to counsel and I am not going to utter another word to you until I see an attorney

263

walking through that door with my name on his client's list. I want counsel and I want him now!"

Dan Barrett didn't respond right away. He picked up his cup of coffee, drew a long deep breath and blew into it. After taking a few sips and a bite from the sweet roll he wiped his lips with the napkin provided.

"Mrs. Vincent, I have some good news and bad news for you. I'll share the good news first. The good news is that you are in the Federal Building in downtown Chicago. Aside from various government agencies it houses the federal courthouse and all its support systems. There are at any one-time hundreds of lawyers present in its rooms and hallways. Aside from all that if you were able to walk a short four blocks north you would run into the Chicago Civic Center where much of the litigation both criminal and civil takes place. There are hundreds of lawyers there to choose from. That's the good news. Unfortunately, here's the bad news."

"The bad news is I don't give a white rats ass about you, about lawyers, about judges, about politicians. I especially don't give a damn about your constitutional rights. As far as I'm concerned, they don't exist. Listen very carefully to this next bit of information." Barrett's eyes narrowed, and his thin lips tightened. "I have been personally authorized, and I mean personally authorized from the highest offices of the federal government to do with you as I wish, how I wish and when I wish to accomplish my goals of bringing a peaceful, if possible, resolution to the terrorist actions taking place in Odell."

"No one, and I mean no one knows you are here except those very few involved in bringing you here. As far as anyone else is concerned you may have been whisked away by sympathizers to your husband's cause, by his co-conspirators or well-meaning old war buddies. You may have been the victim of a random home invasion, burglary gone wrong or . . . you may have been kidnapped by well-intended vigilante patriots incensed by your husband's band of terrorists. And very soon we'll be having another press conference. We'll be asked about your whereabouts and what we know. I promise you Mrs. Vincent I will bring all these possibilities to their attention. I will deny to the high heavens that we know anything about your location and will pledge to everyone listening that we are doing all we can to locate you because you are a person of interest to us."

"Here's where this whole scenario turns very ugly Mrs. Vincent. Once that news conference is over. Once those cards have been played, we can never return you to your previous life, to your family, friends, neighbors, husband. Once that happens our options are going to be very, very limited if you get my drift."

"You want a lawyer? You think you're going to lawyer up on me? No, I don't think so Mrs. Vincent. I don't think so at all. No lawyer, no judges, no politicians. It's just going to be you and me."

Stomach churning, her fists clenched beneath the table. Gretchen tried ever so hard not to stare lightning bolts through his eyes into his brain. No wonder Madison agreed to do what he was doing. No wonder the country needed to shed the shackles of the federal government. She focused on Barrett. O'Brien was just a local lackey as far as she was concerned, and she did the best to exclude him from her life by totally ignoring him.

"Do what you must Mr. Barrett. Without counsel, you will never get another word out of me." She felt she'd called his bluff.

"Perhaps you're right. Perhaps. Then, perhaps you need additional time to think about this. Perhaps this conference room is not the best venue for us to

265

share knowledge with one another." Looking to his left at O'Brien he asked what both men knew was a rhetorical question. "I wonder, Captain O'Brien, if we have another venue a little more austere where the staff's sole purpose in life is to encourage communication?"

With that both O'Brien and Barrett got up and walked out of the conference room leaving Gretchen Vincent there to stare at the checkerboard patterned wallpaper!

Several hours later, Mike O'Brien was the first to re-enter the conference room. He held a large glass of ice water. He offered to get one for Mrs. Vincent who accepted the invitation. Minutes later a staffer came into the room and placed the drink before her confirming her suspicion that the room was wired. After a few swallows she broke the silence by thanking O'Brien for the drink. He nodded his acknowledgment. Fifteen minutes later, Agent Barrett re-entered the room with a diet coke can in hand.

"Oh, brother." Gretchen thought. "Here we go, good cop, bad cop. Can they really think this will work?" They did, it would.

"The last time we spoke Mrs. Vincent, I think I let my emotions get the best of me. This has been a very stressful few days for all of us. I used the word perhaps several times. I'll use it just one more time, I think. Perhaps, we got off on the wrong foot because I've not handled things the way I should have. Maybe I need to identify for you the one thing both you and I have in common. We each need information. Information is power, and I need the power to resolve this mess as soon as possible without any further bloodshed. No more lives must be lost, no more blood must be shed in those farm fields."

"You need information too. And I'm going to give some of it to you now so that you know we are not playing good cop, bad cop like any reasonably

266

intelligent person would think. I know you are a pretty smart woman. I know a little of your background because I've read your file as well, though it is considerably less thick than Colonel Vincent's." He let loose a small grin. "Here's the information you need. You already know that Colonel Vincent was wounded last Sunday afternoon. You may or may not be aware of the fact that the young reporter with him had most of her head blown off. The weapon used to kill her and wound the Colonel was a Korean War vintage M1 rifle. It is a brutally powerful weapon. Colonel Vincent sustained a very significant wound to the face and is in grave condition. He is currently in Loyola Foster McGraw Hospital just twenty minutes from us."

"As you saw for yourself his wounds are to the head and they are grave. He is listed, as of yesterday afternoon, in gravely critical condition. I have personally spoken with each of his surgeons and the other doctors managing his care. We're advised that all that can be done for him medically has been done and is being done. Now it's a matter of will power. Now it's a matter of those intangible things that will determine if the last lines of his letter telling you his spirit will always be nearby or if you will be bringing him home. I think he needs to see you, to know you are nearby. I think you may be the only medicine now that can help him, save his life."

She flinched. He saw it in her eyes. He'd seen hundreds who sat in that chair or similar ones' flinch. Most folks would never pick up on it. Sometimes it was the small almost imperceptible way the carotid artery in the neck began to pulse harder, sometimes it wasn't even a physical thing; he could feel it in his gut, his being. No doubt her countenance shifted just a bit. He continued just a little bit more to give her the opening she was looking for but hadn't found yet.

267

"Maybe you and I digging our heels into the sand, playing at this game is the wrong way to go about this. Maybe we each need something from the other that we can't get anywhere else in the entire world. You and I maybe need each other more than either of us knows. We must have the same goals even if we feel we have to go about them at odds. All I want is to resolve this like you do, peacefully. It's what the President wants, it's what the country wants, certainly it's what the innocent people of Odell want and though your husband is a warrior, it must be what he ultimately wants, or he would have blown that place to holy hell by now."

"Is he conscious?"

"He has occasionally gained consciousness but not for very long periods of time. He's asked for you. That's one of the reasons you're here. You should also know that if he does survive his wounds, he's going to need extensive re-constructive surgery. It's not going to be an easy road for him or for you. I've spoken with his doctors and they've assured me he can be put back together again if he can survive the trauma of his wounds."

"Listen, I've spent hours going over his file and yours. I know almost everything about each of you individually and as a couple. You've been together since high school. He cannot survive without you and I doubt you can without him. It's a love story for the ages your stories are."

"But it all still boils down to you and me. How's this going to shake out? It's largely going to be up to you. Are you going to work with me? Are we gonna shut this thing down peacefully? Are you going to go to your husband's aid? What do you have to say?"

After a very long pause, "You know, Agent Barrett, I'm conflicted. Part of me, the wife part, wants to break down and cry and beg you to take me to him.

The other part, that part, doesn't trust you. You and I both know that I'll never be able to bring Madison home again. Our lives are shattered and can never go back to what they were once."

She'd been easier than Barrett or O'Brien had expected. All Barrett really wanted was to get her off the "Never another word" square. She was off that and she was going to cooperate. It might not come in big gulps, but it was going to come.

"Don't say that. Look let's face facts if you want facts. You nor I know how this is going to shake out in the end. What we do know is if we can get the guns lowered, if we can stop the saber rattling on both sides and get men to talk, anything can happen. As much as I dread the thought of it, as much as I want to vomit when I think of it, politicians are going to enter this, that's what's going to bring this to an end. Negotiations take place. They take into consideration things, facts neither you nor I are even aware of. We can't predict, but given his stellar military career, his dedication to this country even his dedication to his cause though I disagree with it, I'd put my money on the Colonel. Many possibilities could still come to fruition to bring him back to your arms and home. We can't move forward without thinking that's possible. But I need to talk to you in detail. What's it going to be?"

Gretchen sat quietly staring at the table before her. Barrett and O'Brien were careful not to press the issue, so they sat still and stared out the window watching puffs of white sails glide slowly up and down the blue waters of Lake Michigan. It didn't take very long before they had their answer.

"I don't know how I can possibly be of any help to you, Agent Barrett. I'm a military wife. Over the course of his career, Madison's been all over this globe, involved for the government and military in God knows what. I learned

269

early as a young bride not to ask questions. Surly you must know how that is with a wife from personal experience. How much does your wife know about your responsibilities? I'm sure you don't run home and discuss your cases with her. I just don't know what I can say to you that will be of any value."

"Little things, Gretchen," Barrett addressed her by her first name for the first time. She needed to feel like a partner right now. "Little things can help us understand the entire situation. Let me be the judge of what's important and what's not. I want to go back several years and talk to you about your travels, associates, relatives, guests at your home, vacation destinations, etc. There's just a ton to be gone over. Lunch is on the way. After lunch you go ahead and get showered and cleaned up if you like. I've arranged for you to stay in another "apartment," one with more creature comforts that a woman could appreciate. Let the agent with you know what else you might need."

"We'll need to move to a different conference room, what the heck's wrong with these building engineers? It's always colder than heck in here. If you need a sweater or something let the agent who comes for you know. We'll find a different room that's a little warmer and more comfortable. Then let's just spend some time and see if we can figure this out, ok?

"When will I get to see Madison?"

"As soon as possible. I've already sent my request to Washington and as soon as I hear back from them, I'll get you in a squad car and have you on your way to him. Let's reconnect at two o'clock. I may be a little late. We're having supplies dropped into Odell this afternoon and I want to make sure that goes off without a hitch. If I'm delayed, I'll get word to you."

Barrett and O'Brien got up and left the room. On the way down the hall to the elevators O'Brien said, "We've got her. I do believe you are the best damn

270

liar I've ever met in my entire life!" Dan Barrett didn't answer, but there was a smile his face.

After they left the room, Gretchen Vincent got up, smoothed her wrinkled skirt and walked to windows overlooking Grant Park. She stared at the mass of people on Michigan Avenue heading to offices before she turned to watch Barrett and O'Brien disappear down the long, sterile hallway. "Well they were way easier than I thought they'd be," she thought

Chapter XIX

John Coffin walked slowly into Colonel Vincent's office. "How ya feeling today, Chief?"

"Well, I've been better, thought a few hours in here would help the fog in my brain dissipate. Have some stiffness, but Drew's got the pain under control. Just can't stand lying in that bed a second longer. Did you get the law out of Dodge?"

"Yeah, we handcuffed him to Petracha. He wasn't none too happy about it, but we drove him over to Grandmother's house to remind him how appreciated his cooperation was going to be. He and the shooter go way back. No doubt there was some kind of communication between the two of them. I noticed Ralph and his wife way up front Saturday morning while you were speaking. In any event, I think it's a good call. He doesn't know why he was moved out and the feds will have to expend some time trying to figure it out themselves. You were right, better to remove him."

"Barrett wanted to talk to you. Said he wanted to discuss the details of the supply drop. Told him anything he needed to discuss about that he could discuss with me. He didn't take it very well and told me to have you contact him as soon as you were up to it. Told him you were up to it, you just didn't have anything to say to him unless he was calling to capitulate to our demands. He hung up."

"Well, that wasn't very nice of him was it?" Vincent flashed a grin. "But if you think he's in a foul mood now, wait another two or three weeks when the town cupboards run dry. Then the heat's really gonna turn up on the whole gang of them.

"Yeah, and I supposed he was just fishing for information about your

272

status. After all, they don't really know squat. You could be lying on a slab in Miller's meat locker for all they know."

"Or all they wish," Vincent smiled weakly again.

"Speaking of food shortages, today Sergeant Major Manning is arranging for the federal re-supply drop. He's handling the logistics. Food distribution will be done through the Miller's IGA. He's got two guys working on that. Captain Drew will oversee the pharmaceuticals; they're to be distributed through the field clinic. Four choppers will begin the drop at 1600 hours; should be done by 1640 or so. Tom's having them lay it down in the soybean fields just east of town. And we've got serious eyes on it, Sir"

"Good, don't use a large contingent of our men to lug that stuff back to town. Round up some of the locals and have them give a hand. Let them use their own trucks if they want. They'll be glad to drive them. Plus, if they're working alongside our guys, the personal contact may build some bridges, which couldn't hurt. What's new in town? Pick up any scuttlebutt? Morale?"

"Not terribly important but, yes Mary Odell wants to know if you were up for a dinner delivery yet. I told her I didn't think so and that most of your diet is still soft. She insists she could conjure up some homemade soup that would speed your mending and cheer you up. Seemed like a pretty genuine offer, Sir. What shall I tell her?"

Vincent thought for a moment.

"Tell her thank you very much. Ask her if she has a date Friday night and if not, might I come by instead? I should be able to get around without walking like a drunken sailor by then. Get my dress blues ready so that we make her feel important."

"Are you sure you're going to be up to that Sir?"

273

"No, but it's important, John. I'll make it if I have to crawl. It's not often one is invited to dine with the President's grandmother."

"Yes, Sir, I'll let her know right away. Is there anything else you need or that I can get for you before I make rounds?"

"No but schedule a cadre meeting for tomorrow at 0630 hours here in the office. I think it's important the noncoms and men to see that their commander is not lying in bed drooling on himself while they man the front lines. I'll want to hear the usual reports from each of the units at that time. How are the boys looking, John?"

"Our guys? Our guys are just fine Colonel, though there was a little groaning about sending Petracha out. I've addressed that best I could. I think they understood. We look to be ok."

"We're all on schedule with everything else? My nephew is doing well?"

"Yes Sir. All is as according to plan."

"Great John, great. And thank you for stepping up this last week. I appreciate your help and want you to know you handled that press interview as well as anyone could. They have to be running in circles right now. The recipe is good. All we have to do now is add time. Time and unfortunately a little blood. That's always the key to freedom. . . a little blood."

"And as far as Barrett is concerned let him stew. We've got another week or two before the town starts to feel any pain. And it's gonna take some pain to make that boy in Washington get off his butt. He hasn't felt any yet. All he's felt so far is . . . the fear of pain."

"Okay, let me know when the drop's completed and the perimeter is locked down again. And make doubly sure the men keep their eyes peeled for any funny stuff?"

"You bet Colonel. We've had two briefings about it already. We're wired pretty tight, there won't be any shenanigans."

# # # # #

At four thirty that afternoon, Dan Barrett and Mike O'Brien were walking down a long hallway to the conference room on the forty third floor. Gretchen Vincent was waiting for them in a more pleasant room.

"What did Petracha have to say?" O'Brien asked.

"The same thing over and over again. "Captain Mario Petracha, RA51-592-258". All we've got out of him so far is his name, rank and an army serial number. Sounds like a freaking robot. A few days of isolation will give him some time to think. And when he comes to the realization that Vincent just sentenced him to life in a federal prison or worse, that will loosen his tongue, but I think it's going to take some time. We're retrieving his military file now. We'll have that here by the end of the day, the rest should be here no later than Friday."

"Sheriff Odell is in debriefing still. He hasn't got much to tell us that we don't already know. He's been under lock and key since invasion morning. Kept him locked up in family room of the mayor's house. First real light of day he's seen since the town square meeting. The only significant thing that we've found out is that Dick Ralph told him some time ago when the Scotts-town/Brady Bill passed he was never giving up that old M1 from Korea. He caught Ralph's eye that morning and nodded to him. Ralph took it upon himself from there."

"That's all we have so far but our guys are working with him to see what else he may have. I still can't believe they served him up like that. I mean, why would you do that? And Petracha, is he a Trojan horse? It's just too neat

275

we're not seeing something."

"What we know is that Petracha's a first-rate soldier. Came out of Dix advanced infantry training, did the Screaming Eagles thing, combat decorations, a purple heart or three and honorable retirement four years ago. He's been in and out of the Mideast more times than a Saudi Prince in the last few years and that has me nervous. That's the reason the CIA is trying to justify involvement. They're desperate to get their mugs on the six o'clock news and the President is getting a lot of heat from several cabinet members to let them into the mix. And if they get their mugs mixed up in this God knows what the hell they might pull. What we've got to do is fill in what Petracha's been up to, who he's been up to it with and what his role is if it's beyond the obvious."

"Where's he from?" O'Brien asked.

"Southwest side, a Chicago boy. Comes outta little Italy. His parents run a neighborhood meatball joint on Cicero near 63rd street. You know where Santucci's used to be?"

"Yeah, I used to run to that neighborhood all the time. It was just four blocks down from a great jazz joint, The Dry Martini. Ever been there?"

"No, not a jazz guy, but I wish I could pay it a visit right now!" Barrett meant it as he reached for and opened the door to the conference room where he saw a much more relaxed and refreshed Gretchen Vincent. She'd been shown to a more comfortable "apartment", allowed to freshen up. New clothes that were brought to her perked her up as much as the large salad and sandwich she'd ordered. She looked almost calm, friendly, Barrett thought when he and O'Brien entered the room.

"Mrs. Vincent! You look like you've had a chance to catch your breath. Are you feeling better?"

276

"Yes, I am, Agent Barrett. Thank you for the refreshments and change of clothes. Not sure how you got my sizes right, not sure I want to know," she smiled briefly. "Look, I still don't know how I can be of help. The only thing I intend to do is be honest and get this over with as soon as possible so I can visit my husband. Have you any word yet from Washington?"

"No Ma'am, we haven't, but the President is a busy man. There are a million things going on aside from this matter. We know it's important to you. And I have nothing more important on my agenda, but we just have to be patient. I am supposed to join a conference call later today or this evening. They haven't given me a specific time yet, but I'll let you know when I do."

"I have had updates from Loyola and Colonel Vincent is resting comfortably. The doctors seem to feel he's improving. I don't know but as close as you two have been perhaps he can feel you're close by. I promise we'll get you there as soon as I'm given the authorization to do so."

"Well, thank you in advance then."

"Is there anything you need, another drink or something to nibble on as we go along?"

"No, no, I think I'm just fine."

"Shall we begin then?"

"You may proceed with your questions."

"Thank you. Now, just so you know Captain O'Brien here may also join in and ask a few questions as we go along. Mike and I have worked many cases together. We're comfortable with each other. I trust him and his judgement. I've asked him to be here because of that and because of his knowledge of Odell. He's also an insurance policy. He'll make sure that neither you nor I miss something important, any little thing that may bring our mutual goal to fruition. Are you comfortable with that?"

"Yes, I suppose. Whatever it takes to bring this matter to an end; to avoid any more bloodshed. To bring all those involved back home to their families."

"Great," looking at O'Brien, "we're all on the same page. Let's see, where shall we begin? So that I know more about you than I've read in your dossier, tell me in your own words about your hometown, your family, school friends, things like that."

"What? You want me to go back to my childhood?" She smiled, "What on earth does ancient history have to do with anything?"

"Well, let's start there and move forward. It helps us get to know you, gives us an idea about the accuracy of your memory. Could help us with not having to verify or double verify later facts. All of us have different levels of accurate recall when it comes to long term memory. Believe me it's important. Little things may seem unimportant, but when we move up the timeline in retrospect they may be very important. It's part of the process, trust me."

"You're stretching it a bit, Agent Barrett, but I'll do the best I can without boring you or myself to death. I'm thinking about something I read a while back. About going home, about even visiting it in your own mind. Remembering it like it was when you were just a little girl growing up in a very protected home, a privileged home really. The author said, "you can't go back home. It's there, but it's not yours anymore. It belongs to other people, a different generation. After all these years you're only a part of home's history. Home has become a garden for the next generations' memories and you. . . you are just a weed." I'm feeling like a weed right now . . . a big weed."

"Understandable, but let's remove that feeling. Go ahead and tell us about your family." All Barrett really wanted to get out of this first session with her

278

was to determine the level of truth she was going to be dishing out. He was going to have every detail checked and double checked to make sure when she said something the following day that he could give it a truthfulness grade. Right now, though, he wanted to see how much she was willing to share and more importantly how much she was not willing to share.

Gretchen Vincent then began a long account of her personal family history. She described her moderately privileged upbringing in Saratoga Springs, New York, a large home on the lake with guest house, boats and other water toys. Her physician dad practiced cardiology in a resort town known for its history of luxury and opulence. The famous racetrack there and the natural springs thought to have medicinal qualities in the late 1800's, brought tourist from as far as Europe. Many of New York's wealthiest kept palatial estates about town and the beautiful rural pasture lands surrounding it.

For a long time, dad's practice was the only cardiology group within fifty miles. A long trip to Albany would be necessary to find another group nearly as qualified or as highly regarded. Mom was very active in the community, all the right clubs, all the right places. Brothers and sisters all excelled at sports and academics. Her two older brothers, both physicians, specialize in plastic surgery. Each made Los Angeles home with their growing families. Her dad was sorely disappointed they'd opted for the cash and fast lifestyle of the west coast instead of going into his specialty and perpetuating his practice. But he got over it eventually and did his best not to bring it up at family reunions at least after those first few years.

Her youngest sister lived in Virginia and was the executive assistant to the Docent at Monticello, Thomas Jefferson's home. That caught Barrett's and O'Brien's attention. She was someone who'd need examination, someone to

279

focus a background check on particularly.

Three hours into the family history and a plethora of mundane follow-up questions to mundane information Barrett hit her with it.

"Gretchen, by any chance do you know a guy by the name of Mario Petracha?"

"Oh God, yes!" She laughed. "Do I know Mario Petracha? Surely Agent Barrett you know he was the best man at our wedding. If the Colonel has a best friend, Mario would be it!" She smiled. And then almost immediately her face changed. "Now why would you be asking me about that old loaf? Don't tell me he's with Madison? Of course, he is. Where the hell else would he be?"

All Barrett and O'Brien could do was stare at her.

# # # # #

Glen Garnet had been trapped in God forsaken Odell for the last nearly two weeks. He wasn't happy that he'd been rounded up before he could make it back to the farm. He knew his elderly parents would be worried sick about him. But he reasoned, they'd soon figure out that he'd not made it back from the town store that Saturday morning. And as long as his name didn't show up on any casualty list published by somebody, he was relatively sure his dad would put the facts together and figure out that his son was held in town and wasn't gonna do anything stupid. So, here he sat in the basement family room of the owner of Tractor Supply cutting red warning flag cloth into strips. When he'd used up all the material, he gathered the strips up, put them into a small white plastic trash bag and headed out the back door.

When Glen had been hustled out of Pat's bed that first Saturday morning after the town square address, he headed to Tractor supply, he wasn't alone.

Several other young men and boys had been hanging around the front of the store as well as those in the store with him. Most of the young bucks had stuck together as the townsfolk were allowed to go their ways; Garnet and the young farming bucks were, after all, different than the people who worked in town. Always had been. Attend a Future Farmers of America meeting at school or go to the fall dance sponsored by them and you'd note the dominance of the farm teens. You probably weren't going to see Gus Morgan, his girlfriend nor many of their friends in attendance. There wasn't any animosity really, it was just a cultural thing. Town folks were headed off to college and other parts of the world unknown and the FFA boys and girls were, well married already . . . married to the land like their ancestors had been. So, Glen and his band of 18 friends who were either in the store with parents or hanging around outside seemed to just naturally gravitate towards one another . . . and stay that way.

Whatever he may have been perceived to be, Glen was a leader, a born leader and so he assumed that role with these young folks. They immediately looked to him and his decisions. And besides, he was already a bit of a folk hero with the young people ever since that day he dumped that load of manure into Ralph Kletzial Mustang. Yes, Glen Garnet was a guy to be looked up to, admired really.

So, leader Garnet called a covert meeting, a social evening in disguise, a dance. But the real purpose of the meeting was to discuss 'the plan'. The plan had been entirely Glen's brainchild and he was quite proud of it. He knew it was good because the moment he unleashed it on the others, it had nearly unanimous acceptance. There were only two fellows who weren't sure of the wisdom behind it, but they were soon swayed by the court of peer opinion. Now, all they had to do was to pick the time and place to roll it out. And

Wednesday evening at a dance sponsored by the auxiliary women of St. Paul's Church that's just what they did.

Mary Duke Odell was there serving chocolate chip cookies to the young people. Refreshments were also provided by St. Paul auxiliary ladies and the other two churches in town. Even, believe it or not, a donation arrived from Millers IGA. That is to say from the boys of the ARM. Large quantities of lemonade, Gatorade and soda arrived in the back of a jeep. Two young soldiers, Glen noted not much older than himself, unloaded the cases and brought them to the table compliments of Colonel Vincent. Glen watched them attentively along with his "boys" who were staged around the social hall dance floor.

Whenever a young woman wanted to dance with a young man she simply walked over to him and tied one of those red bandanas provided by Garnet around the neck of a young man. No one refused it, whether he wanted to dance with that particular gal or not. The evening curfew was suspended or rather extended 'til midnight to accommodate the festivities. Extra patrols were on alert but kept a low profile. At midnight everyone headed to their various homes, even the temporary guest homes.

# # # # #

After he composed himself, and it took all the strength he had to not let an outward expression give away anything that he didn't want revealed, Barrett asked, "well it's not just a name we've run across during our intel gathering. We noted here of course as you pointed out that the Col and Captain Petracha were in several campaigns together and they seemed to be close associates professionally and personally. What can you tell us about him?'

"I could tell you I wouldn't want to be caught on the wrong side of him in a

282

dark alley. He's as gentle as a dove around those he cares about, but a viper to those who cross him. He's fiercely loyal to Madison. They've been in campaigns all over the world together. South America, Asia, Mideast, places I don't know how to pronounce, places I don't even know how to spell, places I'm not sure I could locate on a globe and places I don't even know about, I'm sure. All I can tell you about Mario is that he's like family. I'm surprised that some evenings I don't roll over to find him between Madison and me." A slight smile showed itself. "God help the fellow that tries to harm the Colonel if Mario Petracha is around." Then a serious, concerned expression replaced the smile. "Is he alright? Please tell me nothing's happened to him?"

"He's fine Mrs. Vincent. In fact, would you be surprised to learn that he's right here in the federal building just a few floors down from where you're sitting? If you like, after we are finished here, I'll take you down to see him. I can't promise to let you speak with him yet, but you'll be able to verify that I'm not lying to you. Not about him, nor your husband. Now, let's get back to your family's history with Captain Petracha?"

"Well, Madison met Mario right out of West Point. I think Mario was his first Top Sergeant and when Madison made Captain, he requested Mario to be his Top and he was until he attended officer candidate school and received his own bars. Now, he wasn't always with Madison, but whenever he could pull enough strings Mario was at his side."

"He retired just a few years ago. His wife died from injuries sustained in the Twin Towers. She was just on a touristy trip to New York you know. One of those damned strokes of bad fortune. We all almost died when we heard she'd been trapped in the second tower when it collapsed. They never found her body. Mario seemed to melt into oblivion after that. The Col did everything he could to talk him out of it, but it just took the fire out of him. He was often a guest at our home for months on end. He'd hike up into the mountains, go fishing or canoeing on the river for hours on end. Most days were ended with a smile after dinner, some small talk and retiring to his room for a ballgame on television or some reading. On weekends he'd disappear. Then after nearly two years of staying with us he just up and disappeared. Madison said sometimes a man just needs time."

I'd guess the last time I saw him was the day he left our home about two years ago. Packed his bags, gave me one of his giant bear hugs and a kiss, told me he loved us and rode off into the sunset. After that, we got occasional postcards from all over the world. Never any pictures, but postcards. Sometimes they had odd messages, like Merry Christmas right after Easter, but that was just Mario goofing around. Madison always thought his messages were so funny. Cute, but not knee-slapping, funny for sure."

Barrett was just about to delve into this new treasure chest of information when a young aid walked into the room and whispered loud enough for Gretchen Vincent to hear.

"Sir, your call from Washington will be coming through in about twenty minutes. Director Cellini wishes to talk with you before it begins."

"Okay, I'll be right there." The aid left the room. "Mrs. Vincent, I don't know if you overheard that or not, but I've got to beat it upstairs pronto. This may be the green light we've been waiting for. Will you please excuse us? I'll have you escorted back to your quarters and as soon as I'm done with the call I'll have them drag you back down here. There's no keeping this call waiting, if you know what I mean."

"You're right. We surely don't want to keep that call waiting. Please let me

284

know what they've said as soon as you are able to."

"I promise you. As soon as I speak with the President and get his permission to take you out to the hospital, I'll let you know. Fact is, I'll personally ride with you to visit the Colonel." He smiled at her. "We're making progress. We're making progress. As soon as we wrap your interview up we'll be able to get ahead of the game. I can just feel it. Something you know, something small may be the key. And maybe between us three reasonable thinkers we can bring this thing to a conclusion sooner rather than later."

"Look, Mrs. Vincent, I know a woman like you must hold sway over her husband. You may be the only person on earth who can reason with him. We need you, he needs you and as corny as this may sound to you. . . our country needs you."

"Well, I don't know that anyone holds sway over Madison Vincent once his mind is made up, including yours truly, but I agree with you. Whatever is going on doesn't make sense to me; there has to be another way. I don't know how Madison got caught up in this. He's always been so patriotic, so level-headed. I'll be delighted to talk to him to see what can be done. Just get me to him, Agent Barrett. Just get me to him."

"Of course. Now get some rest and I'll get back to you as soon as I can. Most likely it'll be an hour or two. We'll rush it along as soon as possible."

The two men left the conference room, as soon as they were out of earshot Barrett turned to O'Brien.

"There's no Washington call, but I'd like to have another crack at her when she's not so refreshed. Let's meet with her in Judge Schenk's chambers at 1:30 a.m. Want her to have a good look at the inside of a federal courtroom on the way. She could be spending years in one alongside her husband, so she

285

may want to familiarize herself with it."

"Perhaps I'll dangle the Petracha carrot in front of her. I may even let her have a few moments with him. That little tidbit about him being an old family friend really ratchets up the deal a bit doesn't it? I want another shot at him as soon as I can. Let's see how he reacts when I tell him his best buddy handed him over with a note pinned to the back of his shirt that accuses him of murder. Yeah, let's drop that bomb on him and see if his tongue will loosen beyond his serial number."

"You go ahead and get some rest 'til then."

"You got it." O'Brien responded, "I'm gonna make a call to the district and to the wife. I'll meet you in your office around 1:00 a.m. if that's good with you? If you need me prior to that, let me know."

"Nope we're good. Try to get a little shut eye as well. That's what I'm needing to do. I'm not sure I still have a family anymore. It been so long since I've seen them!" Barrett said with a slight grin.

# # # # #

Very early the next morning Barrett sat in Judge Schenk's chair with his elbows propped on the large mahogany desk. "Yes, the President is aware of your desire to see Colonel Vincent and he's not unsympathetic to the Colonel's need to have you at his bedside as soon as possible either. But he's reluctant to grant that permission today."

"We know how important it is to you. So, here's what I've done, and I hope you know it's a huge move for me to make. His chief of staff, Mr. Halderman, is here in Chicago. He's doing some public relations things with the local media. He's also very close to the President and is giving him the eye on the ground that the President feels he needs. Halderman is a man he knows he

286

can trust."

"As soon as we got off the phone with the President, I pressed upon Halderman the need for you to have some time alone with the Colonel even, even if it's just fifteen minutes, a short visit. I think I convinced him to convince the President that you are an innocent victim here and that you needn't be punished because of the misdeeds of others. Halderman is leaving Midway Airport for Washington in three hours, so about five o'clock this morning. He's promised me he would do whatever was necessary to twist the President's arm for you. I know he'll keep his word. He's one of the few people back there one can count on once he gives his word." Barrett took a deep breath. "I know you're disappointed."

"You're damn right I'm disappointed. I'm being jerked around here Agent Barrett. I'm not stupid. I can't think of one reason to sit here with you another second without counsel and speak another single word to you!" She said angrily.

"I know, I know. But let's not take steps backwards. It will help no one. Not me, not you, not the Colonel, no one will benefit from that, no one. Listen, why do you think I hauled you down here at this ungodly hour? For my health? I'm dead beat tired. I'm sure you are, and I know Mike is. Look, you want to see your husband. We want to see our wives, our children our own beds. We're not gonna get to do that until this thing is under control. That's why you're here. I kept my word to you. I didn't let you swing in the wind until later in the day, so we could get some shut eye. If I didn't care, you'd still be sitting in your quarters until I had gotten eight hours of much needed sleep. O'Brien here hasn't seen his family in weeks. Only a phone call a few days ago right Mike?

"That's about it."

"Perhaps you're telling the truth, Agent Barrett, but this seems like hollow promises to me, stalling to me."

"Let's see if I can add some meat to them then. What would you say if I told you I've arranged for you to spend some time with Mario Petracha later this morning? I've done that, I'll make it if it will add any credibility to my promises to you. I can make that happen this morning, right after he's been fed and had a chance to shower, shave and all that. Deal?"

"Mario Petracha *is not* my husband Agent Barrett," she responded emphatically.

"I know, I'm trying my best," Mrs. Vincent, "to negotiate this web of craziness. I'm doing what I can to present a course that will eventually bring about a reunion with your husband."

"I'm not sure it's a course I can live with, a deal." She responded and drew in a deep breath. "I do believe if I smoked, I'd love to have a cigarette right now." Then silence reigned in the conference room for several minutes after she swirled about in her chair and stared at the plaques on the judge's wall. O'Brien and Barrett stared at one another and at the back of her head for what seemed like eternity. From experience each one of them knew it was best to let the silence stay in the room until she broke it. Whomever speaks first loses.

"I would like to see Mario. I think it would help calm my nerves right now. Let me think about it. I need a minute," she turned around towards them in her chair and played with a button on her sweater.

She sat quietly in one of the three leather chairs that sat across from Judge Schenk's desk. She listened to O'Brien breathing. He looked tired, worn out.

288

He was a bit older than Barrett, but at this time of day, in the low lights of the judge's inner sanctum he looked much older. Both men showed signs of the stress they were under. And God, she thought, if they look that bad, I wonder how bad I'm looking.

"Ok Agent Barrett," she said after several more minutes though it seemed like five days to the two men. "Where do we go from here? What do we need to talk about at this time of day that can't wait until all of us have had some rest and can think more clearly?"

"Perhaps you're right. What's the sense of carrying on at this hour when we're all so beat. I just wanted to sit with you to deliver the President's answer face to face." Looking to O'Brien for his agreement which came immediately Barrett rose from his chair. "But just humor me about one thing first. This Petracha is an enigma. Read a little about him before the President's call. He's such a patriot! His military record is impeccable. He's never disobeyed an order in his life. I just can't get my head around a man like him . . . for that matter, a man like your husband getting so far off the straight and narrow. I'm speaking about line of command things you know?"

"Well, all of this is a bit of a mystery to me as well, Agent Barrett. I don't know what I can say about Mario Petracha that would be of any use to you. We've known him forever like I told you this afternoon. He's been a lovely, wonderful family friend."

Before she could say another word, an ashen faced Agent Randolph blasted through Judge Schenk's door with a note in her hand. She ignored everyone in the room except Barrett. She immediately thrust a note into Barrett's hands then stood waiting for instructions.

As Barrett read the note both O'Brien and Gretchen could see the blood

289

drain from his face. And then it turned the most crimson red either one of them had ever seen.

"Oh my, God! What in Sam bloody hell was that moron thinking?"

# # # # #

Colonel Vincent was fast asleep when the blast from the first explosion nearly shook him out of his bed. Suddenly, his room was as bright as the noon day sun. He scrambled for his glasses and radio just as Captain Tom Manning burst into his room.

"Colonel, we've got boogeymen inside the wire!"

Colonel Vincent knew that meant they were under attack and the enemy was somewhere, at some point, inside the perimeter.

"Where are they, Tom?"

"We've got a large blast in the drop zone east of town. Not sure if it was dropped and overlooked from this afternoon or if it was shot in here from a distance. There are boots on the ground though, 'cause we're taking small arms fire from that area as well."

"Is that moron in Washington insane? Make sure Hauser keeps the town on lockdown so we don't take any civilian casualties. Let everyone know, and I mean everyone, that once we've alerted the entire town to stay inside out of the way that anyone found outside will be considered a legitimate target and we've issued orders to shoot to kill. I'll be in the command room in two minutes."

"Sir yes, Sir. We're returning fire, and in the process of locking the town down. Claymores are going off on the east side as well. Rodriguez says it doesn't appear to be a large number of them based on the amount of fire, maybe squad size. It's madness, we're gonna chop them to heck. Meet you in the command center."

Manning then rushed out of the room and downstairs to the main floor of the VFW building where the ARM Command Center had been established.

Minutes later, Vincent walked into the room which was a buzz with radio traffic. Manning was pacing back and forth listening to reports. As soon as he saw Vincent, he turned the room over to him. "Sir, Lt. Rodriguez's directing return fire at an unknown number of intruders. His current estimate is that there's about thirty or so troops on the ground. Initially, they laid down a fairly significant amount of small arms fire. It's tapering off a bit now. We've given them an angry answer. The blast, probably some C4 came from the soy fields, just southeast of where the supply drop took place this afternoon. It looks as though that's a diversionary move though."

Vincent knew it was a serious incursion, but he also knew his men would crush an assault force that small. Fifteen minutes later a report of small arms fire on the southern perimeter was taken from Larry Schnecksnider.

The radio cracked. "We got an attempt at penetration on the line Captain Manning."

"This is Colonel Vincent, Captain. Give us an assessment as soon as possible."

"Yes, Sir, right now it's so small it seems they can't be serious. We're laying down some heavy return fire, not meeting with much resistance."

Vincent was puzzled because someone was mounting an assault that had absolutely no chance of victory. Who in heck would be nuts enough to attempt whatever they were up to? The VFW building was located on the southwest side of town. Was someone trying to take him out? The crack of inbound small arms fire was steady though not overwhelming. Each time there was a

291

burst loud voluminous response could be heard from ARM forces.

"Colonel, this is Rodriguez. We've sent out flanking squads and have got these boys just about surrounded. We can pinch them off and eliminate them or wait until daybreaks and take some prisoners. What do you want me to do?"

"Pin 'em down. Keep their heads down until dawn so we can get a real good look at 'em. As soon as day breaks, I want you to let loose with everything you have. Aim high. I wanna scare dirty drawers on em. They need to see what their commander sent them in to. As soon as they get a whiff of what they're really up against demand surrender from them. If they refuse, eliminate them. Let their blood be on Washington's hands. But if I have my preference, I'd like a few prisoners to exchange if we need them and to interrogate to find out what the hell's up."

"Yes Sir. You got it," Rodriguez replied.

Colonel Vincent turned to the radio call of Schnecksnider.

"Colonel, some of these civilian buildings are taking sporadic fire. I've gotta shut these guys down pronto."

"Get it over with Captain. Shut em down now."

As soon as that order was given a deafening level of small arms, automatic weapons fire, claymore mines and mortar rounds jarred the early morning air just south of Odell.

The initial explosion forty minutes earlier followed by automatic weapons and small arms fire drew some of the curious townspeople out of their homes. Others knew better and sought refuge in the basements of their homes. Captain Paul Hauser and his men drove through the streets of Odell warning everyone to move back into their homes. This was not a drill. Live rounds were flying about sometimes chipping off huge chunks of wood and paint from buildings

292

on the south and east sides of town. Odell was under attack by the government? A few cries demanding the stoppage of violence followed some people in doors, but most just wanted to get the hell out of harms-way. The loudspeakers barked orders to get inside their home. People were cautioned to lie prone on the floor and to hide behind furniture or to seek below ground level cover where possible.

Another twenty minutes was all it took for Rodriguez's men to stop incoming fire. Only an occasional, random pop of a weapon could be heard. But all that did was to let him know there were still live bodies out there hunkered down well enough to avoid night vision scopes. Several bodies could be seen lying in the darkness of the field, at least ten that his men could count. Initially the incoming fire had been insanely furious. It was as if the enemy didn't even know its target or if they did, they had bad intel and the fire had no real direction or purpose to it. Unfortunately for them, whoever they were, they'd suffered the consequences of mixing it up with seasoned combat vets. Rodriguez couldn't help but think how stupid it was to yank on the tail of a tiger. Firefight? He had a hard time calling it that, it was more like a suicide mission.

He reported to Vincent.

"Colonel, we've got it under control here. Won't be able to do a body count 'til morning as we're still taking some sporadic fire. But its calmed way down. They've taken several casualties. There's no movement at all now. We'll clean 'em up at daylight. I'll bring you prisoners or bodies, Sir, whatever they choose."

"Good job Captain but keep an eye out for the insertion of possible reinforcements. Captain Schnecksnider is dealing with probing of the southern perimeter. If anything spooks you, shoot first then get back on the horn to me."

"Yes, Sir," his radio clicked off. In between bursts of the automatic weapon from the phone tower, claymore mines once again exploded along a fifty-yard wide line two hundred meters south of town. The gas station was a large ball of fire. Unfortunately for the intruders, it lit up the newly plowed fields they were trying to hide in. No matter how low to the ground they clung for cover, there was really no cover there. There were only shallow rows of black dirt to hide in.

It didn't take Schnecksnider long to determine that the strength of the intruders was no more than twenty men. Several were dead, the rest in shock. Daylight would demand their surrender. They'd have no choice.

# # # # #

Colonel Vincent sat in his office leaving the clean up to John Coffin. The hours left before dawn seemed to him like days. Staring back and forth from his cups of coffee to the clock on the wall over the giant fireplace at the opposite end of the room didn't speed the sun's course in the eastern sky at all. He hadn't heard the report of any weapons for two hours when his radio cracked.

"Colonel, it's all quiet. We're about to send men out to have a look. As far as we can tell there's no fight left in these guys," John Coffin said.

"Roger that, get me a fire fight report as soon as possible. Did we sustain any casualties?"

"No, Sir, none to speak of. Williams in Alpha took a bit of shrapnel, some brick fragments coming off one of the old warehouses on the southside. Captain Drew's already got him patched up and back to his tent. Other than that, there's nothing to report."

"Alright, keep me posted. I want a full report ASAP." The Colonel responded.

The lull now left him more time to contemplate the motive behind the confrontation. Rodriguez was right. This wasn't a legitimate firefight. What kind of moron sends in a platoon-sized outfit to challenge a battalion-sized combat group. And then lets them go in there outgunned. Certainly, by now the Feds had to know, more than generally speaking, the arms strength of his group. Satellite imaging can read name tags these days. He knew that, and they must know that he know. There was no need to go to extraordinary measures to conceal weaponry. It was what it was. They weren't getting into town unless his men let them in, or they decided to exterminate his men and all the townspeople with them. And he knew that wasn't going to happen. This was a catastrophically stupid move. No military man could be behind it. This was a politician's move. That's what it was. That's what it had to be. And if it was, whoever that idiot was, he should be tried for murder, because that's just what it was sending those men in like that.

Only in the most dire, emergent combat scenarios would a military man ever consider such a move. The thought of it sickened him. They had to be brave men to have followed those orders or they had to be ignorant about the "enemy!" Vincent was sad about that. Occasionally, only occasionally he thought about enemy casualties. They had families and loved ones, wives, husbands, children. Most all of them just wanted to be home taking care of their families, living their lives. Nobody wants to die for his or her country. Soldiers, for the most part, die for their comrades, a fact he learned a long time ago. But the Colonel was a warrior and warriors are not privileged to have such thoughts. Warriors, fight wars. And like one politician recently said, "they knock things down, they kill people." That's what warriors do.

Tom Manning had, had a busy night as well. Aside from running messages around the command center, he'd been to all four perimeters gathering firsthand intel. Live rounds whizzed by his head on several occasions bringing to the forefront of his mind the seriousness of the cause in which he was engaged. It was dead serious he thought. On the way back to the command center that morning as the sun was starting to rise over the eastern soy bean fields, he couldn't help but remember a quote he'd read in college attributed to Benjamin Franklin, "There is nothing quite as exhilarating as being shot at without result!" He wasn't sure if the quote of author was accurate, but he was damned sure the sentiment was.

It was odd. He often thought as a combat infantryman, that he felt safer on the battlefield engaged in combat, a weapon in his hand, lives in his hands, than he felt at some rear command headquarters far removed from the action. It was better to be out there with the tracers flying about than it was to be in an office wondering when and if they would reach him there. Maybe catch him with his pants down sitting on some toilet, God forbid!

He stuck his head into Vincent's office and said "Sir, you doing okay? Anything I can get for you?"

"Top, these dang antibiotics are tearing my G.I. system up. Can you get me something from the clinic to settle this down? And it's about daylight. Is Captain Coffin here yet?"

"No, Sir, but I can get in touch with him if you like. He was headed over to check the recon results with Captains Rodriguez and Schnecksnider. He's been gone a while so I'm sure he'll be back momentarily. If you like I can get a hold of him and hustle him up?"

"No, Top. He's doing exactly what I asked him to do. Let's let him do his job. I'm just anxious sitting here, I guess. Get me some anti-acids and when you get back stick around for a bit 'til John gets back. That is unless you have something that needs your attention this morning."

"There's always something that needs the Top's attention," he grinned. "But I'd also like to be around when Captain Coffin comes in to report."

"You're always welcome for report Top. Thank you." Sergeant Major Manning headed for the door and injected. "You know Colonel that Coffin is as anal as they got!"

"Yes, I do, Top. That's why he's my exec," the Colonel smiled and then added "And that's why you're my Top. Now get out of here and get me some meds."

Three-hundred years later, or so it seemed to Vincent, John Coffin knocked on the Colonel's door and walked in, Sergeant Major Manning in tow. Coming to a swift attention with smart crisp salutes Coffin said, "Colonel I've completed rounds and am prepared to report, Sir."

"At ease, gentlemen. Let's move around to the conference table. Top, do you have something for me?"

"Yes Sir, right here, but Captain Drew said to take this stuff with something to eat, so I've got the mess crew cooking up something easy for you."

"Thanks, Top. Please gentlemen, have a seat and bring me up to speed."

"I've taken reports from both Captains Rodriguez and Schnecksnider. Captain Stewart's men are still on full alert, but we had no incursions from our northern perimeters. We're keeping an eye on it though, Sir. I've also walked the fields with each of the units. Squads have been sent out for body count and recovery and for the securing of prisoners. We've also got Captain Hauser who is conducting a house-to-house, building-to-building search to make sure no one slipped through the lines and has taken up a position inside the town

297

limits. We'll double check enemy troop numbers once we have a chance to interrogate prisoners, Sir."

"Here's what we know so far. There were two groups of twenty men, one group on the eastern perimeter and one on the southern. They are not infantrymen, Sir. According to one prisoner who's already chirping like a mockingbird, they are members of an elite SWAT unit of the Illinois State Police. They were here to secure the freedom of Mary Odell. It appears that this whole fiasco was centered around rescuing 'key' citizens of the town. This is about as stupid as it gets, Colonel."

"Of the forty men engaged with our troops twenty-seven of them were killed in action, five are critically wounded and eight are being held in the sheriff's jail for processing."

"My God! It's hard to believe anyone could be so friggin stupid!"

"We're in the process of loading up the wounded troopers for transport to Dwight for medivac on to local hospitals."

Coffin and Manning could see the anger rising in Vincent's face.

"No, we're not doing that. You get hold of Barrett and tell him he can come get them. I want it done right in front of the American public. When I give the order, I want those men taken on stretchers over to the interstate and laid in a row on the highway. Barrett can come pick them up, by God. I ought to insist he come do it personally. In fact, that's a great idea. Demand that Barrett come get them personally, or he can watch them lie there on the road and die while we broadcast it all over the internet."

"Before we bring him inside our perimeter, I want two things done. Have Robert Cox get in touch with the boys and girls from One America News and let them know they can have a twenty-minute flyover to cover the pickup.

298

Secondly, I want you to have the men load up the KIA's and carry them back out to the fields and place them where they found them, as best they can remember. Tell Cox to let One America know they may include the fields in their twenty-minute flyover photo shoot. If . . . and this is a big if, Captain Coffin. Have him tell them if One America does a good job, they'll get an exclusive on our press conference Friday night. If they don't, we'll go back to our friends at Fox and see if they're interested."

"When Barrett comes to get those wounded, I want the highway lined with six Jeeps carrying M60s on each side of the road. Let him ride the gauntlet and see what we're all about just in case those boys lying on the ground don't convince him. I think it will. Any questions?"

"No, Sir."

The Colonel sat quietly for a few seconds before he spoke again. The anger he'd struggled for years to control left his face. His voice softened; his eyes narrowed. One could see his brain kick into gear.

"Ever hear of a boy by the name of Harvey McKay?"

"Can't say as I have, Colonel," Coffin answered.

"I have." Piped up Manning. "He's some kind of business guru out of Wisconsin, I think."

"Close but no cigar," a surprised Vincent responded. "Minnesota. At least he made his bones there. Ran one of the biggest envelope factories in the country there and also helped produce one of the Olympic games we hosted. Not sure which one though. Well, old Harvey wrote a book called 'How to Swim With The Sharks Without Being Eaten Alive.' Read it a long time ago when I was a pup. Lots of people management advice; helped me through my growing years of being an army officer. One of the things he said in this book

299

that I've use a million times is this. . . "When you are weak make them think you are strong. When you are strong, make them think you are weak." 'Til now, 'til this very moment I've been an advocate of that advice. But we are strong and we're gonna show them jackasses in Washington just how strong."

"Now to these prisoners for a moment. First, Captain Coffin I want you to personally supervise the interviews of these prisoners; see that they're treated appropriately, right?"

"Of course, Sir."

"We want a tally of body count, prisoners and original troop strength. Make sure we've got the numbers right and that no lone wolf is running around out there risking injury to our men or the townspeople."

"I'm dying to know who the idiot is that put this debacle into motion. We need as much intel from this as we can get. You know what to look for Captain. I don't know why I'm micro- managing you on this assignment. Not like this is the first rodeo for either of us is it? Look, just make it plain to these guys that none of them are going home. Many of them may never see their families again . . . ever . . . if we don't get complete and total cooperation from them".

"Lastly, that I can think of, after One America gets photos of those dead troopers, gather the bodies up and store them in the local funeral home. If that fills up, we'll put them in the meat locker in the local IGA. We'll have plenty of time before we have to bury them here if we must."

"And then as far as Barrett and the media are concerned we won't release names 'til we're damn good 'n ready. For that to happen, we need to see some movement in the satisfaction of our demands. Until then, they can sweat and endure the grilling of relatives. They'll just have to guess who's alive and who's in the cooler."

"Okay then if we're about done here, let's get to it."

"Well, Sir, we're not quite done. You were on such a roll I didn't want to interrupt you."

"What gives?"

"No other way to put this, Sir. You won't be needing your dress blues for dinner Friday night. Mary Odell caught an incoming, darn near blew her head clean off. Not much left of her. Guards found her seconds after it happened. She must have wandered out onto her back porch to see what all the ruckus was about."

Vincent did not respond to Coffin's announcement right away. He picked up a pen and began reading through some papers laying on his desk.

"Is there any word on my wife?"

"Nothing additional Sir. They still have her locked away tighter than a drum."

"That will be all gentlemen."

Chapter XX

Frank Halderman and Dan Barrett had a car wreck on the forty third floor of the federal building. Halderman's flight turned around and headed back to Chicago the instant he heard about the debacle that had taken place in Odell. He had only the scantiest details and was rushing to a video conference with Governor Hinshaw, members of his staff and the state police when he ran flush into Barrett in the hallway just around the corner from the conference room.

Dan Barrett had seen some crazy things in his professional life, riots in Detroit, Chicago, St. Louis, a couple assassination attempts on local governmental officials, all kinds of crazy white collar, political crimes and all the madness that surrounds those behaviors. But he'd never seen the equal of utter stupidity by a public official. His heart was beating so hard, his mouth was so dry, his blood pressure had to be so high, he wasn't sure he'd be able to articulate a word when he got into the room.

"Do you know any more than your aid shared with me earlier?" Halderman asked.

"No, sir. You have all the information I have. I guess we're gonna learn what the heck the thinking was when we walk through those doors."

"Well, just let me do the talking. I've been on the phone with the President and he's madder than hell. Let's see what Hinshaw has to say for himself."

Barrett didn't respond. He just pushed through the double doors to the conference room ahead of Halderman. As soon as he entered the room, he saw Peter Hinshaw on a large screen sitting behind his gubernatorial desk fidgeting with several pages of paper and a number two lead pencil. A few aids and administrative assistants sat out of sight of cameras against the wall behind the south end of the conference room table. The only other person in the room was Mike O'Brien who was in full dress uniform as one would expect since he was being addressed by the boss.

"Thank you, Michael," were the only words Barrett caught when the doors swung open. Halderman never had a chance. The beet-red-faced field agent in charge lost it. For the first time in his career he didn't really give a damn about his career. "You!" pointing at the governor. "You, are you the crazy, incompetent, stupid SOB who sent 40 tactical officers into a firefight with a battalion-sized group of heavily armed combat veterans? Are you nuts? I swear to God, if you were here, I'd slap the living hell out of you, you incompetent moron! And I don't care if you have an army of state police protecting you . . ."

Before he could utter another word, Halderman had him by the elbow and was directing him to a chair at the conference table. He knew he had to rein him in but very much enjoyed hearing him say what he himself wanted to say.

"Let's all calm down a bit here, Agent Barrett. This isn't going to get us anywhere. What's done is done no matter how bad it might or might not be, the proverbial horse is out of the barn." Barrett couldn't take his eyes off the Governor who, doing his best to remain calm, had a very pronounced bead of sweat forming on his upper lip.

"Mr. Halderman," the governor purposely omitted Barrett from the salutation. "Mr. Halderman, I assure you that our intentions were the very best . . ."

But before he could even finish the sentence, he was cut off by Halderman.

"Governor Hinshaw, I've just gotten off the phone with the President of the United States of America. Quite frankly, I've never seen him so angry. It doesn't matter that you are a member of his party or not. It doesn't matter that

303

you delivered this state for both his nomination and eventual election. What matters to him now and the most is the safety and well-being of the citizens of Odell. And while it is unspoken, can't be spoken, you and I know how much that old woman means to him. I pray to God for your sake that not one civilian casualty arose out of this mess, especially her. I can assure you that your political life will be as dead as a rock if any citizen blood spilled. Now, governor, tell us what happened and why. And do it as briefly as possible. I have a plane waiting on the tarmac at Midway."

"Mr. Halderman as I was about to say before I was. . . you rudely interrupted me, we felt that things were moving just a little too slow in Odell. I'd consulted with senior advisors and the head of the state police department. I was increasingly concerned for the well-being of the President's grandmother especially since she is an older, frailer woman. No one could give me any assurances as to her well-being, safety. Our thinking was if we could create a minor distraction on one of the borders of town, we could get a tactical unit in there and get her out of there. It would be a moral victory; the President's grandmother would be safe and at the same time we'd show the country that these thugs couldn't just come into a town and terrorize it with impunity."

"And frankly, Mr. Halderman, I want to remind you that I am the governor of the State of Illinois. This is Illinois ground we're standing on and I resent being called to task like this, like a schoolboy. And all for an honest attempt to rescue members of the President's family. Your boys," looking directly at Dan Barrett, "have done nothing, absolutely nothing, to bring this matter to a close. It's been nearly two weeks and all that's been done, Mr. Halderman, is talk, talk to these traitors! Talk's cheap and the lives of some three-thousand citizens of my state are at risk! From the reports I'm receiving Mr. Barrett hasn't even been able to get productive dialogue in place."

"You're damn right we sent some men in. We didn't sit on our asses waiting for some break in the clouds to deliver those innocent people. And if we have to take that approach with the press and the public, that's just what we'll do. At least we did something. God knows what atrocities are going on in that town. We're not just going to sit by and watch valued members of our citizenry brutalized by some rabid-back-hills, red-neck militia faction and not do anything about it."

This time it was Halderman's turn to show emotion, but he didn't, at least not very much. "You know Peter" intentionally leaving off the title. "You and I have known each other for a very long time. We've been through some up and down political times and have always managed to come out alive. We're survivors, aren't we? So, because we have that long friendly history, I'm going to do you a big favor."

"I'm going to share something with you. We're going to handle the spin on this. We're going to get you out of your own way on this one. Since my installation as chief of staff and over the course of the last few years of this administration, we've made a few friends. We're going to call in more than a considerable number of chips to cover up this gross stupidity of yours. And you, my friend are going to sit there, keep your mouth shut until you're told to open it and do what you're told. If you don't, the entire weight of the presidency is going to come pounding down upon your head so hard your nose will be poking out your wingtips. Don't you dare make a peep until you hear from someone from my staff later today."

"Did you honestly think sending in state troopers against eight hundred soldiers was going to do anything aside from getting them killed? Did you honestly think about anything except putting some coins in your political bank? In all my years in politics I've never seen anything more ill-advised or poorly carried out. Frankly, Peter, it borders on murder. Let me repeat that. It . . . borders on murder. I'd hate to go on record saying that about a valued and beloved fellow servant of the people of the great state of Illinois, but by God I will, and you will win the title of the biggest fool of our generation. Let's face it Peter, three, count em, three of the last four Illinois governors are either doing time or did time in the big house. Do you catch my drift?"

The conference continued for another twenty-three minutes wherein the pathetic details of the failed rescue attempt were laid out for Halderman and Barrett. The governor finally ended his report Halderman issued a curt "Thank you, Governor Hinshaw. We'll be in touch. In the meantime, please wait for instructions from the White House."

With that he clicked the off button on the video conference and turned to Barrett. Taking him by the elbow, he ushered him out of the room. The two walked down the long hall in silence before Halderman finally stopped dead in the middle an empty hallway. He turned towards the FBI agent.

"Poor performance, Agent Barrett. Very poor performance. For a man in charge of an entire field office, a horrible performance. You are supposed to have better control of yourself and your emotions. For now, and hopefully forever we'll let this rest here between you and me. And, of course, the few unfortunates who were in the room, whom I dearly hope to keep their mouths shut. But both you and I know no one is going to pass up the opportunity to share the fact that a lowly FBI field office employee just called the governor of the state a stupid ass! It was a very poor performance indeed."

"Yes, sir, it was." Barrett wasn't going to argue. It hadn't been one of his better moments. There would be no "but" in that sentence. It ended there.

Halderman hesitated waiting for the "but" to come and was glad when it didn't. Taking Barrett by the arm once again he said, "Come with me, I'm going to share something with you. You mustn't forget the moral of this story but forget who the principals are."

"You bet."

"Many years ago, when the President and I worked for a large law firm in Chicago we were asked to attend a wake for one of the managing partners' parent. When I arrived, I noticed the President in a corner with some fellow I'd never met before and I'd met just about all his friends and family by then. Old buddies for sure, maybe someone from college or law school. They were engaged in an animated conversation for a wake I thought. Others had been drawn to the two old friends it seemed. The give and take went on for some time. Finally, as I was about to leave the President approached me and asked if I could give him a lift back to the office. The wake had taken place all the way out on the other side of DeKalb, so we had a bit of a ride back downtown. We talked about this and that and then I remembered the guy at the wake. I said, 'Hey who was that guy you were speaking to in the corner?' He responded with something like 'What guy, who are you talking about?' I said. "The buddy. The guy you had your arm around and were joking with. Maybe a friend from college?' And then the President gave me my first glimpse of his future political prowess."

His eyes steeled, and he said to me "I hate that scum bag. One of the most despicable fellows I've ever met. He works in our Springfield office. Has tried to derail me several times. I think mostly because we come from the same part of the state and he's stuck there with all the political hacks and we're in the big city office where all the action happens. I've had the pleasure of having to tolerate him and his antics for years. I've finally gotten through to the executive committee members and next month it's going to be my absolute pleasure to fire his butt."

"He'd floored me; I thought for sure they were old buddies and told him so. His eyes softened a bit and he put his hand on my shoulder and said to me. 'Frank, Frank. Never and I mean never let your enemies know they're your enemies, . . . and there was this long pause. Until your knife is being drawn across their throat.' "

"The difference between you and me in that conference room Agent Barrett is that you don't have a knife. Not yet anyway. I do so I drew mine. Understand?"

"Sir understood, yes." Barrett answered quietly.

A few more hallways negotiated found them at the doors to private elevators surrounded by security agents for Halderman.

A still embarrassed Barrett said, "So I need to do a full report to Cellini. But first I need to get in touch with Vincent in Odell and explain that this was a renegade situation. See what I can do to salvage credibility with him and to see how he responds. What do you want me to do or not do other than that?"

"We're gonna have to determine the casualty numbers and identifications as soon as possible. How can I deal with the press until we know more detail? We've had no additional word from the men inserted, is that correct?"

"Right. Communications ended right around the time your plane was taking off. At that time all we knew was that those men were pinned down taking heavy fire and that there were indeed some casualties, but no count. We don't know if any of Vincent's men were injured or killed. Heck, we don't even

308

know if Vincent himself is still alive. Coffin has been keeping me away from him. He may not have survived the assassination attempt, or he may be in worse condition than they're letting on. I need to get to him somehow."

"Oh, something tells me, Agent Barrett, that you're gonna hear from him alright. And it's not going to be an invitation to the prom. Reach out, but don't be surprised if he decides to set the timeline for contact. Keep me posted, of course. Listen, Barrott, you have a direct line to the President here. Use it judiciously."

"Yes sir. The first thing I'm going to do is head down state with staff to the police district headquarters and make sure our people are in control there. Then I'm going to get Vincent on the line somehow come hell or high water."

I guess before I even do that, I've got a personal call to make. We've got his wife locked up downstairs. We'll need to bring her up to speed with limited information. We've also got one of his company commanders downstairs and it seems that Vincent and this guy have professional and family history. I may take her down to see him for a little face time and see what it jars loose. Especially with news that there's been fire on the ground. After that's taken care of I'll try to be on a chopper within the next two hours and I'll have you and Director Cellini briefed before noon."

"And Sheriff Odell? Has he been moved someplace quiet and secure? We'd like to put word out that he's been released. Make it look like its progress on our part. We'll need to keep details close to the vest."

"Yes sir. He's tucked away in a very comfortable suburban home. We're working on telecom with the President this afternoon if you think that will be okay."

"Set it up. I'll see to it that it goes through."

"You keep Director Cellini on top of things, but don't forget to keep me at the top side of that loop, you understand?" Nobody knows anything including your boss before I do."

"You bet. I'll personally see to it."

"Before you head downstate I'll have my guys in contact with the Governor's office to make sure you don't run into flack with local law enforcement. By the time you get there they'll know you chewed Hinshaw's butt. These men aren't stupid. They will have sorted out what kind of orders sent their buddies into that trap. Knowing you stuck up for them should sit well with them and bode well for you. Anything else I need to know before I head back out to Midway?"

"No, sir."

"Good luck to you, Agent Barrett." A very serious looking Halderman disappeared behind closing elevator doors.

As soon as the doors closed, Dan Barrett was on his cell to the office a few floors below. Once on the phone with his administrative assistant Judy Kaye he said, "is Mike O'Brien around?"

"Oh yes sir. He's been here since your conference call with the governor. Do you want to speak to him?"

"No, not right now. I'll be there in just a few moments. What I would like you to do is to get one of Swanson's rookies and one of Lovemoney's on the horn and have them meet me at my office in five minutes."

"You bet, sir. I'll have them here waiting for you."

Ten minutes later, Dan Barrett arrived at his office. In the outer office Kaye sat at her desk shuffling a pile of papers while two obviously anxious, young agents paced back and forth. Mike O'Brien sat in one of the four guest chairs sipping on a cup of coffee. As soon as Barrett entered the area, he addressed the two agents. "Gentlemen, how are you this morning?"

"Fine, sir, fine," both men replied.

"Are you up for a very important assignment this morning?"

"You bet," they looked at one another.

"Great," he smiled then looked directly at Mike O'Brien. "Get this piece of crap out of my office. Personally, escort him to his home. If he resists in any way, cuff him, detain him. And if he requests an attorney, let him call one when you get permission from me to do so. Any questions?"

"No sir," both men responded in unison.

Before Mike O'Brien could pull the cup away from his lips and say a word, Barrett proceeded into his office and slammed the door.

'I do have a knife, maybe it's just a pocketknife, but by God, it's a knife," he thought.

# # # # #

Gretchen Vincent paced her two-room apartment prison all night long. She knew something was horribly wrong the way Barrett flew out of chambers hours earlier. O'Brien didn't seem to know squat or at least if he did, he wasn't sharing it with her. It was 7:36 a.m. when a young agent knocked on her door and asked her if she could accompany him to Mr. Barrett's office. She grabbed her sweater and followed the young man to elevators that took her up three floors to a hallway leads to glass doors labeled "Federal Bureau of Investigation." Through an outer lobby and down a series of hallways Mrs. Vincent soon found herself in front of Barrett's administrative assistant.

"He'll be right with you. Won't you have a seat? Is there anything I can get for you, perhaps a cup of coffee?"

311

Though Mrs. Vincent's mouth was dry, her stomach wouldn't let her touch anything heavier than water.

"Just a bottle of water if you don't mind," she responded.

Dan Barrett opened his office door and invited her into his office.

"Have a seat, Mrs. Vincent," he said.

She sat in a buttoned leather chair placed near a twin at the front of his desk. Even during the angst that surrounded the moment she couldn't help but wonder about the provenance of the two antiques.

"I'm afraid there's been an adverse development in Odell Ma'am. It seems that your husband's colleagues opened fire on some state police officers, and several may have been injured or killed. We just don't know the extent of any casualties at this time. I'm going to have to leave for Odell in a short time. I wish I could tell you more, but for now that's all that I know. I'm sharing this with you because this obviously is going to throw a kink into my efforts to get you an audience with the Colonel. I haven't heard from Washington yet, but Mr. Halderman did call and leave a message for me that the President is more than upset. That's not going to help our cause."

"Are you saying that I will not be able to see Madison today?" her jaw line tightened.

"Yes Ma'am. I wish things were different. I wish I could just drive you out there now, but I've my orders and I can't do that. What I am prepared to do is to give you something else until we can get a better handle on the situation."

"What do you think you could offer to pacify me, Agent Barrett?"

"I'm not trying to pacify you. I'm trying to show good faith here Mrs. Vincent. I told you I'd get you out to see your husband as soon as I could. I didn't count on some nut jobs in Odell shooting up the countryside wounding, maybe

312

even killing state police officers. Surely you can see how that complicates things. What I'm trying to do here is to show good faith. I'm wanting to break your isolation as much as I am allowed just to show you that I'm a man of my word."

"I don't believe any men under the command of my husband, present or not, would open fire on police officers without some kind of provocation. I've been around the military for an awful long time, Agent Barrett. I suspect I have a great deal more experience and insight into the workings even psyche of those troops than you can imagine."

Barrett caught that slip of the tongue.

"Really? What is it that you think you know about those boys in Odell that I don't know Mrs. Vincent?"

"Well, I must know something, or you wouldn't take all this time and trouble to trample all over my constitutional rights by keeping me from counsel, sir!" she snipped back at him.

"If you want to regress, we can do that, Mrs. Vincent. Military combatants are not entitled to counsel the same way a civilian is. And right now, you're classified an enemy combatant until I can get that title erased from before you name. Is that what you want me to do? Isn't that what we're trying to accomplish, a meeting of minds to bring an end to this madness?"

"Perhaps, but we're not making much progress from my perspective. All I keep hearing is promises and excuses."

"Which brings me to why you're sitting in that chair. Listen, I could put you in a dungeon and forget all about you until I'm damned good and ready. I could forget you even exist. Hell, if I wanted to Mrs. Vincent . . . from the moment you stepped into that limo in front of your house a few days back . . . I

313

could make you not exist."

Barrett's eyes narrowed as he focused on her. He didn't want to erase progress, but he wanted her to know how grave her situation was.

"But that's not why we're here. We're here to demonstrate mutual trust. I will keep my word to you. I can't control circumstances outside of my sphere of influence. Here's what I'm prepared to do."

"Downstairs in one of the vacant courtrooms two guards are waiting with Mario Petracha. You told me he was a dear family friend; someone you have a long history with. Someone one you can trust amidst all this craziness. He's not your husband, but he's as close a person as I can get you to for now. Maybe you can talk with him. Maybe you can find out who's backing this, what's needed to shut it down, to help meet demands. Whatever information you can glean from him may help us reach a mutual goal and bring you closer to meeting Madison."

It was the first time Barrett used Colonel Vincent's first name. It wasn't lost on Gretchen Vincent.

"Let me see. You want me to go downstairs and pump one of your 'prisoners of war' and see what information I can get out of him for you since I suppose, knowing Mario, he's given you nothing but name, rank and serial number?"

"You are absolutely right on all counts Mrs. Vincent. Anything that I can do to get the information needed to bring this thing to a full conclusion, I will do. If that means getting Petracha to talk to you, so be it. If that means you do that so that we can finally get you out to a severely wounded husband who needs you at his side, you bet your butt that's right. Now, do you want to see him or not? I've got a pretty big headache on my hands and I need to leave for downstate within the hour. I can give you forty-five-minutes with him or you can head back up to your quarters until I return, what's it gonna be?"

Mrs. Vincent stared at him for nearly a full minute.

"You take me to him personally."

What the general public doesn't know is that every federal courtroom is bugged. They are covered from top to bottom, front to back with extremely sensitive microphones to record every conversation held in them. There really isn't any such thing as a "private or privileged" conversation in that environ-ment. The reason for such an elaborate eavesdropping system is to catch Louie the Nose conspiring with Vinny the Chin to do harm to a judge or prosecutor or witness. And to put an end to their plan before it is acted upon. The general public isn't aware of this, but of course, Gretchen Vincent and Mario Petracha were.

Petracha, dressed in bright orange prison garb, cuffed to a chain that went around his waist and down to two ankle braces, sat in the very back row of a line of general public benches. The three burly federal marshals that ushered him to the courtroom set him there purposely, so he and Gretchen Vincent would be as close to a microphone as they could get them.

"Mario!" She called out to him as soon as she made entry through the front of the court room. She ran to him, the three big marshals keeping an eye on her would have normally never allowed her to get anywhere near him. But they had exception orders this time.

When she reached him, she fell onto his big burly frame wrapping her arms around his neck and burying her face in his neck. He could do nothing in re-sponse except to whisper, "it's okay, it's all okay."

"Have you been harmed?" she asked. "How did you get here? Have you

315

heard anything about Madison?"

"I'm fine, I'm fine. I'll tell you all about it in a few minutes. I've not seen the Colonel since he was shot. I've not had any contact or news since Coffin sent me out of camp. Turned me over to the damn Feds like I was a traitor or something."

"Why on earth would he have done such a thing. It's not possible. You've been like brothers for what, twenty years?"

"I don't know why. You'll have to ask him one day. I'd sure like to get my hands around his neck right now. How long have you been here? Are you doing okay? Have you spoken to anyone on the outside? I need to get a message out to family."

"No, no I've spoken with no one. I've been here for days, maybe a week, or weeks. I've completely lost track of time. I may have been drugged. I'm not sure. I've only really seen daylight a few times. They tell me they have Madison in a hospital nearby and that if I cooperate, they'll bring me to him."

"Well Coffin might have sent him out as well. He had a pretty nasty wound, I won't B.S. you. But you know him. It would take a rocket to bring that bull down. Maybe they do have him. Maybe there wasn't enough medical to take care of him in camp. All I know is right after he was shot the assassin and his wife tried to attack me as we were clearing the house. I killed the shooter and when the wife attacked, I knocked her to the ground with the butt of my weapon. She was unconscious last I saw her. Next thing I know I'm in cuffs in front of Coffin for murdering some innocent civilian. I think he's always had it out for me, secretly. Never could figure that jackass out."

"What's next? I mean how on earth did you and Madison ever get mixed up in this? You know no one is more patriotic, loyal to this country than the

316

Colonel is. How could this happen? I've got so many questions I don't even know where to start."

"It's best not to. All you really need to know is how the Colonel is doing and how to get yourself out of here. The rest will all fall into place in due time. One way or another, successful or not the end game is not far off. What we have here is a real Mexican standoff, a circular firing squad. No one wants to pull the trigger. There has to be a negotiated settlement. All the other options are unfathomable."

"What do you mean?"

"Not only are there eight hundred plus combat veterans armed to the teeth in that burg, the entire town has been wired. If there's any attempted incursion into it, Boom! The entire place and everyone in it, including the President's grandmother will be blown to pieces. And get this, that crazy Coffin cuffed the President's cousin to me and dumped him out of there as well. He sent a bargaining chip as big as the Empire State Building out of Odell for free! I don't get it. He's always been more competent than that. I just don't know what the hell has gotten into him."

Whatever! When you look at the entire picture, I also don't know how the Feds end this by any other means than negotiations? There's no way to get into the place, trust me. The Colonel and his buddies have been planning this for years! I don't know the big picture you know, Gretchen. I'm just a damn warrior without a war to go to until I heard from the Colonel."

In another room not far away Barrett, listening to the conversation, sat up straight in his chair.

"He's never said a word about this to me, Mario," Gretchen said in as low a whisper as she could utter. It wasn't low enough to avoid the electronic

317

surveillance, but she knew that."

"No one could say anything to anyone Gretchen. It was as hush hush a thing as I've ever seen in all my career. But back to you. What's your counsel have to say. Have they charged you with anything? They must know by now that you haven't anything to do with this."

"No, no they don't. I don't have counsel They won't let me make a call, nothing. Nobody even knows I'm here. My family must be frantic. Oh God! What they must be thinking. Barrett, the clown in charge keeps hanging the 'enemy combatant' thing over my head, swearing he doesn't need to allow me access to counsel. Has even used a threat on my life if I don't cooperate with them! And here's the stupid thing about all this, I don't know crap! I have no idea what the hell information I could give them that would be of any benefit to anyone. And, if I did, guess what? I'd drop it on them in minute. If I could get to Madison, I would. Truth is I just don't have anything to give them, Mario. Nothing. What am I supposed to do?"

"Name, rank, serial number. That's what you're supposed to do. Think about it. Have they gotten you one step closer to seeing the Colonel? No! Not an inch. Promises, promises. Until you are in a hospital room talking to him, do not give them one iota of information no matter how trivial or seemingly mundane. Nada, you get that?"

"Yes, yes I do. I'm scared. I'm scared for me, for Madison, for you and all those boys in town. Their lives are ruined you know. They can never go home to their families ever again. Can any of us? Is this all worth it?"

"Yes, it is. I guess it is. I thought so going in. After being handed over to the wolves, I'm not sure anymore. I'm just gonna sit tight for now, play the cards I have until the picture gets a whole lot clearer for me. You, sweetheart,

318

you just do the same; sit tight, keep your lips sealed even if you don't have anything to tell these monkeys. The Colonel will survive. You'll see him again. It may take a while and you're gonna have to be strong and patient."

"Ok. I'll sit. But I'm not liking this. I'm not liking that no one told me squat. And now I find myself in this prison a million miles away from my home, my family and friends, my husband, my life. I'm not happy one-bit Captain Petracha do you understand me?" She'd pulled rank with a stern look.

"Yes Ma'am, I surely do."

Barrett only had time to listen in on their conversation for another twenty minutes. They engaged in small chat, strangely small chat he thought for friends who'd found themselves in the midst of treachery that had such potentially catastrophic consequences. How odd that there wasn't more weeping, wailing and gnashing of teeth. He expected more passion, desperation, questions. Something wasn't right.

Turning to Agent Lovemoney, "will you get the chopper ready? I'm going to go up to the office for a few things. Make sure the state police are ready to give me a full report and make sure whoever that is, it's not O'Brien. Clear?"

"You bet. I'll be heading down that way as soon as we get the kiddies back in their quarters and transcripts have been gone over. How long do you want me to let them at each other?"

"The more they talk the more there is to shoot at. Let them go until they run out of steam. Then break it up. And don't be nice about it."

When the elevator doors opened Judy Kaye was standing in front of them.

"Just about to come find you, boss. Your phone volume must be turned off again. Halderman's not even made it back to D.C. yet and he's on the phone again. Said to go get you. He sounds pretty annoyed. He's waiting on your

319

office phone."

"Okay, thanks Miss K. I'll speak with him then I'm off to Odell."

Barrett rushed into his office.

"Mr. Halderman, Dan Barrett here. We were monitoring Mrs. Vincent and Petracha's conversation. Apologies my assistant had difficulty reaching me downstairs. You know how these federal buildings operate."

"Agent Barrett, I've just finished speaking with the President and he feels we need to have a show of force, a counter visual if you will. He's tired of hearing how dug in, how well armed these thugs are and feels the public perception is that we're impotent to do anything about it."

"Well, right now that's about right, Mr. Halderman. We're going to make some progress. We're going to diffuse this thing, but in order to do that with a minimum of blood shed we need time."

"The President is already getting impatient and if we find out that any of those SWAT team members are casualties, he's going to be a very unhappy President. So, here's what he's decided. Director Cellini has been brought up to speed and concurs with the President wishes. President Odell wants the Illinois National Guard called out. He wants maximum media coverage and he wants it now today, this morning. He has been in touch with Hinshaw. We all know he's an idiot and not capable of managing his checkbook, but he's been schooled and is in line. Orders from the President will go directly to him through yours truly. The general in charge of course reports to him, but nothing and we mean nothing will be done unless you and I and the President agree. Do you understand that?"

"Yes, but. . ."

"No buts. You can speak when I'm done. The guard will take up positions well outside the perimeter established by Vincent. It is not our intent to engage or to incite. We merely want the public to see that their government is not standing idly by impotent to do anything. Americans expect a 'can do' response. We have to give them something to bite into and troop movement on the six o'clock news is a hell of a lot better than some reporter standing in a cornfield eighty miles away guessing what's taking place.

"Now, what are your thoughts, concerns. We want and appreciate your advice. Doesn't mean, by the way, that we're always going to agree or act on it, but there is a high level of respect that the President has for you personally. Director Cellini has spoken very highly of you to him."

"I'm not as concerned about the concept as I am about the timing, sir. How are these guys going to know this is just not an escalation or the preparation for the escalation of an already pathetically failed exercise that just ended? Aside from that, sir, we all know these things have political aspects to them. I want to be sensitive to that though I can't let it drive my handling of the matter. So, how does the general public not see this troop buildup as further support of a bungling governor? Surely at some point in time not distant from this moment the media is going to get on to what really happened this morning. And, if I might be so bold, perhaps the President should put some distance between himself and Hinshaw's debacle."

"Well you may not be so bold, Agent Barrett, but we appreciate the thought. I think what you're really saying is, 'as the field agent in charge of this mess I don't want my name to be connected with Hinshaw's stupidity. And since it's my face people see on the nightly news that's just what will happen once the talking heads start talking."

"Have to admit, the thought's crossed my mind, sir."

321

"We've got the spin on this, Agent Barrett. Don't forget, the President is from Illinois. We have a lot of media support there. The Star Tribune headlines this morning are "State Police Ambushed near Odell!" By the time the Associated Press and its affiliates pick up that story and blast it around the world, Vincent's crew will be painted black by so much media ink they won't know what hit them. So, we appreciate your *sensitivity*, but trust me, feel free to be insensitive. Do your job, we'll do ours."

"In the end Hinshaw may have done us a big favor with his bungling."

"Yes, but at what price, Mr. Halderman? I've got a bunch of police officers we haven't heard from in over two hours, men with families that may be in the gravest of danger if not already dead. Last communication from them indicated all hell was breaking loose in Odell."

"Don't think for a moment that we're not sensitive to the potential even possible loss of life here Agent Barrett. We understand collateral damage in our world and that's just what this is. Collateral damage. Don't forget for a second that the President has beloved family members and friends in that town. We're not going to do anything to jeopardize their safety if possible. However, we are charged by the Constitution of the United States and the American people to keep this country safe from terrorism foreign or domestic and that's just what the President intends to do."

"What the American public doesn't know and what I remind you of is that every single day of every year good guys die to make sure this country is safe; it's citizens are free from harm. They just don't get any headlines. They have heart attacks, car accidents, they get lost in some jungle or left behind some, border etc. We understand all too well the phrase "the greater good" so no sense in preaching to the choir. Back to the real issue here."

"The National Guard is going in. The general in charge will report directly to Governor Hinshaw who will not sneeze unless he has authority from the President. He has been so advised and has expressed his willingness to cooperate with anything that is asked of him.

The President wishes you to remain in charge of the issue on the ground in Odell . . . with a caveat."

"What's the caveat?"

"I'll get to that in a second. But first I want to share something with you about the governor's future role in this. I understand your trepidation."

"Years ago, I took a friend of mine fishing with me. After several minutes of silence, I turned around and asked him how he was doing. He responded by asking me how he looked. I told him he looked great. He smiled back at me and said 'Good, because I'd much rather look like I know what I'm doing, than know what I'm doing!' And that's exactly the understanding we have with Hinshaw. He's gonna stay in the back of the boat and look like he knows what he's doing. You'll have no problems with him. Got it?"

"You bet."

"Now, the caveat. I assume you are headed to District 6 as soon as we get off this call?"

"Yes. Lovemoney has the chopper ready as we speak."

"The President wants this order passed along to you. He expects you to speak with Colonel Vincent today. Not some underling, he doesn't care how you do it, what concessions you have to pretend to give, he wants that to happen today. He doesn't even care if you have to get into an open jeep and drive into Odell with a white flag sticking out of your ear. He wants that conversation to happen today. If it doesn't, you will be relieved of your duties and will

323

be transferred to the Anchorage office before the sun sets. He wants a verbal report from you by this evening, seven o'clock eastern time. Do you understand?"

"Yes, sir, we'll get it done."

"We know you will, Agent Barrett. We'll look forward to your report this evening."

As soon as the phone call ended Barrett called Agent Lovemoney.

"Charlie, you're coming with me. Meet me at the chopper pad in five minutes."

Chapter XXI

John Coffin would never barge unannounced into Vincent's office, but he did just that at precisely 0900 hours Thursday morning. "Colonel I think you might want to come have a look at this."

He didn't wait for a reply. Vincent arose from the couch where he'd been resting and followed Coffin out through the lobby of the building onto the front steps that overlooked the southwest section of the town square. There he witnessed a group of young people, red bandannas around their necks, perhaps twenty odd strong marching in formation down Wolf Street. They were led by a young man who appeared to be in his mid-twenties. He carried a blood-red flag and appeared to be the leader and the most intense of the group. Vincent assessed him as such the instant he saw him. On each side of the small group of young people and to the front and rear soldiers from ARM walked with weapons at port arms watching every move.

"What do ya make of this Captain," Vincent asked.

"Not really sure Sir, but I'm just thinking we don't need this right now whatever it is."

"My thoughts exactly, but let's see what they have to say."

As the group got closer to the front steps of the VFW headquarters the soldiers escorting them drew closer and the port arms lowered ever so slightly. The 'click' associated with the removal of safeties from their weapons sent a clear message. There weren't going to be any shenanigans or there would be heck to pay. When the group came to a stop at the bottom of the stairs, Glen Garnet handed the standard over to a young woman now standing at his side. He came to attention and offered the Colonel a sharp salute. Vincent did not return it.

"Good morning. Thank you for coming by. Is there something I can do for you?"

Vincent gave Garnet a hard-unfriendly stare. The morning had already been eventful enough. He wasn't in the mood for a grievance committee. Garnet accepted the slight and understood the reason for it. He'd listened to the firefight through the morning hours and decided that this was the perfect time to meet with the Colonel.

"Good morning Colonel Vincent. My name is Glen Garnet." Looking behind him at the assembled group, we're all from Odell or the farmlands surrounding it. We either live here in town or were on errands here when you and your troops came into town. We've listened to your cause. We've discussed what we feel are the arguments in favor and against you and your men being here. We've decided as a group of concerned Americans that there are no arguments against your presence that stand the test of time."

"Like you, we're fed up with a government that butts its nose too far into the private lives of its citizens and into the sovereign rights of individual states. We agree with you that it's time in the beginnings time for people to take a stand. We know that siding with you and your position will most probably brand us as traitors. That's what Captain Coffin said in his speech the other day. We're good with that. So, as unlikely and as unprepared a group as we are, we come to offer you our support in whatever way we might be of use to you."

Vincent was surprised but didn't want to show any emotion or commitment to the group until some vetting could take place. "Mr. Garnet, we are pleased to have your support. This morning has been an especially busy and difficult morning for us. As you know we came under fire from agents of the

326

government during the early morning hours. We are busy right now sorting all that out including a significant loss of life and wounded on the side of the invading force."

"What I'd like for you to do right now is to return to your homes until we have a better handle on things. I'd like for you to meet with Captain Cox first thing in the morning to see what it is that we might do to involve you further in our cause. I hope you can appreciate the fact that there is just too much on our agenda right at this moment to meet with you. But rest assured, we welcome your approach this morning and respect the bravery of every young person who has shown up this morning. God bless each of you. You are the reason we are here, you and your children and your grandchildren and generations to come."

Turning to Coffin Vincent said loud enough for all to hear "Captain make sure that each one of these young men and women who haven't had a chance to communicate with their family members have a chance to do so today. Also, ask our men to escort them over to the Dinner Bell and get them some food on our tab. Mr. Garnet here is going to need an appointment with Captain Cox. Will you arrange for that to take place in the morning and see if there's any room on my schedule to see him afterwards?"

"Yes Sir. I'll see that that's taken care of immediately."

Vincent, against his better judgement and to the heightened attention of the military escort, walked down the steps and stuck his hand out to Garnet for a handshake. Garnet's smile broadened as he took the Colonel's hand. Vincent then walked past him, though he wasn't sure he had all the strength he needed to and shook the hand of each of the young people who were present. He then spoke to them briefly.

327

"I'm not one hundred percent me yet," he announced. "But if I'm only ninety percent, you have my ninety percent completely. You are, my friends why I, my officers and men have given up our lives. You and millions like you. Thank you so much for coming this morning. You have no idea how much it means to us."

With that Vincent turned around and walked back up the steps and into the Headquarters building.

"Well, I'll be damned!" Coffin said.

"Yeah, get Captain Cox on this right away. Have him vet this kid, get name of all the ones who were with him this morning and check them out as well. If this is not a ruse, it has tons of media potential. Let's get to it. Maybe the worm is gonna turn today. Keep me posted. Cox is going to have his hands full but have him get some of his people on it right away. He may need to 'phone home' to get some of the intel. If he has to, tell him to go ahead. It may be that important."

"I'll get right on it Colonel. Is there anything else?"

"Yeah, let me know when you hear from Barrett."

# # # # #

By the time Dan Barrett's helicopter landed to the rear of District Six's building, the media was frothing at their mouths to learn more about the firefight that had taken place in Odell. The Tribune had run an early edition "Terrorists Ambush State Police". The numbers of casualties and missing in action were not available. Fighting still taking place at the time the article went to press. The unthinkable was happening. All-out war within the boundaries of the state who'd provided the President of all presidents, the defender of the union. And now this. He was being challenged again. Barrett just shook his

328

head when he saw the front- page story. "They're just making things worse. It happens every time these politicians get their hands in the stew. It just becomes a mess."

Walking into the district's war room, he was surprised to see his ex-associate Mike O'Brien standing in the middle of the room watching several monitors and men and women with headsets on. Barrett cast a disapproving glance at Lovemoney who could do nothing but shrug his shoulders.

"Agent Barrett, you might learn this morning that the Gods of the plans see things a bit differently than the Gods of the Cities," said O'Brien without taking his eyes off the monitors or even to make contact with the Federal Officer. He continued, "the governor insists I remain in charge of this district and that's just what I intend to do. Now, you have our full cooperation and I will see that whatever it is you need to diffuse this crisis you will have if we can get it. Like it or not, I'm your guy."

Barrett knew which battles to fight and which ones to avoid. There was one thing more important than this peeing contest. He needed to get to Vincent and this was the only way he was going to be able to. It was 10:30 a.m., time was slipping by.

"I need a report on casualties. I need to be brought up to speed. What do you know?"

His failure to even acknowledge the issue of the commander's presence intimated surrender on that issue so both men proceeded.

"We have nothing concrete. Some of the satellites have picked up what look to be bodies, but we can't tell if they 're theirs, ours or just people dug in. Nothing of real concrete value right now. All I can tell you for sure is that we have dead silence. We've sent messages to Vincent that have had no response.

329

We will attempt another call in fifteen minutes, but we're not optimistic that this attempt will be any different.

"Coffin seems to be the guy in charge, and he hasn't been very cooperative in the past and isn't being so now. Heck, we're not even sure Vincent survived that wounding he took last week. He may be deader than a door nail by now."

"Captain O'Brien, here's what I need. I need a vehicle, a driver and a white flag of some sort. As soon as you get Coffin on the line, I want you to tell him that I'm coming in. I'm coming down under a white flag to talk to Colonel Vincent and if they don't let me through, we're going to have a full, head-on assault and bring this friggin matter to an end right here and now, casualties be what they may. I'm going there unarmed to talk to him to see what we can do to resolve their grievances and I'm not returning until I get to speak to Vincent or the person in charge if that's not Vincent."

"I'm not sure, given this morning's fiasco they will let you in. I'm not sure it's a great idea to expose yourself like this. It's too much of a gamble."

"Captain O'Brien," Barrett said keeping the interaction formal, you said you'd get me what I need. What I don't need right now is your opinion. What I need is what I just asked for. Agent Lovemoney will remain here with you. All I want now is a vehicle, and a white flag . . . or something that can be made into a white flag. Can you handle that?"

"You bet, it's your call."

Twenty minutes later Dan Barrett sat in the rear seat of a black SUV with blue, red and white lights flashing. He stared out at the plowed black fields surrounding the rural district headquarters and wondered what could have brought his country to such a state, a state that compelled enough people to be so afraid that they refused to obey the law of the land, a position held by the vast majority of Americans that some weapons just weren't needed in the hands of the general populous. What was behind the drive of these men who had given up their lives, their liberty no matter how this ended? He just couldn't wrap his head around it all. As he sat staring, wondering there came a rap against his rear passenger side window. It was O'Brien.

"Coffin, says don't you dare start down that highway. If you do, they'll blow you to bits." Darrett opened his door and walked around the front of the vehicle to the driver's door. He opened it.

"Officer, would you please step out here for a minute?"

"Yes sir," the large officer responded after looking towards O'Brien. As soon as he was out of the vehicle, Barrett slid into the driver's seat.

"I can't allow you to take this ride with me, my friend, but I have to go and I'm going." Over the man's objection, Barrett eased the vehicle into gear and out of the parking area. He drove west towards interstate-I55 not all that far from where Officer Fred Ryelts became the first casualty of the insurrection.

Insurrection, terrorists, rebels, patriots, protest, he wasn't sure what terms should or could be used. These men were criminals pure and simple. He didn't care about their motives or their "cause". They'd broken a million laws already and people who broke laws were criminals. And his job was to catch them and turn them over to the justice system. The justice system, men and women better educated, then him would find the right words, the right labels to attach to them. All he had to concern himself with was catching them, shutting this thing down with a minimum loss of life and then, and then . . . go away someplace, far, far away.

What a funny thing to be thinking of at this time. He needed a vacation and he needed one with his little family and he needed it now. "Just stop it dammit, just stop, go home, behave yourselves. Don't you have families? Don't you want to go on vacations with them, too? What's the matter with you guys?" Barrett thought. He took the entrance ramp to Interstate 55 headed towards Odell, Illinois, twenty odd miles away.

He slowed his vehicle to twenty miles an hour. There would be no appearance of hostility. As he drove northward, he first heard the helicopters. For an instant he panicked thinking Hinshaw was up to yet another debacle. Rolling his window down, slowing even slower he stuck his head out the window and saw two news choppers from One America News heading straight for Odell. "Oh God!" He thought, "just what I don't need, a greedy producer sending employees to their death." A quick call to O'Brien settled him down. The "Terrorists" had given permission for the flyover. What were they up to?"

Back in District Six headquarters, Mike O'Brien's eyes bounced between satellite images and the news coverage/speculations surrounding the mornings "ambush." Something deep down in his gut twanged. He knew the headlines were outright lies and he didn't like it. There wasn't anything he could do about it, but he didn't like it.

# # # # #

"He's coming anyway Colonel."

"Good. I'd be very disappointed if he wasn't c'mon in. I want as many jeeps mounted with 60s as we have available lining each side of Prairie Street and the I-55 ramp. I want him to see what he's driving in to. You meet him at the exit and bring him straight here. As soon as he's in your vehicle blow that cop car to hell. He won't be needing it."

"Yes Sir."

"One more thing. I've an idea. Those kids that were here this morning.

Round em up. Distribute all the weapons captured this morning and give them to them. Do not, however give them ammo. Post them around the jail. Give them a little port-arms training. I just want 'em visible for a few hours, maybe 'til the end of the day. Get the leader on board. Explain the importance of visibility and the message we want him to help us send. Let me know how it goes. I think that's it."

Barrett cautiously drove up Interstate 55 until he came to the large crater blown into the highway two weeks ago. Squad cars still littered the highway. He wasn't sure his vehicle would make it off road around the barrier, but it did. Back on the highway and fifteen minutes later he slowed to a stop at the Interstate sign advising the exit for Odell, Illinois was just two miles ahead. He sat there looking at it for a few minutes hoping Vincent's men could see the white flag on top of his vehicle. Taking a deep breath, he eased the gear shift into drive and let his foot off the gas pedal. It became the longest two miles of his life, but he eventually reached the exit. As he turned off for Odell, he got a gander of a welcoming committee like he'd never seen. Eight jeeps with M60 machine guns mounted on them in a staggered line on each side of the street. A command jeep containing Captain Coffin sat just two hundred yards at the end of that gauntlet. Barrett turned off the overhead emergency lights and drove onto Prairie Street. His mouth dried as he looked to his left and right at young men with determined looks in their eyes staring down gun barrels at him. Just feet from Coffin's jeep he brought the SUV to a stop. He looked through the windshield at Coffin seeking permission to exit his vehicle. Though his heart was pounding a million beats per minute, he didn't want his adversary to see the outward evidence of the inner turmoil. He put on his best game face and when he received a nod from Coffin which seemed to carry with it permission to come forward he did just that. Coffin stepped from his vehicle. There were no exchanges of pleasantries.

"Agent Barrett I presume. Please have a seat in the rear of my jeep. Colonel Vincent is awaiting you."

With that Barrett got into the rear seat next to a young man brandishing an assault weapon. He knew these guys were well armed, but one had to see it up close to really appreciate it. And he'd been in a lot of tight situations but none like this. He just kept asking his brain to stop producing so much adrenalin. "Just slow down, just slow down and deep breaths when they aren't looking." It didn't work.

It was a short, quick ride into town. As the jeep carrying the three men rounded the corner of Prairie and Tremont a loud burst of gun fire could be heard. Initially it startled Barrett and he instinctively reached for a weapon that wasn't there. He didn't take it out of the SUV with him, it would have served no real purpose. If these guys wanted him dead, dead he'd be. Within a few seconds his brain wandered to identify what all the gun fire was about. It was the gauntlet of M60s making short work of what was left of his vehicle.

He'd noticed the streets were nearly deserted, but he wasn't given much time to see anything aside from some activity in the center square of town. Military men gathered about in a circle working, weapons laid on the ground off to the side by a stone monument. And then he was at the steps to the VFW, the headquarters of the ARM or whatever they were calling themselves. He went up the stairs and into a large reception area where several young men were sitting at computers and wearing headsets. It looked much like the counterbalance to O'Brien's lot just down the road he thought.

"Please wait here Agent Barrett. I will let Colonel Vincent know that you

334

have arrived."

"Yes, thank you Captain Coffin."

Barrett was glad his voice didn't crack. He waited for fifteen minutes before Coffin emerged from Vincent's office.

"You will surrender any weapons at this time Agent Barrett."

"I have none, you may check of course."

"Thank you, we will."

With a nod two military police types moved quickly to Barrett's side and began clearing him for any weapons, recording or video devices. After a thorough search, Coffin opened a large mahogany door and waived him into Vincent's office.

Colonel Vincent did not look up right away and when Barrett began to introduce himself, he was shushed by Coffin. He was made to stand there for what seemed like a very long time but was only a matter of seconds. Finally, Vincent looked up from his desk, but did not rise out of his seat.

"Colonel Vincent I am . . ." Barrett was interrupted mid-sentence.

"I know who you are, Agent Barrett. What are you doing here?"

"I came here to rectify an error of grand proportions, that being the incursion that occurred this morning. It was a lame unauthorized attempt on the part of Governor Hinshaw to liberate key townspeople including the President's grandmother. I have authorization from the highest offices in the nation to apologize for the effort and to assure you that no matter what you see or hear on the news those same offices have no intention of another episode of like kind."

"Come with me, Agent Barrett."

Vincent arose from his desk and walked past Barrett, through the lobby and out onto the front steps of the legion hall. From those steps the town square was visible and those young men mulling around only a few minutes ago were now standing at port arms in a double line directly in front of the statue of Abraham Lincoln. When Vincent raised his arm, the formation broke in two, opening like a swinging door. Barrett squinted in the morning sun to see what was taking place. Vincent walked down the stairs and towards the men in formation. Beyond them on the ground lay twenty-seven white sheets; blood had seeped through some of them. They lay very still, dead still. All the way to the right of that line of bodies a flag draped coffin rested on a funeral parlor's gurney.

"Agent Barrett, you needn't apologize to me or to my men. We are all combat veterans here. We understand the meaning of senseless casualties. You need to apologize to the wives and widows of those poor unfortunates who you sent here to be slaughtered. This is your deed and the deed of your 'Highest Offices' just as certainly as you each had pulled the triggers yourselves. And you see that last one there, the one with the flag draped over the casket? There lies one of the finest women I've ever met, a treasure of a woman. She was the third woman you've arranged to murder in the last two weeks. Her name, sir, is Mary Duke Odell. When you speak to the President tonight Agent Barrett, be sure to advise him that she was killed by incoming fire and we can prove it. Yes, perhaps one of those young men who lay here beside her shot the rounds that caught her square blowing her head nearly in half."

"Don't you dare apologize to me sir. You apologize to her, to them."

With that Vincent turned on his heels and marched back towards his office.

Barrett stared at the carnage before him. He didn't even try to beg his brain to stop the adrenalin. His knees buckled. His throat tightened, and a foul metallic taste filled his mouth. His tongue seemed to swell, filling his whole mouth so much so that all he could choke out was.

"My God, oh my god!"

Chapter XXII

Four hours later Mike O'Brien was filled with regret that he'd let Barrett drive off in that jeep. But then, what could he have done about it. He'd lost Barrett's confidence, his trust and there were no jurisdictional arguments that could be made to have prevented him from leaving. All he knew now was that he hadn't heard a word from him and the day was moving on.

The outside world had begun to polarize, those who believed the Tribunes' report and those who were yelling "False Flag." Over the course of the day, depending on which media outlet one monitored, and he was watching them all, each side of the equation was gaining supporters. He knew it wouldn't be long before the respective sides would take to the streets and then violence at some level was assured. He knew there was little or nothing he could do to prevent it.

Social media being what it was, caused him to fear that things could get real nasty in a very short period of time. It was more than he wanted to think about, but he had to. At least he had to worry about the local scene. He'd have to let the lying Feds deal with the larger mess they'd created by not telling the truth behind this morning's disastrous attempt at incursion. He shared his feelings with Agent Lovemoney and with his superiors. Some of them bubbled up the same concerns but they got the typical Washington response. "The potential ramifications of the day's events were already being considered by the federal government and "*they*" were "*on top of it*"

At 3:00 O'clock in the afternoon a young trooper approached O'Brien from one of the communication stations in the war room.

"Sir, there's a Captain John Coffin on the phone for you." O'Brien nearly bowled the man over in his effort to get to the phone.

338

"Captain Coffin, this is State Police District Commander Mike O'Brien."

"Commander O'Brien, I wish to advise you personally that Agent Barrett will not be home for dinner. Turn One America News on."

The phone went dead. O'Brien had every screen in the room tune to that media channel in time to hear the lead in "Breaking News."

"One America News has been in exclusive contact with the leadership of the American Revolutionary Militia, a heavily armed and apparently well-trained group of citizens who, as we all know, is now ensconced in the small, rural town of Odell, Illinois. The occupation of that community has been going on now for almost two weeks."

"We are advised by those leaders that in the early morning hours a contingent of the Illinois State Police under the direction of Governor Hinshaw of Illinois and with the complete cooperation of President Odell, initiated an assault on the town. During this ill-fated attempt, a significant numbers of law enforcement officers were wounded and several more were killed in action. Identification of those fatally wounded or injured have not been released by the ARM leadership yet. They also advise that the assault force numbered approximately forty tactical team members. All of those team members have been 'neutralized' according to ARM's public information officer Captain Robert Cox."

"In an interesting twist, ARM claims that the captured members are being guarded by volunteer members of the citizenry who call themselves the "Red Guard'. Obviously, we have been unable to verify that aspect of our report. There does however appear to be a civilian element to the personnel surrounding the local courthouse and jail. We were able to document this during a fly over the town authorized by ARM."

339

"One America News has also been promised that our reporters will be allowed into Odell once the current situation stabilizes. We have no timetable on that occurring and of course we will have to receive clearance from local, state and federal officials. We will keep you posted as that story develops."

"Our air-mobile reporters have been allowed a brief fly-over the town and surrounding fields to shoot film. We have reviewed the video and have sent copies to the appropriate governmental authorities for analysis and verification of what we think we're showing you. We warn our viewers that some of the footage may be disturbing in that some casualties can still be seen lying in the farm fields outside of Odell. Even so, we have severely edited what you are about to see in deference to the officers who may be involved and their families or friends."

O'Brien watched as fly-over film of the town revealed at least a dozen bodies strewn over the newly plowed fields adjacent to the southwest side of town. He lowered himself slowly into one of the conference room chairs as he watched. The battle, if it could be called that, took place no more than thirteen miles northwest of where he was standing, and he couldn't do a damn thing about it. He couldn't stop it, though he tried, and once it began he was impotent to do anything about it. He knew it would be a bloody disaster, but orders were orders and that was that. Now some of his dearest friends, men he'd trained, worked and risked his life with, good men had faced or were facing an unknown fate. His stomach turned as he watched the ninety seconds of video air. The beautiful female reporter's voice chimed back in again.

"Other sources advise us that the governor has called out the National Guard and that the guard is taking up defensive positions surrounding the town. We have field reporters on the way to the various locations we've been

340

told about and are hoping to have some response from the governor's office or from National Guard command. So far, all attempts to reach them have gone unanswered. We'll keep you advised as soon as new information develops. We'll now return to our normal broadcast for a few moments and then we'll return with several experts to analyze these most tragic developments. If new information becomes available, you can be sure that you'll hear it here first on One America News."

His worse fears confirmed; O'Brien's mind filled with worry for the families of those who might not be returning home this evening. He had some hope that there were more captured than killed or wounded but he was a realist and knew what those men were walking in to. He'd heard nothing of civilian casualties so that was an upside. Even if the attempt to rescue Grandmother Odell had failed, at least none of the townspeople have been hurt. And now, what about Barrett? What was up with him; hopefully something that could move this mess in the direction of peaceful discussions?

# # # # #

Barrett thought he'd seen a lot of nasty, shocking things over his twenty-six years as a peace officer, but nothing like this. How incongruous that phrase seemed to him as he was led away from the devastating scene . . . peace officer. Whoever came up with that moniker? He didn't deal with peace, chaos that's all he ever dealt with. Flushing out the rats, dragging them off to jail. Chaos, fifty shades of chaos. And now, here in the midst of all this madness, maybe fifty-one. He should be called a Chaos Officer.

Twenty-seven dead officers covered with white bed sheets, lying there on the cold hard ground in the morning sun was more than any good man could take. And sweet old Mary Odell, that great spirit now lying in a flag-draped

341

box, a glorious life brought to a brutal senseless end. She was not just the President's grandmother, she was the nation's Grandmother. The press devoured any story that came close to touching her. They and their audience just couldn't get enough of her. Three months never passed without some major national or international media outlet doing some kind of spread on her or one of her colorful ancestors. Now those twinkling, beautiful sky-blue eyes were closed forever, and she lay in that box with her hands folded across her lifeless body.

The last thing he recalled as he sat on the cot in that dark cold cell was Coffin asking military types to escort him to his quarters. It wasn't a loss of consciousness as much as it was an assassination of his senses and now here he was in some ramshackle, po dunk town, jail cell awaiting what?

He didn't have long to wait. As soon as Vincent was finished watching the One America News broadcast, he summoned him. The walk from the jail to the VFW on the southeast corner of town wasn't far. Barrett noticed now people lined up in a viewing line outside the local funeral home just down Prairie Street. He presumed that's where Mary Odell was now. The bodies of the slain police officers had been removed, but to what destination?

Young people with red bandanas tied around their left arms could be seen here and there walking about. A couple of them carried weapons, automatic weapons. They gave him the "hard look" when he passed by. Up the steps into the lobby of the VFW where Barrett was made to wait again for twenty minutes or so before he was awakened from deep thought by Coffin's voice.

"Agent Barrett you may come in and speak with Colonel Vincent now."

Barrett did the best he could to put on his tough guy face so as stoically as he could he marched into Vincent's office and waited for an invitation to

342

speak or to sit. This time Vincent rose from his chair when Barrett entered the room. But his gesture was short lived, and he sat back down never taking his eyes off of the FBI agent. When Barrett was comfortably seated in one of the two leather chairs that faced his desk Vincent rose once again and came out from behind his desk and sat next to him.

"Captain Coffin," Vincent said. "Will you please have a seat behind my desk. Stay with us for a few moments. I'm going to need your assistance while I speak with Agent Barrett here."

"Yes Colonel."

Coffin then walked around and sat in the Colonel's chair. He looked and felt uncomfortable doing so. The only other time he'd done that was the few days the Colonel was flat on his back from his wounds.

"Agent Barrett, when you first entered my office a few hours ago you began to introduce yourself. I rudely interrupted you. Perhaps the hour of combat was still a little too fresh in my mind. The point is, however, that introduction though a formality which I should have accepted was wholly unnecessary. I already know you. I know absolutely everything that could be possible for one man to know about a man who was about to become his enemy. You don't think for a moment that we could plan and carry out an operation as big and as detailed as this without having known in advance those people with whom we'd have to do combat in one form, or another do you?

"Your resume is impressive. Homeland security is fortunate to have someone of your professional caliber and morality. This is not personal, Agent Barrett. In another time and another place, it would be my honor to go into battle with you instead of being here aside you as enemies. Be that as it may, I want to share something with you. May I?"

343

Though the question was rhetorical, Barrett felt it was necessary to establish some psychological footing by granting a permission he really didn't have.

"Yes, Sir, go right ahead."

"Thank you," Vincent half smiled. "I find upon more reflection that I did not however properly introduce myself to you. You know me only as Colonel Madison T. Vincent, U.S. Army retired, West Point, all that gibberish about what a wonderful soldier I was while in various theaters of operation. Some service on the record and rewarded for, some off the record, quite nicely and appropriately hidden away from all but God and the angels."

"Like all men, I am much more than that. On the obvious surface I am a husband. . ."

With that he paused and nibbled on one of the earpieces of his reading glasses as he stared at Barrett who could not hide his discomfort no matter how hard he tried.

"I am also a father and grandfather. I am a fisherman. Did you know that?" He didn't wait for an answer. "I love photography and the scriptures. And above nearly all those things, Agent Barrett, I am a patriot. I love my country, this country more than you or the ilk's of you, who have never spilt blood for it, will ever comprehend. My men share my same passion for her, our country. Yes, you have never bled for her, but your profession is noble and someday you may be called upon to do so. Let's hope," Vincent smiled weakly "that the call does not come very soon."

"The reason I let you through our perimeter instead of blowing you to tiny pieces, Agent Barrett is twofold. First, so I could more accurately identify myself to you. You know, beyond the dossier thing. So that in case of some odd turn of fortune you are able to speak to your President again, whether that's through Cellini or Halderman or personally, you can let him know what a dangerous man I am and that I am in command of some very dangerous men, warriors and patriots every swinging one of them."

Barrett showed no response to the mention of his superior or Halderman. There must be an insider he thought. How else would he know that he'd been in direct contact with the President's chief of staff?

Vincent knew immediately where his mind was going. "Are there insiders, Mr. Barrett? We're professionals. We have at our disposal some of the world's most incredibly intelligent men and women. We've done our homework; we know what we're doing. That's all I'm going to give you. It really doesn't matter who. It's a matter of a needle in a haystack and you guys don't have all the time in the world to find it anyway."

"But I digress, I am not just the commander of this unit, I am the chief commander of this entire army. You are not facing the difficulties of just this beautiful little town. You are looking at the front edge of a civil uprising beyond your wildest imaginations. You won't be shocked to learn, will you, that the cells we have stationed all over this country awaiting a signal from my command have been in the works for several years? From before the beginnings of President Traitor's presidency in fact."

Looking across the desk at Captain Coffin he continued, "John, you have one of our secure phones on the desk in front of you. Will you please call the east coast for me?"

"Sir? Are you sure . . .?" Vincent cut him off.

"John, make the call." He said tersely. "Put it on the speaker phone."

"Yes, Sir." The phone rang five times before a deep male voice answered

345

it.

"Good afternoon, Colonel. How are you feeling?" the voice at the other end of the line answered.

"I'm just fine. I'm going over some paperwork while I get a few moments to breathe. Just remind me if you will, share the current troop strength under your command?"

"Yes Sir. We currently have, as of last week forty-five hundred souls. All willing to lay their lives down for family, God and country Sir. Is everything well with you Sir? Is there anything else you need?"

"Thank you. All is well. Just needed my memory refreshed. That will be all the information I need for now. I'll be in touch. Keep us in your prayers, we need em."

"Will do Sir." The voice responded, and the call ended.

Vincent turned to Barrett, "I can make that same call to twenty-seven different states and get similar or greater number responses, Mr. Barrett. Do you think posting the National Guard in response to the ass whipping you got this morning is going to deter us one bit? Do you not understand that if we were to suffer irreparable defeat here in Odell, tomorrow there would be twenty maybe thirty towns just like this town in the cross hairs? Do you see me trembling?"

"Here let me show you something. John come back around here and sit next to Agent Barrett."

Reaching into his desk drawer Colonel Vincent pulled out a large copy of the Bible. "Do you?" he asked.

"Occasionally, I'm not a student of course, but we attend regularly enough I guess."

"Good, that's good. It's important for me to know. I read a bit every morning. Sometimes at night, too but not as often. Ever heard of the story of David and Goliath?"

"Of course."

"Good again!" Vincent said with enthusiasm. Let's do a little Old Testament reading, shall we?"

Barrett couldn't take his eyes off the man. He couldn't tell if he was a stark raving lunatic or a charismatic raving lunatic.

"Here it is. I Samuel Chapter 17. You of course know the back story. Those nasty Philistines were trying to destroy the Lord's folks, that would be the Jews. And they're facing one another across the valley. The Lord's people aren't so keen on going to battle. So, one day some Philistine clown says, "here's what were gonna do. We're gonna send out our best guy and you send out your best guy and whomever wins, wins the day. And the loser's people will become the slaves of the winners' people. You with me so far Agent Barrett?"

"Yes, Sir, so far I think I follow."

"Good. Well then this is sort of like the situation we have here today. You and the President's gang are the Philistines. We are like David's group, the Lords people. But do let's continue the narrative. It says here in verse forty-two when Goliath first saw David he scoffed at him. Laughed at him, Agent Barrett. Do you know why Goliath laughed at David?"

Barrett was getting a little uncomfortable.

"Yes sir. He laughed because David was so small and appeared to be weak and was not a soldier."

"Perfect, perfect! Do you see the parallels here? I know this is sounding a

347

bit trite but bear with me while I make a not so obvious point. Goliath says, because he is so big and strong and has so many weapons of war that he is going to feed David's carcass to the fowls of the air and the beasts of the field. In other words, there's going to be nothing left of him. Utter and total destruction. No one will ever even know that David existed. Sorta what you fellas are thinking. Just you're trying to decide how you can get away with it and not reveal your Goliath identity, right?"

"Of course," Vincent continued, "You and I both know what happened. David ate him up. David and the Lord ate him up with one rock. There's lots of lessons here to learn, Agent Barrett, and many of them are obvious. I could appear like some religious nut and tell you David won because the Lord was on his side. I won't tell you that though I believe that to be true. No, that's not the point of this little scriptural lesson. The point is found in verse forty. Let me read it to you, it's beautiful. Speaking of David . . . 'And he took his staff in his hand, and chose him five smooth stones out of the brook. . .' There it is, Agent Barrett, the moral of the story! Tell me what it is."

Barrett looked hard at him for a few seconds. "Is this a joke?"

"Do I look like I'm joking?

After a long pregnant pause Barrett responded quietly, "No."

"Then tell me the great moral lesson to be gleaned from verse forty."

"I'm not sure under the circumstances I get it."

"Let me help you. David knew the Lord wouldn't let him down. He knew he couldn't lose this match. But listen to this very carefully, Agent Barrett, *He picked up five stones, not just one.* David God Bless that little boy! Even he knew better to go into battle unprepared for a miss. He knew maybe that first shot wasn't going to be true to the mark. Maybe it would just wound that big bully. Maybe he'd need another shot and another and another and even another. But you can bet David knew he wouldn't need any more than that. Thank God it didn't take any more than one shot to bring that bully to his knees, ya know Agent Barrett? It only took one. Now do you understand what I'm trying to tell you."

"Yes Sir, I think I do."

"Good, good. Now we can talk as two men who understand one another."

Vincent leaned back in his chair and took a long drink of coffee through a straw resting in his cup. His jaw ached, but he wasn't going to let Barrett see the pain.

"So, Mr. Barrett, do you think we give a white rats butt about the lies the Trib headlines vomited forth this morning? Don't these morons know we'll have video evidence documenting just how this thing started? Don't they know that when the survivors that are sitting in that jail over there realize what a slaughter Hinshaw sent them in to, that they'll rat that old corrupt SOB out and the President and Halderman and their friends with them? Young man you've become the drum major in the lying puke parade!"

Vincent got up from behind his desk and began to walk around the room. He wanted Barrett to know he was mending. "A mentor of mine when I was a young captain gave me some advice. He said to me Madison you show me a fellow who will tell the smallest, tiniest little white lie and I'll show you . . . a liar. We're going to show the President and his political cronies to be the liars they are. You can thank him for adding one more 'smooth stone' to our sling bag."

Vincent returned to his leather chair and stared at Coffin. Taking another long draw on his coffee he waited for Barrett to speak.

349

"You told me, "Barrett said "you brought me in here for two reasons. I think I have a handle on the first. What's the second?"

"Ahhhhh you're not going to like the second I'm afraid."

"Try me."

"The second is to inform you that you will not be home for dinner tonight."

"What are you talking about? I drove here under a white flag. I trusted you to be men of honor. Where's the honor in this? This is an act of cowardice. The press will eat you up for this. You'll gain no support by keeping me here. The President . . ."

"The President, what? The President is as impotent as you are. What's he going to do? You sit there and rant about honor, Mr. Barrett? You tell me about the honor it took to lie and swindle the citizens of this country with backroom deals to get the President's agenda passed. You want to know when you're going home to Ellen and the children, Agent Barrett?"

"Yes, Sir, I do."

"On the same day, Agent Barrett, you release my wife."

"Captain Coffin, remove the prisoner."

"Yes Sir."

# # # # #

In 1973 Jim Croce described the southside of Chicago in one of his most popular songs. It was the home of Bad Bad Leroy Brown and it was according to the lyrics "the baddest part of town." That makes for a good lyric, but everybody who knows anything about the city of Chicago, including the residents of the southside, know that the westside of Chicago is indeed the baddest part of town.

Charlie Lovemoney was from the westside. He could have been the Leroy

350

Brown Croce wrote the song about with one exception. Croce once described his "Leroy" as never having climbed the knowledge tree. Charlie Lovemoney graduated first in his class at Holy Trinity High School and moved on to Roosevelt University where he received his undergraduate degree in criminal justice graduating in the top ten percent of his class. He was one bright boy and his station as second in command of the Homeland Security division of the Chicago office put his career on the fast track to a successful future. Anyone who had dealings with the big man knew he was no one to trifle with.

When Dan Barrett didn't check in at the appointed time and O'Brien got Coffin's phone call, he knew he needed to be back in the Chicago office as quickly as possible. As soon as he reached his office, he called an aid into his office and said, "Get Petracha up here right now."

Fifteen minutes later the strapping figure of Petracha stood in his doorway. "Captain Petracha, my name is Charles Lovemoney. I am second in command of the Homeland Security office here in Chicago. Will you please come in and have a seat?"

Looking at the two agents who accompanied him Lovemoney said, "Gentlemen, please take the cuffs and leg chains off Captain Petracha".

"Captain, come in and have a seat." He repeated motioning to a chair. "Can I get you something to drink?"

Petracha stared at him for a few seconds before he answered. "Yes Sir. I'd go for a cup of coffee and if you'd add a sweet roll to that or something, that would be just fine with me. Thank you, Sir."

"Gentlemen, please fetch something from the cafeteria for the Captain and add me to the list of customers as well."

The agents hesitated. Lovemoney could tell they were not wanting to

351

leave him alone with Petracha, unguarded and against protocol.

"It's fine gentlemen. We are two old soldiers, seconds in command. We're not going to get into any fist fights."

He smiled then looked at Petracha over his black rimmed glasses. "Are we Captain?"

"Not unless you start it, sir." Petracha half smiled back.

"Well then we'll be just fine. You fellas get us some refreshments. It's been a hellava day for all of us. We're both tired men and we need to chat with one another with clear heads. Are you up to some chat, Captain now that you've spent some time with Mrs. Vincent?"

"It was very kind of you fellas to let her come down and say hello. Of course, you know I've counseled her to keep her trap shut since you guys won't let her speak with counsel."

"Yes, we know what you've counseled her. She's not our main concern. Doesn't appear to have a lot of the answers, though we'd love to win her over. We think she could help us bring this matter to a more peaceful conclusion than it's likely to be, given how things got off to a start this morning."

"I wouldn't bet the farm on that."

"Why would you say that, Captain?"

"Just don't think she's your gal. And I don't know much about what occurred this morning Mr. Lovemoney. And I'm not in much of a talking mood myself, but there are a few things you should know that I do know. Wanna here 'em?"

Surprised at Petracha's sudden verbosity. "Of course, Captain I'm all ears."

Lovemoney smiled. He was talking for the first time beyond the military serial number name and rank he had been repeatedly offering and that was a start.

"Guards talk. Don't care if it's military guards or civilian. Don't care if its local county jail guards or state prison. Doesn't even exclude the fancy Dan's you got around here. And as a result of that, I know two things for certain." He paused, "you listening?" he smiled.

"Of course, I'm still all ears."

"First, there is no way in hell you have Vincent. If you did, I'd know about it. So, that's a load of crap I didn't share with Gretchen."

"And how's that Captain?"

"How's what?"

"And how is it you would know whether or not we have Colonel Vincent locked away in that hospital and I assure you we do."

"And, how's that? How would I know that? You'd never guess; you wish you knew. But I can tell you one thing for absolute certain, if you continue to keep this charade up, keep lying to me, you can have the boys stick the coffee and rolls where the sun don't shine, put the chains back on and lead me back to quarters. I know that serial number by heart and from this moment on that's all you'll be hearing out of me."

After a few moments of fiddling around with pens and papers on his desk Lovemoney responded, "Okay I hear ya. Let's start all over again. Let's suppose I agree with you that we don't have Vincent. What does it matter?"

"Matters enough that you lied to me and to Mrs. Vincent about it."

"Life is all about 'quid pro quo' Captain. It's no giant surprise that we would hold a carrot out to Mrs. Vincent in hopes of gleaning something, anything to bring this mess to a halt. There has to be some way beyond armed violence to shut this down."

353

"There is, meet the demands of the people of the United States and arrest those crooked rascals who shoved this law down their throats. Throw them rats in jail where they belong. Repeal the law and everyone goes home and lives happily ever after."

"Pie in the sky, pie in the sky, Captain. Surely, you know that's not possible. We have the kidnaping and holding against their will of nearly three thousand American citizens! We have the murder of civilians, law enforcement officers shot, some killed. We've got the confiscation of property, the beating and bullying of the civil rights of those townspeople 'til I don't know where to stop. Really there's so many crimes involved here that I don't think I can name them all. And do you really think this is all going to go away? We're just going to send senators and congressmen off to jail, reverse a law that's been legally enacted and go home because your boys have taken over a town in the middle of nowhere Illinois?"

"Listen, let's get really honest here. That town doesn't mean a damn thing to anyone in Washington and I mean anyone aside from the intrinsic media value it represents in a million different scenarios. It's all about the 'greater good' Captain. If we have to sacrifice three thousand souls to save the union what do you think is going to happen? In the final analysis if we have to bring sufficient troops into play and civilian casualties are sustained, they are all going to be laid at your feet, Vincent's feet. The government of the United States is going to come out of this looking like heroes, victims, defenders of liberty and this ARM is going to be exposed for what it is, a bunch of red-neck, rebel militia fringe that threw a deadly temper tantrum because a vote didn't go their way!"

Petracha laughed out loud. It was the first time he'd done so in weeks he thought.

"We're back to the serial number game Lovemoney," he said intentionally dropping the former salutation of Sir. "I'm not going to sit here and debate the merits of our cause with you, but I will tell you one thing. You're wrong, so wrong. If you think this is one little isolated event, if you think this is just bunch of angry backwoods radicals looking to stir the pot you couldn't be more off course. And you will see in short order just how wrong you are."

"But there is one thing you're right about. I don't think the government is going to use common sense and do the right thing here. They never do. So, here is what your biggest problem is going to be. Are you ready for this? There is not one soul in Vincent's group that does not know they are going to die or spend the rest of their lives in a federal prison when this is all said and done. These men have all said goodbye to their mothers and fathers, to their wives and children, to their girlfriends, their homes, fishing in the summer hunting in the fall, to Thanksgiving to Christmas, to anything and everything they've ever loved. Think about it. Do you really think this is just some little rag tag outfit made up of redneck misfits? If so, you're in for one hellava surprise."

Petracha sat back in his chair and watched Lovemoney as what he'd just said sank in. While he stared back at Petracha the two agents returned with coffee and two sweet rolls.

Petracha leaned forward "You think, Agent Lovemoney, I could have a cigar or two to light up?"

"I'd very much like to accommodate you, Captain Petracha, but this is a federal building and as such there is a no smoking policy."

"Can one smoke outside the building?"

"Yes, one can. If one wasn't a prisoner."

Petracha looked at him and at the cup of coffee and the sweet roll sitting on the front side of Lovemoney's desk. He hadn't touched either. He sat up straighter in the chair. As big a man as Lovemoney was Petracha was even bigger. "There is a smoking area outside the building. Maybe there's one on the roof also. You know, so very special prisoners can have a drag on a good ole cigar?"

Lovemoney saw it coming and struck a preemptive blow.

"There's no way in hell you're leaving this building for a second. And there's no way you'll be allowed to smoke in here. So, put that out of your mind."

"RA51-295-258."

He stood up and slowly pushed the untouched coffee and sweet roll off the desk. The crash brought the two agents outside the door running. He turned to them arms outstretched and offered his wrists.

# # # # #

Two hours later Captain Petracha and Agent Lovemoney stood on the roof of the federal building taking long draws on Cuban cigars. The sun was setting over the western horizon. Long straight lines of lights moved out from the city in every direction as far as one could see. In a way, thought Petracha, they look an awful lot like the plowed fields that surrounded Odell.

"You never told me the other thing," Lovemoney offered after a long silence.

"The other thing?"

"Yes, downstairs you told me there were two things you knew for certain. One was that Vincent wasn't in Loyola Hospital. What was the other?"

"Oh. The other was . . . this morning those cops shot first. No way Vincent would have given away his positions to an insurgent group of unknown strength. Wouldn't have happened that way. You can take that to the bank. Somebody pressed that perimeter with bad intent. Then there would have been no mercy. You don't know the guy like I do. It didn't go down the way you folks are trying to sell it."

Lovemoney continued to draw on his cigar in silence as he looked over the edge of the building towards the western horizon. Petracha threw his over the eastern side of the building and watched it fall forty-five floors to the alley below. He spits the taste out of his mouth. He'd never smoked a day in his life. "Disgusting habit," he thought as he once again stretched his wrists out towards the agents guarding him. He smiled inwardly as they led him off the roof back into the stairwell. If they'd have really done their homework Lovemoney would have known that.

# # # # #

Early Friday morning while Colonel Vincent was having breakfast, Coffin knocked on his office door. "Come in John."

"Colonel One America News is flashing a breaking news story to be aired after this next commercial. Has a live feed of Mike O'Brien standing outside of District Six? Not sure what he's up to but you may want to tune in."

"Yes. Get Captain Cox in here. Vincent turned to the laptop on his desk and found the live broadcast. Cox walked into the room with a stoic look on his face.

"Any idea what's going on here, Captain Cox?"

"Sir. I'm hoping it will be good though O'Brien looked pretty grim on the lead in shot."

357

"Well, let's see what's in the wind." Vincent leaned back in his leather chair and sipped his cup of morning coffee.

"Good morning ladies and gentlemen. This is Karen Cook reporting for One America News. I'm standing outside of District Six headquarters with Commander Michael O'Brien of the Illinois State Police. Commander O'Brien is about to read from a text he's prepared and has agreed to answer a few questions after his remarks. Commander O'Brien, when you are ready."

"My fellow citizens of the great State of Illinois and to those across the length and breadth of the United States. You, along with most of the world, know of the tragic events that have taken place in our district over the last nearly two weeks now. Our officers, men and women along with myself have worked tirelessly around the clock with other law enforcement agencies, including those of the federal government to resolve, to try to bring to a peaceful conclusion the occupation of the town of Odell, Illinois."

"Yesterday morning a tragedy of epic proportions occurred. News reports, both print and broadcast have disclosed that an unknown number of law enforcement officers were either killed, wounded or taken captive by the forces occupying that town. We have now confirmed that between twenty and perhaps as many as twenty-five officers have been mortally wounded. Several more have received less severe wounds and are being released for treatment at local hospitals at this very moment. A few more, perhaps as many as six of seven officers remain as prisoners and we hope are being well cared for."

"We do not have specific identities of the killed, wounded and prisoners at this time, but the state police will release that information as soon as it becomes available to us and we have made proper notification of family members. We are currently negotiating terms for the release of the deceased and

358

the prisoners."

"At this time, I want to correct an error in the reports that have been presented to the public and to share with you other most tragic news. First, the police detail that suffered such casualties at Odell yesterday morning were not ambushed by the occupiers of that town. They were dispatched to Odell by the governor of the State of Illinois over the objections of myself and many others in leadership in the state law enforcement community. If any of those individuals wish to come forwards to identify themselves and to corroborate this statement, I will leave it to them to do so. The object of the mission was to liberate Mrs. Mary Duke Odell from capture. The governor had concern for her as a woman of advanced age with some significant health issues. Knowing she was the grandmother of the President of the United States, he wished to ensure her safety."

"It is my most very sad duty to inform you this morning that Mary Duke Odell died from wounds she suffered in that attempt. All information we have at this time suggests she was struck by friendly fire and died instantly. Our prayers and condolences go out to the President and his family and all of her friends, extended family, fellow citizens of Odell and, the United States of America and indeed the world over. All of us who knew her loved her and will miss her."

"I have chosen the certain end of my career to share this information with you, because it was the intent of the government, both local, state and federal to mislead you about the events in Odell. And they have so done. I am not endorsing nor condoning the actions of those in charge of the seizure of Odell, but I cannot and will not be an instrument in the hands of those who wish to deceive the American public."

"Therefore, I immediately resign my position with the Illinois State Police, a law enforcement agency which I have loved and served faithfully throughout all these years. I will miss the thousands of faithful brave officers with whom I have served and am very proud of."

"Thank you for your time. God Bless America."

Karen Cook's microphone looked like it was going to fall out of her hand it was shaking so hard.

"Commander O'Brien, are you absolutely sure that Mrs. Odell died in the assault on Odell yesterday morning?"

"Positively. I've seen incontrovertible photographic evidence of the remains of Mrs. Odell and the service officers. The photographic evidence has been reviewed by our experts and was verified as authentic. The President has been notified of course."

"You stated that the information released to the media surrounding the events that led up to yesterdays' violence was inaccurate and that it provided in an intentionally inaccurate picture of what took place? In other words, someone in the government lied to us and to the American People."

"That's correct."

"If true, can you tell us who was behind the misinformation?"

"No Ma'am. I'm not going to get into that. I'm not privy to who decided to release the story that those officers were ambushed, but it's simply not true. I'm not going to get involved in any of the political wrangling of this mess. I just want the American people to know the truth behind what happened and to decide for themselves what to do about it. The cleanest way I could think of while minimizing personal repercussions was to bring the truth to the attention of the media."

"Well, isn't it going to be just your word against those of your superiors and or the words of state and federal officials?"

"I suppose it could be. But, thank God there are survivors and they'll be able to rehearse for you what their orders were and who issued them. Some of those men and women were my friends and they knew that I and several other members of the law enforcement community were against the plan to try to extricate Mrs. Odell. Certainly, if any professional thought we were contemplating such an attempt there are available military or paramilitary options that would be certainly more capable."

"Can you share with us the names of some of the people who were involved in the planning of the failed mission, who was in the room, on the video screens? Give us any idea who the plan originated with?"

"No Ma'am and I'm about done here. I don't think I have much more to offer you and will let you folks in the media and other law enforcement bodies do their jobs to answer those questions for you. Thank you for allowing me time this morning to share this very painful news with you and your audience. Again, my deepest regrets and sympathies for all those officers and their families and for President Odell, the Odell family and the citizens of Odell. God bless America."

Vincent turned to Robert Cox,

"Captain, you, Sir, are a bloody genius! Great job, great job. How on earth are they going to get around that. Heads are gonna roll, by God, heads are gonna roll. What's our next publicity spin wise Captain?"

"I'm thinking we'll send an invitation through Barrett to his office to secure the remains of the KIA's and the body of Mrs. Odell. In exchange for that we demand the release of Mrs. Vincent."

361

"No, don't go there. In exchange for the bodies we'll want to see an acknowledgment of the wiretapped conversations we've supplied them with and that an investigation is ongoing on each of the politicians we've identified. We'll also demand a withdrawal of the national guard troops although they will never agree to that. Let's show the tip of the olive branch and see what they come up with. The prize is their invitation to talk. That's what we want. Bring Barrett over here this afternoon. We'll let him call home in the morning."

"Yes, Sir," Cox replied. I've already sent word to O'Brien that Barrett will be allowed one phone call within the next twenty-four hours and that it will most likely take place tomorrow. Had to give him that along with the photos of Mrs. Odell to get the press conference out of him."

"That's fine, but we're not releasing Mary Odell's body. We're going to have a funeral and viewing right here in Odell so the citizens of this country, her fellow townspeople and relatives can pay their due respects and see just what those lying SOB's did to her." Turning to Coffin, Vincent's lips thinned. "Check on my nephew."

"Sir, yes Sir."

Chapter XXIII

And the last place Dan Barrett ever expected to find himself this cool, but bright sunny Saturday morning was sitting in a high-back leather chair behind Colonel Madison T. Vincent's desk. For a fleeting moment he wondered if he'd exceeded the President's expectations! His cuffs and leg chains had been removed. He'd been allowed to shower and shave, he was even given a fresh shirt. A cup of coffee sat in front of him though he never drank coffee. A glass of orange juice half empty next to the coffee cup seemed out of place. A video camera on a tripod faced him and the little red light told him it was recording.

"You may now place your call, Agent Barrett," a voice from the darkened side of the room spoke. "Just one call so make it a good one."

The last person Charlie Lovemoney expected to hear from that Saturday morning as he sat in his office waiting to take a conference call with Halderman and Cellini was Dan Barrett. "Charlie, its Dan. I'm ok. I have a few minutes but wanted to check in with you and ask you to be sure to let Ellen know that I'm fine and that I'm being treated well. I hope to be able to give you another call later today and am sure I'll be home most likely tomorrow morning, depending on my talks with Colonel Vincent. We ran a little over yesterday and it looks like it will take at least a day or two before I can wrap this up. As much as possible at my level, anyway. So, tell her not to worry if she doesn't hear from me 'til tomorrow night or so okay?"

"Yes, I completely understand. Are you really alright?"

"Yes, yes I'm fine. I hadn't planned on staying, but the Colonel extended an invitation that was too good to turn down, if you get my drift?"

Lovemoney knew exactly what he was saying. There's no way Barrett would be incommunicado for so long on a voluntary basis.

363

"We're going to resume talks in a few minutes, and I hope to be able to report positive movement. You know as well as I that I can't promise much, but I do have the eyes and ears of Washington and know that they'll listen closely to any proposal I make to these gentlemen."

Lovemoney responded, "yes, I know for certain that the highest levels of government are anxiously awaiting your report. In fact, I'm just about due for a conference call with Director Cellini and Frank Halderman. They've been very concerned that you've not reported in and that you were being held against your will. As we both know, the government has limits and the kidnaping of a federal agent on top of a thousand other felonies might just be the straw that breaks the camel's back."

"Well, that's simply not the case, Charlie. Things are tense here no doubt, but we are engaged in fruitful dialogue. So, don't let anyone get a hair trigger finger do you hear me?"

"Yes, just expressing some reasonable worries boss."

"Colonel Vincent and his men have treated me with the utmost respect and I'm looking forward to getting back to the table with them this morning to iron out further details and to present proposals we can all live with."

"Have you had an opportunity to see the news?"

"No. Most all outside communication has been cut except here in the headquarters building so after discussions and an evening meal, I hit the rack. What's up?"

Well, Vincent and his boys should be in a good mood, because your old buddy Mike O'Brien held a news conference yesterday afternoon and blew the lid off of Hinshaw's plan to liberate Mary Odell from the town. He laid out the raid, not too much detail mind you, but he threw a bunch of folks under the bus for sure. Not sure how Springfield or Washington are going to handle it but much of the news media is livid calling for everyone's resignation from the President to the governor. All hell's breaking loose."

"I'll see if I can't catch up some today during a break. I've got to sign off now and get back to my hosts. Just let everyone know all is going well, slow but well and I will touch base with you later this afternoon."

"Okay, boss. I gotta run too. Judy Kaye's got the Feds on the line."

# # # # #

The reality of the matter was that Dan Barrett spent a fairly miserable night on a bunk in the town jail in a cell next to the tactical officers who'd been taken prisoner. Most of them seemed to be in shock and spoke very little. When they did, they didn't include him in their conversation. As far as they knew he could have been the mastermind creep who dumped them into certain failure. A meal resembling some kind of meatloaf, a potato, a slice of bread and a bottle of juice was all any of them received. For the month of April, it was unusually cold that night and no one made any effort to turn on the heat. By the time the sky began to lighten he found himself begging for rays of sunlight to warm up.

What was he going to do? He had no real negotiation authority, they had to know that. He really was nothing more than a chess piece. And they could use him, move him, play him any way they wanted to. As he thought about it the only real thing he could do was act like he knew what he was doing. Offer whatever it took, within reason. Learn what he could, observe and do what was needed to get the heck out of there in one piece. He counted minutes for the sun to rise. It seemed like forever. After a quick cold shower and fresh clothes that were waiting for him on his cot. He sat quietly until a young guard with two armed escorts entered the cell area and distributed black cups of coffee. No words were exchanged with any of the prisoners. The coffee was poured and handed through the bars while the other two escorts stood at port arms watching very carefully. When they got to Barrett's cell the young man poured the coffee and handed it through the bars.

"Sir, I have been asked to advise you that you will be called upon around 1100 hours. Please make use of the fresh clothes that have been provided. You will then be escorted to Colonel Vincent's headquarters at that time. Is there anything else you require?"

Cognizant of the scarcity of provisions for the other prisoners it took him no time to respond in the negative. The officers in the other cells watched the exchange without comment and remained seated with their backs to him. He didn't think from the vibes he was getting that it would be wise to make contact even though he was sickened by what they'd been through.

At 1115 hours Barrett sat in the outer offices of the headquarters building. Captain Coffin entered the room through a hallway and greeted him.

"Agent Barrett good morning. Colonel Vincent will speak with you as soon as he gets here." Colonel Vincent entered his office shortly thereafter and nodded to Barrett as he passed by. "Captain Coffin is my Kool Aid ready?"

"As we speak Sir."

"Thank you." Turning back to Agent Barrett, "Good morning Agent Barrett. I won't insult you by asking you if you were comfortable last night or if you slept well. I'm sure neither is the case. Now, we have to figure out just what to do with you. To be perfectly frank none of us considered the possibility that a federal agent would be so unwise so as to fall right squarely into our laps. And to top that all off that it would be "The" federal agent in charge of

366

homeland security for this part of our great nation. And thus, the man in charge of destroying us. Or at least communicating our demands to those in charge who would have us good patriots slaughtered."

"Yes, Colonel you seem to have some dilemma as to what to do with me. But, perhaps I could offer some suggestions?"

"Yes, do tell me what the President is doing to meet our demands?"

"You know I can't speak for the President or anyone else for that matter, but I do have his ear as well as other influential people in Washington. You must also know that as a result of the press conference Commander O'Brien held yesterday that people are embarrassed. You are a man like myself, Col Vincent who has spent much of his life doing his duty and staying as far away from politics as possible. I suspect you find them as repugnant as I do."

"But as studious men we have, of necessity, many occasions to observe behavior. And we each know when the heat turns up and the media gets its jaws set into one's buttocks, they will do whatever they can, whatever is expedient to loosen the grip. There is always room for talk. Wouldn't you agree?"

"There is always room for talk." Vincent agreed.

"Let's discuss what I can do. I can bring to the authorities at the highest level the demand for a complete investigation into the behaviors of those behind Scottstown/Brady. I can and will become a voice for repeal of the law and you know as well as I do, Colonel, that those politicians who may scream for it in public can often be persuaded in private to get behind a movement to repeal it. Especially, Colonel if indictments or potential indictments are waived under their noses. No, I can't promise anything, but you know how this works. You and I've seen it a million times. You know as well as I do that President Odell is going to throw Hinshaw under the bus by the time the

367

evening news hits the air. And one of his boys, probably Halderman, is going to be sitting in the driver's seat stomping on the gas pedal."

"What more can I offer? I don't know. You have to have known as well as your men that there will be repercussions. Nobody's so stupid to think that we're all just going to be good boys now and go home. I know your men are prepared to make ultimate sacrifices. The question is now can we prevent that from becoming a necessity and can we even give some of their lives back to them. Yes, there will be trials, there must be. But where there are trials there can also be acquittals, there can be plea down bargains, there can be good time served for bad time. This does not have to be an all-or-nothing deal Colonel. There's still time to salvage your position and save your men. Give it some thought."

"Your men have families who depend on them financially . . ." Before he could go any further Vincent interrupted him.

"Agent Barrett, you needn't go there. We're aware of those needs. They've already been provided for. No one can ever replace husband, father or brother, but we knew before coming here that we'd not return. All I can and will tell you about that is that this movement is so large that each family of each man I have here in Odell and elsewhere in the country is provided for on a very long-term basis. I apologize for stealing that thunder, but it's not an issue that hasn't been identified and addressed by our side of the equation."

"I understand, Sir, and will forego that aspect of my plea to you. All I'm trying to say is that there has to be some quid pro quo here. There will have to be a dismantling, a lessening of tensions and a full return to the ballot box and not the ammo box. There's still time for dialogue and I may not be the right guy to be so engaged, but somewhere someone has to be. Do you agree?"

368

Vincent leaned back in his chair and lit up a cigar, "I think the discussion that we've had is too theoretical, you admit that you have no authority to offer any of the things you propose. The discussion is at a level too low to accomplish what each of us wants most. We'll mull over what you've suggested, but there's nothing new, nothing that we've not considered ourselves long ago and far away. I'm not even sure what you think you were going to accomplish by even coming here, Agent Darrett?"

"Nothing more than to sit face to face with you and to see if there was room for reasonable men to have reasonable discussion that may lead to more discussion that would avoid more bloodshed."

"Well, if that's the case, you have accomplished your mission. There may be some room for discussion. But make no mistake you are not leaving here until my wife leaves the federal building. Do you understand that?"

"Yes, Sir, I do. I'll ask Agent Lovemoney to have that done if I am allowed to make contact with him this afternoon as I so advised him."

"You may and then we'll discuss the conditions of the mutual release. In the meantime, when you make your report to Lovemoney this evening, tell him the return of the remains of the tactical officers and two of the prisoners will require the release of my wife and the total withdrawal of the national guard troops first. Then we'll talk about what we're gonna do with you."

Vincent leaned back in his chair and took off his glasses. He wiped his face with a clean white kerchief, the wound though healing still hurt like the blazes. Not only was he still unable to eat most solid food, anything the least bit salty set the wounds on the inside of his mouth afire. His neck ached from the wrenching impact of the bullet that struck him, and an ever-present headache varied in intensity from a low, dull, throbbing nuisance to a migraine intensity that required him to lay down in a blacked-out room. He blinked a few times before speaking again.

"And let me be clear about this. We have absolutely no fear of the guard. We will absolutely bloody those boys. Those weekend warriors will not stand a chance against my men. It will be a slaughter of epic proportions should any moron try something as stupid as yesterday morning was. Do you understand?" He didn't wait for a response. And Vincent had no expectations that his conditions for release would be met. In fact, he was counting on that they wouldn't be.

"We don't want to hurt those boys, but that's what will happen. We want them removed, because we don't want to lay that much bloodshed at anyone's feet. If they aren't withdrawn and an attack of any magnitude begins, their blood will be on your hands. When you take upon yourself the responsibility of coming here you take upon yourself the accountability for what happens as a result of your visit. Besides, you want to see them removed so that the possibility of any additional talks stays on the table, no matter at what level or in what venue."

"Speaking of that one last thing, if any additional talks are to take place, since you suggest that they might with those having more authority than yourself, you should know that no person, not even the President of the United States himself, will be allowed to step one foot inside the perimeter surrounding Odell. We permitted your arrival, but you're damn lucky we didn't blow that vehicle up with you in it. Be absolutely clear on that point when you report."

As Barrett was being escorted back to the jail, he felt very pleased with himself as he took stock of the last day and a half. The President had ordered him to meet with Vincent and that's just what he'd done. He'd not only met with him but found it surprising that Vincent was willing to listen to anything he'd had to say. This was extremely surprising considering the botched raid, the attempted cover up and the installation of the national guard just miles from their perimeter, no matter how much of threat they were or weren't. If he could just exert enough reason to get them to speak with the real power brokers, maybe there could be a peaceful ending to this madness.

Yes, he was very pleased with himself until he reached the steps of the jailhouse and felt the sting of a rifle butt slam into the left side of his face. The pain was not only excruciating, it was so surprising and intense that he felt the world swirl, flashes of blinking lights and then a crash to the ground that opened a gash over his right eyebrow. When he awoke, he was in his cell with bandages in place. A guard was with him and water and medicines were on a small table just outside the bars.

# # # # #

Captain John Coffin was monitoring the various news feeds, gloating a bit about the predicament governmental officials found themselves in with various media outlets. Even the liberal press was up on arms about the disinformation that had been disseminated. They knew that could not have happened without the President's knowledge and approval. The White House had scheduled a news conference for Sunday morning.

"Yes" Coffin thought. "Schedule, it when most people will be in church or on the golf courses, in their cars heading to various locations to get away from news just like the one he was going to make. And don't forget, Mr. President, to pre-select the reporters who'll be asking the questions and the questions they'll be instructed to ask."

371

That's when the door burst open and the young guard said in a loud voice. "Captain, you better come right away. We've had an incident."

The young man didn't wait for an acknowledgment, he turned and dashed out the door. By the time Coffin reached the top steps of the staircase leading to the sidewalk he could see a gathering of soldiers in front of the jail which was located just across the town square. He walked hurriedly towards the crowd, arriving in time to see a bleeding and unconscious Dan Barrett lying on the ground.

"What in sam hell happened here," he barked.

The crowd parted even farther to reveal two other young guards who had an arm bar lock on an angry, red faced Glen Garnet.

"You men get Agent Barrett inside and get the medical people here right away."

Turning towards Garnet and his guards he glared.

"What's this all about Mr. Garnet?"

"That damn fed gave me 'a hard look' Captain Coffin."

"A what?"

"You know, a hard look. He looked at me disrespectfully, so I thought I'd teach him a lesson. He won't be doing that anymore." Coffin could hardly believe his ears.

"I ought to cut your ears off young man! Where are you staying?"

"I'm staying with Lou Cucci's grandparents." His tone had quieted considerably realizing how angry Coffin was.

"Mr. Garnet, consider yourself under house arrest as of this moment. You will be escorted to your friend's home where you will stay until I personally give the order for you to be free to move about. We do not, understand this,

372

we do not assault prisoners of war. You will have to answer for your actions at some point in time, but for now you can be damn thankful I don't have you shot on the spot. GOT ME?" Coffin screamed the last question.

"You men, get this moron out of my sight." Turning to the rest of the young people who'd been asked to pretend they were guarding prisoners, Coffin addressed them. "Nothing like this will happen again as long as we are in charge of this village. Do you all hear me?"

He waited as his eyes moved over each young person. All nodded their heads in agreement. "This is not schoolyard playground time young people. People can die here. Yesterday morning several did. You will have respect for that fact and conduct yourselves accordingly."

And then after a long pregnant pause and a 'real hard look,' Coffin dismissed them to return to their posts.

"You will all take your orders from this young corporal here and if there are any incidents of like kind, I'll dismiss your organization and send you all packing."

Coffin then turned to the group of soldiers who had gathered in response to the assault. "Gentlemen, who was assigned to escort and protect the prisoner?"

Two riflemen stepped forward.

"Sir, we were, Sir."

"What happened here, gentlemen?"

The taller of the two men replied, "All was fine, Sir, until we reached the steps. We never saw it coming. The kid stepped forward, yelled 'Bastard' and gave the prisoner the butt side of his assault weapon before we could do anything."

"Your duty was to escort and protect the prisoner. Your inattention led to an assault where the intent, thank God, wasn't fatal in nature. You failed in your duties. Report to the statue of Lincoln on the opposite side of the square. You will guard him and remain at attention until word is sent relieving you of that assignment. Perhaps this order will assist you in learning the importance of your responsibilities."

The two men barked "Sir, yes, Sir" before they raced across the square to the statue of Abraham Lincoln where they snapped to attention and remained in that position until midnight. When the clock on the tower at the northeast side of the square struck midnight, a shadow of a figure walked to the soldiers who's been standing at attention for just over twelve hours. Quietly, respectfully, without any other words the figure said, "Gentlemen, thank you for your service. Dismissed."

The men saluted and marched away in step with their weapons at port arms. Coffin thought to himself, "how I love these boys."

Chapter XXIV

". . . In conclusion Director Cellini, all I can tell you in addition is that Agent Barrett sounded well. There's no question that he's being held against his will, but at least he has them talking. His main concern is that he had no authority to offer anything and, so he didn't know what he could accomplish."

Halderman had taken the lead in the conference call that was now in its second half hour. "Well he's going to call back this afternoon, right?"

"Yes, Sir, that's what he told me. We've a recording of the call of course and that's being analyzed. Sounded to me like he was in some distress, but not overwhelmed. Who wouldn't be?"

"And he did indicate that he was speaking directly with this Colonel Vincent?"

"Yes, yes sir, he did. I'm sure that Vincent was on the other side of the discussion table as we were speaking, if not listening in."

"That's good. At least we know who we're dealing with and that we don't have to go through one of his subordinates. Was he able to communicate anything about troop strength, how things look in the village, the morale of the people anything else at all?"

"Nothing at all Sir. I'm sure he was being very careful knowing that the conversation was being monitored. I'm going to go back and review the tapes. They're being cleaned up and copies with and without background noise will be in the air to you via secure emails within a few hours. We're nearly finished looking for anything in the background that the natural ear can't pick up."

"This is what's important. This is to be Barrett's top priority. We don't care what has to be promised to achieve it. You somehow have to get this message to him. Listen very carefully, Agent Lovemoney. *Get the Snakes Out Of The Nest!* Once we get them out of the nest, we can chop their heads off. Once Vincent is captured or dead, preferably dead, they will all wither away and die. My instinct is that he's the glue that holds this thing together."

"If we can get him and one or two of his key guys out of there all kinds of other options open up to us. Somehow you've got to get that message to Barrett and he's got to get them to come out." Halderman's voice was emphatic.

"We're looking at this from every angle we can think of and the think-tank boys are plotting out all kinds of scenarios, but it doesn't take a genius to figure it out; there's no way we can go in there without massive civilian casualties. And of course, they know that. We've got to get that risk off the table somehow, anyhow. And here's the scariest scenario. And they know this as well. At some point in time, under some circumstance, no one and I mean no one is going to occupy American soil, take Americans prisoners and make demands on the President of the United States without a full-scale assault to take that soil and those Americans, dead or alive, back."

"Now, you have two cards to play yourself Agent Lovemoney. You've got the wife and Petracha. Get with them today and offer whatever you have to offer them for their complete cooperation. Use those two to clear out the nest. I'm also convinced they are the key to our achieving our goal."

"I'll get right on it, Sir."

"Right then. Director Cellini do you have anything further to add."

"Just one thing, Mr. Halderman. Charlie, I think the best card for you to play is Petracha. You already have him talking. Offer what's necessary to unlock this thing for us. He must know what the hot buttons are. Move him over from the Dark Side and find out what he knows. Use any method, do you

376

understand me? Any method make any promise. We don't care what you need to do. The President is more than beside himself that his Grandmother is dead. He's beyond furious. He wants to see these traitors standing on the gallows with ropes round their necks. . . the sooner the better."

"I got it, Chief. I agree. We'll get to Petracha and unlock him. You have my word on it."

Halderman had the last word as politicians always do.

"Ok gentlemen, we all have a lot of work to do. Let's get moving. Agent Lovemoney, we'll wait to hear from you. Get in touch as soon as you have something positive to report. Good afternoon, people."

The phone went silent as Lovemoney looked out over an almost quiet Dearborn Street on a Saturday afternoon. He had no idea that Barrett was lying near unconsciousness in a jail cell with one hell of a headache.

Lovemoney agreed with Cellini. Petracha was going to be the key to moving things off center, but Gretchen Vincent had been locked away in her quarters since the assault Thursday morning. She had to be a basket case. They needed to get her out of there. She might still prove to be an asset at some level.

"Miss Kaye, get the car ready and have two agents meet me in the garage with Gretchen Vincent in thirty minutes."

Before she knew what hit her, Mrs. Vincent was being hurriedly ushered into a black executive looking vehicle with dark-tinted windows. As soon as she bent over and popped her head in, she noticed the giant African American man sitting on the opposite side of the rear seat. "Where are you taking me? Are we going to see Madison?"

"No Ma'am, we are not, but I do have some good news for you. Agent

377

Barrett is with your husband and some short discussions have taken place that could at least be the beginning of the end of this mess. The Colonel is still not in good enough shape for the kind and length of discussions needed, but he's at least aware that some conditions are being met. And more importantly, that you are here and are scheduled to see him as soon as we can get authorization from Washington."

"Do tell? And you are?

"I am Agent Charles Lovemoney. I work with Agent Barrett and am second agent in charge of homeland security for the Chicago Office."

"Really? And, Agent Lovemoney, why am I supposed to believe anything you say?"

She crossed her arms and stared out the tinted windows of the SUV. She was shocked to see the vehicle exit the building from an underground parking lot onto south Dearborn Street. She focused on street signs; left on Jackson. The vehicle moved slowly in the light Saturday afternoon traffic across the bridge over Grant Park. When it came to a halt at Lake Shore Drive it turned right and headed south. Landmarks familiar from previous trips to Chicago with Vincent passed by on the left. First the Museum of Natural History which she'd visited, while Madison was attending a convention several years ago, then Soldier Field where the Bears play, McCormick Place the huge convention center where dinner was served all those years ago. All located on the beautiful south city shoreline of Lake Michigan.

"Where are we going?" she demanded.

"I thought you weren't talking to me, Mrs. Vincent."

"Just answer the question, Lovemoney, or I'll open this door and jump out. Then you can explain that to the press tonight."

"I'm sure that's not possible. The driver is the only one who can allow us to open these doors, but just to show you my good intentions Mrs. Vincent we are going. . . to lunch. A late lunch albeit, but lunch. A perfectly wonderful Italian place, my favorite in the whole city. It's called Piccalo Mundo. Ever hear of it?"

"Surely, you're joking?"

"Nope, I'm not joking. I've ordered from Washington to interview you once again at the most immediate moment. I've been up for nearly forty-eight straight hours, I've eaten nothing but the rotten vending machine sandwiches from the sixteenth floor, a cup of coffee and a sweet roll with Mario Petracha. And I'm so damn tired Ma'am that I can hardly remember when that happened. So, you and I are going to kill two birds with one stone. If you don't want to talk, that's just fine with me. If you don't want to know how Colonel Vincent is doing and what he's had to say that's just fine with me too. You can sit there across the table with your mouth shut and watch me devour a great Antipasto and some of the best lasagna in the entire world or you can join in and we can have a nice lunch together, have some pleasant conversation and maybe even a glass or two of a nice wine."

Lovemoney then stared out the window at one of the poorer neighborhoods on the southside as they drove by U. S. Cellular Field, home of his beloved White Sox. He couldn't help thinking that in a few weeks they'd be hosting one of the first home stands of the year and for the first time in many years, as many as he could remember, he may not be there with his two girls.

Gretchen Vincent watched the lake slide by in silence as the black government car continued south on Lake Shore Drive. It was no more than a twenty-minute drive when the Museum of Science and Industry came into view.

379

She'd not been there since a little girl on a family vacation and Dr. York, Daddy, walked with her for hours through its hallways, down into its coal mine and even through the bowels of a World War II submarine; it was gone, no longer a part of that exquisite place. She wondered where it was as they turned off onto 54th street and then quick right and left turns brought them to a halt in front of a small but elegantly furnished restaurant.

Floor-to-ceiling windows afforded a view of the park across the street between the eatery and the museum. Someone was pulling shades down. Two men in suits and sunglasses stood on either side of the entry way. She knew there were others who couldn't be seen, but she didn't focus on that. She was wondering how she was going to handle the large man in the seat next to her. To talk or not to talk, that was the question.

"Mrs. Vincent, will you please join me for lunch?" With that the right-side door of the vehicle popped open and Lovemoney was out in a flash. Before she could respond, her door opened, and a hand reached inside and took hold her elbow. It helped her in a less than gentle way out of the car and directed her towards the restaurant.

Once inside it took a few seconds for her eyes to adjust. The shades on every window had been drawn. Looking into the restaurant she counted only twenty-four tables, covered in white linen, each sporting a lovely small display of flowers. To her left was a small grocery-store-like counter displaying all sorts of olives, hams, cheeses and other goodies. Large cans of imported olive oil graced shelves and next to them bottle upon bottle of wine. Lastly, almost immediately to her right and behind her, was a large display of the various deserts, mostly chocolate this and that. The place smelled divine. Lovemoney was soon approached by a smaller Mediterranean looking type with a slight accent.

"My Paisan! How good to see you again. Please, please, we have a table for you and your guest."

"Thank you, Anthony. We hope we've not caused too much inconvenience."

"Any friend of yours is a friend of ours. And when Mr. Halderman called, well who can turn him down a favor, you know? And remember don't forget he works for the President of the United States, our friend. And, of course, the President used to come here often. He's from down there where all this trouble is brewing you know?"

Then all of a sudden Anthony realized he was talking too much and fell silent.

"Please, please this way, right this way. He escorted Lovemoney and Mrs. Vincent through an otherwise empty restaurant to their table.

Clear goblets of water and menus were brought to the table by a waiter who immediately retreated to the other side of the room and stood against the wall waiting for a signal.

"Mrs. Vincent, they have a very nice dry white wine here that goes very well with anything tomato based, Pinot Grigio. And I have to admit, there is no place in this country that has a lasagna as light and airy as you'll find here. So, if you don't mind, I'll order some for us?"

She couldn't resist. She was starving for some decent food and she was going to have some, damned Petracha's advice.

"Yes Sir, I'll have a glass. I'm tired and I'm hungry as well. I'll drink and eat with you and you can tell me what my husband has to say. But before we go much further you will have to prove that what you are telling me is true.

381

That indeed Barrett is with the Colonel and that he is doing well. All Barrett ever did was make promises to me and then excuses when he didn't come through on them."

"I will tell you what the Colonel has had to say, and I can prove it to you. But you should know first and foremost this is why I've brought you here. The Colonel is almost out of the woods medically! He is up for short spells, eating some liquid diet stuff and even walking to and from the latrine. He seems to be regaining his strength. I can absolutely, positively prove it to you and will do so before the day is done. That good news is worth a drink. I'm damn sure it is."

"Here's what we'll do. You give me a question, something only you and the Colonel will know the answer to. And tonight, after I get a report from Agent Barrett I will send the answer from him to you. If there's a code word or anything secret that you'd like him to say or to identify, I'll bring the answer to you personally or if I'm unable to deliver it myself, I'll have our administrative assistant, Ms. Kaye, personally deliver it. How's that sound?"

Her mind raced for a question.

"I have it. The bookstore in New England. We always enjoyed a drink there. Tell me what it was we used to drink and where we drank it?"

"I will pose the question and get the answer for you today. That's a promise. And that will prove that what I'm sharing with you about his health is true and that indeed Agent Barrett is with him as we speak."

"Now let us order some lunch and chat for a bit and hopefully this thing will be over before either one of can shake a tail. What do you say?"

"I'm suspicious, but I'm more hungry than suspicious right now."

Lovemoney thought he caught a glimpse, a whisper of a smile. He liked

382

this lady, felt bad for her. She's mixed up in a mess of epic proportions and not a hell of a lot she can do about it.

"I don't blame you and to be perfectly honest I'm more hungry than curious!" he laughed out loud. "So, let's eat. I will bring you up to date about the Colonel. I will have obeyed my orders and done my duty. Soon we can get back to the business of getting each of our lives back to normal. What do you say?""

Mrs. Vincent raised a wine glass, not enthusiastically nor very high, but she raised it and said, "I'll drink to that."

"And I as well."

# # # # #

He'd done his duty! Halderman asked him to re-engage her and he had. He'd watched or listened to all her previous interviews. He'd spent hours talking about her with Barrett. There just wasn't anything there. Nor did they find anything when they reviewed her emails, phone records, travel and purchases history. A complete review of her computer, her accounts and electronic tracings left no cause to inspire him to waste any more time on her. If he could gain her confidence, establish rapport with her, he'd consider the effort a success. At some point in time he could use that relationship as an inroad to the Colonel.

The real card in his hand was Petracha and if he could get to him to open up, just give him a glance inside the movement, give him something, maybe he could see an Achilles' heel. Then he could blow the lid off this entire case.

"Judy, have a couple of the boys bring Captain Petracha up to the conference room first thing in the morning. Let's do a sunrise breakfast. I gotta get some shut eye. Wake me up only when the boss calls or if we get a call from

Washington."

"Yes Sir, get some rest. I'll screen for ya."

"Good, give me at least three or four hours?"

"You bet. I'm going to have Patti relieve me in a few hours. I need to get home, get some sleep and freshen up as well, but I'll bring her up to date."

Eight hours later blurry-eyed Lovemoney staggered out of his office. It was nine o'clock in the evening. A few small lights were on in the outer office. A cleaning maid was vacuuming the hallway near a water cooler. His eyes were still adjusting to the light, focusing on the lights of the city when Patti Jankut walked around the corner with a cup of coffee in her hand.

"Good evening sir, did you sleep well?"

"Didn't Barrett call?" he asked as he took the coffee from her.

"No, Sir. He didn't. The only call that came in was from the director. When I told him, you were sleeping and hadn't received a call form Agent Barrett, he told me to let you sleep. That you needed some rest for clear mind. He did ask me to have you give him a status call in the morning. Are you going to go home now, Sir?"

"Yes, I think I will. I haven't seen my place in so long I'm not sure I'll recognize it. Make sure Petracha is in the conference room downstairs at 6:00 a.m."

"Yes Sir, good night. I'll pack up and head home for the evening as well as long as there's nothing else until morning."

# # # # #

Nine hours, later Mario Petracha paced back and forth in the same conference room where Gretchen Vincent met Dan Barrett nearly two weeks ago. The sun rising over lake Michigan greeted Petracha the same way it had her.

384

When Charlie Lovemoney walked into the room the sun was just breaking the horizon casting a blue hue over all of Grant Park and the yachts lined in neat rows in the harbor next to the Shedd Aquarium.

"Good morning Capt., Petracha. Thank you for meeting with me on a Sunday morning," he smiled weakly.

"No problem agent Lovemoney. I was up anyway. You never get over the military rise times you know?"

"We have coffee and rolls on the way. Should be here any minute. While we're waiting I'm going to cut to the chase. Take a look at those sailboats over there. That's the Chicago Yacht Club harbor. To the right is Shedd Harbor. Nice boats, huh?"

"Looks pretty inviting, you bet."

"I'm a water guy Captain. When I'm off duty, I'm out there on my boat with the family or on one of the rivers in Wisconsin, sometimes Michigan, upper peninsula of course. Got to ask you a question. It's just got me curious as hell. Do you mind?"

"Not at all, shoot away."

"What does it feel like to know you will never walk outside a free man ever again? That you will never smell the fresh waters of a lake like that or feel the grass beneath your feet? Like the grass in the park. What's it feel like to know you'll never feel the soft caress of a woman's hand ever again? If you look far enough south Captain Petracha, you see over there? Over there's Lake Shore Drive. If you drive just twenty minutes south there's the best Italian restaurant in all of Chicago, maybe even in the entire country." Lovemoney paused for a long time. "What's it feel like to know that all that has gone from your life never to return again?"

385

Petracha stared at him.

"Never liked water much."

Then much to Lovemoney's surprise he walked around the conference table and sat down in one of the good boy chairs.

"I never liked chairs too close to the floor," he smiled.

Lovemoney had to keep pace, no, exceed pace with him.

"Well maybe not, but I never met an Italian in all my life in all the world, and I've been all over the world Captain. Never met one that didn't go nuts for good Italian food. And you're not going to lie about that to me. Don't even try." Lovemoney hinted a little smile.

"What's the dancing all about agent Lovemoney? Let's just cut the crap and ask what you want, and I'll decide whether or not I want to give you an answer. None of this is going to work. I'm a military man. Deprivation is part of the deal. You'll find most good military men and women have mastered that in themselves. We may not live to see the next sunrise. We may never hold our wives or husbands again. We may not see our children or parents or brothers or sisters. Do you really think I'd give a crap whether I could never suck on some spumoni again? C'mon man. It's gonna take a hellava lot more than that!"

The men were interrupted by an agent delivering coffee and a tray filled with a variety of sweet rolls, energy bars and small bottles of juice. The two men remained silent while the food was set out before them. They remained in silence while each chose from the assortment. Interestingly, Lovemoney found himself on the wrong side of the conference room table. He didn't think it was accidental.

"The Sun's getting up. Would you like me to get those blinds for you?"

Petracha asked him. Then he knew it wasn't accidental.

"No, I don't think that will be necessary. We won't be here that long. The President has a news conference at ten o'clock and I must call Washington before that. So, indeed I should cut to the chase Captain. First, let me apologize for trying to hold a carrot out to you. I mean who could have imagined that you'd not miss a nice cold spumoni?" he grinned. "But let me tell you what I can do."

Lovemoney stood up and turned around. Looking out the tall windows at the Sunday morning waterfront he said.

"What I can do Captain Petracha is give you all that!"

And he pointed to the lake front. "Have you out of here a free man in a week. I can have you on a plane to any location in the world with enough money to keep you happy and safe for the rest of your life. One hundred percent immunity. Sounds like a bribe doesn't it? It's not. t's quid pro quo. Something for something. You give us something that will help us end this thing and we'll give you your freedom."

Lovemoney saw a flinch. It was small, but it was there, and his years of training and experience knew he'd hit a soft spot.

"I know that at one time you were close to Madison Vincent. I get that. I also know that he turned you over to us branded as a murderer of innocent civilians. We don't even have your side of the story. But . . . but Captain Petracha if you will give me your side of the story, if we can live with it and if you'll help us, give us something, anything that we can use to end this without having to go into Odell with force, you will have our gratitude and that of a grateful nation. And that of innocent lives saved. What do you say?"

Petracha took a long draw on his coffee before he stood up and walked

387

over to the windows. He was a man used to making quick decisions, he'd saved his life and the lives of his men on many occasions by making good decisions under a great deal of stress. "Will you put that in writing?"

"Yes."

"Will you put that in writing and sign it in front of counsel of my choice?"

"Yes."

"And he will walk out of here with copies properly signed by the attorney general of the United States and the attorney general of the State of Illinois?"

"I'll have it done by noon today."

"Ralph shot Colonel Vincent in the face through a window in his house. My men and I were patrolling that part of Odell at the time. He came out the door of the home for a second shot. The colonel's jeep was moving out of view and the girl was in the way. I had my weapon up and dropped him, shot him dead with one shot to the chest. It was an easy shot really, I wasn't that far from him. When he came out of the house either he didn't see me or didn't care. Bet he does now."

Petracha turned from the window. "I could use a cigar right now" he grinned. "While I was checking him, I noticed movement to my right. Suspecting an accomplice, I whirled around and swept up with the butt of my pistol. The impact was pretty severe as you can imagine. Unfortunately, it was his wife. An elderly woman. I didn't know she was just running to his side most likely to check on him. She looked too frail to survive that strike and as you now know, she didn't. I think she survived in a coma for a day or two before they buried her."

"The Colonel was down and his next in command, John Coffin, and I have never seen eye to eye. Don't know what version he got of the events. I was

388

never given a chance to give mine. Next thing I know I'm in cuffs standing behind an ambulance with that big lug of a sheriff, the President's cousin. It pulled away and left me staring eyeball to eyeball with the state cops. You know the rest. Is that a good start?"

"It's good enough for me. I can't believe it won't be good enough for Washington."

"Well, I'm thinking the Ole man could have saved my skin. After all, I've saved him on more than one occasion and in more dangerous places than most of the world even knows about. If Ralph had gotten off that second shot we'd be looking at a repeat of Dallas, you know? Vincent would have been deader than a rock".

"I mean, by now Vincent's had a chance to get a message to me . . . or for that matter to you guys. Looks like I'm left here hanging out to dry, comforting his wife while my butt's looking at a probable death penalty. Doesn't seem fair to me, how about you?"

"Nope. Doesn't seem fair to me either Captain. Looks like you've been sold out. And while it's not my place to give you any pause for second thought, it could be that Vincent's injuries are bad enough that your old nemesis, Coffin, is running the show. When I spoke to Agent Barrett yesterday however, he didn't indicate that at all. Vincent's still the commanding officer for sure. Nah, I guess your old buddy has sold you down the tubes, sorry."

"Now, we need to talk, but before we do, I want you to hear this." Lovemoney got his cell phone out and dialed four extension numbers. "Judy? I need you to get the legal eagles on this right away. We need to draw up immunity papers for Captain Petracha. I'll need them reviewed by them and then signed by Attorney General Swanson and then get a hold of Hinshaw. I'll need

389

him to cooperate with our legal and use his good offices to have the Illinois Attorney General sign them. I'll also need signed copies to go to Captain's Counsel. I'll have him brought by your desk on his way back to quarters in a little while.

"Now listen to me. This all has to be accomplished by end of business today; let's say five o'clock. I want the signed papers in Captain Petracha's hands by then. You'll have to call Cellini and have him get a hold of Halderman. Tell them that I personally guaranteed the immunity agreement for the Captain I want legal to call me, so I can give them the particulars. There'll be an undisclosed amount of reward money that we are working on now that must be approved by the Captain and his attorney as well. We need a ton of people on this ASAP. Call me if you or legal have any questions. I'm sure you will, but we've got some things to wrap up here and then I've got to get up to my office for the President's address and news conference at ten. Ok?"

"Yes, I'll get right on it. I'm sure legal is gonna have a ton of questions like they always do, but I'll do my best to answer them before I interrupt you."

"I'm sure they will. And I'll need to review it before it goes anywhere. Just the standard template, I'll pencil in some detail. Okay, get to it, Miss Kaye! And thank you in advance for your day off and getting this done. It's very important. Have a good morning."

Turning to Petracha while he disconnected the call with Barrett's assistant.

"You tell me who you want to represent you. But remember one thing when you make that selection. Right now, no one knows you're here. No one except your ex-compatriots in Odell and Mrs. Vincent. So, whomever you choose, make sure that boy has tight lips. Otherwise you will be hounded by the press for the rest of your natural life."

390

"It's my brother. He's got real tight lips. And Agent Lovemoney, I do want some people to know I'm here, was here otherwise . . . if I were to have an unfortunate accident in a few weeks, months or years . . . well you get the drift, right?"

"Yes, I do. I understand where you're coming from. No problem here."

"And you have to understand up front that you will definitely be called upon to testify extensively as a government witness. You do agree to testify, don't you?"

"No. Sir, you never mentioned that, and I do not. I might as well put a target on my forehead and walk into Odell right now. The deal is I give you some information and you use it however you want to end this. I'll give you details to check out and when they're verified, "poof" like in Poof, not Puff, The Magic Dragon." I'm gone. I don't need no witness protection program. I don't want anything to do with you feds. I know how to hide myself. Don't think for one second, Sir, that I like you or your boss or your bosses back in magical mystery land. Give me a bowl of water and just like Pilate, I'll wash my hands and disappear."

After a long pause, Lovemoney said, "We have a deal Captain Petracha."

# # # # #

Ten o'clock a.m. - White House, Washington D.C.

"My fellow Americans. Thank you for inviting me into your homes this Sunday morning. The events unfolding in Odell, Illinois, over the past fifteen days have made it important to clarify some erroneous reports that have found their way into various media outlets. I also want to share with you the current efforts taking place here in Washington to resolve this terrorist act".

"First, I want to thank all of you for the outpourings of sympathy expressed

391

to myself, my wife and extended family over the tragic and untimely death of the matriarch of our family and as many feel, the matriarch of our country, grandmother Mary Duke Odell. She raised me from the time I was a young boy. She was a kind and gentle woman whose life was spent in the service of others. She was a blue-blood patriot committed to justice, fairness and equality. She was a champion of women's rights, civil rights and care for the poor and underprivileged in society, especially the children. I am going to miss her angelic influence in my life. I know that she had so many friends in Odell and the surrounding area that she loved dearly. She also loved you. And while she protested the attention, I know each and every interview that saintly women agreed to, brought secret smiles to her face. She loved and appreciated the secret service details assigned to her and treated them as if they were her own kin. I know you will miss her as much as I will. It is indeed one of the great tragedies of my life that she suffered such an untimely and cruel death at the hands of heartless men."

"I'm going to take a few minutes this morning to speak to you about the terrorism that is taking place in Odell. I call it terrorism, because that's what it is. Whenever citizens of this great country are harmed with premeditation or put in harm's way that's all it can be called, and it will be dealt with accordingly. That same despicable and treasonous occupation of the town of Odell, that resulted in the death of Grandmother Odell has also taken the lives of at least two other citizens of the town and maybe more."

"There was also the wounding of others and now just this morning we've learned of the deaths of at least twenty law enforcement officers sent to investigate living conditions existing in the town and to ensure the safety of its citizens. While currently some confusion exists surrounding the events that led up to the gun fire that occurred Thursday morning, a full investigation is under way to determine who sent those state law enforcement officers into such a dangerous environment and what occurred once they arrived there. We are working closely with state and local officials to determine where lines of communication may have broken down and to make sure they will not again."

"As your President, I want to promise you that those responsible will be punished. They will be captured, and they will be prosecuted to the fullest extent of the law. I want to make this perfectly clear to you and to those responsible. I promise you and them that every resource of the Federal Government will be brought to end this treasonous act of cowardice and terrorism and mete out the justice their actions demand."

"Your President wants you to know that since the events in Odell began now just a little over two weeks ago, we've been in constant contact with the leaders of this terrorist group and that progress was being made until the unfortunate eruption of violence Thursday morning. I wish I were at liberty to discuss details, but you will understand the sensitive nature of our discussions and that we will need additional time before we can share more with you. However, I do want you to know that our efforts to avoid bloodshed have been unceasing since the very beginning. We have at this very moment high level discussions taking place in Odell with the hope of avoiding additional, senseless violence and to preserve the lives of innocent civilians and law enforcement personnel who carry the responsibility of protecting the citizenry."

"Let there be no mistake, however, it would be most unwise for any enemy of the United States, foreign or domestic, to perceive our willingness to befriend reason and common sense as a weakness. And as long as I'm President, no one will blackmail the United States."

"We must focus on Odell, but we are also determined to prevent any other community from suffering at the hands of similar treasons. To that end, my administration has been meeting with the Attorney General of the United States and his staff, counsel for the office of the President, members of congress, governors and constitutional scholars to discuss an executive action that will tighten up even further the importation and sales of weaponry such as is being used against the citizens of Odell and the country at large."

"We will shut down the use of firearms that go beyond normal, logical recreational hunting and target shooting purposes. Our law enforcement officers must not be asked to confront illegally armed individuals or domestic terrorists in the execution of their daily responsibilities. We must become more a people of peace and peaceful conflict resolution. We need to redefine ourselves from frontier mentality and frontiersman depending on arms for day-to-day survival to men and women who depend on rightfully elected officials' whose sworn duty is to protect and preserve their liberties. There must be, and I agree we must better earn the trust of our citizens. Duly elected representatives of the people so identified through legitimate electoral processes have a sacred, time proven duty to provide such assurances."

"Perhaps to the world, our country needs a newer, better definition of the words liberty and freedom. For certain the American people are much in want of one. We make declarations of liberty and freedom but in using those words do we all refer to the same thing? It has been a struggle since the founding of our great nation, contested many times this thing called liberty. I declare, as do the great majority of our fellow countrymen, that we are at liberty to go to the local mall without fear of slaughter. I declare that we are at liberty to send our children to their schools without having to arm our teachers and principals. I

394

declare that we are at liberty to attend a concert, or a seasonal festivity without fear of masked cowards slaughtering us. I declare that we should be able to go to Miller's Grocery Store in Odell, Illinois, on a Saturday morning without fear that a mob of cowardly terrorist won't wrest away from us the very most basic constitutional liberties millions have fought and died for."

"I agree with the greatest president this nation has ever had, Abraham Lincoln, when he said liberty means different things to different people. And I am here to tell the terrorist of Odell that the gods of liberty and freedom are here to stay and to define liberty in no uncertain terms differently than the gods of terrorism."

"Friday morning, after consultation with Governor Hinshaw of Illinois, we concurred with his decision to assign two units of the national guard to the Odell area. We can promise the citizens of the state of Illinois that those responsible for the atrocities in Odell will be going nowhere. They will not be spreading their venom elsewhere. There will be no more hostages or murders. We will, by God as my witness, negotiate from strength or destroy with power if that is the course we are led to."

"That favorite son of Illinois, President Lincoln once, said about having reverence for the law and impliedly the process of law '. . . let it be preached from the pulpit, proclaimed in legislative halls, and enforced in courts of justice.' And, in short, let it become the political religion of the nation; and let the old and the young, the rich and the poor, the grave and the gay, of all sexes and tongues, and colors and conditions, sacrifice unceasingly upon its altars."

"We believe in reverence for the law and the process of law. We have a sacred duty to preserve and promote that reverence and we will not bow to the offenders of all that is sacred and dear to us and our most basic liberties."

"After meeting with our resources in the intelligence community we have come to the very sad conclusion that an operation the size of this operation in Odell, utilizing sophisticated weaponry, alongside other military assets could only have been organized by, supported and encouraged through foreign enemies of the United States. As a result of many hours of research, discussion and review the administration has come to the conclusion that bringing the Central Intelligence Agency into the equation will widen our investigative efforts and assist the Federal Bureau of Investigation who has performed above and beyond the call of duty. The Central Intelligence Agency's involvement will speed up that investigative process as well. Again, all the resources of the government are being used to contain and eliminate this threat to the peace and safety to each of you, our fellow citizens."

"May God bless you my fellow countrymen and women, may God bless the souls of our dear brothers and sisters in Odell, Illinois . . . and may God have mercy on those murderous traitors responsible for the death and injury of so many of our citizens. Good day and know that the prayers of your President are with you."

When the President concluded his remarks, much to the consternation of the press corps present, he abruptly turned and walked away. One reporter was heard to mutter, "well so much for the freedom of the press to ask our President a few questions." Several reporters yelled questions to the President looking for more Odell details and especially about the executive action he'd alluded to. Others wanted to know more about the lies surrounding what was now being called the failed "Police Invasion" of Odell. What none of them could see was the color draining out of the President's face as he turned and walked down the long hallway to the Oval Office.

Chapter XXV

"What the Sam living hell do you mean, Mr. Director?" the President said as he slammed a pile of papers down on his desk, startling Cellini.

"What I mean, Sir, is that Frank Halderman called me this morning from Bethesda. His wife runs early every morning. When she got back to the house, she went upstairs to take a shower and the water from every faucet in the bathroom ran red. She then found the same thing in the rest of the house. Naturally, it frightened her. Then the next thing she did was wake up the neighbors. They had the same problem, so she called the police department who immediately responded to the Halderman residence. They've called city services who are on the way."

"And so, both you and Halderman didn't think that was important enough for me to know about before I went before the American public and completely failed to address that event. Please tell me it's not connected to those SOB's in Odell."

"We didn't want to disturb you while you were rehearsing for your address. And our thinking at the time was that it could have just been a stupid high school prank. Unfortunately, we now know that it's not."

"Are you telling me the water source for all of Bethesda has been polluted?"

"I'm afraid it's not just Bethesda, Mr. President. It's the entire northwest quadrant of the District of Columbia!"

"Again, what is the connection? How do you know it's just not some nutball copycat?"

"We have evidence that it is . . ."

"That it is what?"

397

"We have evidence that it is connected. At least we strongly suspect that it is connected because, someone left a signature card on the door of the town hall, big red letters on a black background, ARM. We were hoping it was just a copycat sympathizer until a few minutes before your address concluded. Then we got word from the west coast that a similar card was left in Sonora, California. The entire region's water supply is running a crimson red color, right in the breadbasket of one of the states' most productive agricultural areas."

"I don't need a geography lesson, Director; I know where Sonora is."

"Yes Sir."

"Are you positive it's those crackers in Odell?"

"Yes, as much as we can be at this time. Identical card taped to a downtown store window. Timing is too close not to be a coordinated effort. But there is some good news. We've identified the contaminate. Thank God, it's only red food dye. They're just sending a message this time. And the message is there's more than just Odell to be concerned about."

The President walked around his desk and sat down as he pushed the intercom button on his phone. "Yes, Sir, Mr. President, how may I help you?"

"Get the Director of the CIA over here immediately?"

# # # # #

Dan Barrett watched the President's address in his cell on a laptop provided by a middle-aged guard. He'd turned the screen, so his fellow prisoners were able to watch the address as well. Only a few of them muttered a weak thank you before returning to their own private conversations. As soon as the address was over the same guard opened the cell door and removed the computer.

398

Fifteen minutes later Captain Robert Cox entered the outer cell.

"Agent Barrett, will you please accompany me?"

Barrett, though sporting a black eye that had turned yellow and purple around the edges, was feeling a bit feisty after viewing the President's remarks.

"Oh, yeah Captain whatever your name is, as long as you can guarantee I won't get my brains bashed in while I'm under the watchful eyes of your elite guards!"

"We'll do our best, Sir." Cox replied flatly. "Now get up and move out."

Barrett stood, exited the cell and found himself surrounded by two additional guards. He was placed in hand cuffs and leg irons. He started to protest but a quick harsh look from Cox quashed the thought immediately. Discretion being the better part of valor he offered his wrists like he'd seen many prisoners do during his career.

"It feels weird," he thought as he was being led out of the building and assisted into an, oversized, black SUV whose windows were so darkly tinted, so no one could see inside.

"Agent Barrett, Col Vincent requests that you join him and Captain Coffin for a brief field trip."

His mind raced, "A field trip?"

Once he was buckled into the vehicle, Cox joined him. And then as it is in most military situations, they just sat there without moving. Five minutes pass ten and then after nearly twenty minutes of sitting in front of the jail without any noticeable command the vehicle lurched forward. He decided to say nothing, to show no emotion.

"Let's just see what these boys are up to."

The vehicle drove north on Wolf Street. It wasn't until they passed the Dinner Bell Restaurant that pangs of missing home and family hit him. He couldn't remember the last time they'd had just a quiet dinner together. For a few minutes Odell disappeared and all he could think of was Ellen and the kids.

When he finally returned to the present, they were driving slow enough that he could see after-church patrons enjoying a Sunday afternoon brunch at the Dinner Bell. They looked as though their world was as normal as could be and that Odell and themselves were not the focus of worldwide media attention. Even those milling around outside seemed to have not a care in the world. Made him wonder if this was all staged for his benefit; it wasn't. But it was most likely facilitated by Captain Cox's ability to bring in fresh food supplies for the citizens in return for the bodies of some of the dead state troopers.

They drove in a circle around the town square three times. There was also a group of what appeared to be heartier souls milling around the front door of Blintz's bar. As barbecue smoke drifted through the air and into the SUV, his mind drifted again to his own backyard and how he wanted to be with his family.

By the last circumnavigation of the town square, people were beginning to note the repeated passing with curious stares. Barrett wondered about the circuitous route. And then the last time around as the vehicle made a right turn and headed west, he noticed a crowd. Cox ordered the vehicle to a halt just outside an old white house with a small picket fence of the same color. On the screened in porch sat a flag draped coffin. He'd seen this house before on the news, it was Mary Duke Odell's. The crowd waiting across the street was there to pay their respects. Eventually, all of the town would show up, those satisfied customers of the Dinner Bell, even the inebriated from Blintz's. It's what one does in a small hometown; look after one another even off into the eternities.

Mary let it be widely known that when she passed the last place she wanted to be seen was in musty old Flynn's Funeral Home. She didn't particularly have anything against the Flynn boys, in fact one of her niece' kin was married to one of them. She just didn't like the smell of any funeral home. And then there was "all that walking around whispering thing. Heck the dead can't hear ya! And there's just that nonsense of walking around mumbling like that! Reverence don't mean ya gotta chat at each other like yer next up! The whole thing gives me the creeps. Just put me in the box, close the door, say a few nice words and get it over with. I won't be needin' no long, drawn out affair. But, you can just bet I'll be close by with the angels screaming Thank Ya, Jesus!"

And so, at 1330 hours Colonel Vincent ordered that every member of his officer cadre would be in dress uniform to attend her self-orchestrated viewing. Each member of the eight-hundred-man battle group would also pass by, a company at a time in formation as a sign of respect. Posts would not be left unattended, but it was important to Vincent that the town knew that he and his men respected this grand woman. After the troops had passed and were withdrawn, local clergy would care for the rest of those who'd come to pay their respects.

Barrett took the scene in, but he was determined not to speak. He sat in silence with Cox for four minutes and fifty-eight seconds staring at his watch. And then the driver again without any noticeable order, but seemingly in obedience to one, pulled away from the Odell home. Driving in a westerly

401

direction, Barrett was surprised as they passed under Interstate 55 past the telephone tower on the west side of town. A rural-looking road running north and south soon came within view. A left turn took them down that tree-lined road at least two miles out of town. The road dead ended at a farmhouse surrounded with old oak trees and a dark green lawn. It looked so peaceful, but it also looked as if no one was home and hadn't been for some time. No one had been. It was the second home of Dick and Ruth Ralph. They had rented it and toyed with the idea of a bed and breakfast. Now it just sat there at the dead end of the road looking out on rows of newly plowed cornfields.

Barrett looked out the window as they pulled into the grass and gravel driveway and saw several people milling around about two hundred yards west in the field. He quickly counted seven with shovels and a group of ARM soldiers standing nearby, perhaps ten of them. As he focused on the scene, he was distracted by the noise of a second vehicle. It was Colonel Vincent's jeep with Coffin sitting beside him in the rear seat. Both men were in dress uniforms, their chests lathered with medals.

Robert Cox turned to Barrett, "Sir, will you please come with me?"

He opened the door to his side of the vehicle and stepped out. Soon thereafter two burly guards opened Barrett's door and assisted him in a less than gentle manner out his side of the vehicle. He marched with mini steps to the front of the SUV where he was asked to remain standing. He looked at Vincent's jeep, but they never glanced in his direction. So, there he stood not knowing what to expect, but dread started to slowly fill his chest and ooze its way up his throat. He watched the figures in the distance; they were digging. Digging what? And then it hit him. . . they were digging a grave.

His pulse rocketed out of control. He didn't know a human heart could beat

402

that fast, so fast he couldn't catch his breath. His mind raced to a few days earlier when he got out of that state police car and how he begged his body to cut off the adrenalin. He thought he pulled it off then, but there was no doing so now.

His mind dashed to his three little ones. He was never going to see them again. Oh my God! How can this be? These men can't be seriously thinking of executing me. And then an image of his wife, Ellen. She had been, was, still is his high school sweetheart. How in God's name was she going to survive without him? She would he knew, but he begged his brain to not even think about it for another moment.

And then, in a flash, just like it had all started the angst began to subside. His training? He wasn't even sure of that. But suddenly there was a brain shift.

"Please God, don't let them see my fear. Please make sure I die like a man, in a manner that she'd be proud to tell the children about. Please, God, if you're there and you hear me, don't let these knees buckle. Then he decided he would die with dignity. Let me take this like any good American would."

It's funny all the things that will run through a man's mind in a millisecond. But if you've ever stared the death angel in the eye you know it's possible. And that's exactly what Danny Barrett was staring at, the death angel. . . it just wasn't his.

"Here, have a look" Coffin's voice startled him out of a million scenarios all running around his mind at the same time.

A pair of binoculars were in Coffin's hand and were being held out to him. Barrett grabbed them and spun about directing his attention to the people in the field. They were digging a hole; it was long and deep. Seven of them, four men and three women. All of them wearing a red scarf around their necks.

403

"Any of them look familiar Agent Barrett?"

Barrett scanned the group again. There on the left; there he was. The jerk that smashed his face in two days ago.

"Yeah, the tall one on the left. He's the kid who rifle butted me the other day."

"Yes, he and a few of the others were caught stealing food stuff from Millers warehouse and the rest thought it would be a keen idea to steal some 'munitions. That didn't go very well for them."

Coffin then took the binoculars back from Barrett.

"Did you see the President's address to the nation this morning."

"Yes, Sir, I did, but you know . . ." He was cut off.

"No buts, Agent Barrett. I just want to know if you saw the damn address?"

"Yes, yes I did."

"Our demands have been met with nothing but more lies, murder, deceit and threats. And now more corruption, the National Guard the CIA? Were this not so serious my friend it would be laughable. He must think we are playing with him."

"No, that's not true."

"He must think we don't mean what we say?"

"I'm telling you he doesn't think that at all, he understands where you're coming from. I've spoken with his chief of staff personally on several occasions!"

"He has to be a complete idiot!"

"No, that's not it at all, Captain Coffin. You and I both know there are words and deeds for public consumption all the while real intent must be kept under a basket for the time being. It's just huff 'n puff and I'll blow your

404

house down stuff. Politics, that's all."

"We don't think so."

"Captain Coffin, you know, you must know there's not a damn thing he can do that won't divide the country more and cause untold, unneeded bloodshed. You must know that. He has such limited options he's got to be peeing his bed at night."

Coffin looked at him for a minute and then cast his glance in the direction of the field. He nodded his chin in an upwards direction as if to call Barrett's attention to what was going on in the field behind him. Barrett's head turned, and he now saw seven young people in a line with their shovels blade down at their sides. A God-awful voice rang out an order. The military men raised their weapons in unison and shot. All seven of the young people fell backwards into the hole they'd been digging.

Coffin did an about face. As he was walking back towards Vincent's jeep, "The Colonel requested your presence for dinner this afternoon right after we attend Mary Odell's viewing."

# # # # #

Petracha had spent five hours too many answering Lovemoney's questions the best he felt he could. The most he really knew of any significance concerned the military strength of the men entrenched in Odell. He was, after all just a military man, a warrior. If you wanted to know anything about that, he was your guy and he had in fact shared with Lovemoney everything he knew about troop strength and weaponry, everything he knew. The information both pleased and terrified Lovemoney. He couldn't see how this was ever going to end without some kind of blood bath.

Petracha wasn't privy to the global aspects of putting the force together he told Lovemoney. The financing, the support mechanisms in place or for certain the size and scope of ARM were way beyond his "need to know". He told Lovemoney he'd been approached by Vincent on a fishing charter boat off the Florida Keys. It was there he first learned of the plan to take Odell and force the government to acknowledge that the campaign for the Scottstown/Brady Bill was a scam forced down the throat of the electorate. He'd been recruited solely for his military expertise, his leadership of men and his loyalty to Colonel Vincent. It was Vincent that talked him into this mess he complained.

But Petracha did know a lot more than he was letting on. He knew that there were others poised to strike at the drop of a hat, but he was going to hold that card in his pocket until he was safely out of the building on his way to somewhere unknown. As he got up to leave the conference room, he signaled for Lovemoney to cut off the recorders, all of them.

He leaned on the agents' desk and said, "Now, I'm going to give you my get-out-of-jail-free card. This is worth more than anything you've heard so far, this afternoon and I don't want my voice on any damn recording spilling this to you. Deal?"

"Deal."

"Gretchen Vincent. She's the key. She's the only weakness the ole man has. f you want to get Vincent out of Odell, she's your bait. She's the only chance you have of getting him to the table to talk and my best guess is you'd love to have him right here?"

"Would be nice."

"He's gonna scream hellfire about coming out of there. There's only one other person that could convince him to do so."

"And who would that be?"

406

"Yer lookin' at 'em. He may have tossed me out of Odell on some bad intel, but he and I go back a long way, a long, long way. We've survived some battles, literally and figuratively, he and I and one thing I do know, he trusts me. If I tell him he needs to get here to rescue his wife. If I tell him she's sinking fast under all this pressure and that I'm worried for her health."

"If I tell him she's . . ." a short pause before he smiles and continues, "If I tell him she's refusing to eat, and even tube feeding is not doing the trick. If I tell him that she's dying, he'll figure out some way to come running. He's gonna raise hell about it, scream to the rooftops, but he'll come if I tell him he will never see her alive again if he doesn't. And you my friend, can take that to the bank."

Lovemoney didn't take long to take to the idea.

"How could we get him here physically. He's gonna be suspicious as hell."

"Yeah, he'll come armed to the teeth. He's a warrior and he's not gonna lay his guns down. And he'll still have Odell hostage. If he comes under a white flag and he knows doing that will keep you fellas away from his headquarters, I'm pretty sure he'll come. He's gonna squeal about if for a few days like I told ya. He's gonna tell you to stuff it and that until demands are met he's not doing anything, but give him a few days to mull it over and he'll come around. He may bring an aid or two. Coffin won't come because he's second in command. He'll bring one of the younger ones who he trusts but can do without if things go south for him. But he'll come."

"You get the word to him through Barrett that I need to speak to him, and I'll bring him to you. But here's the caveat, don't cross me or there'll be more blood running in the streets of Odell than you can imagine, and it will be your black face on the front page of every newspaper in the free world. And they

407

won't be singing your praises. You'll make Waco look like a day at the freakin kiddies' pool Charlie."

"You don't have to worry about that Captain, I said we have a deal and we do. I've got to run this by my superiors, and they have to run it by theirs. You know the dance. But I like it. If we can get Vincent to leave Odell, we can work on the next steps to be taken. Is that about all now?"

"No. When I get him to come, when he gets here, he's going to want to see her. When he does, he's going to know he's been duped. And that's ok. He's here and he can do nothing about that once he arrives. Give him, give them some time. Fifteen minutes, half an hour I don't care. But I want my time with him. Not private mind you. I want to sit across the table from him and look him in the eye, so he knows I'm the one that brought him here. And then, when we've all had our little cup of tea together, Mrs. Vincent and I go, at the same time, together. I mean out of here with an armed escort as far as the front door and nobody following us. Vincent will bring an extra vehicle, he's not gonna trust you guys. Have him bring Barrett in an extra car and we can do an exchange outside right in front of the building in broad daylight. Have my brother there, have whomever you want to take charge of Barrett, then Mrs. Vincent and I drive off into the sunset. Then forget about us."

"We have no deal concerning the release of Mrs. Vincent."

"We do now, or we don't have any deal! Look, you've grilled her 'til she looks like a swiss cheese sandwich. She's got nothing. She knows nothing; you've said so yourself. Let her go. I'll turn her loose and she can come home when this all settles down. That's the deal Agent Lovemoney. You want some time to think it over?"

"Yes. I'll think it over."

"Good. I'm going up to the roof with the boys for a cigar, wanna come?"

"Uh . . . no, no thank you."

"Okay. One more thing now that I think of it."

"Yes?"

"The ole man, Colonel Vincent?"

"Yes?"

"Don't underestimate him. That would be the worst thing you could ever do."

"I won't. Now I have one more question for you."

"Yeah."

"What's your deal with Gretchen Vincent? Why do you care about her?"

"I don't. I just want to see the look on his face when I walk out of the room with his woman."

# # # # #

When Dan Barrett arrived back at his jail cell, he noticed a suit, a freshly pressed white shirt and tie hanging in his cell. There was a note attached to it. "Agent Barrett, we felt you could stand a fresh set of clothing before joining the Col for dinner. If there is anything else you need, please advise the guards who will get word to me right away. It was signed "Captain Coffin."

"These guys are nuts, oh my God, certifiable frigging crazies!" he thought. "He'd witnessed the execution of seven innocent, teenaged children and these mad men wanted him to join them for dinner? Dinner? How could he even think of food? How could they think of food? All he wanted to do was vomit and then lay down and go to sleep. His brain had never raced faster, his training seemed worthless. There were no rules here, nothing could prepare anyone for dinner with these crazed, murderers! This was insane." His thoughts were interrupted by one of the guards.

"Agent Barrett, if you'd like we've been authorized to take you down to the showers to clean up. Or if you would prefer to get some rest first, just call when you are ready. Chow with the Colonel is at 1530 hours Sir. We shouldn't be late."

All he could do was stare at the young man before he fell backwards onto his cot.

"Insane."

Two hours later a baton rattling along the bars of his cell woke Barrett from a sound nightmare-filled sleep.

"Agent Barrett, we're running a bit late if you wish to shower and shave before joining the Colonel, Sir."

"Yeah, what the heck happens if I decide I just don't want to join the Colonel for dinner?"

"That wouldn't be a good idea, Sir. The Colonel has a temper and doesn't like being disappointed. Surely, you got that point this morning in the fields."

The guard didn't look like he was kidding. Remaining stationary on the cot for some time, Barrett finally sighed in resignation.

"All right. Lead me to the showers."

A half an hour later with two days of sweat and grime removed, clean shaven and suited up, Barrett exited the jail for the second time that day and got into the same black SUV that had chauffeured him around earlier in the morning. This time he wore no cuffs and had no chaperone, only the driver. Once the vehicle got underway, he noted almost immediately that they were not headed in the direction of Vincent's headquarters.

"Driver, where are we going? I thought we were going to dinner with the

410

Colonel?"

"We are, Sir. We'll be there in just a few minutes."

With that announcement the vehicle turned left onto Prairie Street and headed a few blocks west. When it reached the corner of Spencer it turned right and came to a halt at the end of the block in front of a large white Victorian home. Standing outside at attention were two guards in full army dress uniforms, white gloves and all. All Barrett could think was what the hell was going on? The driver remained seated while one of the guards walked to the side of the vehicle and opened the rear passenger door for Barrett.

"Sir, Colonel Vincent awaits your arrival. Please step into the parlor on your left as soon as you enter the home. Someone will be there to escort you to the dining room. Thank you, Sir."

Barrett took a long, deep breath and looked around the street. It was lined with large, old oak trees whose new green leaves rustled ever so slightly in the springtime breeze. The rest of the street was quiet, too quiet for a Sunday afternoon, but given the circumstances nothing seemed ordinary or out of the ordinary in this town. Everything was so screwed up he couldn't tell what was up or what was down. Of course, that's just what Colonel Vincent wanted of him.

The home smelled old, clean but old. It had been on that corner for over a hundred years. The old woman who owned it had offered its use to Colonel Vincent the very first day he'd come to town and given the speech from the backend of that flatbed truck. What a striking figure he cut she thought; reminded her of her husband when he came home from World War II. Now she sat in an upstairs bedroom staring out the window at the two guards who were protecting her house while the most handsome Colonel Vincent had guests for

411

dinner. What an honor, what an honor she blushed.

Another guard, unarmed, again in full dress uniform soon approached him as he stood in the middle of the parlor.

"Sir, won't you join the Colonel in the dining room? Right this way."

Barrett followed the young man down a narrow hallway aside a dark staircase towards the rear north side of the house. When the escort came to the dining room entranceway he halted and turned to Barrett with an outstretched arm inviting him into the room.

As soon as Barrett hit the entrance and turned to his left, he was greeted with a sight that buckled his knees! The soldier reached out to steady him. Colonel Vincent rose from his seat alongside Ellen Barrett and the three children.

"See Mrs. Barrett, just like I told you, your husband's in good shape except for that shiner. Some folks here in Odell just don't like anything about the federal government. But don't you worry we took care of that rascal this morning, didn't we Dan?"

Not waiting for a shocked Barrett to respond, "Heck, he looks a lot better than I do! Having to dine with two beat up scarred old soldiers like us makes me want to apologize to you Mrs. Barrett, I really do!"

At the sight of their father the three Barrett children ran to embrace him. Their grasps jolted Barrett out of shock enough for him to hug and kiss them and assure them that yes, daddy was fine, just working with the Colonel on some very important business. And, yes, after dinner they could go see the army men if it was okay with Colonel Vincent. With a child hanging on to each leg and one around his waist, he made his way past the empty chair across from his wife and crushed her in his arms.

412

"Are you okay Baby?" he asked her.

"Why yes, we've been treated wonderfully by the Colonel. Couldn't wait to see you."

Looking over her shoulder to Vincent, "How on earth did you get here?"

"Charlie, Charlie Lovemoney left a message on the answering machine this morning that he was sending a car for us, so we could come see you. The arrangements, you know, had been made and that we were to put on our Sunday best and get ready to have dinner with you. So," she smiled, "here we are. Isn't it wonderful? Your eye looks so sore. You are well though, aren't you?"

"Yes Baby, I'm fine."

"Well," piped in Colonel Vincent, "This is what Sunday's all about, being with family; going to church, sitting around the table for dinner with each other. Too many families in our country have gotten away from that, don't you think Dan?"

"Yes, Sir, I believe you're right," was about all Barrett could muster at that point. His heart was still beating two hundred beats per minute.

"Well, lookie here," Colonel Vincent said, "let's have us a good ole fashioned Sunday dinner together. Then, Mrs. Barrett, we'll let you and your husband have half hour or so, no an hour or so together before we get back to work. Does that meet with your approval, Dan?"

"Why yes, Sir Colonel, that sounds just fine with me. And when the hour is over. . ."

"When the hour or so is over, we'll see that the family gets a nice ride back home, delivered to the front porch all safe and sound. You have my word on it. I promise you. Is that all right with you?"

"Yes Sir. Yes. Thank you for bringing Ellen and the kids here."

413

"My pleasure. What do ya say, let's eat?"

During the next two hours dinner was served, and dinner conversation was had between Colonel Vincent and his guests. He expertly avoided any conversation having anything to do with the occupation of Odell by him and his troops. The dinner chatter was kept light and Barrett, of course, took note of it also guiding any talk away from politics or the occupation of Odell. Ellen Barrett was no dummy. She knew something had to have kept Dan from calling her over the last few days. So, when Charlie left that message as brief as it was, and she was given the opportunity to come see Dan for herself, she wasn't going to ask any questions that could injure whatever talks he was engaged in. She quickly realized that some topics were strictly off limits, so she avoided them the remainder of the stay.

After the long dinner Colonel Vincent made his apologies, offered Dan Barrett and his wife and children some alone time which was closely observed by guards placed at a distance. Barrett knew better than to let on what his real status was to Ellen. Yeah, some hot head kid had taken a swipe at him because he was the Federal Government guy, but Vincent had punished the kid, and all was forgiven. The rest of the hour was spent on family matters. Ellen, as bright as she was, voluntarily remained in the dark.

At 6:45 p.m. she and the children kissed Dan Barrett goodbye and slid into the back seat of the same black SUV that bore the insignia of the FBI on the side of each door that had picked them up earlier in the day. They drove off into the dusk with children, arms waving outside each of the rear windows. Would it be the last time he ever saw them? That's what Dan Barrett was wondering.

He was still wondering that when he was escorted into Colonel Vincent's

414

office an hour later. He was too exhausted to want to know anything more than his cell and his cot. Vincent was behind his desk looking over a map which he quickly folded when he saw Barrett entering the room.

"Please have a seat Agent Barrett. I trust you enjoyed your visit with your family?"

"Yes Sir, I did. Thank you."

"You're welcome. They are a beautiful bunch. You are a lucky man. You have a beautiful wife and adorable children, all-American Americans. I applaud you."

And then a few moments of silence. "I have a wife also, do you know?"

The question stung Barrett.

Every interrogation technique came to mind. Vincent thought the agent was pretty easy to read for a trained professional, but then they'd scrambled his brains pretty good that day. Inwardly he smiled.

"Do you?"

"Yes, Sir, I do know Mrs. Vincent."

"Well, then, perhaps when this is all over and we have, peacefully without further bloodshed, returned to our respective homes, you to yours with your sweet wife and I to mine with my Gretchen . . . do you know her name is Gretchen, Agent Barrett?"

"Yes, of course Colonel Vincent. What's the point of all this?"

"Well the point is, Agent Barrett, I wonder, how do you think it would feel to know that you'll never have that opportunity again? What do you think it would feel like to know for certain that you'll never see those little arms waving goodbye again? Or to feel the softness of your wife's cheek as it lies in the crook of your neck, to feel her breath on you, to smell her. How do you think

415

that would feel my young friend?"

Barrett's pulse increased. "It wouldn't feel very good, Sir."

Vincent's head dropped a little, staring at a legal pad he was drawing circles on, round and round and round. And for the first time since he'd met the man, Barrett saw some emotion. "You're right. It doesn't feel very good. Let me tell you something. I want you to know this in case you survive this mess. It's important to me personally that at least one of you feds understand; even if it's lowly you. That you understand that that bastard who ranted on and on this morning calling us traitors is a liar who is doing his best to steal the true liberties and freedoms of the citizens of this country. And me and my men and ARM are not about to let that happen."

Agent Barrett, now that you've had a taste, now that you have just an inkling of what that feeling might be like, please understand that each man under my command knows that feeling, because every night when he lies his head down to sleep he feels that feeling. He pictures them the way they were the last time he saw them, just like you are now that you have, perhaps, seen your family for the last time. Each one of my men made that choice *willingly. . .* chose to never sit at a Sunday dinner with his wife, children, parents, brothers or sisters, friends ever, *ever again*. They chose it, Agent Barrett. They have their free agency and they chose it. And my dear enemy, they made that choice for . . . for you and those sweet little children of yours."

"You work for a gang who wants to take away choice, every choice eventually, free-agency. They started with the little ones, no prayers in schools, no pledge of allegiance either, let's not stand for the flag, let's disrespect the national anthem and all those who died for it, let's shove mandatory insurance down their throats but exempt themselves, give 'em unending overly

416

burdensome taxes, especially on those who could stand it the least. They've imprisoned millions with a sense of entitlement in exchange for votes. Our veterans stand in endless lines to get substandard medical care, care for wounds sustained defending this country while those morons in Washington send billions of dollars to nations who burn our flags and shout 'death to American' in their streets!"

"The American public is fed up Agent Barrett. I'm fed up, my men are fed up. We're fed up with minority rule. We're fed up with your bosses stealing our voices, our rights, one at a time and then one more at a time, bigger and bigger until soon laryngitis is all we'll have."

After some pause, Vincent raised his eyes until they met Barrett's.

"What if I took the choice to ever share a meal with your family again away from you Sir?"

Barrett swallowed hard, no use in hiding it. "I wouldn't like it, Sir."

"No, I wouldn't expect you would."

Vincent stood up with his cup of coffee in his hand. He moved around to the front of his desk and then walked slowly towards the door. He turned around and said, "I'm going to do something unconventional, Agent Barrett. I'm going to allow you to call Lovemoney right now on my personal line. It's not monitored, the only one in Odell that's not. You get him on the line and tell him I'm running out of patience. Either we start seeing some progress to-wards meeting our demands instead of this constant volley of lies and huff an' puff 'I'm gonna blow your house down' crap from the President . . . or we're gonna start executing people."

"You know I'm capable of that you, don't you? After this morning you can't possibly have any doubt about that do you? Because if you do, the

417

greater good demands that I assemble another line up for you to witness until you are convinced that I am capable and willing."

"Seeing those young people die, looking at Mary Duke laid out in that coffin has given me my fill for the day. Yes, Sir, I want to see movement and if I don't my temperament is going to get a hellava lot sourer than it already is. Any doubts?" Vincent stared long and hard at him.

"I have no doubts Colonel. I'll make the call as soon as you want me to."

"I'll step out, you make it."

Of course, Vincent had no intention whatsoever of allowing Barrett to make that call without listening in and Barrett wasn't naive enough to think that he was. All he wanted to do was to get to Lovemoney and do whatever it took to calm this insane murderer down. It was 7:30 Sunday evening and it had been a very long day, but he couldn't let the mental and physical fatigue he was feeling hold him back.

Lovemoney was sitting on the couch in his office staring at the remnants of a submarine sandwich and a few potato chips on the coffee table next to several bottles of diet coke. He was wondering when, if ever, he'd have a hot home cooked meal again. He was just about to call his mother like he did on every Sunday evening since he'd left home, when the phone rang, and two other agents walked into the room.

"Lovemoney" he answered.

"Charlie, this is Dan."

"Dan, are you, all right?"

"I'm fine and I've a ton of information I want to share with you but first I want to know what the heck you were thinking sending Ellen and the kids into this mess?"

418

"What? I don't know what the heck you're talking about. They were there? Are they out? I'd never send them into that snake pit. You have to know that!"

Lovemoney had no idea that Barrett's family had been in Odell nor that they were now home, the kids tucked away in bed and Ellen working on laundry.

"You mean you didn't send a car for them?" Two rooms above Vincent and Coffin allowed a smile.

"No never."

It sobered each man as they realized Vincent's men had been inside and outside the perimeter four times that day without their men, including the National Guard, having any idea that it had happened. Had they been out before and how?

"I guess that's not important right this minute, but please have someone get hold of Ellen and make sure she and the kids are home safe. Do that right away, will you?"

"I've got someone on it right now. I'll know in a few minutes."

"Look, things are heating up here. Vincent feels there's been no serious consideration of the demands. It's quite tense and the President's address did nothing to de-escalate the feelings of frustration here in Odell. I witnessed the execution of seven, maybe eight innocent young people this morning in a field just southwest of town. He's threatening to execute more citizens if they're not taken seriously."

"You've got to do something. We've got to get some dialogue going. Believe me they're dug in here in numbers. We've even got Stockholm syndrome starting to show its head. The people are starting to develop relationships with these guys, the propaganda effort is working. Kids are running around with

419

red bandanas tied around their necks in support. Cripes, some of them are even acting as guards at the jail. I've seen it firsthand."

"It's going to take some high-level actors that have the authority to make some concessions and get things moving. There's no way whatsoever to move these guys out of here by force without massive civilian casualties. The whole town is wired, at least that's what I've been told and right now I have no reason to doubt them. What's your take from there?"

"I've spent a long time talking to Captain Petracha. He's shared some very interesting intel." Lovemoney knew "the boys" had to be listening as well. "The thing that has each of us concerned right now is that Mrs. Vincent has gone on a hunger strike. She's saying no counsel, no food. We've had medical monitoring her but she's failing notwithstanding our efforts to convince her to eat. Next thing up is more tube feeding, but I gotta tell ya I'm real concerned for her. Personally, I don't think she knows a damn thing about what's going on here. She just wants to get to her husband and there's little chance that she believes us that he's nearby. I've spoken with Cellini and Halderman and neither is convinced to turn her loose or to allow counsel at this time." He paused to listen for a familiar noise from a third-party listening in. There was none.

Knowing they were listening anyway he continued, "Petracha says we should send a delegation to Odell or some nearby neutral spot. Has to be done covertly or the damn press will have a field day with it and likely screw up any progress before it can even be obtained."

"No not ever. There's no way they'll let anyone near this place. I'm not sure Vincent will buy that. The next government agent or representative that approaches the perimeter will be shot on spot. I've been reassured of that. He trusts none of them and so far, who's to blame him. What about District Six

420

headquarters. Its close and each side will have reinforcements nearby?"

"I don't know. You see if he'll buy it. First, we gotta know he'll talk, then we've got to know who he'll talk with, any venue he'll consider and timing. You're in the best position to answer those questions. Our preference is that we have them come here. It could be done under cover of darkness. I'll see who Halderman and Cellini wants to represent the President. He may have the attorney general come, but we've got to keep this away from the press."

"Look if Vincent will come here under a flag of truce, under a promise that he can return to Odell until something is worked out, maybe, just maybe we can get his wife cut loose from here. Maybe we can do a covert exchange. You will be allowed to walk out in broad daylight and she'll be released to go home to her parents with the explanation that she was doing her best to be an intermediary?"

"We have to get the powers in Washington talking with these folks. There has to be a solution. And look, I gotta tell ya something. There have been events, harmless at least for now, on both coasts. hey're connected to ARM. It may be just a couple nut job copycats or sympathizers, or it may be another part of a larger thing. We just don't know. The President has asked the CIA to engage with us to see if there are overseas tentacles attached to this thing. You know that's gonna complicate this beyond all get out. Just what we need those cowboys running amuck. No guessing what they'll turn up or make up if they don't turn something up. We have to get people talking before they get too in-volved."

"I agree, Charlie. I just don't know if I can convince Vincent to trust any-one enough to make a trip out of this place. They're so dug in What's the ad-vantage to them?"

421

"I don't know, but Petracha says he knows these folks pretty well and he's more than concerned about Mrs. Vincent. In fact, he spends much of his time when he's not in his cell sitting at her bedside. Maybe if we can convince him to speak with Vincent, he can convince him to come under a white flag and begin talks. Ideally, if he does, we can send his wife out to a hospital for treatment and then home. I'll work on this end, you do so on your end."

"Here's what else I'm going to suggest, and you can pass this along to Colonel Vincent. I'm going to suggest that we covertly bring Halderman in. There's no way the President or Vice President can come, but if we bring in Halderman and the attorney general it'll be a start, a darn good start."

"The attorney general can take whatever evidence they have against the named politicians who allegedly bought the votes on Scottstown/Brady and run with it. Promise an independent transparent investigation. If they uncover the dirt on these boys and girls that ARM says it has then corrective political action can follow, maybe a revision or repeal. Anything that can bring this to the beginnings of the end. You run this by Vincent, get some recommendations from him, add your own and see if we can make it happen. One thing's for sure. I agree with you; everybody has to agree. The only sensible way to end this is diplomacy."

"Next time you call, I'll have Petracha available to speak to Vincent if he's willing. I'm not sure he'll want to speak to Captain Petracha, but he thinks he can convince Vincent to come rescue his wife and at least begin dialogue."

"Here's my last concern. If we lose her, I'm afraid all hell's gonna break loose." Lovemoney and Barrett spoke for another thirty minutes. Barrett told him everything that had happened since the last time they'd spoken. Some time was spent on the execution of the seven teens early Sunday morning and

Barrett's concerns that the mass murder was just the beginning of such desperate actions. In fact, he'd been promised so. And . . . no he didn't know when or if ever he was going to be allowed to leave Odell. He thought it more likely than not that he'd be leaving in a pine box.

"Dan, Tell Vincent, Lovemoney's tired and getting impatient. . . 'I can let Mrs. Vincent wither away to skin and bones and not give a damn. Give Colonel Vincent that message. All of us can play bad ass if that's what he wants. Give me 'til tomorrow to put together a proposal. Call me tomorrow afternoon as close to five o'clock as you can."

"Will do Charlie. Take care and I'll call you tomorrow."

"Dan, we've just confirmed that Ellen and the kids are home. We've got a detail parked outside the home for the duration. Just wanted to let you know before we go."

"Thanks. Needed to hear that."

Five minutes passed between the end of the phone call and the time Vincent walked back into his office. Once he sat down in his chair, he looked at Barrett.

"How did it go?"

"It went, Sir. I asked Agent Lovemoney to contact Washington and see if we could put a proposal on the table that might be appealing enough to you to initiate some dialogue. We both know, as we've agreed before, that there'll be the public position and the real position. I've asked him to bring some high-ranking government officials who'll have both the President's ear and authority to move this stalemate off center. Hope that's what you were looking for, Sir."

"I didn't say so, but if conversation will lead to movement on our demands,

I'm a reasonable man and will entertain your proposal. But let me be clear about any conditions that must be adhered to before I'll consider anything. First no law enforcement officials are to be present and whoever the government representatives are they must have rank. Second, no one is to come near the Odell perimeter and whatever the venue, it has to be neutral. Third and finally, significant demands satisfaction proposals must be on the table. Don't waste our time. Understand?"

"Agent Lovemoney is working on it as we speak. We're going to try to have something worth speaking about by tomorrow afternoon if that meets with your approval."

"It does. And now let me share something else with you before we call it a day, Agent Barrett. And we can both agree it's been a long, stressful one. Know those young people out there in the field that got executed this morning. The ones that made the vomit stick in your throat?"

"Yes?"

"Why, Agent Barrett, did you stand by and not do a damn thing to save those innocent kids? What the living hell is a matter with you?"

"Me? What? What the hell could I do? What the hell is the matter with you? You murdered those kids in cold blood. What did you expect me to do? What could I do?" Barrett barked back angrily in disbelief that he could be accused of doing nothing!

Vincent sat back in his chair and lit up a cigar. He hardly ever smoked, but he wanted one now.

"I know Agent Barrett. I know. You couldn't do a darn thing. Could you?"

"No, you know I couldn't, or I would have."

"Yes, I do know that, and I know that you being the kind of man that you are would have if you could have; even, Agent Barrett, if it would have cost you your own life. Isn't that so?"

"Yes, you're damn right its so, Colonel."

"But do you know why you couldn't?"

"It's obvious Colonel. I don't know what you're getting at. It's obvious, I had no means." Vincent drew a long tug on his cigar and exhaled. He picked up his cup of coffee and drank from it before he answered Darrett again.

"It's not obvious. If it was, you'd be ashamed of yourself and those jack asses in Washington, you want me to meet with."

He paused again staring at Barrett with a look of disbelief in his eyes this time.

"You couldn't Agent Barrett, because you were outnumbered by a superior force and because *we'd disarmed you.* You, my friend, were just like those innocent folks in Lidice's town square when they stood by, just like you, helpless and watched hundreds, all the men and boys of the village, get slaughtered right in front of their very eyes. Husbands, brothers, sons, nephews shot dead, bodies heaped upon one another and burned to ashes, right in front of their womenfolk."

"You couldn't do a damn thing. The only solace you have Sir, the only peace of mind that I'm going to give you tonight, so you can sleep in spite of your impotence is. . . is that the entire thing you saw this morning was a charade, an object lesson. The fire went over their heads, they fell backwards into a grave lined with bed mattresses."

"How did it feel, my friend, to be so impotent in the face of insane tyranny? Not so good, not so good did it?"

Barrett didn't know what to say. He just sat there staring at Vincent. All he

425

could really think was something he didn't want to think, couldn't think, didn't dare think. And that was this, "Could these maniacs have a point?"

After a very long, pregnant pause during which Vincent knew sometimes the best answer was no answer he said, "in one half an hour I want you to get back on the phone with Lovemoney. I want you to reinforce for him that we need to crap or get off the pot. They are going to do something, get something moving, or it will not be long before we blow this entire town to kingdom come. Any questions?"

"I'll make the call."

Chapter XXVI

Barrett and Lovemoney spent the better part of Monday and Tuesday trying to convince authorities in Washington to meet with representatives of ARM, in particular Colonel Vincent. Lovemoney spent hours on conference calls trying to convince Cellini and Halderman that "discussion" didn't equate to "negotiations."

Everyone knows the United States doesn't "negotiate" with terrorists foreign or domestic. It was such a tiring battle.

They had all agreed that any attempt to end the Odell occupation by force would involve a decision that made massive collateral damage inevitable and, worse yet, acceptable. Everyone equally agreed that it would be political suicide to make such a decision. There was a sense that the botched tactical squad invasion as it was now being referred to, began a tip in public opinion. The media overwhelmingly condemned the Odell takeover, but they had to admit the "man on the street" was beginning to get more and more suspicious of the reactions of Washington. The President was already losing approval ratings points on a daily basis, some angry that he'd not gone into that town and kicked some butt, some angry that he'd not addressed the allegations made by ARM that were becoming the suspicions of more and more Americans.

The fly in all this ointment of course was precedent and repercussion.

Halderman said to Cellini during one conference call, "Look, let's say we go in there and have tea with these traitors. What's to say we come to some agreement. It's not going to ever happen without prosecution and incarceration. If these guys think they're just gonna fold up their bed rolls and go home to momma and the kids, they're more nuts than I think they are."

"The President and I and the rest of his cabinet have discussed this ad

427

nauseam. Let's say we do have a meeting with these folks, and all's resolved. What happens next week when some group of crazies decides they don't like the color of the dollar bill, or a vote for aid or the creation of a dam? It opens the flood gates for every whacko in the world to try the same exact thing!" Lovemoney had run into that argument or versions of it time and time again. He was so tired of talking to the walls that he didn't know what to do. He didn't know what to do until 0437 hours on Wednesday morning the third week of the occupation of Odell, Illinois.

Colonel Vincent, Capt. Coffin and Captain Cox were standing on the second-floor balcony of the VFW headquarters just before St. Paul's Catholic Church was blown so sky high that citizens on the east side of Kankakee forty-five miles away saw the bright glow of an orange sky. Had the three men not been sheltered by a large cement column they surely would have sustained serious injury. State troopers at District Six headquarters thought they were under attack. So, did the citizens of Odell. It had been less than a week since the night air was filled with gunfire! National Guardsmen were placed on red alert, guns were at the ready and artillery pointed towards the town from every direction though that was more for the news boys than for conflict purpose. Almost every window in every home on the south side of town was cracked, shattered or blown out completely. People's immediate, though not entirely intelligent, reaction was to flood out into the streets. Some though, dove for the shelter of their family rooms or cellars.

Almost immediately after the explosion young soldiers in jeeps patrolled the streets reassuring the residents that it was just a gas main. At least, that's everyone's best guess. And thank God Father Moore had been given permission to travel up to Mokena to celebrate the 150th anniversary of the

428

establishment of the Franciscan Sisters of the Blessed Heart. He was uninjured and safe nearly forty miles away. And Colonel Madison T. Vincent was more than happy to suggest the trip exception, so he could blow Father's church to smithereens!

All the prisoners in the jail, including Dan Barrett, thought for sure the government had begun another attempt to unseat the hold on Odell. He shuddered as he pressed his ear to the grey mason brick south wall of his cell. The window was too high to see out, but after a while he was able to pick up bits and pieces of conversations.

He could hear jeeps flying back and forth and loudspeakers reassuring people. Gas explosion, that's what he heard and while his head was still swimming his heart rate started to slow. Wouldn't that be what he needed while trying to calm these boys down, trying to get them to the table? Another misguided unsuccessful run by force at them. Who knew how in God's name they would retaliate with!

A few minutes after the debris settled, Colonel Vincent turned to Captain Cox, "Captain do you think Agent Barrett is awake at this hour?"

Captain Cox, doing his very best to subdue a grin replied, "My best guess, Sir, is yes. I'd say he was very much awake."

"Good, then please deliver a message to him for me. Tell him to call Lovemoney at 0700 hours. He can share with him the unfortunate news of the natural gas explosion resulting in the utter destruction of St. Paul's, the church his President helped to arrange national landmark status for. You can tell him that if the President, Halderman and Cellini don't quiet the saber rattling and get to the table, another church most probably connected to that same faulty gas line is going to blow up tomorrow and another one the day after that and

429

another one the day after that."

Barrett was still standing on his tip toes trying to hear pieces of conversations taking place outside the jail when Cox walked in. As soon as Barrett saw him, he rushed to the cell bars spuing question after question, not waiting for an answer.

"What was that? Has anybody been injured? We heard it was a natural gas explosion. What blew up?"

"Unfortunately, St. Paul's. And it was not natural gas."

And then he delivered Vincent's message to him.

"The Colonel will enjoy breakfast with you at 0700 hours. After breakfast you will call Lovemoney and clarify what took place this morning. You will have him deliver this message to the liars in Washington. Number one, if the President doesn't like the message, do something about it. The guard is nearby, we assume they're ready. We are as well. Number two, if Gretchen Vincent dies, Colonel Vincent will set in motion events that can only be described as widespread armed insurrection on a scale the President could never fathom. And the beginning of those events will be the complete, utter and total destruction of Odell and all of its fine citizens. It will be for 'the greater good'. Number three and this is the last point, eliminate the delay, shut down the rhetoric and initiate good faith negotiations towards a reasonable, peaceful resolution of our demands or suffer the consequences and let them fall squarely on an increasingly unpopular Presidency."

"Good morning to you Agent Barrett, we expect you in the Colonel's dining room shortly."

With that Cox executed a crisp about face and left the room. Barrett stood with his aching head pressed against the cold steel bars of his cell for several minutes. He remembered from his training all those tortures, mostly the mental ones that he knew could never break his spirit. And now all he could think of were those prisoner interrogation films he'd watched from past wars and how he'd secretly disdained those men and women who apologized to the enemy, denounced their country, said whatever they'd been forced to say. Now he understood what it meant to have one's brain turned to mush. He walked back to his cot and fell on it. He'd never get another full night of rest his entire life no matter how this turned out. All he could do was to think of a warm safe embrace with his Ellen. Exhausted, he fell back asleep.

# # # # #

The breakfast with Colonel Vincent and Captain Coffin was as crazy as he'd imagined it would be. Bataan rattling his cell bars, dressing hurriedly and shaved, then driven to the dining room, cold greetings, reiterated demands and then, "Agent Barrett, here's a cell phone, return to your cell. Get a hold of Lovemoney and don't come back here until you have a reasonable proposal. I expect that the battery will run out in about twenty-four hours. If we don't hear from you, we'll assume Washington has no interest in our demands."

Colonel Vincent wiped his lips and left the dining room. Coffin followed him shortly thereafter but not before giving Barrett additional advice.

"Dan, may I call you Dan?"

"Yeah sure."

"Dan, look the Colonel is no man to be trifled with trust me. When I tell you this is much, much bigger than this little isolated town. You need to get these guys to the table to discuss our demands or all hell is going to break out all over this country. Surely by now Lovemoney knows what happened in Bethesda, the entire northwest quadrant of D. C. and in California?"

431

This was the first time Barrett had heard anything about either of the two events.

"No what? What happened there?" he asked dreading the answer.

"Oh, not much. Just a little exercise to let those folks know the more global reach of our organization should it be necessary. Now listen. The Colonel and those closest to him are beginning to believe based upon the President's rhetoric and the lack of positive response that there is no interest in a peaceful conclusion to this matter. Unfortunately, it's going to fall on your shoulders and Lovemoney's to convince the powers that be to change minds."

"You must know Colonel Vincent didn't bring your family here just, so you could have a lovely family Sunday brunch with them. He wanted you to know what ARM is capable of if necessary. Back in my day they called it AT&T. Ya know? Reaching out and touching someone. We are capable of some real havoc. All that can be avoided, but you must get back here before that cell phone dies or parts of this town is going to start to disappear. Good luck."

And then he was out of the room, so fast Barrett didn't have time to respond. All he knew for sure was he had to get to work with Lovemoney. He knew their conversations would once again be monitored, but he didn't care anymore.

Over the course of the next several hours of continuous phone calls, negotiations and begging they'd reach a plan acceptable to Washington. Now they needed to sell it to Vincent and his gang of thugs. Barrett sent a guard to Vincent's office asking for an audience. An hour later he was brought before Vincent, Coffin and Cox sat in a corner of the office and didn't say a word.

"Agent Barrett, you have news for me?" Colonel Vincent asked.

432

"I do Sir. I hope it's a first step. I'm not sure it's going to be everything you want, but it's the best I could do in the time allotted."

"Well, let's hear it."

"A meeting is proposed. We know it cannot be held here. We considered State Police District headquarters and a few other neutral sites, but we didn't think it would be in the best interest of Mrs. Vincent's health to move her until she has agreed to take nourishment and is stronger. We felt if we could let her know you would be coming to see her; she would accept food and end her hunger strike. If she has a few days that will give her time to recover her strength. And if we offer you time with her with a guarantee of safe passage you will allow us the preference of venue."

"And just what venue do you suggest?"

"None other than the federal building downtown Chicago."

"Are you crazy?"

"No, Sir. Hear me out. It has many advantages for both sides. First it is close to good medical care. Mrs. Vincent will not have to be transported far if she is in need of it. I promise you she is being looked after as well as can be right now, but even if she agrees today to recover, she's going to need monitoring. Second, we can control flow in and out of the area better than anyplace else. We'll cordon off blocks of downtown so that no vehicle or pedestrian traffic can enter the area. This will assist with your security and the security of the officials who have agreed to come from Washington. Third, we will provide helicopter service from anyplace in Odell or the surrounding fields to the rooftop of the federal building. No one will get anywhere near you or your men. Fourth, you will have a document signed by the attorney general of the United States vouching for your safe return to Odell immediately after the first

433

round of discussions."

"The only caveat that has been placed on these meetings so far is a complete blackout of the press. No one must know they are taking place or that the officials involved have ever set foot in Chicago. It's a start, Sir. It's a start."

"You're right, it's a start. It's a damn poor one, but it's a start. There are some issues I don't like. The first is the venue. I'm going to be awfully far away from my men. I'm going to want Captain Coffin with me and that may be problematic for us. Don't get me wrong there won't be any leadership issues in Odell, I just don't like the smell of it. My gut tells me no."

"We can fix that, Sir. We can include language from the AG that will in effect create a stand down from any and all actions against Odell forces. And don't forget, Sir, you still have nearly three thousand hostages. It's not like that's going to change if you take a day-long field trip."

"Who's going to attend from Washington?"

"Cabinet members. The Secretary of Homeland Security, the Secretary of the Interior and the director of the FBI, Mr. Cellini."

"You're asking me to meet with two cops and a farmer?"

"Sir, these three individuals have the President's ear. They're cabinet members who could fill any number of positions within the administration. They're very capable people from all walks of the private sector, who won't necessarily be missed from Washington for a day or two and who's personally volunteered to attend!"

"Let's look at my proposed list of attendees, Agent Barrett. The President's Chief of Staff, Halderman. After all, he's the guy who's been calling the shots for the President. He's the guy who's denied my wife counsel and her liberty. The attorney general, he's the fellow who's supposed to make sure our

434

government isn't corrupt and has failed miserably. And the Vice President, he's most likely President liar's successor."

"Why would you even come to me with the list of nobodies you propose. When you get serious about the government's representatives proposed to attend, Agent Barrett, let me know."

Vincent knew his list, for the most part was as impossible as was Barrett's proposal, but that's how negotiations work.

"I don't like the venue Agent Barrett. I don't like the venue at all. Work something out. But because I see that you are making progress, I'll extend the time you have. For today you have saved a portion of Odell. Now get back to work and I will see you tomorrow evening."

# # # # #

"Halderman, Cellini, the deputy attorney general of the United States and the attorney general for the State of Illinois. That's as best we can do. And the deputy AG will come only if we agree to meet in the federal building. It's as good a group as we can get Colonel. It's the last call. I promise you we've done and said everything we can to make this a meaningful sit down. The deputy attorney general will be bringing with him a proposal to identify a special prosecutor to immediately begin an inquiry into allegations of the corruption your demands have made. You will, of course, be asked to turn over whatever evidence, names of witnesses, etcetera you allege to have."

"Well that's all for discussion at the table isn't it, Agent Barrett? We won't be making concessions of any kind until we find like kind at the table. But we agree to the principal parties."

"I also have Captain Petracha on the phone waiting to speak to you. He has important information that he said you would accept as the truth coming only

435

from him. Will you take his call?"

"Yes, I'll take the call." Vincent jaw tightened, and he looked at the agent with a cold stare.

Barrett slid the cell phone across the dinner table to the Colonel.

"Captain Petracha, this is Colonel Vincent. What can I do for you?"

"Good afternoon Colonel. I wanted you to know that I just came from a visit with Gretchen. She isn't well; I've seen her in better shape. I'm sorry I did so without your permission, but I told her you may be coming to see her within the next few days. She perked up appreciably. I had to tell her that Colonel because I felt she was determined to carry on with this hunger strike thing. You know I love her, both of you. I always have and always will. And I wasn't going to let her die like that. It was the only thing I could do to buy some time for her. Though I may have spoken out of turn, it was with inherently good intentions. She looks as bad as she did when you guys were in Ecuador and she got that parasite. Pretty emaciated. You need to come see her."

"I also feel you got some bad intel about me, for whatever reason, but given what you had and knowing who you are, there are no hard feelings and I want you to know that. You know I have always walked a clean line and would want you to know that I did so with the civilians who attempted to assassinate my commander. That's all I have to say about that."

"As far as your wife is concerned, I can only urge you to consider coming to see her. Maybe some good can be done on all fronts if you do. That's all I have to say, Sir."

"Captain I appreciate your words of concern for Gretchen. I am not sure I can fulfill your promise to her. There is a greater good here to be dealt with and we cannot afford to let personal feelings and relationships interfere with

436

objectives. As a soldier, I'm surprised that basic principal has slipped your mind. In fact, I find it odd. Nevertheless, we will know within the next few days whether or not we can come to mutually acceptable terms for a meeting."

"Captain Coffin has asked me to consider the less dangerous possibility of a video conference. And that is now beginning to have some appeal to me."

Out of the corner of his eye, Vincent watched Barrett's heart sink. He wanted nothing more than to get eyeball to eyeball across the table from Hal derman and the deputy attorney general.

"Nevertheless, we're still working on details. I would like to see my wife, even if it's for one last time, but that can't be the impetus for a face-to-face meeting with the proposed principals. We will get back to our discussions here and Agent Barrett will let his superiors know of our decision. Is there anything else you wish to share Captain Petracha?"

Petracha shot a look and a smile at Lovemoney that couldn't be seen by Colonel Vincent, but Lovemoney thought if he had, Petracha's life wouldn't be worth the proverbial wooden nickel. "No Sir, that's about it."

Petracha slid a piece of paper lying on Lovemoney's desk towards himself and wrote on it "A million dollars says he'll be here by Sunday morning! Call my brother in to sign the papers."

Over the next two days, negotiations, arguing and resisting each other continued long into the evening hours. Oft times Colonel Vincent wasn't present. They continued to wear Lovemoney and Barrett down with delay, lack of sleep and sessions at all hours of the day. One began at 0300 hours and lasted fifteen minutes during which time it was decided that the Colonel would be allowed to carry a side arm with his formal dress uniform. Discussions reminded Barrett of the Vietnam Paris peace talks where days on end were spent deciding the shape of the conference table that was to be used. Finally, he conceded the odd request, but had no intention of allowing this guy to walk into the federal building containing top government officials with a weapon strapped to him.

After endless additional hours of discussion concluding at 0245 hours Friday morning Vincent turned to Coffin and said, "What do you think, John?"

"I think it's worth a shot Colonel. I'm not sure it's a good idea that I go with you. Perhaps Captain Cox would be best to go and as second in command I remain here. If anything goes awry, if someone decides to get cute. . ." "Coffin shot a glance at Barrett, "you know you could rely upon me to move this thing forward."

"You're right, of course." Turning to Robert Cox who for the most part sat silent off to the side of the large office, "Captain Cox, how do you feel about a trip to the big city?"

"I'm game, Sir." Turning back to Barrett the Col continued. "Agent Barrett, there may be a few more details to work out. I will let you and Captain Coffin do that. But before I leave you to that task, I have a few remaining conditions, deal-breaking conditions."

Barrett's head dropped a little. That's all he'd been hearing for the last forty-eight hours.

"Well, your boys have their requirements, I have mine. Number one, I'm not liking the venue at all, but if we agree to go to the federal building, there will be no chopper ride. There will be no police escort, nor will there be any closing of any expressway. We will make the journey this Sunday morning beginning at 0600 hours. We will travel in two vehicles. Agent Barrett will ride in my vehicle, Captain Cox will ride in the second vehicle with a driver. We want no special attention given to or drawn to our two-vehicle convoy. The point of entry to the federal building is subterranean. Captain Cox and his driver will park outside the front entrance of the building. You will have that cordoned off so as to accomplish that. Should anything look out of the ordinary Captain Cox, you will radio Odell and immediately leave the area. Do you understand?'

"Yes Sir."

"Agent Barrett, here's my last non-negotiable demand. After I've had a few moments with Mrs. Vincent, she is to be escorted downstairs, out of the building and into Captain Cox's vehicle. She will then be transported by him to a hospital we've already chosen to receive whatever care that's necessary. When that's been accomplished she is to be transported by our people back to her home. Is that agreed to?"

"That has not been part of our discussions, Colonel Vincent, but I will do my very best to see that condition met."

"Yes, I believe you will. In fact, I'd bet my life you will." Then after a short pause, "yours as well."

# # # # #

"Captain Coffin, are we all set to go?"

"Yes Sir. Captain Cox is having breakfast with Agent Barrett. The vehicles are filled, armed and ready as well. I expect we'll have sunrise around 0545 hours and you are set to depart at that time. The state police out of District Six will have only one or two vehicles on the sides of the interstate all the way up to the Cook County line. They're present only to offer aid should there be some need. There will be no escort, lights of any kind. As far as anyone passing by they will appear to be the usual traffic detail vehicles. Odell is secure.

439

The men have been advised as well."

"If anything should go awry, you have your orders. You address the men on my behalf and let them know how proud of them I am. They know, but you reinforce it. There may be a need to move out of Odell in as few as two weeks should things go well. It has been my pleasure to serve with you Captain Coffin."

"I have in my desk a written order. It is an order promoting you to the rank of major. You deserve it; it's probably long overdue. Well, not probably. If I'd not been so frenetically busy over these last two years I wouldn't have been so neglectful of that obvious oversight. I have left instructions that you are not to remain in that rank for more than a year before another rank elevation. I'm sure that order will be executed by our commander if I am not able to do it myself. Now, let's you and I go have breakfast ourselves. Then I'll get dressed and we'll get this show on the road."

As they walked out of the Colonel's office and to the small dining room the Colonel stopped and turned to Coffin, "have you let One America know?"

"Oh, you bet, Sir. They're happier than pigs 'n slop," he grinned.

# # # # #

After a quieter-than-normal breakfast, Colonel Vincent lit up another rare cigar and said, "Let's go for a walk around town, John."

It wouldn't take more than an hour to completely circumnavigate it and that's just what Vincent needed. So, off they went and during the course of that early Sunday morning stroll they only stopped three times. The first time was in front of Richard and Ruth Ralph's house.

"I'm sorry this happened to these good folks. He was defending his home,

440

his town and way of life. He didn't get us, did he?"

"No, Sir he didn't, but at least he wasn't afraid to do something in his 'beginnings time.'

"You're exactly right. A good soldier, always."

Vincent took his military hat off and put it under his right arm. After a few moments of silence, he put it back on and he walked away.

"I remember her lying on the medical cot just a few feet from me. I saw her in and out of my consciousness and wanted to reach out and hold her hand. I couldn't. She'll always be in my mind."

The walk continued until it reached the ruins of St. Paul's Catholic Church. Vincent stood silently for a long time looking at the still smoldering embers, the smoke rising from piles here and there and the so obvious and distinct smell of C4 explosive that none of the civilians connected.

"Damn shame, damn shame, John."

"Yes Sir. Enough to make one sick."

John Coffin had attended mass there twice while in Odell. After last Sunday's mass he stayed behind and joined Father Moore for dinner and some sipping bourbon on the back porch of the rectory. They weren't two men engaged in the turmoil that had brought them together, they were just two Catholic boys talking salvation.

"Greater good Sir. Greater good, right?"

"Yes John, 'the greater good.'"

Still staring at the hole in the ground where the old church used to stand, Vincent said, "Who ever came up with that stupid phrase ought to be shot. I've used it so many times during my forty years in the military that just to think of it makes me sick. You know what it means, John?" The question was

441

rhetorical, "It means that whoever says it is going to do whatever the hell they want to regardless of the consequences, moral or otherwise. They do it because they can do it. It's the biggest lie of all perpetrated on the recipients of 'the greater good.' It's the 'frig you', there's nothing you can do about it. I'm as guilty as the liars in Washington. I've used it for them, I've been the executive in charge of 'the greater good' more times than I can count, in more countries than I can even admit to being in. What a load of BS!"

He threw the now unlit soggy butt of his cigar into the hole that used to be St. Paul's and resumed his walk around Odell.

When the two men had come nearly full circle Vincent stopped again.

"It's a pretty little town isn't it? I mean, it kinda reminds me of the little place I grew up in. It doesn't have the terrain of course, but it has that small-town atmosphere that I love so much. Good people here. Salt of the earth, representative of most of the good people across our country. All they want to do is make a living, fall in love, have a family, live peacefully happily ever after and have the damn government leave them alone. The last thing they want is us coming to town. We sure turned it upside, down didn't we. Greater good!" Vincent smiled weakly.

He stopped purposely this last time outside the white picket fence that surrounded the home of Mary Duke Odell.

"Yes, Sir, we sure did turn it upside down but one day, just like the citizens of Lexington and Concord these folks will be remembered as the beginners of times when the country was restored to the people like it was designed to do. Liberty and freedoms already lost and those that would have been lost had we not acted will be their heritage and our legacy. What are the words of the 'American Moses'? 'Now is the time, this is the place and we are the people.'"

"Yer, preachin' to the choir, Captain Coffin."

Vincent smiled and then he turned towards Mary's house again and came to attention.

"Mary Duke Odell, you are one of the finest women I have ever met in my life. I expect to meet you again sometime soon and when I do, I hope you will treat me not unkindly and know that while it seems so very at odds with you, my presence here was for you."

With that Colonel Vincent executed a crisp salute and walked the few hundred yards back to the headquarters building.

Captain Robert Cox, Agent Dan Barrett and two drivers stood on the front porch of the VFW headquarters building. When they reached the bottom steps Col Vincent greeted each of the men. He thought of all those present, Barrett seemed most relaxed. He was sure he was relieved to be getting the heck out of there.

At the bottom of the steps were parked two Conquest Knight XV armored vehicles. When Barrett first saw them, he uttered a low whistle to himself. Each one of those specially equipped, top of the line security vehicles tipped the scales at around $650,000! It became apparent why Vincent didn't want a police escort to Chicago, no one could touch the occupants of these vehicles unless they had a tank to do it with.

"It's a good Sabbath day morning for a ride wouldn't you say Agent Barrett?"

"Yes, Sir, I would say so. I'm more than ready," Barrett smiled weakly.

"Well good. Maybe by the end of this day we will have you home with Ellen and the children for dinner. I don't expect I'll be an invited guest," he quipped trying to keep the moment light.

443

Barrett had come very close to spitting out "and I hope you with yours." but caught himself at the last moment. He knew that Vincent was never going to have that opportunity again and Vincent knew it as well. But the remark demanded a response.

"Well you never know Sir. I'd say that depends on how good a negotiator you are."

It even made Vincent smile.

"I'd guess I'd have to be one hellava one! But it would make my day, indeed it would make my day. Well what do you say gentlemen, shall we get this show on the road?"

Vincent, Barrett took seats in the back of the first XV and Captain Cox and a driver took the front seats of the second. Colonel Vincent exited his vehicle on the spur of the moment and walked over to Captain Coffin.

"John, hold down the fort my old friend."

And with that he gave him a kiss on the right cheek, stepped away and saluted his dear old combat side-kick and reentered the transport vehicle. Coffin followed him. When he reached the side of the vehicle Vincent rolled the window down.

"Colonel Vincent, Sir, the men wanted me to give this to you." It was a walking stick, commonly known as a 'short stick' in Vietnam.

"Well, what's this for?"

"We thought Colonel that you might want to make them think yer weak!" a large grin spread across Coffin's face.

Sliding the walking stick through the window Vincent studied its ivory carved head. "Well, Captain Coffin, we certainly wouldn't want to give them that impression, would we?" The blacked-out window rolled back up.

When he settled into the vehicle, he laid the gift from his men between him and Barrett. It was symbolic. His briefcase on the floor in front of him and with a cup of coffee in his hand he turned to his riding companion and said, "Are they ready for us?"

"Yes, traffic on I-55 is light this time on a Sunday morning. There are no major events planned for downtown so pedestrian traffic will be light. There will always be some joggers in Lincoln and Grant Parks, but that will be light as well."

"Rehearse for me again the procedure for entry."

"We'll be coming into the downtown area from the southwest. We're going to take a back way into the heart of the Loop. We'll travel up Canal Street to Adams over to Dearborn. Captain Cox's vehicle will pull into the designated area in front of the building. There it will be searched and cleared. We will proceed a few hundred feet down Adams to the underground security entrance. This vehicle will then also be cleared. Once cleared, we'll be escorted into the sub level of the building. When we exit, your driver will park the vehicle and then he'll be escorted back to Captain Cox's vehicle. He will not be coming inside with us."

"Once we are safely inside the building, we will proceed to Mrs. Vincent's quarters. You will be allowed as much time as you wish with her. We'd like to request that we keep as close to the meeting start time as possible though because of the schedules of the attendees. After the meeting has concluded, we will escort you back upstairs and you can then spend as much time with Mrs. Vincent as you wish. Once your visit has concluded we have made arrangements for her to leave the building and she will be taken to Northwestern Medical Center for a complete examination and any needed treatment before she is released. Once released she is to be taken to Midway Airport where a private jet awaits. She will then be flown into Albany, New York and taken by car back to your home in Bemis Heights. It was the best I could do, Sir. I know it's not in perfect tune with your wishes, but it's the best I could do. And in the end, the results you wanted are achieved."

When it came to lying, Barrett wasn't nearly as good as Vincent. And when it came to interviewing prisoners Barrett was very good, but he hadn't had nearly the experience Col Vincent had. So, at the end of the plan rehearsal, Vincent knew nearly every word the federal agent had told him was a lie as soon as he started talking. Vincent watched very carefully as Barrett's carotid artery picked up speed and intensity. His respirations per minute went up as well. And they both went up as soon as he started to spin his tale about Vincent's wife.

"Agent Barrett, I appreciate your efforts on our behalf. I know Mrs. Vincent will be happy as well. Listen, I understand the chain of command of things as well as anyone. I know you have your orders and have had to make some tough calls. It's never been personal with us. I know you personally would never trample all over an American citizen's constitutional rights had you not had orders to do so. I trust you, Agent Barrett, we trust you. If I hadn't had a measure of you over the last few weeks, we wouldn't be taking this ride together, trust me." The words stung Barrett.

Soon, only fifteen minutes into the ride northwest up the interstate they passed Dwight, Illinois, there was a District Six state police car sitting in the median strip. It looked like nothing more than a Sunday morning speed trap. Twenty minutes later as they passed Joliet a Will County squad was sitting on the overpass bridge keeping an eye on the two-vehicle convoy. Neither caused

446

any concern to Vincent. Just as they were circling the bend north of Joliet the skyline of Chicago came into view. If Barrett had been watching, he would have noticed Vincent's carotid artery going nuts. But . . . no one was looking.

A Cook County squad came screaming by, lights flashing siren screaming. It got the Colonel's attention for a few seconds and then he relaxed as he realized it was just a typical county call who was completely impervious to the two XV's moving down the highway. Then he concentrated on one of the world's most beautiful skylines, lake fronts. He'd been there many times over the course of years, mostly on vacations and business trips. The last few times were tactical. The closer they got he thought of the 'Loop', a nickname for Chicago's heart of downtown. It came about from the fact that an elevated train that began in the north side of the city traveled down through the city, made a semicircle and headed back north along the eastern side of downtown. Most all tourists took the train at one time or another.

The vehicles exited the expressway at Canal Street taking the route outlined by Barrett earlier. Vincent's mind drifted. Drifted like it shouldn't drift, but he couldn't help it. His thoughts turned to her, to everything about her, her smile, her eyes, her smell, her laugh, her touch, her feel. If ever the phrase, 'she completes me' was true, it was with her. And now he would soon see her, hold her, kiss her. But it would be for the last time. He knew it and the thought just about killed him. He resolved that she would not see that in his eyes. She would only see joy, pure unadulterated joy at being with her. That would be his gift to her.

The two XV's slowed as they drove side streets until they came to Jackson Boulevard. A right turn and then moving even more slowly for a half a mile to the intersection of Dearborn Street. There Vincent noted the signal from Cox

447

that he was turning left towards the main street level entrance of the Federal Building. Cox's vehicle came to a rest between sawhorses that sat outside cement barriers that prevented vehicles from getting too close to the building. Two Chicago police officers were all that could be seen by the front doors of the building. It was as discreet as Vincent wanted it to be. However, as soon as Cox's driver shut off the vehicle federal officers dressed in black combat fatigues moved in out of nowhere and with bomb sniffing dogs and other search tools to clear the vehicle.

Vincent's car proceeded down Jackson Boulevard another 100 feet and then turned left down a steep driveway that led to the government underground parking. The area where high profile federal criminals are brought in for trial has the strictest security protocol. Before Vincent's vehicle is allowed to proceed, another group of federal officers approached his vehicle and swept it both inside and out. It was the only time during the trip that Vincent felt really uncomfortable. Standing there at the bottom of the ramp while the officers did the vehicle check left him feeling pretty vulnerable, but it was over quickly, and he soon re-entered the XV and was in the belly of the beast.

As they pulled to a rest at the bottom of the ramp in front of two glass double doors several federal officers stood with weapons at port arms. Colonel Vincent reached over and touched Barrett on the arm before they got out.

"Agent Barrett, I have a favor to ask of you."

The remark surprised Barrett as much as the personal touch.

"Of course, what is it? If I can do something for you I will."

"Last Sabbath day I had your life in my hands. I needn't have restrained myself because it was never in danger no matter what you thought or what we caused you to think. In any event on that day I granted you a day with your

448

family. Firstly, so that you could have it, but secondly to allow you to participate in a teaching moment. And," Vincent grinned, "you have to admit it was one hellava teaching moment."

"Indeed, it was Colonel, not one I ever care to repeat."

"I've never been a man to procrastinate much. I dearly want to see my wife as much as you wanted to spend time with yours, but there's business to conduct. I know important people are coming here to size me up, to see what can or cannot be done. We need to get about that business. That being the case I don't plan on spending more than fifteen minutes with Gretchen as much as I'd like to. Maybe I can spend some time with her before you release her for medical care?"

"Yes, of course."

"Well, thank you but that's not the request. The request is that I would like you to personally take me to her and to remain outside the room until it's time to go in to meet the others. I don't know anyone else here, don't trust anyone. Our visit would be less stressful to me if I knew you were nearby. Can you grant me that request? I just want fifteen minutes of your time. After that you may go wherever it is they want you to."

Barrett looked Vincent directly in the eye.

"Of course, I will do that for the both of you."

He wasn't being as gracious as it appeared on the surface, he was being a smart interrogator. Everyone who's ever done an interrogation or who's held a prisoner knows that the sooner you can get things on a personal level, the sooner you can get that individual in your debt, the better. And Barrett was just about to put Vincent in his debt after all he'd put Barrett through. "Let me call upstairs right now."

449

With that he called Lovemoney to explain what he'd be doing and that they would actually be in the conference room earlier than anticipated. Turning back to Vincent he said, "We're good to go. In fact, nearly everyone is here. We're ahead of schedule and your desire to get to talks will work out just fine. The only person who is not on premises yet is Mr. Halderman. He had a political obligation in St. Joe, Michigan, yesterday and stayed overnight. He'll be arriving by chopper within the next half an hour or so. Anything else before we take you up to meet Mrs. Vincent Sir?"

"No, Agent Barrett, but thank you."

The vehicle then parked three spaces down from the entrance. The driver was immediately escorted out of the building to Captain Cox's XV. And then the rear doors to the vehicle opened, Vincent and Barrett got out under the watchful eye of several federal agents. Immediately inside the double glass door was a rather austere reception desk behind which sat an enormous federal marshal. Behind the marshal elevator doors open and waiting. Barrett escorted Colonel Vincent into the elevator and the doors closed. It was just the two of them on Barrett's home turf now. He was feeling pretty good about it.

"How ya feeling, Colonel?" he asked.

Vincent responded, "to be totally truthful with you Agent Barrett, I'd rather be on my pond, in my boat back in Bemis Heights."

There was a small smile on his face. Barrett noticed that he didn't look a bit nervous. It impressed him.

The doors opened, they exited and took a left down a long hallway and then another left, and soon beautiful Lake Michigan and Grant Park were in sight through massive glass walls. Then they came to a set of doors. At the last one on the right Barrett stopped.

"I think Colonel, I'll step down the hall a way and let you knock on this one."

He understood the emotion of the moment for the Colonel and wanted to give him some respect. And it wasn't all a lie. God knows he didn't agree with almost anything the Colonel and his men or movement stood for, but he had to admit this guy had guts, he had conviction, he loved his country and he was one smart old bird.

Colonel Vincent straightened his gig line, took off his cover and knocked on the door to room number three. He heard footsteps, a series of locks being unlocked and the creaking open of the door. And there she was the most treasured thing he'd ever seen in all of his sixty odd years. His Gretchen!

Chapter XXVII

Gretchen Vincent fell into her husband's arms, burying her face in his neck. She clung to him weeping quietly for several minutes before either of them could say a word. It seemed like they'd been away from each other for years. But then for the last two years at least that they'd been away from each other more than they'd been together. Vincent clung to her, his face pressed into long blond hair. He'd wondered if he would ever see her again. Her face planted in his neck, tears wetting the color of his dress coat was one of those really rare occasions when he'd seen her so emotional. He listened for her heartbeat but couldn't hear it through her sobbing and her kisses of reassurance. As they held each other they both thought the same thoughts; they couldn't get close enough.

Hours earlier when she'd been assured that he was on his way, she scurried about like a schoolgirl on her first date. She showered and washed her face again before applying just a little make up. A simple white spring dress with small pink flowers had been provided by one of the female agents who regularly looked in on her. It was perfect. Her hair hung straight with a little natural curl and famed her perfectly sculpted face. It was the same look that Madison had fallen in love with all those so many years ago. She wore the simple gold necklace that she had on the day the FBI took her from her home in upstate New York.

They embraced for several minutes just inside the doorway before they took each other by the hand and retired to a small couch provided in the sparsely furnished apartment. It was then she first noticed the ragged indent on his left cheek corresponding to the healing entrance wound on his right one. His eyes had that raccoon look that accompanies the healing of some really black eyes. There was still a yellowish tinge to his left eye and his right eye still sported some darker discoloration. She ran her fingers over each side of his face and kissed them. Was he well? "Well enough" he replied and went back to their embrace. She looked wonderful and he had known all along that all that chatter about a hunger strike was a ruse.

Knowing they were being video recorded they kept their conversation in whispered tones close to one another the entire time. Finally, as the time allotted by the Colonel was nearing its end Gretchen took him by the hand and said "Darling, shall we invite Agent Barrett in for just a few moments. I would dearly like you to have a few words with him before we part."

The Colonel looked at her for a few moments and drew a deep breath. "She outranks me" he thought before he smiled and responded.

"Yes, that's a good idea. I'll get him."

The Colonel opened the door and looked down the hall where he saw Agent Barrett staring out a large window. The Colonel's voice startled him.

"Agent Barrett, would you join us for just a few moments before we go downstairs?"

Barrett turned away from the window.

"Yeah, sure, on my way," as he began walking towards the Colonel. When he entered the room a very healthy-looking Mrs. Vincent was still sitting on the couch. She patted the spot next to her inviting her husband to rejoin her. A kitchen chair had been pulled up right across from the couple.

"A hunger strike? A hunger strike?" she chuckled. "Who in God's good name came up with that one?"

An embarrassed Barrett blamed it on Lovemoney.

"I'm sorry, we just had to get people talking. We did what we could do to

453

make that happen."

"Well, all is forgiven on that point, Agent Barrett, but my husband does have a confession of his own to make don't you, Madison?"

"Yes, yes, I do. Come closer Agent Barrett. We do know we're being listened to, but what I must tell you is for your ears only at this point. In time it can be shared with anyone you like." Barrett scooted his chair in as close as he was encouraged to do so. His knees were less than an inch from the Vincent's.

"Obviously my wife has never been on a hunger strike. And of course, I've always known that. You see, we've never been to Ecuador together and she's never had a parasitic infection. At least, not that I know of. Have you honey?"

"Oh no dear, never anything like that" she responded. And then almost as if they were in a different place, time and circumstance, "unless you count that time we ate at your aunt Michele's and nearly died of food poisoning?"

Vincent smiled broadly at her. How he loved the spunk in this woman. She did outrank him. She really did. He then turned his attention back to Barrett.

"I never came here for her."

"I understand what you were trying to accomplish. I'm a military man, I get the 'doing my duty' thing, though your lies do cause me discomfort. What makes me uncomfortable about them right now is the ease with which you and your cohorts lie so easily and so liberally trash the guarantees of the constitution of the United States. That has me real troubled. I mean, if I can't trust you to be a man of your word, how do I know that Odell is not under attack right now and that you are about to arrest me for treason and a whole host of other trumped up charges?"

"We are not, Sir. Odell is under no threat and all the parties agreed to are in the conference room awaiting your arrival except Halderman who should be here within a half an hour or so. I promise you. We're just trying to get parties to the table, that's it. Lovemoney has worked very hard to meet your requests about that."

"Perhaps so. Perhaps not. So, here's what let's do. I want to discuss the immediate release of my wife. Last Sunday, while you were having dinner with yours, our men, the same ones that picked her up were busy. They were busy loading the foundation of your house with so much C4 that it would blow it, everyone in it and in fact anyone within five hundred yards of it to Oz. You understand?"

Barrett's face drained of blood for the millionth time since he'd met this man or, so it seemed. Vincent didn't give him an opportunity to respond.

"Yes, of course you do. I couldn't have made it any plainer. Now those C4 explosives are timed to go off in exactly one hour. In Captain Cox's XV downstairs is a control panel. It folds down out of the rear panel of the front seats. On that control panel are two fingerprint-activated buttons. One for Mrs. Vincent and one for . . ." and there was a long pause. "One for Captain Petracha. The only thing that can prevent those explosives from going off is if both Mrs. Vincent and Captain Petracha activate those buttons within ten seconds of one another.'

Vincent paused. He wanted Barrett to realize what a pickle he was in.

"Do you understand me Agent Barrett? You've had my wife's life in your hands for several weeks now. In fact, she has shared with me the fact that you've even threatened her life! How does it feel, Agent Barrett, to have some bully threaten to kill your wife and children? You needn't answer that."

"Here's what we're going to do to save your family. You're going to call Lovemoney right now and have him bring Petracha to the front door. You are

455

going to have an agent come get my wife and take her to the XV and send them off. You wonder of course what guarantees you have. You don't. You will simply have to believe that I am a greater man of honor than you. Make the call Agent Barrett or I will declare your family an enemy of the state and blow them all to hell. Don't think I won't do it."

Barrett knew he wasn't kidding. He called Lovemoney who at first protested until Barrett gave him a direct order and told him he would explain later. He then turned to Vincent.

"Colonel please don't injure my wife and those innocent children," he pled.

"I don't want to. As long as you get my wife and the Captain out of here, I promise you they will be safe. We'll get them out of there and remove the C4. Simple as that.

"Captain Petracha is on his way down." Barrett responded. "I will personally take Mrs. Vincent down with your promise they will not be harmed."

"You have my word."

"Will you come with us or do you want me to have you escorted to the conference room?"

"I will come with you, so I can say goodbye to my wife."

The three of them then left the room and went to the main elevator bank. As they were exiting the elevator on the main floor the elevator next to them opened and off stepped Captain Mario Petracha.

As soon as Petracha saw Vincent he instinctively snapped to attention and saluted. Vincent returned in kind and then something happened that Gretchen Vincent had never seen happen in all the years she knew these two good men had known each other. Mario Petracha quickly moved forward and kissed Madison on the hand. Madison kissed each of the large man's cheeks and they

456

embraced the way that only warriors gone to battle together can understand. Then Captain Petracha went forward and after a brief hug stood behind Mrs. Vincent.

Agent Barrett opened the front doors and stood by waiting for Mrs. Vincent and Petracha to exit. When Petracha passed him, he grabbed him by both shoulders and kissed him on the left cheek. It startled Barrett, but he had no time to respond.

Colonel Vincent moved forward towards his wife for what he and she both knew would be their last kiss on this earth. They kissed and then hugged and kissed again and then quietly wiped away tears. And then Gretchen Vincent abruptly turned on her heel, walked out the door and into the rear seat of the XV waiting for her. The vehicle backed out of the barricade that had been provided, backed onto Jackson Boulevard and sped out of sight. When Barrett turned around, he saw the Colonel standing at attention, stoic, majestic. He'd never seen anything like it in all his career.

"Shall we go upstairs Colonel?"

"No not yet Dan. I have one more request of you. Thank you for escorting my wife to freedom. I owe you and I am a man who never is comfortable with debt. I am not a debt-free man but would like to be so. I want you to call and have your car brought around. Don't worry, it's not for me, it's for you. This is very important. There is a package waiting for you on the exit ramp of Interstate 55 and LaGrange Road. It is being watched over by some of my men right now. It is absolutely imperative that you pick it up within the next half hour. If more than half an hour passes, they are instructed to destroy it and leave the area. That's all I can tell you."

"It's a wild goose chase."

457

The Colonel laughed, "yes we've put you through the mill, but this is not a goose chase. Do it, young man. You will be grateful you did; your family will be, and your country will be."

Against all logic, against all training and reason, Barrett decided that he needed to trust this man one last time. After all, he was done. He was never going back to Odell. He knew that and so did the Colonel. The President would announce his capture that evening on the news and demand the surrender of the rest of those traitors remaining in Odell. He'd gotten the snake out of the nest. He'd take a chance and do what the old man asked. His car was called for and he got into it. Before he pulled away he took one last look at the Colonel. The last time he saw Vincent he was being escorted into an elevator heading to the thirty-seventh floor conference room.

But just before Barrett left for his vehicle, the Colonel turned to him and said something odd.

"Agent Barrett good luck to you, young man. Say goodbye to Ellen and the children for me. And remember this is the rest of your career. When things look the darkest, when things are helpless and hopeless, God can and will 'trouble the waters.'

# # # # #

The elevator doors opened on the thirty seventh floor and Vincent stepped out and followed his young escort down a long hallway towards "the" conference room. The large glass windowed eastern wall of the building allowed for plenty of sunlight. It was good to see the bright blue of the lake melt into the paler blue of the morning sky. It was a beautiful morning. When they reached the end of the hall they approached the doorway to the conference room. The escort stopped and presented his arm to allow the Colonel entrance, but

458

Colonel Vincent stopped and insisted the younger man precede him. When he'd done so Vincent walked only to the entranceway, then stopped. Lovemoney was there, a few other agents, the invited officials and two secretaries, all staring at him. He waited silently. After a few awkward, silent moments one of the young agents slowly rose to his feet and stood as if at attention. One by one each of the people in the room including Lovemoney joined him. When all were standing Colonel Vincent looked at the first young man and said simply, "thank you for your service young man, I feel more comfortable knowing another military man is present." He turned towards Lovemoney "Agent Lovemoney, I don't see Mr. Halderman and his cohorts."

"No Sir, Colonel but they are on the way via helicopter. Mr. Halderman and the rest should be here in a very short time, minutes really. In the meantime, is there anything I can get for you?"

"Two things Agent Lovemoney, thank you. I'd appreciate a glass of orange juice. A large cold glass and if you don't mind very much and I'd like to switch sides of the table with you. I prefer facing the lake. No soldier, no real soldier ever, ever sits with his back to a window." he smiled. Lovemoney knew it was going to be a long day and was already wishing for Barrett's return. "Of course, Colonel whatever we can do to accommodate you. Agent Barrett had to step away momentarily but will return as soon as possible. He will join us as soon as he can."

"That will be fine. Dan and I have gotten to be good friends over these last few days. I think he's a fine young man. He's got lots of promise, maybe politics are in his future. I think he has all the abilities, don't you?" Vincent didn't wait for an answer. "We'll just have an orange juice and wait for the big boys to show up. But you should know beforehand Agent Lovemoney, this is going to be a very brief meeting. Short 'n to the point, like a country music song as they say. . . three cords and the truth."

When the orange juice arrived Colonel Vincent rose from his chair behind the conference room table and walked to one of the large glass windows over-looking the lake. He stared out at the beautiful Chicago shoreline. He could see as far north as Evanston and as much as it churned his stomach as far south as Calumet City and the steel mills. "She outranks me, she certainly does" he smiled.

And then watching a few white sails far out on the lake he thought "It is a beautiful morning to die, may God Trouble the Waters. And then his attention was drawn to a tiny object in the sky on the eastern horizon far away. A heli-copter? Halderman's heading towards the city.

# # # # #

The XV carrying Gretchen Vincent and Captain Petracha sped down Lake Shore drive in and out of very light, Sunday morning traffic until it reached side streets and twenty minutes later slid through the blue-collar community of Calumet City. There near the lake was an industrial harbor used mostly for shipping coal and steel. All of the grain silos were now empty and rusting skeletons of past economic boom times. Now they afforded much needed shel-ter and a perfect view of the Chicago skyline against a beautiful bright blue morning sky. Sunlight bounced off buildings that lined the park and lake front.

Petracha turned to Mrs. Vincent and said, "Your husband has to be the best liar I ever met." He never took his eyes off the skyline.

"Yes, Captain, I should have forced him to stop hanging around with you years ago" She paused and then continued. "He is also the most honest, dear, bravest man I ever met. I do love him so."

460

"Me too Ma'am. Me too!" he smiled.

"Yes, I expect so and knowing Madison, the way I do, Agent Barrett's speeding down I55 like a bat outta hell right now."

"Good for him, Ma'am. Good for him."

Indeed, Barrett was speeding down the Stevenson Expressway, lights flashing, sirens blaring. He hadn't quite made it to the LaGrange exit when he first noticed vehicles in the northeast bound lanes screeching to a halt. At first, he thought there had been a horrible accident. Then came a brightening of the highway, like it was under a giant spotlight. Then, in his rear-view mirror he saw the flash of a million suns. Then he felt a vibration and then there it was in his rear-view mirror.

He'd only made it just beyond First Avenue exit. He'd never make it to La-Grange. Frank Halderman was a lot less lucky. He was only out 3 miles over Lake Michigan when he saw it. It was the last view he'd ever have.

Just minutes before Petracha sat in silence until he heard Gretchen Vincent ask Captain Cox one question. "Captain Cox, is my nephew ready?"

"Yes Commander."

The nephew she was referring to was a small nuclear device built into the body of the XV that Colonel Madison T. Vincent driver had parked deep in the basement of the Chicago Federal Building. It was so powerful that it would take out nearly a third of the buildings on the south side of the downtown area and make the rest uninhabitable for God knows how long. She looked at Petracha for a long time. There were tears in her eyes yet there was strength there as well.

'In the beginnings time when men and women do nothing to save liberty and freedom they and their children and grandchildren become slaves to those

461

who would wrest those liberties from them, even if one at a time. It is time now Captain Petracha to assure liberty for our children and grandchildren, for their children and for our country now and forever. It is now time for the beginnings of restoration. It is for . . . the greater good."

For the first time in a long time Petracha answered with a short military response. "Yes, Commander Vincent." He then let the panel down from the rear seat in front of them. They looked at each other and then placed their forefingers in each of the buttons and pressed. The blast was enormous, white hot, thunderous. The Federal building melted almost instantaneously on the spot, others around it collapsed immediately. The sound wave shook the XV Commander Vincent and Petracha were in all those miles away hidden behind tall cement grain silos. Several minutes passed before Gretchen Vincent could speak. She had to swallow hard a few times, tears overflowed her eyelids, but she bit her lower lip, gained her composure and spoke authoritatively to Petracha as she barked out the order.

"Captain Petracha, call Captain Coffin and tell him as soon as the National Guard leaves Odell to respond to Chicago to get those men out of there. Evacuate according to plan and put in a call to the east coast. It's time to shake up Washington."

Dan Barrett got out of his car. He looked on with horror as the mushroom cloud shot up from the south side of the loop. He turned around and looked back down the southwest direction of the highway and realized in an instant that Odell was never the target. He leaned back against his vehicle and prayed that this was not the beginnings of what he thought it was. And if it was, thank God Madison Vincent wasn't around to lead it.

And then his mind raced to his own home and what might lay there. He called into the local police department who confirmed there had been a large blast on his block and that they were in the process of responding to it. He raced towards whatever remained of his home and family all the while screaming and cursing Vincent.

# # # # #

A day after the nuclear blast leveled a significant portion of the southern side of downtown Chicago, the FBI and units of the National Guard descended on Odell, Illinois. The FBI agent in charge who entered the town after it was determined to be safe was Agent Dan Barrett. He headed straight for the deserted VFW hall and straight into Col Vincent's office. It was empty except for an envelope that lay in the middle of the Colonel's desk with his name on it. Barrett opened it carefully and read it.

"Dan,

Your family is safe and sound in the old house where we dined with them last Sunday. Wanted to make sure they were out of harm's way. You are one of the few who knows the full truth. I bequeath it to you. Do with it what you will. And always remember Agent Barrett, ". . . After the fire, a small still voice."

Colonel Madison T. Vincent

American Revolutionary Militia

p.s. get on the right-side Danny.

Barrett folded the note and placed it in his shirt pocket as he raced out of the VFW towards his family.

> "The best way to take control over a people and control them utterly is to take a little of their freedom at a time, to erode rights by a thousand tiny

463

almost imperceptible reductions.

In this way the people will not see those rights and freedoms being removed until past the point at which these changes cannot be reversed."

Adolph Hitler

About the Author

Born and raised in upstate New York, a retired Chicago business executive, Mr. Vines now resides with his wife, Judy, and their two puppies, Miss Blue and Bob in a Nashville suburb. He is also the author of "Theophany", an international spiritual thriller and "Sacrament", a murder mystery set in Chicago. With his latest work "The Iscariot Fields", he hopes to encourage meaningful, civil dialog surrounding the issue of gun control and domestic terrorism. He is also a passionate public speaker using anecdotal techniques to motivate and inspire his audiences.

You can contact him at:

Facebook:
MJVinesAuthor

Twitter:
MJVinesAuthor

Email:
MJVinesauthor@gmail.com

Other Works by Michael J. Vines

Sacrament

Theophany Kindle Version
Amazon

Theophany – Paperback Version
Amazon

Made in the USA
Monee, IL
05 March 2025